WANNABES

by Michael Logan

Cover and interior design by Natalie Grant.

ISBN-13: 978-1530075010

ISBN-10: 1530075017

First edition, March 2016

www.michaelloganbooks.com

Also by Michael Logan

World War Moo
Apocalypse Cow

"I want my children to listen to people who fucking rocked. I don't care if they died in puddles of their own vomit. I want someone who plays from his fucking heart "

Bill Hicks

1

February 3, 1959

Murmur crouched beneath the wing of a Beechcraft Bonanza 35 light aircraft at Mason City Municipal Airport, cursing the flurries of snow blowing into the human face he'd been wearing for two weeks. Two centuries of deskbound drudgery in Hell's Souls Receiving department had been spent dreaming of this moment: when he would lurk with murderous intent in the world of man instead of stamping forms until his wrist ached, squabbling over whose turn it was to make the tea, and gluing his colleagues' staplers to their desks when they nipped out to the toilet. He just hadn't expected this longed-for moment to be so bloody cold. He was sorely tempted to set himself ablaze to ease the chill that nipped at the toes and fingers of this fragile body, but knew he couldn't risk it. Even though midnight had passed, a cigarette glowed in the shadows of the control tower and the technician who'd refuelled the plane had only just slouched off around the corner.

Not that he'd be in any danger if he were to be spotted; he could incinerate any foes with an insouciant flick of his wrist. He'd been practicing this gesture for decades during imaginary battles with angels—without actually firing, of course, since these fantasies usually took place in his bottom bunk at the office dorm and the cost of any damage incurred would have been deducted from his pitiful wage. His fingers itched to unleash a crackling fireball for real, but leaving a trail of smouldering corpses wouldn't comply with Satan's command to keep a low profile. There was also a good chance that the fuel the sloppy worker had sprayed over both fuselage and tarmac would catch and set the plane alight if he indulged himself. The aircraft had to take off in order to come down far quicker than the pilot intended, so Murmur hugged his armpits and consoled himself with the knowledge that there would soon be burning wreckage upon which he could warm his hands.

As if the cold wasn't bad enough, his cells longed to fly apart from this everyman American form he'd assumed and reassemble in the comfortable, if lumpy and unattractive, pattern of his true shape. The strain was a thousand times worse than having to suck in his saggy gut, as he'd felt compelled to do under the disgusted gaze of the drill sergeant on his first day of field training just a few weeks ago. Still, the perishing cold and effort of holding sway over his mutinous molecular structure was a small price to pay for this opportunity. The vagaries of chance had set him free to spread woe and, as a welcome bonus, finally given him unlimited access to high-quality alcohol. Hell's upper echelons enjoyed exclusive access to the good stuff, while low-borns like Murmur had to make do with fermented harpy piss, which tasted just as bad as it sounded and caused apocalyptic hangovers. A bottle of Martell XO Extra Old Cognac awaited him back at the New York hotel he'd set up in. He intended to shutter the windows, relax into his flabby demon form, and let the alcohol spark a warming burn in his gullet as soon as he'd completed this evening's assassination, which would undoubtedly be the first of many. Next time, though, he would pick a target in Florida, or at the very least bring along a thermos and a nice thick blanket.

With the boozy treat in mind and the coast now clear, he yanked open the door and climbed into the four-seater plane. He scanned the controls, mulling over what to monkey with. The twin joysticks were tempting, but sabotaging those might only make the plane skitter off the end of the runway. Cutting control cables or damaging the fuel lines would show up as obvious sabotage in the post-accident inquiry. His gaze fell on the gyro, which the pilot would use to figure out the aircraft's orientation to the earth. A spurt of flame roiled across his cheeks as he smiled. He extinguished it and the blistered skin healed instantly. He'd have to get better at keeping his emotions under control if he planned to remain on Earth for any length of time.

Murmur hawked and, like a hell cat coughing up a fur ball, spat a glob of viscous red phlegm into his palm. The sticky sphere sprouted arms and legs, tiny eyes and a grinning mouth. He held the avatar out to the glass covering the gyro. It leapt onto the dashboard and reverted to its fluid form to squeeze through the cracks. The fragment of his soul had barely reformed and clambered up the side of the gyro when the wind carried the chug of an engine and another flurry of snow in through the open door. Murmur clambered out and retreated into the shadows before headlights from the car trundling along the airport approach road swept across the plane

Minutes later, four men walked up, hunched against the inclement weather. Murmur's sensitive demon eyes had no difficulty recognizing his targets. The pilot climbed in first, leaving Buddy Holly, Ritchie Valens and The Big Bopper to eye the aircraft. Murmur had to concentrate to avoid flames of glee erupting across his face at getting three pioneers of Rock'n'Roll for the price of one. Holly had quickly become an obvious choice for the first killing—his songs on every radio station, his name in every newspaper, his trademark glasses adorning the faces of fawning copyists across New York. Murmur had tracked him for over a week, looking for his chance. It had come that evening when the singer arranged for a plane to take him to his next concert date. Murmur knew from his years of processing incoming souls that planes came down often, particularly amidst rancid winter weather. When they did, there were rarely survivors.

'You sure this here contraption's safe, Buddy?' said Valens, a broad-faced man with a curly coif held immobile in the wind by copious amounts of hair gel.

Holly adjusted his thick, pointed glasses and grinned. 'What's the matter, Ritchie? Getting cold feet?'

'You know I ain't flown before,' Valens said.

'Never mind cold feet. I got a cold face, cold hands and cold balls. Let's get in before something drops off,' said The Big Bopper, the oldest and chunkiest of the trio.

'Yeah, come on,' Holly said, holding up his overnight bag. 'I got a bagful of smelly socks that need washing before they grow fungus.'

'Just make sure you keep that zipped up. That plane don't look too roomy, and we don't need your cheesy feet stinking it up. Chances are I'm gonna puke anyway,' Valens said.

Holly teased open the zip and shoved the bag into Valens' face. The other man batted it away and they boarded the aircraft laughing. The nose propeller began to whir, building in speed and volume until the plane started its taxi to the runway. Murmur shoved his hands deep into the pockets of his heavy black overcoat and strolled to the end of the tarmac strip, more for the sake of creating a dramatic scene to replay in his mind later than operational necessity. The plane accelerated and wobbled into the air a few seconds before it reached him, passing no more than ten metres over his head. He spun round and watched the taillight recede into the distance. Now came the tricky part.

He tilted his head and reached out to the avatar. He'd never tried to control one in a fast-moving target and, even with the training fresh in his memory, it took several fumbling attempts before he synched with the tiny saboteur. The plane was fluttering along no more than six hundred feet off the ground, the pilot pulling back on the joystick as the musicians clutched at the edge of their seats. The avatar, which had been clinging to the gyro's casing, dropped onto the ball and began to run. The gyro shifted off-centre and to the right. The pilot moved the controls to compensate and the plane dipped and banked towards the blank canvas of the earth, devoid of any lights in the rural surroundings. When the aircraft had sunk to less than 200 feet, the avatar responded to Murmur's coaxing and broke into a wild sprint. The gyro swivelled and the pilot automatically followed its lead, sending the plane's nose down to a 45-degree angle.

After a few seconds, Murmur saw the pilot's eyes widen as he made out the dark shadows of trees rushing beneath the wingtip. Before the pilot could yank up on the controls, the right wing clipped a thick branch. Murmur looked out through the avatar's eyes at the four pale faces, mouths screaming holes, as the plane juddered and flipped out of control. Then he withdrew his consciousness and listened to the distant sound of the crash—a loud thud, the screech of tearing metal and a succession of smaller impacts as the plane tumbled to its final resting place. He spread his hands and the airfield blinked out of existence as he flitted to the crash site.

The crumpled wreckage of the aircraft had come to rest against a wire fence. It hadn't exploded on impact as he'd expected, robbing him of both the heat he needed and that extra element of anecdotal spice. He supposed he could just lie and invent a roaring bonfire of rockers when he got round to writing his autobiography. He reclaimed the soul fragment, letting it scamper out of the ruined aircraft, up his arm and into his nostril before inspecting his handiwork. The mangled fuselage enfolded the dead pilot in its metallic embrace. The Big Bopper lay motionless a short distance away in the field demarcated by the fence. Murmur had to track back to find Holly and Valens. They lay spread-eagled, battered and bloody snow angels on the white rutted ground. Holly's glasses were nowhere to be seen.

A snowflake landed on Holly's eyeball, melting in the body heat that had yet to leave him, and ran down his cheek like a tear. Only the soft creaking of the plane settling further into the earth disturbed the snow-thickened silence.

'Nice and quiet,' Murmur said. 'The boss is going to be very happy.'

Secure in the remoteness of the location, he relaxed his control. Flames ignited on his lips, spreading up to his cheekbones and playing around the bottom of his eyes. Then he was gone, leaving behind the after-image of his fiery smile leering down on the still bodies, the music gone from them forever.

2

Barry Deckhart flexed his muscles against the ropes that bit into his arms and legs, straining to create some wiggle room. The bonds didn't budge. He held the tension anyway, his woozy mind distracted by the splendour of his rock-hard thighs and calves, which had won so many trophies for Chelsea and secured the affections of his pop star-slash-model wife. With the aid of the Oxford English Dictionary, Barry had assigned his legs many adjectives down the years—'heroic', 'intimidating', 'majestic', 'sumptuous' and 'monumental' among them. Today, he decided, they were 'gladiatorial'.

It was only when he smiled that the gag bit into his cheeks and brought his attention to bear on his unfamiliar surroundings. Somehow he'd ended up naked and lashed to a sturdy chair in a windowless room illuminated by the soft glow of a floor lamp and a flickering television screen. A purple-streaked fashion mullet poked up like a diseased cockatoo's crest over the back of a leather swivel chair, and a pale hand groped for the half-eaten Mars Bar that lay on a low glass coffee table.

He dredged up his memories of the evening from the moment he'd stepped out into the chilly January night after a fund-raising dinner for sick kids, at which London's high society had splashed out to dine with Britain's top celebrity couple. Cynthia had rushed off to catch a flight to Budapest for a show and the kids were at the hotel with the Polish nanny. He'd slipped on a baseball cap and shades before climbing into his Mercedes Benz S-class. He kept to the speed limit as he crossed town to the Camden flat he and Prudence rented under the name of a well-paid personal assistant, just another wealthy Londoner navigating the late-evening traffic. While being famous was utterly fabulous, sometimes you had to blend in—especially in a city where packs of tabloid photographers roamed like wild dogs in search of fresh meat. When he climbed out of the car and walked down the empty side street to look up at the flat, the curtains were glowing with a sensuous, welcoming light. His mind was already slipping between the silk sheets when footsteps scuttled up behind him.

The blooming paparazzi followed me, he thought.

He pirouetted with the grace that had flummoxed many a defender, already picturing the scandalous red-top headlines. Instead of the flash of a bulb, he glimpsed a syringe glowing orange under the street-lights. And then he'd woken up here.

Barry gathered his thoughts as best he could, still suffering from the after-effects of whatever had been used to drug him, and considered possible motives. Cynthia and he had long agreed that casual dalliances on both sides were fine as long as they didn't become public and affect their profile, so it couldn't be the revenge of a scorned wife. Ransom seemed more likely, although foolish since his disappearance would prompt a massive manhunt. He scanned the room. The walls were the same contoured green foam that coated the recording studios Cynthia had dragged him to during their courtship. A microphone stand, two gleaming black speakers and a mixing desk were arrayed around the room. On the wall hung a blown-up photograph of a round-faced woman with flowing curly hair, squinting and smiling into the sun. Beneath the picture was a dedication:

Remember what Henry Wadsworth Longfellow said, 'Fame comes only when deserved, and then is as inevitable as destiny, for it is destiny.'
You deserve it – Love, Mum.

None of it gave him any clue as to why he'd been brought here. Whatever the reason, he should have been in bed with Prudence, watching the faded stars scrabble to reignite their careers on *Celebrity Public Eye*'s eviction night special. His kidnapper was watching the same show. On screen, a middle-aged man, whose thinning shoulder-length hair brushed the shoulders of a tight yellow shirt, was crooning to a sofa of minor celebrities, scrunching up his face and apparently trying to crush a walnut in his clenched fist. His name was Jackie Thunder, a singer Barry vaguely remembered from the early nineties. The kidnapper's attention remained on the TV screen, so Barry began to rub the ropes against the chair, hoping the blaring speakers would mask the noise.

Jackie Thunder sat propped up on a fluffy pillow, surrounded by his housemates, and curled his lips up into a poor approximation of a carefree grin as the camera panned around the semi-circular sofa.

Please don't let it be me, he thought.

Ageing glamour girl Nicole Andrews placed her hand on his inner thigh, while Pete Flaxenburg, master of the straight-to-DVD realm and owner of Hollywood's most-Botoxed face, slung an arm around his shoulders in a display of mock solidarity. Jackie wanted to snap the wrinkled fingers that betrayed the ham actor's true age. He knew Flaxenburg had nominated him; he could sense it in the patronizing pats the American doled out.

The voice of the presenter, Lysa Singh, boomed through the speakers embedded in the garish red walls. 'Housemates! The votes are in and have been counted. I can reveal the first person to be evicted from the *Celebrity Public Eye* house is …'

In the ensuing pause, Jackie glanced at the other nominees up for eviction: Jeff Black, who was famous for being married to somebody who was famous for being famous, and Marie Stubbs, who like Jackie had taken the charts by storm years back only to end up on the scrapheap. She was tugging at a lock of straightened black hair with one hand; the other clutched the sofa, knuckles starkly white against her light brown skin. He wanted to wrap her in a hug and tell her it would be fine. It would have been a lie. Whoever got kicked out would face a plunge back into anonymity, another chance at a comeback smothered beneath the dust of a thousand fragmented dreams.

Still the pause went on, stretched far beyond the bounds of decency. Jackie's clamped teeth were beginning to ache. Jeff looked like he was going to vomit, with any luck into Flaxenburg's lap. Finally, Lysa let the axe fall, '… Jackie Thunder!'

His lips and cheeks succumbed to gravity and tears spangled his eyes. He remained motionless as the housemates crowded around to deliver their Judas kisses, his mind stunned into white noise. When Marie drew him to his feet, a tear trickled down his face and jump-started his brain back into life. Hubbub rushed in—condolences, excited chatter, the announcer counting down the seconds until he had to leave. Marie wrapped her dainty hands around his lower back.

'Milk it for all it's worth,' she whispered into his ear, 'then maybe we can do a duet when I get the boot.'

He nodded, planted a kiss on her forehead, and turned to where two of Lysa's headset-wearing minions were waiting to lead him away.

Get it together, Jackie boy, he thought. *This is your last chance to wow them.*

He took a deep breath and held it until the tremors running through his body subsided. He belted out the first lines of *Miserable Lie* by The Smiths as he walked the gauntlet of faded musicians, washed-up soap actors, cocaine-snorting socialites and plastic-boobed models with pretensions of acting careers. He blew kisses at the camera between lines and willed his leaden legs to dance up the stairs. He felt like a man climbing to the gallows, only it was his career that would dangle from the noose.

When he emerged onto the walkway, where speakers pumped out a thumping beat over the orchestrated bedlam of cheers, applause and boos, the energizing heat of the mob vaporized his despair. He froze as spotlights crawled over and around him. Three weeks ago, the cashier at Tesco had barely acknowledged him when he shuffled through with a basket of the supermarket's own brands. Now, thousands were drinking in his every move. Even the haters only had eyes for him.

I'm home, he thought.

He launched into his trademark twirl and point, managing not to wince at the twinge of pain in his lower back, and skipped into Lysa's outstretched arms.

The first section of the post-eviction interview focused on Jackie's memorable moments in the house. They showed a clip of the arm-wrestling match with hard-man-footballer-turned-actor Victor Cole, which Jackie won by planting a distracting sloppy kiss on his opponent's lips. Next up they flicked through the many moments of flirtation with Marie, including a spot of footsy in the Jacuzzi. Finally, the screen ran a montage of him singing: *It's Raining Men* at the male beauty contest, during which he almost passed out due to the effort of tensing his puny muscles; *Feeling Hot Hot Hot* while everyone was asked to cram into a tiny sauna for an hour to win ten bottles of champagne; and *I Predict A Riot* as Victor and Plastic Face almost came to blows over who would take up the challenge of licking a can of whipped cream off Nicole's boobs in under thirty seconds. Jackie was miffed they didn't screen his barnstorming performance of *(Everything I Do) I Do It for You*, which showcased the raw emotion of his ballad voice, or any of his own new compositions, all of which were sure-fire hits. The irritation threatened to spill over into a tantrum when Lysa broached the subject of why he'd been put up for eviction.

'So, Jackie,' she said. 'You must want to know why the housemates nominated you. I'm not going to beat about the bush. It was your singing.'

'What do you mean?'

'You did sing. A lot.'

'I'm a singer, so I sing,' he said. 'What's wrong with that?'

'I'll let the housemates tell you,' she said, and turned to the big screen.

Flaxenburg's face filled the diary room camera, the increased scale of his features bringing a corresponding growth in Jackie's desire to smash his face in.

'I'm nominating Jackie because he sounds like a cat being strangled,' the actor said in his muted voice, caused by the Botox that held his facial muscles in its neurotoxin thrall. 'People of Britain, vote him out or you'll get to hear what he sounds like when he's really being strangled.'

The next four clips were equally cruel. Jeff claimed Jackie's singing made his fillings ache; Nicole confided that she thought whoever had told Jackie he could sing was tone deaf; and chick-lit author Mary Svenson, whose latest book was languishing in the bargain bins, said she wished she wasn't so feminist and owned knitting needles to ram into her eardrums. Small-time comedian Alfie Anderson, up last, got the biggest laugh.

'I'd rather play Snap with Captain Hook than listen to Jackie sing,' he dead-panned.

Jackie tried his best to be a good sport and chortle along with the mocking audience laughter being piped into the interview room. He could only let out a succession of winded grunts, as though he was being punched repeatedly in the stomach.

'Do you think that's fair comment?' Lysa said.

She wanted him to lash out, but he'd agreed with Phyllis, his loyal manager of over two decades, to play nice when evicted—at least at first. He would meet Phyllis tomorrow to figure out what approach to take for maximum publicity. If that meant slinging muck in the tabloids, he would do so. They needed to pick their targets carefully, though, for attacking somebody too popular could backfire. Anyway, he knew he was a great artist. His single *Your Eyes Are Mine* had topped the charts for six weeks back in 1990. A rotten singer couldn't perform such a feat, unless they did a Milli Vanilli. Jackie hadn't gone down that road.

Before putting forward the only sensible explanation for his eviction, he had to lose the desire to let fly. He did what he always did in moments when he needed to be calm. He imagined himself alone beneath the spotlight in a cavernous darkness, his sole companion a glittering silver microphone. When he sang a note of absolute purity and beauty, the microphone sent out an expanding sphere of blue light that banished the darkness and bathed him in its peaceful incandescence. When he opened his eyes, he no longer felt the need to vent.

'I'm not surprised they voted me off,' he said.

Lysa raised an eyebrow. 'Are you saying they're right?'

'No. You've seen *The Weakest Link*. They vote off the strongest, not the weakest, to make it easier to win the money. It's strategy.' He spread his palms. 'Same thing here.'

The audience whooped and applauded, but Lysa wasn't about to let him squirm off the hook. 'So why do you think the public voted for you to go?'

Jackie knew why the public had chosen to eject him over that talentless scrotum Jeff, who stripped to the waist at every opportunity to display his washboard stomach and rock-hard moobs. Jackie's body looked like a wax dummy left too close to a radiator. It was image over content, sex over art, youth over experience.

Jackie couldn't speak his mind, as an attack on the public would destroy what little chance he had of salvaging something from his early exit. Instead, he chose to compare himself to Marie. 'Look who I was up against. Marie is a sweetheart. Who could vote for her?'

Awwwwwwwwwwwwwwww!!!!!!!! went the audience, and Lysa segued into the flirting.

Jackie hadn't lied about his feelings for Marie, a talented and beautiful woman who'd been washed ashore on a remote musical island by a tidal wave of girl bands whose thrusting crotches and bouncing tits hypnotized people into missing their lack of musical ability. He hoped she would win, although he didn't think it likely. She had eschewed plastic surgery, so a little pouch of skin dangled beneath her chin and her nipples didn't point skyward at the perky angle required for stardom these days. Such imperfections didn't matter to him. Gravity always won in the end, as his body proved. She was still gorgeous.

After a few minutes of chit-chat, during which Jackie dropped heavy hints he would like to get together with Marie after the season ended, the interview wrapped up. As the camera cue lights died, Lysa flipped off her microphone and slipped a hand under the strap of her swish purple dress to scratch her armpit. Her black bobbed hair swung as she dug in with her long nails.

'Oh, the relief,' she said, ruby-red lips pursed in satisfaction. 'Jackie, I'm sorry you got kicked off. You were far more entertaining than those other boring sods.'

'So what happens now?'

'You pick up your hefty fee and hope for the best,' she said, climbing to her feet.

The studio lights dimmed as technicians wound up cables and threw covers over cameras. Jackie stayed seated. What did he have to rush off to? A quick last pint down at The Macbeth with his cronies, who would admittedly make him feel better for a while by taking the piss? A cup of tea, his mother's panacea for every disappointment, in the former council flat they shared in Hoxton? That would help too, but he would later be stuck with another night in his bedroom, going through his scrapbook for the millionth time.

Lysa regarded him as he sat there, hands folded in his lap and staring at the camera that was no longer transmitting his image across the country. She let out a sigh and placed a hand on his shoulder. 'Tandy Carston's having a little do down at Aura. She won't mind if I bring you along.'

At the mention of the supermodel and the selective private club often stowed to the gunwales with stars, Jackie snapped his head round like a terrier catching sight of a bone from an elephant's leg. 'Really?'

'Totally. Tandy loves the show. She'll be stoked to get a gander at you in the flesh.'

Jackie bounded off the seat and held out his arm to Lysa, who took it with a smile and led him out of the darkening room.

As the show finished and the kidnapper's hand reached for the remote, Barry had come no closer to loosening the ropes. He knew he had to try something drastic. He planted his bare feet on the concrete and heaved, prompting a metallic squeal from the bolts holding the chair in place, but no movement. His captor turned off the television, sending the corner into shadow, and walked into the light cast by the lamp. Despite the orange Hugo Boss shirt and black jeans he wore on his slightly chubby body, he looked utterly ordinary. The haircut framed the face of a drone in his mid-twenties: cheekbones submerged in flab; dull brown eyes studded into pallid skin; a shapeless dollop of a nose; a down-turned mouth that arced over the absence of a chin. He reminded Barry of the Lego men little Dean loved to play with. No matter how many wigs or new outfits you inserted into the slots, their features remained flat approximations of a human face.

'Hi, Barry,' the kidnapper said. 'You're awake.'

The squeaky, nasal voice sounded strangely familiar, as well as just strange. Barry had a feeling he'd heard it before, although he couldn't recall where and when. All attempts to bring back the memory ceased when his captor lifted his hand to reveal a scalpel pinched between right thumb and forefinger. Barry's calves no longer felt so gladiatorial.

'Sorry about all this,' the kidnapper said, waving the gleaming metal instrument at Barry's bonds. 'It's nothing personal. I'm actually a huge fan.'

The scalpel swished to and fro as Lego Man approached. Even if Barry had been able to get an intelligible sound past the gag, his tongue would have been too numb to do more than mumble.

The kidnapper brought the blade towards Barry's face. 'I've got one question. Answer it, and this will be over in a jiffy.'

Barry wanted to sit tall and show no fear. His body would not obey, shrinking back as far as the bonds would allow. The blade sliced through the gag and the captor pulled out the rubber ball it had been holding in place. Barry gathered up as much saliva as he could muster and spat until the taste of rubber faded. Then he filled his lungs to bawl for help. Lego Man just stood there, tickling the back of his hand with the scalpel. After a minute or so of futile shouting, Barry remembered the soundproofing.

Panting, he looked up at the kidnapper. 'Why did you bother gagging me?'

Lego Man licked a finger and smoothed down an eyebrow. 'I wanted to watch Jackie Thunder be evicted in peace. I voted for him.'

Barry hadn't voted, but he saw the chance to build up a rapport with his unsettling captor. 'Me too. He's awful.'

The kidnapper clapped his hands like an excited infant. 'I knew we had things in common!'

Barry smiled, his facial muscles creaking with the effort. 'I'm sure we do. Maybe if I knew who you were we could figure out more things.'

'Oh, I'm nobody.' A smile crooked Lego Man's lips. 'You're going to help change that.'

'I have tonnes of money,' Barry said. 'My missus will pay up, no questions asked.'

The kidnapper pouted. 'This is more meaningful than a ransom.' He paused, regarding Barry's body. 'Which one is it?'

'What?'

'Which one gives you your power?'

Barry frowned. 'Which what?'

Lego Man breathed deeply through his nose and lowered the tip of the scalpel to rest on Barry's upper arm. 'Which tattoo makes you famous?'

A new possibility occurred to Barry, one that sent warm relief coursing through his limbs. He was on *Punk'd*. That was why the voice sounded so familiar. Somewhere in the shadows there would be a camera. One of his celebrity chums would be in the next room, watching the video feed and chortling.

'Alright, you can come out now,' Barry called. 'I've rumbled the joke. Who set it up? Was it you, Brad? George? I hope you at least asked the producer to fuzz out my family jewels.'

No door opened, no presenter came out with a microphone and a wide grin.

'There's no point filming now I know what's going on,' Barry told Lego Man, who still loomed over him. 'Untie me. This chair's freezing my arse off.'

'You're not on television. For once.'

Barry continued to exhort the producers to stop the cameras. Still nobody came. As Barry's certainty grew weaker so did his voice. This was real. When he'd stepped up to take a penalty in the World Cup, the hopes and dreams of a nation on his shoulders, his pulse had barely risen. Now his heart felt like it could burst from his chest and bounce across the room like a casually kicked football.

Lego Man moved the cold point of the scalpel to rest on a faded yin-yang symbol on Barry's shoulder.

'Is it this one?' he asked. He moved the scalpel to the Kanji script running up Barry's forearm. 'Maybe this one. What is it? Some kind of magic phrase?'

'It's my son's name in Japanese.'

Barry's thoughts turned to his two beloved children. No matter what he got up to, he always made sure he got back in the morning to deliver a kiss to each sleepy little face when they woke. If he was not there, they would be frantic.

'Please, let me go,' he said. 'My kids are waiting for me.'

The unheeding scalpel shifted through each of the remaining six pieces of body art, each time leaving a cold dot on the skin. It came to rest on the Sanskrit etched into Barry's stomach.

'What does this one say?'

Barry, his thoughts rendered sluggish by panic and the remnants of the drug in his system, struggled to remember what the squiggly lines meant. 'It means, "The greatest mastery is self-worth." No, I mean, "The greatest worth is self-mastery." I think. God, I don't know. I only got it because it looked cool. My tattoos don't give me any power, honest mate.'

'Liar, liar, pants on fire,' Lego Man said.

'It's not the tattoos,' Barry said, trying to keep his voice from cracking. 'I'm just good at football.'

'Loads of people are good at football but none of them are as famous as you. That's not a coincidence. Now, don't be a greedy guts. Tell me which one it is.'

Barry had cried once in his adult life, when his three-year-old daughter contracted pneumonia and spent days fighting for her life on a drip. He battled the tears that threatened to come again as the full extent of his captor's insanity seeped in.

'I swear, they're only tattoos,' he said between hitching breaths.

'Maybe he doesn't know,' Lego Man said, cocking his head and petting the back of his mullet.

Barry seized upon this indecision. 'That's it, I don't know, so it's pointless keeping me here. I won't tell anyone if you let me go. I promise.'

The kidnapper's eyes glazed over and his attention drifted elsewhere. 'You're right,' he said, clearly not addressing Barry. 'They always lie.'

The scalpel was dropping towards the Sanskrit text as Barry's captor appeared to be talking to an imaginary advisor. The footballer pulled his stomach in as tight as he could.

'Take them all?' Lego Man said. 'That'll be icky.' After another pause for a voice only he could hear, he nodded. 'Of course I'm committed. If you say I have to, I will.'

His eyes snapped back into focus and he reached around Barry, avoiding the footballer's desperate attempts to catch his eye and remind him he was about to slice up a human being. He leaned close enough for Barry to get a whiff of the musky yet sweet scent of Deckhart, Barry's own brand of aftershave.

Barry had enough time to shout 'No!' before a needle stung his neck and darkness claimed him once more.

When Jackie walked into Aura behind Lysa, he had to steady himself on the wall. He'd never been to the venue, but at the height of his fame he'd been to many elite clubs and restaurants just like it. The atmosphere was always the same, regardless of the décor, fashion or music. Underneath the smell of leather, rich food and burnished wood lurked the crackling electricity of A-list celebrity.

Around the tables were gathered the cream of the British acting world, singers whose albums went platinum, an array of models and a smattering of business tycoons. Their skin glistened with the pampering of a thousand lavish spas, shinier than the cutlery strewn around the empty plates, and designer clothes hugged their perfect bodies. Jackie felt giddy, blessed and deeply inferior. When Tandy slunk towards them on legs so long she crossed the room in a few strides, he cringed behind Lysa like a nervous toddler.

'Lysa,' Tandy said in her polished middle England accent. 'We watched the show. Brilliant, *comme d'habitude.*'

The pair exchanged air kisses as Jackie looked around for the toilet. Once, long ago, this had been his world. Now he felt his blood bubbling like that of a diver emerging too fast from the depths. He needed some time alone to acclimatize and remind himself he belonged here, not clawing at a Casio organ in seedy pubs.

Tandy peered around his human shield, one tweezed eyebrow arched above a feline green eye. 'And who have you brought? Could it be the man of the moment? How marvellous!'

She grabbed Jackie's wrist and yanked him out. 'Look who's here. Jackie Thunder, callously ejected from the *Celebrity Public Eye* house. Oh, you must sing for us, Jackie, your big hit. What was it called again?'

'*Your Eyes Are Mine,*' Jackie said, his arm hanging limp in the model's clutches.

'That's it. I remember making my dollies dance to it.'

She winked at the crowd, raising a few titters.

In normal circumstances, Jackie would have been all over such a request. But these weren't normal circumstances. The club was packed with people whose current fame eclipsed his even when he was at his most popular. Now he was just somebody who'd resorted to *Celebrity Public Eye* to revive his career—an insect in their eyes.

'Well, I'm not sure ...'

'It's my party, so what I say goes.' Tandy turned to the DJ. Her mellifluous voice dissolved into a barking order. 'Andy, play Jackie's song and scare up a microphone as well.'

'I'll need a few minutes to download it,' said the DJ, a dreadlocked youth with a face full of piercings. 'If I can find it.'

'Super.' She turned back to Jackie. 'That'll give you time for some Dutch courage. The bar's over there. It's free, so don't worry about not being able to afford it.'

She skipped off, treating Jackie to a view of her gorgeous buttocks wrestling each other beneath a clinging black skirt.

Jackie found himself with nowhere to go. Lysa had squeezed onto the last free seat between Oscar-winning actress Cathy Green and cheeky London rapper Splicer. It had only been a few hours, but he found himself missing Marie. He headed for the bar. Though he'd promised himself many times that he would take it easy on the booze, he ordered a Zubrowka. A second swiftly went the way of the first.

Take it easy, he thought. *You're in now.*

A third vodka was sloshing around his stomach by the time the DJ thrust a microphone into his hand.

Tandy stood up and clapped her hands. 'Come on, man, give it to me.'

Jackie tried to summon up his calming image. It wouldn't come.

I can't do this, he thought.

But when the opening guitar chord progression kicked in, climbing from Am to D, and the synthesizer swelled, he lifted his head and let his voice rise in synch with his younger self on the recording.

Your eyes are mine, sparkling like wine
Our love is divine, our fates are entwined
Your lips are mine, full and so red
Our love is pure, it will last 'til we're dead
Your heart is mine, it beats with our passion
Our love is eternal, never out of fashion

He forgot he was nothing more than post-dinner light entertainment. The melody was pure and everlasting, the words ripe with meaning. His eyes squeezed shut as he reached the chorus and his fist clenched, pumping out emotion from the deep well within.

Your eyes are mine, my eyes are yours
My eyes are yours, your eyes are mine
We'll stay together, 'til the end of time

Verse followed chorus, until the final minor chord died away. Jackie, spent, opened his eyes to find Tandy's lips trembling with suppressed emotion. The other stars were still, looking down at their laps or staring off into the distance, entranced by the splendour of the song.

You still have it, you old dog, Jackie thought as Tandy rose to her feet and led the room in applause and merry laughter.

By the time they made the short hop to Embassy in a fleet of chauffeur-driven Mercs, Audis and Aston Martins, Jackie was plastered. He'd squeezed in beside Tandy at Aura and, egged on by the model, regaled the table with his old exploits: the parties, the women, the occasional drunk-driving conviction. As he held the celebrities in his spell with tales from the past, he knew he would soon be writing a new future for himself.

He lurched from Tandy's car outside Embassy and held out a hand to help the model rise to her feet. They crossed to the entrance, where a burly bouncer with an incongruously gentle face manned the rope holding back the plebs from the smoked glass doors leading into nirvana.

'Jackie, is that you?' the bouncer said.

'It is indeed, Kev, my good man.'

Jackie had for a few months the previous year tried to perform the miracle of getting into Embassy, only to be rebuffed by Kev each time.

'Kevin, Jackie is mine tonight, aren't you, my love?' Tandy said. 'Be a dear and let us through.'

The bouncer unclipped the rope and stepped aside.

'Watch yourself, mate,' he whispered to Jackie as they swept past.

Once inside, the orgy of booze continued. Soon Jackie was swooping around the dance floor, giddy with delight. After a while, Tandy cleared the floor and guided him to the middle, where she demanded he do his twirl and point again and again. At one point, the vodka and champagne swirling around his stomach almost came up. He swallowed the vortex of bile and kept spinning. The show only stopped when Lysa guided him back to the table with an arm around his shoulders. He rested his head on the wall, relishing the celebrity sweat moistening its cool surface, and watched Lysa say something into Tandy's ear. Soon they were arguing, glancing in his direction. Jackie let out a happy burp.

He must have fallen asleep, for the next thing he knew the house lights came up and the revellers began to melt away. Through the thinning crowd, Jackie saw two Tandys head for the exit. He clambered to his feet with the aid of the table and followed. As he came out of the club, Jackie spotted a posse of photographers. Tandy was too far away for a photo opportunity, so he lurched towards quirky songstress and renowned party animal Fleur, who'd exited at the same time. He intended to put an arm around her for a chummy celebrity snap, but she stepped away at the last second and his hand docked with her right breast. Lenses clicked and bulbs popped.

'Keep your mucky paws to yourself,' Fleur said, stamping on his foot. Luckily she was built like a twig, so it didn't hurt. Jackie lost his precarious balance nonetheless, stumbling back into Kev's arms. The cameras whirred again.

Tandy, who'd turned around to see the show, laughed long and hard before diving into her car to avoid the photographers now swarming her way.

Lysa appeared and gave Jackie a quick peck on the cheek. 'Sorry. I should've known better. Good luck with your career.'

She skipped into a waiting Mercedes and sped off. Her young assistant, who looked like she'd been standing outside the club all night in the bitter cold, handed him two twenty-pound notes.

'Whatsh thish?'

'Taxi fare,' she said. 'Try not to spend it all in the kebab shop. Or puke on it.'

With that, she too departed.

Jackie craned his neck to look at Kev. 'Fuck, you're shtrong. Even your fashe has mushles.'

'I'm getting you a taxi. You're bladdered.'

'I'm shelebrating mate. I'm in, me. One a the gang. Back to the top. I'm gonna be a mehmba of this eshtablishment. Tandy shaid she would vouch for me.'

'She was taking the piss, mate. She was the organ grinder, you were the monkey.'

'Thatsh not true. I'm gonna be famoush again.'

'Sure you are, Jackie.'

'Famoush,' Jackie repeated, and allowed the bouncer to drag him to the taxi rank on the corner, already on the way to sleep.

Barry woke up one last time. His bloodshot eyes focused on the man standing in the middle of the room, holding a scrap of patterned cloth up to the light between his thumb and forefinger as if it was a pair of dirty underpants. He recognized his son's name and realized the cloth was his own skin, his tattoo, sliced from his body. He didn't look down, not wanting to see his beautiful body ravaged. He knew he was dying, could feel it in the numbness below his neck, in the way his thoughts sputtered and fizzed.

Lego Man bent over the table and scraped at the underside of the skin with the scalpel, retching as he did so. When he'd added a sliver of saliva to the puddle of vomit that lay on the floor, the killer swiped at his mouth with the back of his hand and unsteadily broke into the first lines of *We Found Love*. The dying footballer almost remembered where he'd heard the grating voice, but the memory dissolved before he could grasp it. His thoughts turned instead to his funeral.

Cynthia would be the perfect weeping widow, careful not to let the tears drip onto her little black dress as she hugged his sweet kids. He almost lost it then, knowing for sure he would never see them again, but he didn't want to give his killer the satisfaction of seeing him unmanned. Instead, he willed himself to focus on the bigger picture. Hollywood's top stars and the world's most-famous footballers would line the front row, all suitably distraught, while the public would flank the streets in their tens of thousands. Bouquets of flowers would build up in wobbly towers across the country in spontaneous tributes. It would be a bigger send-off than Princess Diana's. In the seconds before his eyes closed for the final time, Barry smiled beatifically.

3

Jackie had never tasted a badger's arse, but when he awoke face down on the sofa he came as close as he ever had to sampling that culinary horror. He was still dressed in last night's outfit, which reeked of stale booze and did nothing to settle his churning stomach. When he tried to sit up, a searing headache informed him that remaining horizontal would be an excellent plan of action. He groaned and tried to suffocate the pain with a cushion.

'Morning, son.'

He opened one eye to see his mum wielding a metal tray bedecked with Scottie dogs cavorting through a tartan-fringed field. Agnes hadn't lived in Scotland since Jackie was three, which explained her love for such twee tat. Stuffed Highland dancers, snow globes containing plastic castles and pictures of glens and mountains littered the two-bedroom flat on the third floor of a block on Purcell Street. On the tray sat a cup of tea and a jammy scone. With all the ease of forty-two years of intensive mothering, Jackie's mum hooked a small wicker table with her purple-slippered foot, slid it across and laid the tray down inches from his throbbing head.

She was short and stocky, with a stern, square face that concealed a loving nature—the kind of no-nonsense Scotswoman who would happily batter a knife-wielding mugger senseless with her umbrella and give him money for a taxi to the hospital afterward. Even though she was one year off her seventieth birthday, red still tinged her hair. Her little legs were strong, although knobbly with varicose veins from a lifetime of standing behind a bar pulling pints. Jackie's father had been a small-time musician, bringing the joy of music into the home, but little cash. He'd played keyboards and guitar in weddings bands, and picked up the odd session gig, but the massive catalogue of songs he'd written never made it to the wider public. Agnes had brought home the bacon.

Jackie had so many happy memories of his father: plucking guitar strings as a toddler, sitting on a broad lap as a gentle hand guided his across a keyboard, sneaking into a pub at fifteen to watch a gig. Jackie still owned dozens of cassettes of his father's compositions, but he rarely listened to them. There was too much pain wrapped up in the music. He couldn't put them on without visualizing his father's skeletal body in the earth, put there by the drunken swerve of a car late one Saturday night. After his father's death, Agnes had been forced to work harder to replace his meagre income. When Jackie found fame and started trying to kick cash back to her, she refused to take it. She'd stayed behind the bar right up to her sixtieth birthday, and still did part-time cleaning work.

Jackie levered himself up and brought the lukewarm tea to his lips, avoiding the crack on the rim.

'Thanks, Mum,' he said, his voice so hoarse he sounded like he was doing a Tom Waits impression.

'You look like you needed it, Archie.'

At the mention of his real name, Jackie sat up further to begin the fruitless task of persuading her to stop calling him by his birth name. Archibald Thorpe didn't suggest star quality, after all. The undertow in his stomach prevented him from taking it any further.

'So you got kicked off that daft show,' she said, perching on the arm of the sofa and rubbing his head.

'Afraid so.'

'Ach, never mind. Those reality shows are rubbish anyway. They're just an excuse to stare at people without getting punched in the coupon.'

'That only really happens in Glasgow.'

'Aye, well. It should happen everywhere. I hate nosy people. Anyway, now that you're up, Phyllis called. She said you've to ring her.'

'What time is it?'

'Eight o'clock.'

'Fuck, that's early.'

Jackie's mum tapped his head, sending a fresh blast of pain rampaging through his skull. 'No F-word in my house.'

'Mum! You know you shouldn't do that.'

Agnes rolled her eyes. Jackie couldn't stand physical pain: the mildest pin prick felt like a Saturday night stabbing, and banging his knee was like being bludgeoned by a baseball bat. It wasn't cowardice; his father had suffered the same condition, as had his father before him. He'd been in one fight at school, which ended with him writhing on the ground after a soft punch. The injury had ached for days. His pride took longer to recover. Since then, Jackie had avoided conflict through a combination of performing, joking and, on two shameful occasions, running away as fast as he could.

Although Jackie knew his ailment was very real, a succession of doctors had been unable to pinpoint any problem. Agnes produced her own diagnosis: Jackie, like his father, was a big Jessie. He'd learned to live with it, carefully manoeuvring around sharp-edged furniture, avoiding sports and keeping as far away from needles as possible. Only Agnes's fast hands caused him any pain these days. Yet he lived in dread of the day when he might suffer a real injury—a broken leg or a deep cut from a knife. He could only hope that day would never come, for he suspected his heart would burst with the agony.

Once the pain had backed off, Jackie dug out his mobile and rang his manager.

'I take it you're suffering?' she said.

He grunted once in the affirmative.

'Not as much as your career's going to suffer after last night's performance. What were you thinking?'

'What you on about? I behaved myself during the interview, like we agreed.'

'You don't remember?'

Jackie replayed the previous evening's events, and ran into a blank after entering Embassy. 'Did something happen?'

'You could say that. Grab a shower, munch a dozen Paracetamol and get down here pronto. And for fuck's sake, don't look at any websites.'

The phone went dead.

'Good news?' his mum asked.

'The exact opposite, I expect. Help me up. I've got to get ready.'

One hour, three cups of tea, two jammy scones and a hot shower later, Jackie sat on the underground, trying to sway in time with the rocking car to minimize his brain's contact with the inside of his skull. He became aware of a smartly dressed woman in her early thirties staring at him and shaking her head.

'Disgraceful,' she said.

'Are you talking to me?'

'No, I'm talking to the other sex pest sitting beside you. Oh wait, there isn't one.'

Before Jackie could ask what she meant, the train braked on its approach to King's Cross St Pancras. He got up and lurched onto the platform. His passage through the tunnels, up the escalator and across the concourse prompted more shakes of the head and pursed lips from women. Once outside, he ducked down Belgrove Street, past a corner building where three workmen were dangling their cups of tea over the scaffolding. One of them spotted Jackie and nudged his pals. 'Oi, Jackie. Next time see if you can grab them both.' He put his hands to his chest and made an exaggerated groping gesture.

A picture began to form in Jackie's mind something to do with camera flashes and cleavage. He was grateful when it slipped away. He had a feeling it might be better if he didn't discover what lurked behind the hangover curtains.

When he got into Phyllis's office, converted from a small flat on Argyle Street next to the Globe Hotel, she laid straight into him. 'Last night was an unmitigated fucking disaster. A catastrophe. A cock-up of epic proportions. Am I making my point strongly enough?'

Jackie nodded and kept silent. He'd been with Phyllis long enough, and made enough monumental mistakes during that time, to know mounting a defence would make things worse. Besides, he still didn't know what he'd done.

'Let me go through it point-by-point. A, you got voted off first, unnecessarily. I told you to tone down the singing. There's nothing the British public hates more than an over-confident prick. That's how you came across, elbowing your way onto camera and singing at the drop of hat. You have to at least pretend to be self-effacing, even if you secretly love yourself. And those songs you sang sucked twelve kinds of donkey cock.' Phyllis lifted her chunky-framed glasses to the top of her head, where they served as an impromptu headband to keep her silver fringe out of her eyes. Normally when she did this, she looked less severe. Today her hazel eyes were popping out of her head. 'Anyway, that was moronic. But we could have dealt with it, without Point B. Have you remembered yet?'

When Jackie remained silent, Phyllis swivelled her laptop around. 'Congratulations. You're the first person in history who managed to make Fleur look sober.'

The first thing Jackie saw was the headline, which ran across the top of the *Daily Mirror*'s celebrity pictures page, STORM IN A D-CUP: JACKIE THUNDER IN FLEUR BOOB BLUNDER.

The picture beneath brought the memory flooding back. Fleur, dressed in a lacy purple top and tiny skirt, looked compos mentis compared to Jackie, despite her smudged eye-liner and the wilting spikes of her dyed blonde hair. Sweat circles as big as dinner plates ringed the armpits of his yellow shirt. The booze had puffed up his face, although not so much that it hid the bags under his eyes. His black hair, dyed to hide the grey streaks, was dishevelled from sleeping against the wall, and the flash had illuminated big white patches on his scalp. His grey eyes appeared to be focussed, if such a word could be applied to his beady stare, on Fleur's chest, where his hand clutched a healthy mound of tit.

'Oh fuck,' he said as he remembered the moment he left the club and the way Tandy had toyed with him. Kev's words about him being a performing monkey flipped up out of the depths, and he knew the bouncer was right. He'd been too drunk to realize it.

'It was an accident. I was only trying to get my picture taken with her.'

'Consider it job done. Seriously, how many times have I warned you that you'll go too far with these stupid publicity stunts one day and get yourself in real trouble?'

Jackie put his head in his hands and stared at the carpet, where crumbs from Phyllis's morning croissant were clinging to the fibres. 'Is it that bad?'

Phyllis sighed. 'No, I suppose not. But I had you lined up to sing in a kids' DVD with The Tinkles, good money too. Now you're the demon tit-grabber of Burlington Street, that's out the window.'

Jackie peeked through his fingers at the picture and turned his attention back to the carpet. 'Can't we use it? There's no such thing as bad publicity, right?'

'That brings me to Point C, which may be the biggest disaster, although this one isn't your fault.' A soft click signalled Phyllis accessing another page. 'Barry Deckhart was having an affair. Oh, and he's missing.'

Jackie scanned the story. Prudence Loveheart, singer with pop sensations Voluptia, had reported seeing Deckhart being bundled into the back of a white van, registration number and make unknown to Prudence, who'd admitted to being pretty far gone on coke and champagne. A celebrity kidnap would have been huge news on its own, but Prudence revealed she'd seen the kidnap from the love nest she and Deckhart used for illicit trysts.

'Cynthia must be raging,' Jackie said, momentarily forgetting his problems.

'Never mind what tits-on-a-stick thinks.' Phyllis stabbed her finger at the laptop. 'That's going to gobble up the column inches in every rag for months, particularly if Dickhard doesn't turn up soon. There's going to be no room for you, unless you find some other tits to fondle. Maybe you could have a rummage around the Queen's withered knockers next. That would do the trick.'

'I'm buggered then?'

'Like a rent boy at a Tory politician's London fuck pad.'

Jackie slid down until his bum hung off the chair. Had he not been so dehydrated, he would have cried. Instead he let out a low moan.

When Phyllis spoke again, the heat had left her voice. 'Look, I'll see what I can do. I'll call the papers, ask if any of them want to interview you. Maybe they'll want to hear your side of the story. In the meantime, I've got you a gig.'

'Where?' Jackie said without moving.

'Near Newcastle, in The Cramlington Ritz. They love you up there.'

'Is that a club?'

'Yes, a very popular one.'

'Why've I never heard of it then?'

'It has a very select crowd.'

Jackie harboured a horrible suspicion where this was going. 'What kind of club is it?'

'A big one. Five hundred punters.'

'It's a bingo hall, isn't it?'

Phyllis paused. 'Well, yes. But it's a really good one. Big cash prizes in the regional link up.'

The self-pity that had been circling Jackie like a vulture eyeing a lost soul in the desert swooped in to land on his shoulder and peck at his head. He slid off the chair and sat on the floor. 'I can't face another bingo hall or crappy little club. This was supposed to get me back on my feet.'

'At least the fee will help pay off your debts.'

'Great, so the bank won't be chasing me. But I still can't afford to move out. I should be a star. Not some loser who blew his money and had to move back in with his mum because everybody thinks he's shit.'

Phyllis rounded the table and put a hand on his shoulder. 'Even the greats have lulls in their careers.'

'This isn't a lull. It's a bloody coma.'

'Something will come up.'

'We keep saying that. It never does.'

Jackie looked at the wall, where a gold disk hung amid a profusion of photographs of Phyllis with her clients. It was for his first and only album, *The Sound of Thunder*. He'd presented it to her when the record went platinum and he got an upgrade. A light sheen of dust covered the glass. He wondered if Phyllis noticed it any more. Jackie had always retained some belief that he would come good again, even amid the unfounded accusations of plagiarism from a little-known German techno band, bankruptcy court and long years of anonymity. He wasn't sure he could believe it any longer. Somehow the knowledge it couldn't get any worse gave him the strength to get his feet under him. He rose and faced Phyllis, who was eyeing him with some concern.

'I would get a day job,' he said. 'The problem is I've got no skills.'

'I wouldn't say that. Maybe you could be a grope-tester for push-up bras.'

They looked at each other, and laughed at the same time. Jackie resisted the urge to stroke Phyllis's cheek, a move that would probably end with a broken wrist. No matter how bad things got, she was always there for him. Not for the first time, he wondered why she stuck with him. He didn't even fit her client profile. She represented independent bands that pushed boundaries, garnering critical acclaim—if little sales. Virtually every time he came to see her, inventive, experimental or plain beautiful music from some new act she'd fallen in love with filled the office. Often he needed to ask who the bands were, but this morning he recognized that the backdrop to their conversation was provided by her current favourite band, The Freelance Whales—all quirky voices, melodic guitars, low-key beats and accordions. Not once had he heard her playing his tracks.

'I'm your worst client, aren't I?'

Phyllis nodded. 'Beyond any shadow of a doubt. You're also my favourite. I'll find you something. I promise. Now come on, let's go for a liquid lunch.'

With one last glance at the gold disc, which stared at him like a huge reproving eye, Jackie shambled after his manager. He lowered his head as they emerged onto the street. For the first time in his life, he didn't want to be recognized.

4

Commuters zipped across the concourse of King's Cross station, clutching newspapers and bagels, lattes and laptop bags, smartphones and tablets. Reluctant to lose momentum, they jinked and weaved like rugby players dodging tackles, rushing for the connections that would spit them out into workplaces across the city. Ringtones blared a digital morning chorus above the babble of hundreds of voices; machines clunked and whirred as they spat out tickets; and the plastic wheels of suitcases rumbled across the tiled floor.

Gareth Jones stood motionless in the middle of the seething mass, dressed in a close-fitting grey jumper, the V-neck of which revealed a black shirt and red tie, and tight jeans that clung to his thighs. While he normally chose his clothes as part of a cohesive look copied from fashion magazines, today the need for tight-fitting garments overrode other concerns: he didn't want the precious cargo taped to his skin to slip out of sleeve or trouser leg and be mashed by tramping feet. Despite the narrowing of choice, the outfit, crowned by his immaculate mullet, still worked. It had taken three washes with L'Oreal Serie Expert Liss Extreme Smoothing Shampoo to remove the matted blood. Now his spiky purple fronds glowed in the morning light slanting in through the roof panels.

The shell was sparkling and ready. He just needed the tattoos, which still raised the faint tickle of nausea in his breastbone and made his skin crawl where they touched him, to breathe fame into it. He put aside the disgust and focused his attention on the Sanskrit tattoo fixed to his stomach, willing it to transform him. As he concentrated, a slight tingle signalled what could be an awakening of the hidden power. He faced the ruddy-cheeked young man in an ill-fitting suit rushing towards him.

'See me,' he whispered.

The commuter's gaze shifted only briefly in Gareth's direction before he passed. Next, Gareth focused on the Kanji script Barry had claimed was his son's name, now running up his arm. He tried to summon its force, narrowing his consciousness down to the few inches of flesh touching the footballer's skin. Two women were approaching, the shoulders of their smart office jackets brushing against each other as they chatted.

'See me.'

A few feet from Gareth, they split and skipped past either side of him, still talking, and melded back together as though the separation had never taken place. He moved on to the thin Hebrew-inscribed band of skin, which he wore like an ankle bracelet. As a girl barely out of her teens, clutching a voluminous handbag almost the same size as her skinny torso, clicked his way on high-heeled boots, he spread his arms.

'See me,' he said.

She looked up, scanning his clothes. When her gaze reached his face, it slid off.

'*Gesundheit*,' she said, and flew past.

And so it went on. He stood there for ten minutes, a dull, flat rock the river of people coursed around. Even when his outstretched fingertips brushed their clothes, the passers-by did little more than glance at him before scattering like startled birds. If he'd taken on Barry's power, he would be the centre of a whirling vortex of admirers, their eyes glowing with awe as they battled to be near him. He dropped his arms. The undeserved cloak of mediocrity he'd worn his whole life remained in place.

All through primary and secondary school, he'd regularly found himself standing unseen on the side of the football pitch as the team captains handed out bibs. When groups gathered to chat in the playground or at the odd party he somehow got invited to, he would hang around on the periphery, guffawing at jokes he didn't understand

and trying to think of something to say. When he did manage to interject, the chatter would do little more than falter before picking up again, his words ignored. Though his chubby body, chunky glasses and parted hair made him a prime target for casual schoolyard violence, the bullies had overlooked him. Gareth's buttocks remained unflicked by wet towels, his glasses unstomped on, his hair unpulled. For a while he set out to invite the beatings that would at least prove he existed. He dressed as strangely as possible and threw his hand up in class at every opportunity. When even the teachers ignored his attempts to be the school swot, he gave up.

While sitting on the sidelines of school life, Gareth tried to convince himself that this ability to go unnoticed was a special power. In his mind's eye, he whipped guns from surprised bank robbers, ghosted into the bases of evil geniuses threatening world peace and foiled countless terrorist attacks. The invisibility fantasies ended one day when, aged fourteen, he was staring at his reflection in his mum's full-length mirror, as he often did when she'd gone out. It started with his fingers. The colour seemed to blanch out of them, revealing bones and ligaments, which in turn faded until they looked like a pencil drawing. It spread up his arms and then his neck and face. He tore his gaze from the mirror and looked down at his fingers. The weave of the carpet was visible through his translucent skin.

He blundered down the hallway to his mum's study, barely able to breathe. He hoped her smell would snap him back. It made no difference. His gaze fell on a craft knife discarded among a pile of the half-finished mosaic tiles she was making to decorate the bathroom. Gareth, sure that any second he would evaporate, snatched up the knife and jabbed it point first into his ghostly forearm. Bright blood trickled across his skin, bringing solidity to the areas it caressed. He closed his eyes and dragged the blade across, the sharp pain reassuring him of his physicality. When he found the courage to look, he could no longer see through his blood-smeared forearm. In the years that followed, as the attacks grew more frequent, he always kept a small knife to hand. Only the gaze of his mum, the one person who ever really looked at him, had stopped him from cutting every day. When that was taken from him last year, slash marks soon criss-crossed his arm.

A scalpel nestled in his pocket in the station, but as he felt the familiar sensation that preceded invisibility run up his arm, he knew he couldn't pull it out. That would attract the wrong kind of attention.

Instead, he bit down on his tongue and dug his nails into his forearm, hard. The numbness backed off a little. Still unnoticed, he took a deep, shuddering breath, and tried to come to terms with both his failure and the fact he'd killed. He hadn't intended to murder Barry; his plan had been to remove the tattoos and drop the footballer outside A&E. But he'd underestimated the trauma the removal of so much skin, and additional flesh gouged out by his inexpert hand, would cause. When he'd pitched the body into the Thames downriver from Teddington Lock in the dead of night and watched the footballer slip below the black waters, he thought it a blessing. Barry, stripped of his magic, would not have wanted to live as a mere mortal, wandering the streets of London unrecognized and unloved. Now that Gareth knew the tattoos hadn't given up their power, a knot of guilt calcified in the pit of his stomach. He did his best to ignore it. After all, Barry could have avoided it all if he hadn't ignored Gareth's letters and emails.

Gareth stuffed his hands into his pockets and, head hanging, shuffled through the crowd. He didn't understand what had gone wrong. When his mum steered him towards Barry, it had seemed so perfect. The footballer's fame was stratospheric, reaching far beyond his ability with a ball. His tattoos must be incredibly powerful. And yet, they'd done nothing for Gareth. Perhaps he needed to perform a ritual to transfer the power along with the tattoos. Or perhaps Barry wasn't the one. Gareth was a singer, not a footballer, so maybe the powers didn't transfer across disciplines.

Either way, he tried not to feel too despondent. His mum had warned him that there may be false starts along the way and he'd already waited ten years for the spotlight to shine on him. A few more months wouldn't matter. Then, once fame finally wrapped him in its warm embrace, he would no longer have need of the knife.

Outside WH Smith, he lifted his head, drawn to the rows of colourful magazines lined up along the shelves. He picked up copies of *Now*, *Heat* and *Celeb!* and, after a moment's hesitation, a Double Decker for some solace. He took his purchases outside. As he walked towards the Euston Road crossing, he saw a group of teenagers pointing and whispering. He followed the line of their bristling fingers, wondering if fate was delivering another celebrity to him. He saw Jackie Thunder, his face pale, hurrying across the road and up Belgrove. He thought about pursuing him, but as far as he knew, Jackie didn't have a tattoo. Even if he had, a *Celebrity Public Eye* reject was not what Gareth needed.

Nonetheless, Gareth continued in Jackie's footsteps for a while, heading for Argyle Square Gardens. Parked on a bench on the other side of the small grassy square from three alcoholics sharing an early-morning beer, he scanned the pages of the magazines. Between soothing bites of chocolate, he scratched absent mindedly where the ragged tattoos, already beginning to waft out a faint smell of putrescence, chafed his skin. Although the pages, so familiar and comforting, were full of celebrities to choose from, he had no idea which one to target next. Yet he wasn't worried. He knew that his mum would show him the way. After all, not even death had stopped her guiding him.

5

Three months earlier

Gareth entered his empty house in East Dulwich and stood in the hallway, held immobile by the oppressive late evening silence. He'd spent seven long months in The Priory munching Lagarctil, talking over his issues in group therapy and listening to doctors tell him he'd suffered a 'psychotic break induced by the loss of his mother and his public humiliation'. Once he'd realized the only way out was to agree with their diagnosis, wrong as it may be, it had been a matter of biding his time until they released him. Now here he stood in his motherless home, officially certified sane once more.

In the week after his mum's death, before his enforced stay in the psychiatric ward, he'd been too busy organizing the funeral in a state of stunned grief to understand how life would be without her. Now he felt it. There was no clatter of dishes or the whistle of a kettle, no brisk peck on the cheek, no music spilling out from the radio she'd kept tuned to Radio 1 to track the latest trends and thus shape his musical direction. Her absence was a crushing weight that forced the air from his lungs and set his skin to fading.

He staggered up the stairs and scrabbled around in his room for a knife. He cut two quick slashes in his arm, where the wounds inflicted in a frenzy of grief after she died had settled into rutted scars. He focused on the bright, clear pain. The building pressure released from the warm blood like trapped steam. Equilibrium restored, he walked to her bedroom, unmindful of the red liquid that dripped from his fingers. The bed was made, all her personal effects still ranged around as if she were still alive. He collapsed onto the mattress and buried his face in the pillows, which retained the faint scent of her hair. He sucked it in, trying to convince himself she'd just popped down to the shops, until his eyes drooped and he fell into a restless sleep.

He awoke early the next morning, fully clothed and with her scent still in his nostrils. The dark waters of sleep hadn't washed away his renewed grief. Downstairs, he brewed a cup of tea and breakfasted on a Crunchie from the stash in the kitchen cupboard, before heading back up to get changed. In his room, he stood before the collection of images that adorned every inch of the walls.

'Hello, my friends,' he said. 'Did you miss me?'

Gareth had amassed the sprawling collage by snipping out pictures from celebrity magazines. Using Pritt Stick, he would paste a passport picture of his own face over the features of the chosen celebrity and stick it to the wall. In his collection, he walked the red carpet with Scarlett Johansson by his side, flung an arm around the neck of Chris Martin, lolled on the beaches of Barbados alongside Cliff Richard, and inserted himself in countless other situations. He eyed the scissors on the bedside table, itching to pick out some images from the magazines he'd bought on the way home. The doctors had banned him from doing exactly that, as they felt it was a contributing factor to the incident. Again, he knew they were mistaken. If there was anything wrong with wanting to be famous, half of the country would have been institutionalized by now. Besides, his mum had seen no problem with this practice, often bringing him pictures she thought would suit his gallery.

He resisted the temptation; he had something else to attend to first. He picked out his most sombre clothes, teased his mullet into shape and headed out the door.

As he creaked open the front gate, his neighbour poked her head out of the window. 'Gareth. You're back.'

'Hi, Mrs Middleton,' he said.

'Are you okay?' she asked, her brown eyes moist with sympathy behind the spectacles that covered the top half of her face.

'I'm fine,' he said.

Of course he was fine. Gareth had only gone to The Priory in face of the stark choice between therapy and prosecution. He still believed that, in his position, anybody would have done what he did. It wasn't enough for that vile man to stomp all over his dreams, humiliating him at the moment he was supposed to transform from a dull caterpillar into a glorious celebrity butterfly. He had to say what he said about Gareth's mum, her sweet old body a few days in the ground. Gareth was not a violent man, but that monster deserved worse than he got, and one day he would get what was coming to him. His supposed victim knew that as well as he did, otherwise he wouldn't have paid for Gareth's treatment.

'It was terrible, what happened,' Mrs Middleton said, as though reading his mind.

Gareth began to edge away. Even thinking about that day brought a mild sweat to his brow.

'The things that man said,' Mrs Middleton said, shaking her head and frowning. 'He should've been put in prison.'

'I'm sorry, I have to run,' Gareth said, now out on the kerb and moving away. 'I'm going to visit Mum's grave.'

Mrs Middleton's face fell. 'Oh, right. Well, if you need anything, let me know.'

He nodded and walked away, fists clenching and unclenching as he fought off the memories that threatened to engulf him.

Light morning mist licked at bare tree branches and curled around the chapel as Gareth walked along the path towards his parents' grave in Camberwell Old Cemetery. He passed a grim stone angel, stubby wings curled up and eyes downcast in grief; a bin overstuffed with rotten bouquets; and a massive Gaelic cross, green-tinged with moss and age. Aside from a bent-backed groundskeeper scooping up armfuls of dead leaves, he was alone.

Gareth placed a spray of white lilies in the pot beside the simple headstone that marked his parents' resting place, then spread a blanket on the threadbare grass and lay down.

'Hi, Mum,' he said. 'Sorry it's been so long.'

He looked at the gravestone. His father's name had been whittled down by twenty years of rancid British weather, while his mum's looked as fresh as the day he'd numbly watched her coffin being lowered into the earth. It had been bad enough back at the house, but here, confronted by the gravestone bearing her name, he knew she was gone forever.

They'd always been close, but their bond had been forged into iron solidity by his discovery of singing six months after his first bout of invisibility. As he'd slouched through the school corridors one lunchtime, he came across a gaggle of excited young girls clustered around Bryan Williams—handsome, talented and way too cool for school. The flirty group was gathered around a poster calling for entries to the school talent show. Bryan was announcing his intention to sing Ronan Keating's *Life is A Roller Coaster*, the previous month's number one. Gareth had never thought about singing. His music collection consisted of two compilation CDs, which he occasionally put on for background noise when he was poking at the latest hobby his mum had suggested. Yet, at that moment, as the girls pinned Bryan with their hungry gazes, he understood what he must do. If he could get up on that stage, they might look at him the same way.

He signed up and rushed home to tell his mum, who was delighted he'd expressed an interest in something. She bought every chart compilation album going. They chose Robbie Williams' *Rock DJ* as his number and spent three long weeks rehearsing in the living room. His mum applauded every note, every faltering dance step, advising and drilling him until the act was polished. She rifled the celebrity magazines for the latest fashions, and brought the full power of her credit card to bear on creating a new look for him. When the big day came, a plague of butterflies assailed his stomach, not so much fluttering as frantically beating their wings and trying to fly up his gullet to freedom. When he set foot on the stage for the first time, the butterflies fell still. Hundreds of gazes were fixed on him, more people properly looking at him than had ever done before. They remained transfixed as Gareth ran through his routine; he felt an incredible sense of rightness.

At the end of the song, amid applause, a teacher walked up to the microphone.

'Thanks to …' He squinted at his clipboard. '… Gareth, for his excellent parody of Robbie Williams.'

Gareth barely heard him. He hadn't felt this solid in months, his feet firmly displacing the tattered floorboards of the stage as he walked off. His mum was waiting in the wings, cheeks burning with pride. She folded him into her bosom, prompting titters from the other kids.

'You're going to be a star, son,' she said. 'I know it.'

When he pulled back, her eyes were bright with belief.

From that day on, he and his mum had thought of nothing else, and for a while he didn't cut himself. Over the next two years, she paid for tuition in vocals, guitar, keyboards and drums. She saw him as a multi-instrumentalist, a Stevie Wonder for the next generation. The tutors changed regularly, Gareth listening through the wall as they told her he didn't have any natural aptitude for music prior to being dismissed. The instruments disappeared as she decided to focus on his voice. After she sent the fourth voice coach packing, Gareth was ready to give up, backed by a reprisal of the self-harm he hid with long-sleeved tops. His mum talked him out of it. The coaches were talentless amateurs who were jealous of his raw ability, she said, and he had no reason to doubt her. She'd never lied to him.

When school ended, there was no question of him getting a job: his mum was a management consultant and a fat insurance policy triggered by the brain aneurism that killed his father left them with money to burn. Yet, despite his mum's ministrations, he continued to go nowhere. He auditioned for countless local bands, never making the grade, and sent off dozens of demo tapes of cover versions to record companies, never receiving a response. He attended battle of the bands events as a solo artist, never winning. He queued for the *Icon* auditions every year, hoping he would one day make the cut and get onto the talent show itself. When his belief began to flag, she'd always been there to pick him up. She'd been the one who held him close, stroking his hair after every failure and stemming the need to cut his arm to ribbons. And now she was gone.

He looked around for a spade, thinking he could bury himself alongside her. Then he heard the voice. At first it was only a whisper below the wind that blew leaves to collect in drifts on the gravestones. It grew ever stronger until he couldn't deny its existence. He flipped over, scrambling away on his hands and knees and staring around him.

'It's okay,' said the voice, unmistakably that of his mum and definitely emanating from the grave. 'It's me.'

'This isn't happening,' he whispered.

'Yes, it is,' his mum said.

'Then they buried you alive! I'll get a spade and dig you out.'

'Gareth, I've been down here for over six months. Do you think I've been living on worms? They didn't bury me alive. But did you really think I would let something as trivial as death keep me from you?'

Gareth, the only semi-rational explanation for hearing her voice denied him, clawed at the earth. He missed his mum so much and wanted nothing more than for her to be there for him, but this had to be a sign of insanity. The doctors were right about him after all.

Yet the voice continued, soft and loving. 'Close your eyes if you want. It'll help.'

He squeezed his eyes shut, afraid that if he didn't he would completely unravel.

'There, that's better, isn't it?'

Strangely enough, it was. With the grave unseen, he could have been sitting in Dulwich Park, as they'd done many times, talking and practicing his scales.

'Tell me how you feel,' his mum said.

'Rotten. I miss you so much.'

'And I miss you, Gareth my love. But I know what will make you feel better.'

He squeezed his eyes tighter, knowing what she wanted him to do. He hadn't sung a note since that awful day. 'I can't. Not after what happened.'

'Forget what that man said. Do you think he knows better than your own mum? You have the voice of an angel, Gareth. Sing me a song to warm me up. It's cold down here.'

She means in the grave, he thought, and almost leapt to his feet and ran screaming from the graveyard. His mum seemed to know what he was thinking, and spoke urgently, 'I know this is strange; you have to trust me.'

A sudden image of her sitting beside him on a sunny day, brown curly hair tumbling around dark eyes crinkled by a smile, flashed through his mind. A wave of calm swept over him. He couldn't deny her, not after all she'd done for him.

'What do you want me to sing?'

'You know.'

Gareth smiled. Yes, he knew. It had been her favourite even before he'd begun singing, and it had swiftly become their song. He cleared his throat and broke into *Hallelujah*, uncaring if anybody were to wander into earshot. Only the murmurs of approval emanating from the grave mattered. Suddenly it was all okay again. This had to be real. The long months of grief, of staring at the creamy white walls of The Priory and hoping she would walk in and make it all go away, were forgotten in the warmth of her love. When he finished, applause pattered up from the earth.

'Beautiful,' his mum said.

There was silence for a while, as Gareth basked once again in the glow of maternal approval. Finally, she spoke. 'You mustn't give up.'

'Why not? You can't help me anymore.'

'Yes, I can. Look behind the gravestone.'

He got up and peered over the stone. On the grass sat shiny copies of *Now*, *Hello*, *Celeb!* and *Heat*.

'Pick them up,' she said.

As soon as he touched the first magazine, a cascade of smells poured forth: make-up and hairspray, the metallic tang of overheating house lights, dry ice and fireworks, fresh sweat trickling down the taut bodies of backing dancers. He reverentially teased open *Celeb!*, forgetting for an instant where he was amidst the smells and images of show business. He first saw it on page seven in a topless shot of Barry Deckhart. Then on page 15, on the back of Britney Spears' neck. It went on and on: page 23, Rihanna's wrist; page 29, Bjork's upper left arm; page 43, Angelina Jolie's left shoulder blade. Mystical tattoos in foreign scripts, each one circled in red pen.

'Do you see what they have that you don't?'

'Tattoos?'

'Yes!'

Gareth crinkled his brow. 'So if I get a tattoo, I'll be famous?'

'Not just any tattoo. These people aren't any better than you, Gareth. They've had help. Those tattoos are special, brimming with an ancient power that brings fame to those who wear them.'

'So if I get one of these I'll be famous?'

'Without a doubt.'

Part of Gareth whispered that the answer to the question he'd been asking for ten years couldn't turn up mysteriously, delivered by his dead mum. And the idea of magical tattoos seemed so far-fetched. On the other hand, every famous person had strange scripts or eastern images etched into their bodies. While he pondered, his mum whispered soothing endearments. He flicked back through the magazine. Where a few seconds ago Robbie Williams had been posing by the side of a swimming pool in tight trunks, Gareth's own face smiled out. This was no scissors-and-glue job. It was a photograph of him in the magazine, his body now taut and muscular, a complicated symbol inked into his chest. The lines flowed and twisted through each other with grace and elegance. The closer Gareth looked the more depth there seemed to be, as though he was wearing 3-D glasses. The symbol seemed to delve deep into his chest and intertwine with his heart. The caption below the image read, *Sexy Superstar Gareth Relaxes After Sell-Out World Tour.*

The last doubts slipped away, like the magazine from his fingers, as the glamour shone full into his face. He rounded the headstone in a daze, sat down, and ran his fingers across the grass. 'How did you know?'

'It doesn't matter. There are things you can't understand, things I can't explain to you. You'll only know when you're dead yourself, and that won't be for a very long time. You have a destiny to fulfil, Gareth.'

The smells of show business came pouring back. 'Yes, my destiny.'

'Good boy. Now, this is very important. You have to find one of those tattoos.'

'How?'

'You go looking for it.'

'Can't you just tell me where to get one?'

'I don't know yet, my love. I'm working on it. You need to work on it too.'

'Okay, Mum.'

'Wonderful. Now, I need you to let me rest while you get on with finding that tattoo.'

'When can I see you again?'

'Come back in two months,' she said, her voice fainter. 'Talking still tires me out. But I'll be thinking of you. Remember I love you.'

'I love you too, Mum,' he said.

No reply came this time, and when he opened his eyes he saw only a grassy mound and cold headstone. The part of him that had refused to believe protested again that he'd imagined it all, but the residual warmth in his stomach that only his mum could generate told him otherwise. Was it really so hard to believe that her love was strong enough to defy the grave? No, he decided, it wasn't.

He stood up, brushing the soil from his behind, and headed home to begin his search, singing *Hallelujah* as he went.

Murmur leaned on the broad trunk of an oak tree, watching until Gareth had passed through the tall iron gates. He sauntered over to the graveside, bent down and placed his palm on the ground. Little gouts of dirt spat up from the earth until the avatar he'd assigned to track Gareth hauled itself out. It stood there, spitting dirt and coughing for a few seconds, before speaking.

'That went well,' it said in the voice of Gareth's mother.

'It did indeed, my little friend,' Murmur said as the avatar climbed up his arm, jumped to his face and flowed into his nostril.

Even given Gareth's devastation at the loss of his mother, Murmur had expected to have to do more than wheel out a few cheap tricks. After all, an average day didn't entail a breezy conversation with the mouldering corpse of a loved one, magical magazines and the promise of destiny fulfilled. Yet the lonely young man had accepted the bizarre occurrences with minimal resistance, no doubt driven by his desperation to have his mother back in his life. Actually, it wasn't that surprising. Murmur had watched *Psycho* many times and understood the power a mother, dead or not, held over a son—which, in large part, was why he chose this method of approach.

Listening to Gareth's grating singing, for the twenty seconds Murmur could stand it before jamming his fingers into his ears, had confirmed that he was the right man for the job. That Gareth actually believed he could sing would have been astonishing had Murmur not already rummaged around his mind in preparation for assuming the identity of his mother. Therein, Murmur saw that Gareth was the human equivalent of an Etch A Sketch. All throughout his childhood, he'd displayed neither imagination nor passion. His mother had tried to foist interests upon him; nothing stuck, erased like a child's scribbles to leave a blankness that ached to be filled. Cupboards in the family home became littered with the detritus of abandoned hobbies: chess sets, paint brushes, tennis racquets, model airplanes, chemistry sets and dozens of other expensive accessories.

Only the singing stuck, and that had nothing to do with passion or ability, just the desire to stop being so anonymous and his mother's determination to support him in the one thing he'd ever shown the slightest interest in. Murmur had gleefully watched a cavalcade of memories in which Gareth's mother built up the boy's unrealistic belief in his own abilities with unconditional love and support. There was nothing special about that, of course. The same thing applied to the tens of thousands of untalented brats who swarmed the *Icon* auditions, each filled with a sense of entitlement and an unwavering belief that their voices were soaring, swooping emotional weapons that would clobber the judges and buying public to their knees in wonder. That's what happened when blind love drove parents to encourage their sprogs to do things they were wholly unsuited for.

Not that he was complaining about this peculiar human trait. Thanks to such ill-advised motherly love, Gareth's inability to think for himself and his desperation to find a lasting anchor to reality, the youth would do whatever he was told to attain fame. Murmur brushed the grass from his knees and stood up, filled with optimism that his recently hatched plan would work. Gareth had brought complications into his life, but he also offered the opportunity to bring about both the crowning glory of Murmur's time on Earth and the recognition he deserved in Hell.

Eager as he was to get going, Murmur knew careful planning and implementation would be required. First, he had to leave Gareth to his own devices for a while. Experience had taught him not to rush such delicate manipulations. The human mind could be a brittle thing, prone to shattering if pushed too hard. For a short-term job, that didn't matter, and Murmur had left a lot of human wreckage in his wake down the years, but he needed Gareth to maintain some basic functionality until he'd played his part.

This fragility, in part, was why Murmur had backed off from his original idea of persuading Gareth he should eat the hearts of celebrities to gain their power. Digging around in ribcages and hauling out bloody lumps of gristle would have pushed Gareth over the edge too quickly, and it would also have made the final stage of Murmur's plan harder to pull off. The more subtle idea for reaping tattoos came to him on a flight to New York, in the first-class seat he always booked when he had to travel with others and so couldn't teleport. He was half-watching the scene in *The Silence of the Lambs* when Clarice Starling inspects the missing skin on a victim's back, and had turned to secure another glass of bubbly from a passing stewardess, when his gaze fell on the tattooed forearm of Johnny Depp, who was sprawled and dozing in the next seat. The two elements meshed seamlessly in Murmur's mind.

Having Gareth collect tattoos was perfect. Virtually every celebrity sported at least one, usually some ridiculous misspelled oriental text or symbol—the very embodiment of the spiritual erosion of Western culture. Humans in Europe and North America had lost faith in their traditional religions, instead looking to the East for some half-baked mysticism to provide the meaning they'd so casually discarded. With such a cultural background, he'd known it would be easy to sell Gareth on the magical power of the tattoos, and as Gareth's coming campaign of mayhem unfolded, journalists would inevitably make the comparison with Buffalo Bill. Media hysteria, essential to the attainment of Murmur's final goal, was guaranteed.

It had been a great morning's work, and he would use the coming weeks to get on with the day-to-day business of running an evil empire and creating a meticulously crafted plan on Microsoft Project to share with Satan. First, however, he had some fun planned. Murmur walked off towards the trees, intending to get out of the line of sight of the caretaker and teleport up to Old Trafford. Today was the big game with Chelsea. If United, whom he'd started supporting in the eighties simply because they had a devil with a pitchfork on their crest, chalked up a victory, the day would be perfect and give United a chance of wrestling the league title back. The problem was that Chelsea were looking pretty good so far; Murmur was beginning to think he should do something about it. Meddling in areas outside his musical remit would be naughty, but Murmur had worked his arse off for the last fifty years in service of Satan, so nobody could begrudge him a bit of moonlighting. An idea formed as to who Gareth's first victim should be, and Murmur cupped his hand over his mouth to allow himself a tiny fiery smile.

As he was about to teleport, he caught sight of Gareth waiting at the bus stop. Though his back was to the graveyard, Murmur could tell from his erect posture that the weight of misery had lifted. An unexpected feeling of kinship welled up inside Murmur. Yes, the human was deluded and without talent, but Murmur knew better than most what it felt like to nurture a dream.

A cold breeze kicked up, sending leaves swirling around his feet and blowing out the flames on his face. Murmur shivered, seized by the certainty that a change was coming, one he couldn't control. He looked up at the clouds scudding across the sky and for one vertiginous moment saw a great eye peering down at him. When he blinked, it became the weak winter sun smearing the clouds with a faint halo. He pulled his coat tighter around his throat. He knew God was up there, although he was equally sure that if there was a greater plan, it did not include him. For fifty years he'd searched for signs that Heaven was aware of his existence and opposing his schemes. He'd seen none. It was only the shift of seasons unsettling him. Thoughts of destiny, of an overarching fate for each individual, were for the weak-willed such as Gareth. Murmur controlled his own future.

And yet, just before he slipped into the continuum, he recalled that it had been a simple quirk of fate that set him on his current course.

6

Early January, 1959

It all began, as events that shape worlds so often do, with a clerical error.

Murmur was squirming on the sculpted plastic of his new office chair, trying to find a position that didn't chafe his buttocks, when the telephone rang. Rivulets of flame raced through the deep scowl trenches on his face. Any time he used the loathsome device, the handset slithered about in his scaled hands and his claws kept slipping from the dialling holes designed for stubby human fingers. The daily struggle was even more frustrating given that demons could communicate through consensual telepathy. Satan, however, insisted that they use phones, pens, typewriters and other technology unsuited to demon physiology to understand, and thus corrupt, humanity. This position, which found him sitting in the uncomfortable chair, was a royal pain in the arse—literally and figuratively.

Murmur made no move to wrestle the phone to his ear. Calls usually meant more work, and only twenty minutes remained until the end of his shift. A pile of forms already teetered in his outbox, ready to be double-checked, cross-referenced, stamped and then sent down to the archives department. Hell never used to be so bureaucratic. When Murmur started as a clerk in 1750, he only needed to fill in the names of the deceased, sin or sins, and appropriate punishment in a thick hard-backed register. There were also far fewer souls to process in that era, before humans invented cures for all sorts of population-controlling diseases and then, as though they realized what a big mistake they had made in doing so, set about developing spectacularly effective ways of killing each other on a large scale. Now the hordes of sinners pouring through the gates stretched the administration to breaking point.

Trapped in this endless cycle of paperwork, Murmur longed for a chance to get out and do some field work. At first, he'd tried to get noticed by being ultra-efficient. This only cemented his position as a useful clerk. For a while, he submitted world domination plans full of intricate webs of deceit and subterfuge to the High Office of Satan. He never heard back. Eventually, he'd settled into the role of an anonymous functionary, shuffling forms and daydreaming about playing a starring role in the Armageddon they were supposed to be working towards.

More than anything, he wanted a mention in the humans' religious texts, which he read voraciously, or a profile in *Fire & Brimstone*, the monthly lifestyle magazine that covered the latest fashions, listed the highest-profile sinners to hit the pits and ran features on the top demons. He devoured the articles on the lifestyles of the high-borns, who resided in sprawling stalactites with hundreds of minions to do their bidding. Every month, before he opened the magazine, he closed his eyes and imagined his name writ large for scurrilous demonic activity alongside the likes of Lucifer, Mammon and Baal. No matter how many times he did it, the rush of disappointment when he opened his eyes to see that his face was not on the cover never diminished.

He knew that he had no hope of fulfilling his dream. For all of Satan's recent modernizing, Hell still ran on the old principles. Only high-born demons or those minions attached to their houses got to represent the infernal machine upstairs. Demons like Murmur, spat out of the spawning pits into a life of servitude, were stuck carrying out menial tasks. He must have processed millions of souls and gone through thousands of quills and biros by now. The ink of the clerk had seeped into his demon soul, which only thrived when bathed in human blood.

The phone rang on through his reverie, prompting stares from the other clerks, so he picked up before somebody reported him for skiving. 'Murmur, Souls Receiving.'

'You took your time,' a female demon hissed down the line.

'We are rather busy down here, you know.'

'Busy picking your nose, probably.' Murmur, who had been idly exploring the inner crevices of one flat, reptilian nostril, yanked his finger out. 'This is Morgane, the boss's secretary.'

'Are you new? I thought Absturia was the secretary.'

'Not your boss. The big boss.'

Murmur sat bolt upright, flames flickering across his brow. He'd never received a call from Satan's office before. He must have done something really, really bad.

'It's a pleasure to hear from you,' he said, trying to figure out what his transgression could be. He'd been late a couple of times the last few months after tying one on with the boys down at the Scalding Tar, leading to one or two sinners being handed down harsher punishments than were warranted as a result of his headache-induced foul humour, but that wasn't a big enough error to attract the attention of the top brass. 'What can I do for you today?'

'You minor demons are all the same,' Morgane said, picking up on the fear in his voice. 'Always cringing and slinking around. You're not in trouble. Satan wants you at a crisis meeting this evening, 7pm sharp in The Stalactite boardroom.'

'Me? Are you sure?'

'Yes, I'm sure, although I have no idea why. You seem like a particularly useless specimen. Just be there.'

She hung up. Despite the parting insult, flames meandered down Murmur's face until they lit up his mouth in a smile. They wanted him in the boardroom. All his years of loyal, and largely uncomplaining, service must have caught Satan's attention. His spirits soared like a harpy caught on the warm updraft from a fire pit.

As soon as his shift was over, he hurried to the modest stalagmite he shared with two hundred functionaries from his department and put on his best loin cloth, a sleek little number made from obsidian rock he'd saved for over a year to buy after seeing it in *Fire & Brimstone*. The authorities didn't want a seething mass of sexually frustrated underlings, which was bad for efficiency, so sexual desire had been bred out of those low-borns not destined for the stud farm. His loins were little more than a device for evacuating his bladder, but that didn't stop him from displaying a basic level of decorum—unlike many of his colleagues, who wandered around with tackle hanging limp and pitiful for all to see.

An hour before the meeting, he announced his destination to all within earshot. As he was about to leave, his gaze fell on the standard-issue organizer on the bedside table. Usually he left it in the office, and had no recollection of bringing it home. He picked it up on a whim, thinking it would add to his professional demeanour, leapt from the porthole and beat his wings towards The Central Stalactite. He would have preferred to teleport, but Satan had instituted a rule that journeys less than fifteen miles be taken on the wing to keep all demons in fighting trim, in case the truce that had kept Heaven and Hell in a fragile equilibrium for millennia was broken. It was just one of the tens of thousands of regulations governing the creaking bureaucracy that was Hell. It was no wonder Armageddon was taking so long to achieve. Even getting a new pen from the stationery cupboard required filling out a form in triplicate.

Within five minutes, his pulse thumped in his ears and the muscles powering his wings ached from the strain of buoying up his body. Years of desk work, and the short commute from office to the adjoining stalagmite, had taken their toll. He dropped his pace until he got his breathing under control. Murmur had never been close to The Central Stalactite, which hung knobbly and gnarled from the roof of Hell's main cavern and was studded with thousands of portholes from which demons issued and entered. A stream of souls fell past the stalactite, pouring from a yawning hole in the cavern roof to the sorting pit far below, screaming and thrashing all the way. This was a new feature. Previously, the dead were herded down a long flight of stairs carved into the wall. As humanity swelled in numbers, this had led to unwieldy tailbacks. The rumour mill maintained that Satan had set to work a team of interior designers killed in a rollercoaster accident to simultaneously solve the bottleneck and give Hell a new look. The human waterfall was the result. Murmur had to admit it added a certain devilish panache to the seat of all power.

A strict hierarchy governed The Central Stalactite, from the less-important ministries at the top all the way down to Satan's offices at the tip, suspended about half a mile above the plains. Murmur swooped towards his destination, still scarcely able to believe he'd been invited. He landed on the entry ledge, waited for his breathing to normalize, and entered the reception area.

Morgane, a petite female demon with a sour face, graced him with a brief glance and tapped her diary with a pen. 'You must be the random. You're early. Go in and wait for the others.'

Murmur padded into the boardroom, which was dominated by a massive oval oak table accessorized with two-dozen functional seats. A leather swivel chair sat at the head, beneath a vivid painting that portrayed Satan as a gargantuan snarling beast whose unfurled wings cast a shadow over a boiling mass of souls undergoing myriad forms of torture. The same picture hung on the walls of every administration office throughout Hell. With a quick glance out of the door to check nobody was coming, Murmur sat in the boss's chair and put his feet up on the table.

'Heed me, you horde of scabrous beasts,' he declaimed to the empty seats ranged around the table. 'There's a new beetle at the top of this festering dung heap, and things are going to change around here. I want a cigar, a goblet of wine and a foot rub, in that order.'

A shadow flitted past the window, accompanied by the beating of wings. Murmur almost tripped in his eagerness to get out of the chair and scuttled to the corner of the room, where he adopted his best subservient pose. The door swung open and in came the boss, folding his wings around his body and turning slightly so the ridged horns curving out from his forehead fit through the opening. In contrast to the portrait's suggestion of enormous size and power, Satan stood only a few inches taller than Murmur, who was himself a rather diminutive demon at just under five-and-a-half feet. Satan's trunk was not particularly bulky or well-muscled, his shoulders were stooped, and the fangs that protruded over his black lips were chipped with age. The effect was rather underwhelming until Satan turned his eyes on Murmur. They were a vivid shade of scarlet, the irises swirling with hypnotic power.

'How are you today, my Lord?' Murmur said, scraping low to the ground to avoid gazing into the depths of Satan's eyes.

Satan thumped towards his chair, claws ripping up fibres from the ragged carpet. 'Fetch twenty goblets of wine, minion.'

Murmur scampered off to do his bidding, following Morgane's directions to the well-stocked bar through an adjoining door. When he returned, the other demons were fidgeting in their seats. The most striking were Baal, with his triumvirate of frog, cat and goblin heads; Beelzebub, proboscis twitching beneath bulbous fly eyes; and Lucifer, whose mouth bristled with far more razor-sharp teeth than strictly necessary—although the other Lords had aspects that would terrify even the bravest of humans. They made Murmur look as frightening as a gecko by comparison. He was barely distinguishable from the hordes of other minions that kept Hell's machinery ticking over: dull-red reptilian eyes, flat nose and wide nostrils, pointy ears and a strip of hair running between the stunted horns crowning his knobbly brown scalp. His chin was a jutting square and he had ragged fangs that didn't quite meet, which meant his mouth hung open and gave him a vacant look that belied his sharp mind.

Still wondering why he'd been invited, he placed a goblet in front of Satan and worked his way around the table before sitting in the last free seat at the far end. Nobody paid him any attention; they were all looking at Satan, who in turn was staring out of the window and cradling his goblet.

'Welcome, my most-trusted demons,' said Satan when he turned to face the assembled group. 'Let's keep this short, as soon I must dine with the Ambassador of Heaven, long-winded dullard that he is. It has come to my attention that there is a pernicious new form of … *music* on Earth, known as Rock'n'Roll.'

Murmur leaned forward. Music in any form, even whistling or humming, was forbidden in Hell. The punishment for listening was instant vaporization, which meant banishment to the void; there was no other side for demons. No reason had ever been given for the embargo, and Murmur hoped he was about to find out. Satan clearly had strong feelings about it, for he'd barely been able to bring himself to say the word "music", his voice wavering and eyes dimming to a bruised purple before he managed to spit it out.

'I have heard of this Rock'n'Roll,' said Beelzebub, his buzzing voice in keeping with his fly-like appearance, 'but I am unsure why it is worthy of our attention. Music has been around for a long time in many forms, my Liege.'

'You are correct, but this is of another order entirely. This thing is … aspirational. It wants people to change, to become better. We cannot have that.' Satan took a sip from his goblet to clear his throat, and continued. 'Even worse, the record player, television and radio allow this disease to rampage unchecked into the homes of humans, where once it was confined to elite cliques or had to be searched out in taverns. Our operatives tell me it is inspiring happiness and creativity in millions of young humans. Something must be done.'

'I sense Heaven's hand at work,' said Baal, speaking through his frog head.

'Perhaps,' said Satan. 'I intend to probe the ambassador this evening, although he will assure me they are doing nothing, just as I will assure him we are doing nothing, even though we both know it is a lie. Anyway, regardless of its provenance, it must be stopped.'

'What do you propose?' Baal said.

'We send a fiery comet to smite them all!' Lucifer shouted, thumping the table for emphasis.

Satan shook his head. 'Always with the fiery comets and the smiting, Lucifer. Do you ever have any other ideas?'

Lucifer's face screwed up in concentration. 'Fiery meteors?'

'That's the same thing,' Charon said.

'No, it is not. Comets are bigger.'

Satan sighed, a deep, hoarse exhalation that spoke of centuries of frustration. 'I have told you a million times, we shall never bring to pass an ever-lasting era of evil by smashing everything to smithereens with comets, meteors or any other large space-based object. That aside, such obvious action would be a clear violation of the truce and could lead to a war for which we are not ready. Need I remind you of the savaging we suffered the last time because we were such a stinking, disorganized rabble?'

Murmur leaned even further forward, his knee tapping against the underside of the table. Along with music, mention of the war was banned, although snippets of information passed between demons in hushed tones. As far as Murmur could gather, the war took place in an inter-dimensional rift specifically opened to create a battlefield, and had been sparked by God's decision to send his son down to Earth, which upset Satan for unspecified reasons. Beyond that, all he knew was that Hell had lost badly.

Lucifer opened his mouth to respond. Satan turned his crimson eyes on him, tiny whorls of fire spinning and pulsating within. Even though Murmur was not directly in the firing line, he could feel the power therein waiting to be unleashed. It was like looking into the crater of a volcano ready to erupt. 'Do not test me, Lucifer.'

Lucifer closed his mouth again and looked down at the table. Satisfied, Satan blinked and his eyes returned to normal. 'I wish to send an agent to Earth to sabotage this movement, with some degree of subtlety.' He pulled out his Filofax and sat with pen poised. 'How are your schedules looking?'

The demons stared at the tabletop and remained silent. Satan massaged his temples. 'Do not tell me you have neglected to bring your organizers again? It is no wonder Heaven has us under its accursed heel. God has a plan. We just mill around.'

'We do not plan! We destroy! We bring chaos!' Lucifer bellowed, already forgetting his chastisement. Murmur was beginning to suspect he wasn't the sharpest claw on the foot.

'Do try to talk at a normal volume,' Satan said. 'I have a headache. You can have as much chaos as you want when the time comes. Until then we need to be discreet and work on our long-term strategy. So, in the name of all that is unholy, next time bring the Filofaxes I got for you.'

Murmur looked down at the Filofax sitting on the table before him. It had become clear that he'd been invited by mistake, and he hadn't wanted to draw any attention to himself in case they kicked him out. Yet here, delivered into his lap by a sheer fluke, was an opportunity to get noticed. He picked up the Filofax and raised it in the air, trying not to let it shake too much. 'I brought mine with me, Sir.'

The demons turned to look at him and he flinched under the combined power of their gazes. Satan's attention was caught only by the leather-bound diary. His lips crackled into a fiery grin. 'Wonderful. Somebody who listens.' Without looking at Murmur's face, he addressed the rest of the table. 'Anyway, I presume you can all at least inform me what you are up to, if that is not too much trouble?'

Each demon gave an excuse as to why they couldn't possibly do anything about Rock'n'Roll, from being too busy installing Castro to getting the Russians into Afghanistan. Satan's brow grew ever lower, and the flames ever stronger, as each demon cried off. Finally, only Murmur remained. He swallowed hard and spoke up. 'I could do it.'

The whole table turned to look at him again. A burst of quizzical fire flipped out above one of Satan's eyebrows as he registered he had no idea as to the identity of the bearer of the Filofax. 'Who are you exactly?'

'Murmur. I work in Souls Receiving. I was invited.'

'No, you were not.'

Satan scanned the other demons. A light of understanding seemed to come on in his swirling pupils. 'Murmur, you say?' He pressed the intercom button. 'Morgane. Can you look down the invitee list for Wormer?'

'Wormer?'

'Yes, spelled W-O-R-M-E-R.'

After a brief pause, Morgane's voice crackled through. 'It's not there, my Lord.'

'But you have a Murmur, yes?'

'Yes.'

Satan released the button and looked around the table. 'This is exactly what I am talking about. We have been sloppy for too long.' He pressed the button again. 'Can you please contact Wormer and ask him what he is doing?'

'He is out of action, Sir,' said Astaroth.

'How so?'

'It was most unusual. He was on holiday, possessing a rich businessman with a villa in the Mediterranean. We do not know how they found him or who carried out the exorcism, but it was a nasty one. He will be laid up for at least two months.'

Satan's horns combusted in displeasure. 'Morgane, you and I need to have a little chat. I am most vexed by this error.' He cut off the intercom and considered Murmur. 'Tell me, have you ever been in the field?'

'Once, my Lord, in the 18th century,' Murmur said, omitting that he'd been an intern, a position won through a lottery system to placate the hordes by providing the false hope of advancement. His only task had been to carry the bags of the senior demon he was shadowing. The job lasted three days before he was sent back for dropping the luggage down a flight of stairs.

'And what did you do?'

'Tried to reignite the plague, my Lord,' Murmur said, before adding in the hope it would make him better suited for the job, 'We gave it to some minstrels.'

'So you have experience killing musicians.' Satan tapped the table thoughtfully. 'I suppose that is useful.'

'My Lord,' said Lucifer, 'surely you cannot be countenancing giving such a task to this worthless underling.'

'Are you volunteering the services of your house?' Lucifer fell silent. 'I thought not. He may be a low-born, but at least he remembered to bring his organizer.'

Satan continued to tap the table and stare at Murmur. His scarlet eyes were mesmeric, and Murmur could almost feel them probing and evaluating deep within his spirit. 'Do you use your Filofax every day?'

'Yes, Sir. Planning is a crucial part of my job.'

Murmur clutched his diary tighter and hoped Satan wouldn't ask to see it. Murmur did indeed love to plan, but as of late he'd had nothing to plan for. Inside the Filofax, Satan would find most of the pages covered with doodles of Murmur at the centre of epic battles with angels, a few entries marking the date of pub quiz nights and a light smattering of work-related notes.

Fortunately, the intercom buzzed and broke Satan's stare. 'Sir, you asked me to remind you when it was time to leave for your meeting with the ambassador.'

Satan checked his wristwatch, another human invention that looked ridiculous on his scaly arm, and slapped his palms on the table. 'Well, Murmur, you are here now, nobody else is free and I do not have time to go running around after this. Honestly, it feels like I do everything myself. I will give you a chance.'

Murmur leapt to his feet, an intense burst of flame searing his lips. 'Thank you, my Lord. I will not let you down.'

'No, you will not, otherwise you will be cleaning out the excrement trenches for the next thousand years,' Satan said. 'I will send a messenger demon tomorrow with the appropriate forms to release you from your duties and arrange for a quick field refresher course. Do not reveal the details of your mission to anybody. Do nothing that can be traced back to us. If you kill somebody, make it look like an accident. Under no circumstances engage in direct confrontation with any angels you may encounter, lest we find ourselves back at war before we are ready. You have exactly four weeks to prove you are up to the job.'

Satan stood up and hurried from the room without another word. The other demons filed out after him, shooting Murmur dirty looks. Baal flicked the Filofax onto the floor as he passed, sending Murmur down onto his hands and knees to retrieve it. When he got back up, Lucifer stood in front of him.

'You made me look bad,' Lucifer said, baring his chaotic mess of sharp teeth.

His contorted face combusted, the flames crackling and popping with the intensity of his anger.

Murmur had always wanted to meet Lucifer, the biggest and baddest warrior in all of Hell, but he'd rather hoped it would be to get an autograph rather than to be the subject of his ire. 'I am sorry, I did not intend...'

Lucifer shot out a clawed fist and grabbed Murmur by the neck, lifting him off the ground. Murmur's shins barked off the edge of the table as he kicked, trying to escape the choking grip.

'What you intended means not a jot,' Lucifer said. 'Hear this, minion: when you fail, and you shall surely fail, I will be waiting to avenge this slight. I will have Filofaxes hammered into your rectum one by one until paper comes out of your nostrils. And that will just be the appetizer.'

With that, he dropped Murmur to the ground and leapt from the window. Murmur sat down shakily, rubbing the deep imprints Lucifer's claws had left in his neck. He remained there for five minutes, trying to make sense of all that had just happened as his heart fluttered like the wings of the fire beetles he'd so enjoyed trapping in glass jars as a young demon. Finally, the overriding feeling of elation damped the fear engendered by the threat down to a manageable level. Lucifer's promised torments would remain nothing but threats as long as he did his job and kept Satan onside. What mattered now, more than anything, was that his dream had come true. He was going to be a field agent.

7

Jackie laid low for the week after his eviction, sending his mum to the shops to bring him cigarettes and newspapers. When Barry's body turned up four days after his disappearance, the papers went wild. The killer had dumped the corpse in the Thames, weighing it down with rock-stuffed plastic bags. Gases released by decomposition finally overwhelmed the makeshift anchor beneath the London Eye, bringing the body up to bob against the riverbank. A Canadian tourist spotted the corpse first; his graphic pictures were splattered over the internet, prompting voyeuristic glee and moral outrage in equal measure. The only recognizable thing about Barry was the mop of blond hair, fanning out like seaweed from his bloated face. Slabs of rancid flesh bubbled up through the ragged holes where his tattoos had once been.

When Cynthia was invited in to assist police with their inquiries, commentators—professional and amateur alike—erupted into frenzied speculation. Had she found out about Barry's peripatetic penis and paid someone to have him bumped off? Did she wield the knife herself in a fit of jealous rage? Would people stop buying her records or would she become more popular? Celebrities with links to the family crawled out of the woodwork to defend, accuse, counter-accuse and generally do a good job of getting their faces all over the news. Had Jackie possessed the slightest link to the Deckharts, he would have done the same. He even suggested inventing a connection. Barry was no longer around to deny they'd met, after all. Phyllis shot the idea down.

Jackie knew his chances of getting positive coverage to re-launch his career were gone. Neither a suicide bombing in Afghanistan that killed four British soldiers, nor a plane crash in India, nor the announcement that a small European Union nation had gone bankrupt could displace the Deckhart drama from pride of place in the dailies and celebrity magazines. On the seventh day of staring at the phone, hoping Phyllis would call with news of an interview request, a proper concert booking or, please God, a recording contract, Jackie contacted her.

'Is that bingo gig still possible?' he said, with no preamble.

'Yes. Your indiscretion has been pretty much forgotten.'

'I'll do it.'

'Are you sure?'

Jackie looked around his tiny bedroom. Every inch of the walls was covered with posters from the gigs he'd played in his heyday—Brixton Academy, Manchester Academy, the Barrowlands and so many others—and pictures of him schmoozing with the stars of the early 1990s. They all had one thing in common: they were yellowed by age, corners curling up. Only the platinum disk still shone, polished every day by his mum.

'What choice do I have?'

'I'll confirm and let you know the details.'

Jackie hung up. He could already hear the cackle of the pensioners and the crinkle of sweet wrappers that would overlay his performance. He lay down on top of his newspaper-strewn single bed and buried his head beneath the pillow.

While the Cramlington Ritz sounded grand, it was actually a squat concrete building, perched on the edge of a weed-tangled patch of waste ground at the heart of a housing estate of equally squat flats. Inside, tables were lined up prison-canteen style in front of a low stage, on a nylon carpet that ensured Jackie received a static shock when he touched the metal pole along the bar. The room smelled of talcum powder and chips with an acrid undertone of old lady piss. The carpet and walls were bright red, so Jackie was grateful he'd cast aside his initial outfit choice, a lightning blue three-piece velour suit, in favour of black leather trousers and silk shirt. He didn't want to cause an outbreak of epileptic fits.

He'd expected there to be more people. After all, Cramlington—a small town on the outskirts of Newcastle, population 39,000—probably didn't offer much in the way of entertainment on a Sunday night. Yet only around half the plastic seats bolted to the tables were occupied. On the plus side, the owner, a rotund Geordie called Jeff in his early forties with hair sprouting from ears and nostrils, greeted Jackie with an old concert ticket and a pen.

'Mr Thunder, I just want to say what an honour it is to have you here,' he said as Jackie signed the ticket. 'I'm a massive fan.'

The brief was from a gig Jackie played at Whitley Bay Ice Rink back in 1990, on a multiple billing with a few artists from the same label. He remembered the concert surprisingly well despite the lines of speed, tumblers of vodka and fat joints he and his entourage had indulged in. The gig came six months after his album hit the top of the charts, so the venue had been packed to capacity. He tried to picture how the owner would have appeared back then: certainly a lot thinner and less hairy. Would he have leapt around amidst the crush at the front, waving his arms and screaming for more, or hung around at the back, smoking a cigarette and tapping his feet? He looked like a foot-tapper, Jackie decided.

He handed the signed ticket back and flashed Jeff a smile. 'Call me Jackie.'

The owner beamed at his autographed treasure as Jackie scanned the half-empty room. He was due to go on in an hour, sandwiched between the small money games and the link-up with other halls, which offered a prize of up to five grand—ten times what he would earn for this gig.

'Do you think it'll fill up a bit?' he said.

Jeff stuffed the ticket in his pocket and shrugged. 'Business has been bad recently.'

'The crowd's quite old as well. I'd expected a few more people our age or younger.'

The owner looked at the ground and shuffled his feet. Jackie took a step away, fearful of the extra charge the discomfited Jeff was building up.

'It's quiz night down at the Blagdon Arms,' Jeff said. 'Cheap booze.'

Jackie heaved in a lungful of static-filled air and let it out noisily.

'Fancy a drink?' Jeff said. 'It's on the house.'

'Do you have any Zubrowka?'

'What's that then?'

'Vodka.'

'I've got Grant's.'

Oh, how the mighty have fallen, Jackie thought.

'That'll do,' he said.

He made small talk with Jeff as the caller droned out numbers and pensioners sporadically wobbled to their feet to hold aloft winning cards. As the time for his performance approached, the discussion turned to his set-list.

'So,' Jeff said, 'basically you're going to play all of *The Sound of Thunder?*'

'I thought I'd throw in a few new songs. Test the waters for the next album.'

Jeff perked up. 'Finally! When's it coming out? Can I get an advance copy?'

Jackie took his turn to charge himself up on the carpet. 'Well, I'm still looking for a deal, but there are a few irons in the fire.'

A woman just behind Jackie yelled 'Bingo!' at the top of her lungs and he almost spilled his drink.

'You're up,' Jeff said. 'Let me introduce you.' He fought his way through lines of pensioners shuffling to the bar and toilet, and clambered onto the platform. 'Ladies and Gentlemen, tonight we are privileged to have the biggest star ever to grace the Cramlington Ritz,' he said into the microphone he'd snatched from the caller. 'Please give a warm Crammie welcome to Jackie Thunder.'

A smattering of dry-palmed applause rippled through the room. Jackie slapped his cheeks a few times and then sprinted up onto the stage. When he took the microphone from Jeff, a blue spark arced to his fingertip.

'Fuck!' he yelled, his voice booming through the PA.

Old ladies paused in their perambulations or stopped their knitting, staring up at him with pursed lips. Jackie tried to pretend the percussive wave that sloshed around the hall was the clicking of fingers from an appreciative audience in a jazz club rather than the tutting of hundreds of dry lips.

'This one's called *Eye of the Storm,*' he said.

He pressed a button on the keyboard, into which the beats had been

pre-programmed, and bore down to send the opening chord farting
through the ageing speakers. Halfway through the first number, it
became clear he was playing for Jeff alone, who'd proven not to be a
foot-tapper and was dancing beneath the stage. The bingo-goers paid
more attention to the young boy in a white shirt and red bow tie who
patrolled the aisles with a plastic tray bristling with ice creams. Their
hungry gazes tracked him; when he stopped they either ransacked his
tray for a Cornetto or aimed a slap at his pert behind. Jeff stepped left
to right, out of time to the beat, clapping and shaking his fat gut.

Is that what I look like? Jackie thought.

He closed his eyes and tried to feel the ghost of the young man he'd
been, so thin and full of energy, within his flabby middle-aged body. In
his mind's eye, he saw the crowd at Whitley Bay Ice Rink—arms held
aloft in adulation, chanting his name, singing along in glorious
synchronization. When the first song ended, he opened his eyes to see
Jeff, sweating and panting, bent over and clutching his knees. The
bingo-goers had gone back to their knitting and novels. None of them
clapped.

The syncopated drumbeat for the next song, a new one hopefully
entitled *It's Thunder Again*, kicked in, followed by a droning Em7. To
Jackie, it sounded like a dirge. He dug his feet into the carpet, which
also covered the stage, and ground them back and forth. Jeff began to
copy him, no doubt thinking it was a new dance move. Jackie, who was
trying to build up a strong enough charge to deliver a fatal shock and
end this misery, dredged up the first note of the melody. It almost
choked him.

8

A gust of chilly wind, made all the fiercer by the ache for smack, set Fleur's teeth chattering as she emerged from Tottenham Court tube station. She edged up against the wall and tried to pick out a dealer from the crowds. She wouldn't be freezing her arse off out here if her manager could accept she needed to use as part of her creative process, instead of hiring a private guard to stop her. He didn't understand the strain she was under. The divorce from her husband festered still; her court case for giving a photographer a deserved boot in the nuts was still pending; and the mounting pressure to deliver a second album that would scale the giddy heights of the first left her sitting alone in her private studio, staring at her guitar—once an extension of her spirit, now a useless lump of wood. Little wonder she needed a little pick-me-up, just something to fight the stress and get her writing good songs again.

She scanned the crowd from her position of anonymity, confident nobody would make her. She'd scraped her spikey crown of blonde hair flat against her skull, abstained from applying thick eyeliner and caked-on lipstick, and covered her skinny frame in matching shit-brown jumper and skirt beneath an old fleece jacket. The prying eyes of the private guard were no longer a problem. She lost him in Victoria

Station, where she walked up to two armed policemen, pointed to her tail and told them she'd seen him leave a suspect parcel on a platform. She'd then ducked back down into the tube station as the cops wrestled him to the ground and headed to her real destination.

It had been many years since she'd needed to hit the streets to score, and she didn't know if the dealers still hung around this area, as they had before she became famous and could arrange for home deliveries. She'd tried to call her dealer that morning to arrange for a clandestine meeting when she woke up with an irresistible craving for heroin, but the call hadn't gone through. She'd instead become strangely certain that Tottenham Court was the best place to go. She figured if she stuck around long enough, any dealers in the vicinity would spot her. They could sniff out junkie desperation as efficiently as a shark could sense blood in the water.

Shoppers sated by their own addiction streamed past, heading home to spend the evening with their families. She pictured herself among them, hurrying back to an unremarkable house in an anonymous suburb where her man waited with a cuppa and a warm, loving hug. She was drifting off the wall, carried into the flow of pedestrians by the force of a recurring fantasy that had grown ever stronger as the pressure to deliver grew, when a familiar figure wound through the crowd. It was that grabby pervert Jackie Thunder, the wispy fronds of his nasty dyed hair undulating in the wind. His next victim, a pretty black woman who also looked familiar, clutched his arm. Fleur was still muttering obscenities under her breath when a little man with a purple mullet leaned against the wall. The shark had found her.

'Evening,' he said in an odd squeaky voice Fleur struggled to hear above the roar of a passing bus. 'Looking for something?'

Fleur's hatred for Jackie disappeared, sucked into the heroin black hole—along with the voice that tried to warn her that the guy could be a copper or a tabloid journo.

'I need smack,' she said.

He smiled, exposing two rows of crooked little teeth, and clapped his hands in a show of exuberance uncharacteristic for a drug dealer. 'I've got plenty. But not here.'

He led her down New Oxford Street. Fleur grew increasingly antsy as they picked their way through the hordes, plucking at the sleeves of her fleece. 'Where we going?'

'To my car. It's more private.'

She followed, fighting the urge to drag him along the road by his stupid mullet to hurry up the process. By the time they reached a small Ford delivery van of the kind favoured by tens of thousands of small business across Britain, parked on the top floor of the NCP parking garage on Museum Street, she'd dug eight crescents into her palms.

'Get in,' he said, lowering himself behind the wheel to fumble underneath the seat.

Fleur threw herself into the passenger seat and stared at the dealer with naked hunger. 'Give me everything you got.'

He pulled out a syringe and glanced around the empty parking level.

'Here, mate, I'm not sharing works,' she said. 'Just flog me the drugs, I'll cook up myself.'

The dealer smiled. 'This isn't heroin. That comes later, Fleur.'

Fleur clutched the door handle, gripped with the certainty she'd been set up. Her first thought was to run, away from the cop or the hidden camera filming the deal. The part of her that cared only for the heroin, regardless of the cost, slowed her down. Before she could pull the door open, he'd hooked an arm around her throat. Fleur's plain flat shoes kicked against the dashboard as she tried to find purchase to push back, but the soles kept slipping off the moulded plastic. She dug her nails into her assailant's arm. His grip did not loosen. The needle sank into her neck and soon the spotless interior of the car drifted away, taking with it her pain.

When Gareth first found his calling in life, he used to shrivel empty crisp packets beneath the grill. When the packets were small enough, he would crumble a few crisps into the bags and hand them out as snacks to his audience of old toys: Cuddles the monkey, Jeffrey the bear, Woof the dog and an array of action figures propped up against the foot of the bed. The toys never strayed from their dutiful task of staring at him as he performed, and though he knew they weren't real, sometimes he forgot his anonymity in their reflective button eyes.

Barry's shrivelled tattoos reminded him of the wrinkled crisp packets as he pushed them around the table top with the handle of a hairbrush. Other memories rushed in through the door to the past: another brush doubling as a microphone in sixteen-year-old fingers, his mum providing a clapping beat; the same fingers holding a real microphone as he focussed on his mum's encouraging eyes in the unresponsive crowd at a local talent show; the same eyes, embedded in parched and withered skin, pinning him from a hospital bed.

He shook his head and focused on the tattoos. He hadn't bothered to put the scraps of skin in the jars of formalin provided for the purpose of preserving them; at the same time he couldn't bring himself to throw them out. They were both a symbol of his initial failure and an incentive to do the job right with Fleur. He glanced over at the singer, who was stripped to the waist and tied to the chair in a straddled position that offered up her back. The tattoo stretched from the nape of her neck halfway down her back, touching the shoulder blades on either side. It advertised its power in the elegant black lines of the petals and the band of swooping, flowing text encircling it. He'd become something of a connoisseur of tattoos in his search and this, he was sure, was the one.

When Gareth had returned home from the cemetery on the day after his release, he did some internet research on tattoo shops frequented by celebrities and headed out to pound the streets. His first stop was Into You in Clerkenwell, where tattoos of all shapes and sizes, from all corners of the world, plastered the bright orange walls. None of them exuded the power of the tattoo he'd seen on his chest in the magazine. That was to be expected. They wouldn't put the magical tattoos on display in the front shop for every pleb to buy. Yet his advances to the tattooed youth behind the counter, which culminated in him waving a large wad of cash and pleading to be let into the club, ended with him being ushered out of the door. Next he tried New Wave Tattoo in Muswell Hill. A review in *Time Out* had informed him that Liam Gallagher, Patsy Kensit and Dave Grohl got their tattoos done there, so it seemed a likely option. This time he was ejected more forcibly after he tried to push his way into the back shop to see if he could locate a lever to a secret room.

Over the coming weeks, he combed the tattoo parlours of London to no avail. After a while, rather than trying the direct approach, he began hanging around the stores and watching for any hint of the magical. He saw nothing. In the evenings, he sat in his empty house, poring through magazines and circling likely tattoos. His collection of pictures began to creep out from his room, like moss in an abandoned building. At night, he lay in his mum's bed, his sweat gradually eradicating every last trace of her scent.

When it became clear his approach wasn't working, Gareth began emailing publicists, managers and agents, asking for the contact details of the mystic who had inscribed the powerful symbols into the bodies of their clients. Each unanswered email added to the nugget of bitterness lodged in his chest. Every night, he stood before the picture of his mum in the back garden, staring at the inscription that promised him glory and asking himself why people who were no more talented than he was should hog all the fame. He began to deface the images of those celebrities he'd tried to contact, scoring angry red slashes across the tattoos they mockingly paraded. Christmas came and went, the festival passed alone with a ready-made turkey meal.

In early January, with his emails still unanswered and his skin tingling constantly on the verge of invisibility, which only regular slashes to his arms warded off, he headed to the graveyard to ask his mum for advice. The time she'd requested to recover had almost elapsed. Sure enough, she was ready for him.

'Hello, my petal,' she said before he'd sat down. 'Any luck?'

'They won't tell me anything.'

'My poor love. I wish I could give you a hug.'

The thought of a caress pricked his eyes with tears. Throughout his life, his mum had been the source of all affectionate human contact. With her gone, he'd taken to riding the tube during rush hour, letting the sway of the carriage press him against the warm bodies packed around him. He would stay on the train until he found a woman about his mum's age and body shape and, at violent lurches, would let go of the bar and allow the momentum to carry him into her. The contact was only ever brief, but if he closed his eyes he could almost fool himself into thinking the arms that reflexively clutched at his torso for balance were his mum's. On one occasion, he found himself in the arms of a prim older woman who wore the same perfume as his mum and found he just couldn't let go. She had to jab him in the testicles with her furled umbrella to release his grip. Fortunately it happened just as the doors slid open at Embankment so he could stagger onto the platform and lose himself amid the press before the transport police arrived.

'Don't be sad,' his mum said. 'We need to focus on what to do next.'

He bit down on his upset, wanting to be brave for her. 'What can we do?'

'Did you really expect them to hand this to you on a plate? They're selfish, holding back the power for themselves. Do you think that's fair?'

'No,' he said, ripping up a handful of grass and tossing it into the air.

'You're going to have to take what you want. Are you ready for that?'

Gareth thought of the way he'd been shooed from the tattoo shops and of all the emails sent off into the void. They were probably laughing at him when it would only take a few minutes of their time to reveal the secret. His face hardened. 'I'm ready.'

'Wonderful. You'll have to do things that mean people will be looking for you. It's going to be hard, and sometimes unpleasant, but it needs to be done. Do you understand?'

Gareth nodded.

'Good boy. You'll have to leave our house and start over. When you go home, you'll find a set of keys on the hall table.'

Gareth began to ask how she'd managed to do this. She cut him off. 'Don't ask me how. Just know that I can do it. Take one suitcase and the keys and go to Sandy Lane in Teddington, to a white house called Klymene. Inside, you'll find everything you need.'

'Can I still come back and see you?'

'No. They might look for you here. But don't worry. I'll send letters and talk to you when I can. I'm getting stronger every day knowing that I can help you. It makes me so happy to think that soon you'll be famous. You can write a song about me.'

Gareth smiled. 'I will.'

'Okay then, my love. Don't waste any time.'

He leaned over and planted a kiss on the earth, willing it down through the layers of grass, dirt and wood to land on the cheek that he imagined still full of rosy life. 'Yes, Mum. I won't let you down.'

Re-energized, Gareth hurried home and packed a suitcase with his favourite posters and pictures, the framed photograph his mum had given him to remind him of his mission, and a carefully folded selection of his nicest clothes. He stopped on the threshold of the front door, looking back into his home of the last twenty-five years. He felt no pang of regret, or sadness. Without his mum, it was nothing more than a skin to be shed on his journey to stardom.

Once on Sandy Lane, he found the house with no difficulty. The key slipped into the lock, and he stepped into a wonderland. The walls were glossy black, the furniture sleek and modern, the television and hi-fi huge and gleaming. The kitchen had a walk-in larder and, apart from the huge fridge freezer, a special fridge stuffed with chocolate treats. His bed was a four-poster with red satin sheets. But it was the studio, accessed by two doors—one from the spacious garage, where a white van was parked, and one from the living room—that set his pulse racing. Recording equipment and musical instruments for the backing band he would soon have at his beck and call dotted the room, which was richly carpeted except for one bare area where a metal chair was bolted to the floor above a drain. Laid out on the table next to the chair were ten syringes, a scalpel, gauze, and a handwritten manual on tattoo removal. Atop the manual sat another letter. When he ripped it open, he found two words: Barry Deckhart.

He understood what she wanted him to do and felt a shiver of disgust. For a second he looked back at the door to the garage. He imagined himself opening it and retracing his steps back to his family home, where he would sit in silence, unable to go to the cemetery after squandering her hard work. Gareth picked up the manual, sat in the swivel chair positioned in front of a huge flat-screen TV, and began to read.

Fleur was stirring, so Gareth began preparing the heroin, following the step-by-step process he'd downloaded from the web. Two weeks after his failure with Deckhart, another letter from his mum had appeared on the bedside table, identifying Fleur as the next target. They'd erred by choosing a footballer for the first victim, despite his fame, she wrote. Gareth was a singer, and therefore the tattoo of another singer would be more compatible. This tied in with what he himself had suspected, so he'd set to following Fleur whenever he could. She rarely left her flat, and when she did a stocky man who looked handy with his fists shadowed her. Gareth had been unable to spot an opening. Then, out of the blue, he'd been struck with the certainty that if he went to Tottenham Court tube station he would find Fleur there. Outside the station, he'd bizarrely once again bumped into Jackie Thunder, but he put the coincidence aside when he saw Fleur.

His mum had told him that Fleur's heroin habit would provide the necessary carrot to persuade the singer to give him her power and had arranged for the delivery of more than enough of the drug to suit his needs. And, provided she cooperated, Fleur would live through the coming hours. Gareth had learned from his mistake with Barry. Next to her bony ankles sat a box full of bandages, ice packs and surgical tape, with which he planned to dress her wounds before dumping her at the hospital.

By the time Fleur was awake and staring around her in confusion, Gareth had cooked up what he hoped was a potent dose of smack.

'Where am I?' Fleur said as her eyes focused on Gareth. 'Did Tim hire you? Is he trying to get me clean again? Tell the self-righteous wanker I'm going to fire him.'

'Don't worry,' Gareth said, holding up the needle. 'This is heroin, in a clean needle.'

Fleur's gaze snapped onto it. 'Thank fucking Christ. Gimme it.'

'Don't you want to know why you're here?'

'You can tell me after.'

Gareth clapped his hands. That she didn't even want to know why she'd been kidnapped showed just how much she craved the drug. 'I need something from you first.'

'I'll give you plenty of money.'

'Why do you people always think it's about money? I just need you to say, "I willingly give up my power to you."'

'Eh? That's it?'

'That's it.'

'I willingly give up my power to you. Satisfied?'

Gareth nodded and jabbed the needle into Fleur's arm. She let out a yelp. 'What're you doing, you spangle? You need to get it in a vein.'

'Sorry,' he said. 'I'm new at this.'

'Gimme a second,' Fleur said, pumping her fist until the tracery of blue veins on her lily-white skin stood out. 'Now, see that blue baby sticking out the bend of my arm? Put the needle in there and make sure it goes up the length of the vein.'

Gareth did as he was told.

'Right, now pull the syringe out a little.'

A cloud of blood floated out into the clear liquid.

'Is that okay?' Gareth asked.

'Perfect,' Fleur said. 'Now ram it home.'

Gareth pushed down the plunger. Fleur let out a long groan and her eyes rolled back into her head. He picked up the scalpel, taking deep breaths until his hand stopped trembling, and began to cut. This time, he only felt the faintest tinge of nausea. The singer didn't react to the bite of the blade, her head lolling around as she mumbled to herself. When he was done, Gareth took the metal tray he'd dropped the flower into over to the table. He swept Barry's tattoos aside and lovingly laid out the dripping skin. His technique had improved. The incision was a perfect circle, and he only needed to scrape off a small amount of flesh to prepare the tattoo for a trial run.

He peeled off his shirt and fastened the tattoo to his shaven chest with surgical tape. He really should have put it on his back in the same position she wore it, but with nobody to help him he had no way to do so. He closed his eyes and stood there for a moment, arms outstretched. Yes, this was it. Her skin was still warm against his and he could feel the tingle as the magic seeped into him. The time for the acid test had come.

It took a minute to turn on the television and boot up the Playstation, and another two to load Sing Star. In that time, his throat flushed with heat as Fleur's talent penetrated his vocal chords. He hesitated over the level, then shrugged and put it to the most difficult. He spun through the songs until he got to Fleur's biggest hit, *Turncoat*. His highest score so far, despite constant practice, topped out at 4100, marking him out as a wannabe. That had never worried him too much, for he knew the game was all about replication and left no room for artistic interpretation or passionate singing. Yet surely if Fleur's power had passed to him he would be able to sing the song exactly as she had.

When the number began, he concentrated on channelling the power of the tattoo. Less than thirty seconds in, he'd scored 750. A scatter-gun of dots surrounded the bars that measured his pitch and timing. They should have been filled in with blue as he nailed every note. He pressed the tattoo closer. It made no difference. The tune was reaching its crescendo when Fleur began to sing. Even in her junked-up state, with blood from her flayed back wending its way between the prominent knobs of her spine, her lungs set every molecule in the room vibrating with joy. The song faded out, and the mocking bray of a donkey replaced Fleur's voice. His final score was a pathetic 2950, only bolstered by Fleur's final intervention. He ripped off the dead skin and hurled it at the screen, where it slid down. He switched off the television and turned to Fleur, who was no longer singing. She hung to one side, drool hanging from her mouth. Low moans of pain escaped her lips. She looked up at Gareth, her eyes uncomprehending.

'What have you done to me?' she said, her breathing fast and shallow.

Blood trickled down the leg of the chair to join the small stream that ran to the drain. Even with bitter failure stinging his gullet, he didn't want her to die like Barry. He had to do something. His roving gaze fell on the heroin works, and he cooked up another dose in the hope it would dull the pain and buy him enough time to get professional help. She was still whimpering when he inserted the needle and pushed the plunger. Her body relaxed. The whimpering stopped. So did her breathing.

'Not again,' he said, and began administering what he hoped was CPR.

After two minutes of puffing air into her slack lips and thumping her naked breasts, he stopped. His heart hammered against a bubble of sick dread in his chest. Did two murders make him a serial killer? He didn't know. All he knew was that he'd deprived the world of an incredible talent. He pulled out his phone and dialled 999. Instead of reaching an operator, he got the voice of his mum, soft and calm, in his ear.

'What are you doing, Gareth?'

It was the first time he'd heard her voice since he moved house, the first time outside the cemetery, and his heart slowed. 'I'm calling an ambulance.'

'What do you think will happen when the ambulance comes? The police will follow.'

'Maybe they should,' he said. 'I've killed two people.'

'They were accidents, Gareth. That's all. You tried to save her.'

'But I didn't. And now she's gone. Her voice, her songs, all gone.'

'The world needs a new star to replace her, somebody else they can idolize. That's you.'

Her voice had dropped in register, the soft and persuasive words slipping down his ear like sweet golden syrup to coat and soothe his panicked thoughts.

'I didn't think of it that way,' he said.

'That's why I'm here. To keep you right. I told you it would be hard, that there would be sacrifices. She's one of them. It'll all be worth it in the end.'

'But I don't want to kill people.'

'Think of the bigger picture, Gareth, of the joy you'll bring to millions when you're famous. Don't you think that's more important? And anyway, she was past it. All her talent disappeared into the holes in her arm. That must be why the tattoo didn't work. The drugs poisoned it.'

Gareth looked at the track marks on Fleur's arms. He'd done the singer a favour. She'd been unhappy: divorced, addicted and struggling to write another album. It was better this way. She would be remembered as a legend rather than some washed-up loser, scratching around for the inspiration that had left her. And when he became a global superstar, he would give back to the world ten times what he'd taken.

'So, what now?' he said

'We keep looking. You take care of the body and I'll see if I can find the right tattoo. Keep believing. We'll get there in the end, and then we can forget all of this.'

The phone cut out. Although Gareth was left alone, he felt calm. He crossed to the body, seeing only detritus that needed disposing of, and began to untie its wrists. As always, Mum knew best.

9

Jackie performed a last-minute manicure with his teeth on a ragged pinkie nail as he waited outside Tottenham Court Road tube station. His suicide attempt had turned out to be as big a failure as his *Celebrity Public Eye* comeback. The static electricity had only charged his thin hair so it drifted up like strands of cobweb, leaving him more eccentrically coiffured than Russell Brand. At least his inability to top himself had left him alive the next afternoon to answer a call from Marie, who'd been evicted. She'd seen his not-so-subtle hints in the exit interview and wondered if he would like to join her for dinner. She left the choice of restaurant to Jackie, her only stipulation that she liked Chinese food.

Jackie had suspected she wouldn't enjoy a greasy chicken chow mein in the red lantern-draped Royal Dragon, so he settled on Hakkasan, which he knew by repute alone. The expensive Michelin-starred restaurant on Hanway Place opened after Jackie's money woes began, but with his debts down to less than two thousand pounds thanks to his TV appearance, he could afford to spend the proceeds of the bingo gig on wooing Marie.

It had taken five changes of clothes to settle on his outfit for the date. He plumped for jeans, a fifteen-year-old black velvet Paul Smith jacket, still in good nick thanks to regular brushing by his mum, and a purple shirt with a subtle floral pattern. It was an understated look for him, yet one he felt Marie would appreciate. He had good reason to be nervous. His last quasi-serious romance ended two years before when the session musician he'd been dating chucked a potted cactus at his head in Fulham Palace Garden Centre. She'd accused him of being a self-obsessed bastard who only seduced her to get an introduction to Sade, with whom she'd recently worked. He'd simply suggested a few times Sade might like to know he was available to fill the support slot on her British tour. What was wrong with that?

When Marie emerged from the exit, he spat out a sliver of fingernail and set off to meet her. She wore a mid-length dark blue skirt, revealing chunky yet shapely legs clad in black tights. Her hair was scraped back in a ponytail, which flopped down the back of her simple beige jacket. A smidgeon of blusher highlighted her strong cheekbones and blue eye shadow had been applied beneath unplucked eyebrows. Her teeth overlapped a touch, pushing her lips out into a permanent kiss-me pout. Kissing her was exactly what Jackie wanted to do. Instead he hesitated a few feet away, unsure how to translate their physicality in the house to the outside world. Marie settled the issue. She hugged him, her short arms barely making it around his midriff.

'It's so good to see you,' she said before planting a kiss on his cheek. 'I missed you in there.'

'I couldn't wait for you to be evicted,' he said, and then backtracked when he realized he'd put his foot in it. 'Sorry, I didn't mean I wanted you to lose. I just wanted to see you.'

Marie laughed. 'I know what you meant, although you're still in trouble. I hear you picked up a floozy while I was on the inside.'

'Did I?'

'Fleur.'

Jackie rubbed his forehead. 'God, that. Look, it was a total accident. I'd had a few, I wanted to get my picture taken with her, I misjudged where my arm was going and suddenly her boob was in my hand. The whole thing was mortifying.'

'You did look a right tit.' Marie kept a straight face for a beat, and then giggled. 'My friends think you're a sex pest. I know you're not like that.'

'I'm not.' He offered his arm. 'Shall we?'

As they turned to walk the short distance to the restaurant, a small man with a purple mullet brushed against Marie. He locked gazes with

Jackie, who had a sudden discomfiting feeling that he should know this man—from where and when he wasn't sure. He walked off without saying anything.

'I think he recognized you,' Marie said.

'He was probably wondering if I was going to fondle you.'

Marie shot him an impish grin. 'Let's not get ahead of ourselves.'

Jackie gripped her arm a little tighter and led her through the crowd.

As soon as they entered Hakkasan, Jackie knew he would have a heart attack when the bill arrived. A staircase studded with orange lights led them down into an open space sparsely lit by overhead spots and glowing slabs of indigo glass embedded into the walls. Carved lattice screens of dark, expensive wood surrounded the eating area, where waiters glided back and forth.

'I've not been here in years,' Marie said as a waiter indicated they should follow.

'Me neither,' Jackie said, which was sort of true if you overlooked the fact he hadn't been here at all.

He tried not to look at the prices beside the long list of dishes, none of which were on the menu at the Royal Dragon. He settled for crispy duck and water chestnut. Marie chose a complicated meal that involved an array of ingredients Jackie had never heard of. He ordered a mid-range red wine, wincing at the price tag, and they settled down to chat.

They'd already swapped basic histories in whispered exchanges in the house. Marie was born in Barbados and moved to London with her parents shortly after. They were the same age, although their brief periods of fame hadn't overlapped. Jackie was on his way down when Marie hit the big-time in the mid-nineties with her warm voice and light acid jazz grooves. Her album sold a tonne and it looked like she was here to stay. Then she made the mistake of taking a one-year break to raise her new-born son, letting her profile fall too low. Like a heart that had stopped for too long, it couldn't be revived. There followed ten years of singing backup for lesser talents, performing to small and partisan Caribbean crowds in London, and a messy divorce.

Jackie filled Marie in on the events leading up to his tit-grabbing moment, emphasizing what a bitch Tandy Carston was. Marie reciprocated with the gossip that Flaxenburg kept whispering sexual approaches once Jackie had been evicted. While Jackie fumed at the American actor's come-on, Marie glanced around the tables.

'Apparently he used to come here all the time,' she said.

'Flaxenburg? If I see him, I'll bloody kill him.'

'No. Barry Deckhart.'

Jackie suppressed a groan. It was still all about that bloody footballer. The funeral had taken place at the weekend, two weeks after his body washed up due to a protracted post-mortem. Cynthia had been released without charge and the service, televised live, proved spectacularly vulgar under her direction. A white hearse drove the coffin past mourners lining the streets of London to Westminster Abbey, where it sat on a raised daises, draped in the Chelsea colours and flanked by two enormous floral footballs. Celebrity after celebrity tried to outdo each other in their grief, several of them picking up the weeping a notch when the camera pointed in their direction. Cynthia forgave and eulogized her husband with a hastily penned song entitled *I'll Always Love You*—released two days after the funeral, priced at £2.99—and then swooned before his football scarf-bedecked portrait as her grand finale.

Speculation over who'd killed Barry, something the police appeared no closer to determining, kept the story at the top of the news. The biggest mystery was why the tattoos had been removed. One psychologist, blogging for *The Guardian*, suggested Barry's killer could be a deranged football memorabilia collector. This line of thought led to the questioning, and subsequent release, of half-a-dozen anoraks who'd already been served with restraining orders for over-enthusiastic pursuits of footballers' autographs.

'To be honest,' Jackie said, 'I'm glad the headline-hogging bastard is in the ground. I got no coverage because of him.'

'Me neither.'

'I can't believe he was selfish enough to get himself murdered as we were coming out.'

Marie issued a short peal of laughter. 'Yeah, he could've waited a few months.'

'What's your manager saying? Did any record labels or producers get in touch?'

'No. John didn't say it out loud, but he thinks I'm past it.'

Jackie slapped the table, setting the wine glasses trembling. 'You're not past it. It's just the charts are stuffed with bloody talent contest winners. You can only get a deal if Murdoch gives the nod. A flatulent monkey could reach number one as long as he said its farts were in tune.'

Marie pursed her lips in shared disapproval at the Svengali who pumped out hit singers through *Icon*, the TV show that plucked wannabes from obscurity. Although ratings were down after last year's scandal and, for the first time in five years the *Icon* winner didn't get to Christmas Number One, the man still exerted a near stranglehold on the music tastes of the nation.

'He's killed it for the rest of us,' she said. 'Back in the day, you had to earn your spurs. We formed bands, wrote songs and played shitty gigs until we got spotted. Now people do a bit of karaoke and they're stars.'

Jackie nodded his head in fervent agreement. When he'd started out, playing music meant hard graft with little chance of making it, as his father's experience proved. Yet, steeped in music from an early age, it had never occurred to him that there might be another career option. He sat down each evening with his father, learning scales and chord progressions, melody and harmony, syncopation and timing. The one time he faltered was after his father's death, when he couldn't even look at a musical instrument. Agnes let him grieve for a month before pulling him out of his funk with a few hard slaps and a reminder that the best way to pay tribute was to do what his old man never could: get a record deal.

Jackie redoubled his efforts. He practised on his keyboard until his fingers ached, strained his vocal cords as he obsessed over finding the right melody, and lay awake in bed at night fretting over arrangements. He gave up his weekends and the chance of a steady relationship to play in dives across Britain. He paid the travel expenses for the loose collective of musicians he used as his backing band out of the meagre wage he earned as a hospital orderly. For three years he sweated blood and, though he never believed he would make it, when he took to the stage and lost himself in the songs he'd created it didn't matter. Then one day a talent scout from Atlantic Records spotted him through a haze of dope smoke at King Tut's Wah Wah Hut in Glasgow and everything changed.

'Spot on,' he said. 'It's a bloody cheat. And all the winners are so bland. If your voice has any character, you can forget it.'

They leaned further over the table, gazes locked.

'If Tom Waits or Nick Cave were starting out now and turned up at an audition, they'd be laughed out of the room,' Marie said.

'They'd rather have some stick insect with a soulless "big voice".'

'Or spiky-haired idiots doing crap covers.'

They snorted in unison.

'Still, we have to keep trying, right?' Jackie said.

The mood lighting accentuated the grim lines around Marie's mouth. 'Do we? It's the hope that gets me, always thinking my break is just around the corner. I don't think I can take being let down again.'

'Don't say that,' Jackie said. 'You're a star. You'll be back. We both will.'

'You think?'

He snaked his hand between the wine glasses and laid it on top of hers.

'Absolutely,' he said with more conviction than he felt.

Marie's face softened. 'Thanks, love. You're a darling.'

The DJ cranked up the funky lounge music a notch in the brief silence that followed, forcing Jackie to lean across the table further. 'So, are you still up for this duet?'

'Sure. Any ideas?'

Jackie indicated the bottle of red wine, which they'd already nearly drained. 'Let's have a few more of these and see if we can find some inspiration.'

As they clinked glasses, Marie turned her hand palm upward and curled her fingers through his. She only let go when the food came.

By the time they were ushered out of Hakkasan on the cusp of the two-hour time limit, they were both unsteady on their legs. Jackie was so merry he hardly spluttered at the bill, which their heavy wine consumption had bulked up to almost three hundred quid. He refused to let Marie go Dutch. When they spilled giggling onto the narrow street, Jackie spotted a lone photographer hurrying their way.

'Hold up,' he said. 'Looks like our first celebrity couple picture.'

She slipped an arm around his waist. 'No groping in this one.'

They walked towards the snapper, smiling broadly as he raised his lens to bear down on them. Their grins drooped when he flew by. Jackie turned to see a woman clad in fishnets, thigh-length black boots and a minuscule pink top that exposed her bra clop down the steps. It was dark and dry, yet she wore sunglasses and held a black-and-white striped umbrella over her head.

'It's Madame Outré,' Marie said.

The photographer scuttled around the singer like a crab, snapping dozens of pictures from different angles while she feigned indifference.

'How can you compete with that?' Marie said.

Jackie detected the despondency in her voice. 'Come on, it looks like she smeared glue on herself and rolled about in a prostitute's wardrobe. And look at that black lipstick. Why'd she only put it in the middle? She looks like a goth goldfish.'

Marie nudged him.

'Excuse me,' Jackie called. 'You've still got soy sauce on your mouth.'

Marie snorted with laughter as Madame Outré raised a tentative hand to her lips. The minder accompanying the star glared at them.

'We'd better scarper,' Jackie said, grabbing Marie's hand and leading her down the narrow backstreet.

They found the solution to their duet dilemma in a bar near Oxford Circus, the fourth establishment they'd visited in an increasingly drunken pub crawl. The pub, to which they were drawn by the wail of a karaoke singer, was a far cry from Hakkasan: real ales and pub food served from behind a wood-panelled bar, fruit machines jammed into a corner, and an ordinary-looking clientele chattering at tables strewn artlessly around the open space. Jackie found them a spot near the speakers, which transmitted the strangled barks of a red-faced office worker with his tie wound around his forehead. Marie had returned from the bar with a Boddingtons and a G&T before he figured out the song was supposed to be *Angels* by Robbie Williams.

'God, he's dreadful,' Jackie said.

Marie held up the photocopied song list. 'Let's show these amateurs how it's done.'

She bent over and scanned the pages, giving Jackie the chance to eye her figure and imagine what she would look like naked. He didn't expect to see the real thing, even if they ended up in bed together. Forgiving darkness suited his body far better.

'What about *I've Got You Babe?*'

'Not my range,' Jackie said.

'*Don't Go Breaking My Heart?*'

'I'm too pissed to sing that fast.'

Marie tapped the song sheet and laughed. '*Ebony & Ivory.* Perfect.'

'Don't you think it's a bit cheesy?'

'Come on, karaoke's all about the cheese. You're Paul and I'm Stevie, right?'

He nodded, and she bounded off to put their names down. They were called to the stage ten minutes later, and as soon as the song began Jackie knew Marie had made the right choice. Yes, the song reeked of Stilton, but it was also poignant and beautiful. As they swayed together, their lips close over the shared microphone, Jackie felt it had been written just for them. They *were* in perfect harmony—and not only their voices, which intertwined sinuously. Her hip rubbed against his thigh and her fingers strayed further up the microphone to touch his. He found himself glad for his long jacket, which obscured his groin.

When the song finished, they lapped up the round of applause and sat back down. Marie's cheeks were flushed. 'That's our duet.'

'You're so right,' he said. 'We can funk it up a bit.'

'Put some heavier bass behind it.'

'More of a beat.'

'We could donate some of the profits to the Campaign against Racism and Fascism.'

'It would sell like hotcakes.'

They fell silent, staring at each other and panting.

'Jackie, we're too old to beat about the bush,' Marie said, 'so I'm just going to come out and say it. I really like you.'

The grin that had been lurking surfaced onto Jackie's lips. 'I really like you too.'

'Do you want to leave these drinks and get a taxi? Back to my place, I mean?'

Jackie leapt to his feet. 'I thought you'd never ask.'

Jackie lay under a rumpled duvet, Marie's naked body warm against his side and her tousled head resting on his chest. He pulled her closer and she stirred, making contented noises deep in her throat.

'That's exactly how I feel,' he whispered and kissed her hair.

Their lovemaking had been drunken and clumsy. He'd tripped while yanking off his trousers. She'd elbowed over the bedside lamp, extinguished by silent mutual consent, as she tried to unfasten her bra. They'd banged heads while both scrambling about the bed for a dropped condom. It had also been glorious—no awkwardness, no sense of inadequacy at each mishap. Instead, they'd cackled and guffawed their way through the whole affair, only turning serious as they approached a near-simultaneous climax.

He tried to remember the last time he'd felt so content. He'd lived with two women he'd thought he loved, received blow jobs from groupies, indulged in a cocaine-fuelled threesome with a movie star and her energetic stunt double, and slept with dozens of women of all shapes, sizes, ages and backgrounds. None of the experiences compared with this moment, because none of the other woman had understood him. He and Marie were cut from the same cloth, had gone through the same rejections, and shared the same dream. All the backstory that couples normally spent months and years filling in was there already, etched within the other's own experiences.

Even her room was spookily close to his. Old concert posters adorned the walls, many of them from the same venues a few years after him. A gold disk hung in the same place as his platinum. The sole difference was the pictures of her son, Brian, who had gone skiing with his father in France—luckily for his tender fourteen-year-old ears, given the racket they'd just made.

'Perfect harmony,' he whispered, tapping his big toe against her foot.

His eyelids drooped and, for a while, it no longer mattered that he wasn't famous.

10

Phyllis and Jackie sat in the Camden Bar and Kitchen, enjoying a late lunch. The fringed red lamps glowed in the early afternoon gloom, casting soft pools of light onto the purple, diamond-patterned wallpaper. Chips of hail pattered against the window, accentuating the cosiness of the interior. Two teenagers were sucking each other's faces off at the only other table occupied in the post-lunchtime lull. In his love-struck fugue, Jackie gazed at the wrestling lips and wished he was engaged in similar activity with Marie, even though the recent marathon of love-making had left him tender in certain areas, which had become unaccustomed to such heavy usage.

Two events had prompted them to emerge from their cocoon: the imminent return of Marie's son and meetings arranged with their respective managers to discuss their duet idea, which four days cloistered away between fertile sheets had reinforced. Jackie hadn't told Phyllis what he was thinking, only suggesting they meet over lunch to discuss a proposal. He wanted to surprise her. He succeeded.

'You are, of course, fucking joking,' Phyllis said, picking up the burger fragments she'd coughed up when he laid out the plan.

Jackie flicked a piece of masticated meat from his chin. 'We happen to think it's a great idea.'

'Are you shagging her?'

'God, Phyllis, you're so crude sometimes.'

'Just answer the question.'

'Yes.'

'Thought so. You've got that dopey "I've been coming all weekend" look in your eyes. It's clouded your judgement.'

'Oh, come on! It's a great song and we've got the whole inter-racial couple thing. Plus nobody's ever covered it.'

'Nobody's covered it because it's two formerly great artists coming together to create a sentimental, turgid piece of claptrap.'

'It got to number one.'

'Three sodding decades ago. The whole racial harmony thing isn't relevant any more. Britain's moved on. Mixed couples are ten-a-penny. Everybody who's going to integrate has integrated and all the mad bastards have joined UKIP or the Jihadis.'

'You're so bloody cynical. Why can't you trust me? I've got a good feeling about it.'

Phyllis jabbed a fork in his direction. 'Cover versions are the slimy shit of Satan, dumped upon this earth to bury real musical creativity under a pile of fetid demon dung. Sure, a few were better than the original, but the vast majority are lazy rehashes by talentless halfwits incapable of writing their own music.'

'I don't care. You're my manager, so bloody well manage me. Talk to Marie's manager and see if you can get somebody interested.'

'No need to get bolshie,' Phyllis said, raising her hands in submission. 'I'll do it. Just understand I don't want you to get your hopes up.'

Jackie puffed out his cheeks and looked at the photographs of old rock stars and movie icons lining the walls. Sid Vicious, forever young, leered down from one side of a mirror. Steven Tyler, in a funky patterned top hat and draped with gold jewellery, pouted from the other side. Tyler and Aerosmith were still touring and recording, even though the singer was sixty if he was a day. Many other geriatrics were still strutting their stuff in skin-tight trousers that clung to their chicken legs. Jackie, at forty-two, was a youngster in comparison.

'What's your secret?' Jackie asked Steven Tyler out loud.

Phyllis coughed up another chunk of burger and looked at Jackie with narrowed eyes. 'My secret?'

'I was talking to Steven,' Jackie said, indicating the poster. 'But since you clearly have a secret too, you can tell me.'

Phyllis shrugged and took another bite to replace the soggy lump that had fetched up against the rim of Jackie's plate. 'I used to be a man.'

'That wouldn't surprise me,' Jackie said, and went back to staring at the poster.

It took four days for the managers to deliver a "no" verdict, a period of such unseemly haste that Jackie suspected they hadn't bothered trying. He suggested as much to Phyllis, who listed the twelve contacts she'd canvassed and, to hammer the point home, delivered verbatim some of their incredulous responses. They ended up shouting at each other. Jackie couldn't understand it, and nor could his mum when he told her. The two of them, plus Marie, were sitting at the kitchen table, taking a break between dinner and the steamed pudding now bubbling away in a battered pot on the small gas stove.

'Ach, what do they know?' his mum said. 'Me and your dad used to slow dance to that at weddings. It's a smashing song.'

Marie, who looked green around the gills after being force-fed an enormous portion of shepherd's pie, nodded. 'That's what we thought, Agnes.'

'Ah well. Never mind. I'm just happy Archie brought you over,' Agnes said. 'I was beginning to think he'd turned into a poofter.'

'Mum!' Jackie exclaimed, as Marie stifled a giggle.

'What? You didn't bring a lassie home for years, and I know those pop stars like to rummage around in each other's y-fronts.'

Aside from shame at his humble surroundings, his mother's habit of stating precisely what was on her mind had stopped him bringing back dates. He couldn't avoid inviting Marie to dinner, though. His disappearance and unusually cheery disposition raised his mum's suspicions he'd met somebody. She threatened to clonk him with a frying pan if he didn't deliver up the lady-in-question for a once-over. He'd warned Marie what to expect, but the outbursts didn't faze her. In fact, Agnes's banter brought Marie out of the slump brought on by the news of their duet's demise. The un-PC poofter comment set them off again, and Marie regaled Agnes with scurrilous tales of the many supposedly straight stars who enjoyed furtive jaunts down to

Hampstead Heath. Jackie brooded over his argument with Phyllis, only coming out of it when Marie got up to go to the toilet.

'That's a great woman you've got there,' his mum said.

'I know.'

She tapped him on the forehead.

'Ow!'

'Don't you go screwing it up.'

Jackie rubbed the injured site, which screamed with the impact of the callused finger. 'For God's sake, Mum, I'm a grown man. I know what I'm doing.'

'Son, sometimes I'm surprised you can wipe your own bum, so don't tell me you know what you're doing. I've watched you grow old and alone, chasing your wee dream of being a star again. Some things are more important than being famous. Your dad, God rest his soul, would tell you the same thing if he was here.'

'At least he wouldn't have hit me.'

'Aye, and that's why you turned out the way you did. If I'd had my way, you'd have got more of this.'

She raised her hand again. Jackie cringed. 'Don't. You know how much it hurts.'

Agnes rolled her eyes as the toilet flushed. She brought her hand back down to her side. 'Just you remember, if you do anything daft I'll tan your hide.'

She turned to smile at Marie as she came back in. 'Who's for chocolate pudding?' she said.

Still too full to consider any antics, Jackie and Marie cuddled on his single bed, listening to a best of the '90s CD on his Linn stereo, one of the few possessions, along with his Korg, he couldn't bring himself to sell when the creditors came calling. The five-grand hi-fi was wasted in the small apartment. It needed to be cranked up to show its worth, but a former Royal Marine Commando with a foul temper and forearms that made Popeye look like Olive Oyl inhabited the upstairs flat. The last time Jackie turned the volume up beyond a whisper, the marine had threatened to throw him and the stereo out into the central courtyard. Any time Jackie sat down in front of his keyboard to compose, he listened for the creaks of his neighbour's constant prowling. Only when it was silent did he feel comfortable enough to let the chords, and his voice, ring out. It hardly produced an environment conducive to creativity, although he'd still managed to record some classic tracks he was sure people would love if he could find a way of enticing more than three visitors a day to his website.

Every few hours, Jackie checked Myspace, Facebook and Twitter for new followers, and tried to hook on to every trending topic. When he came out of the *Celebrity Public Eye* house, he'd almost burst with excitement when he saw he had 20 new followers on Twitter, bringing him to a grand total of 389. When he checked to see who was following him, the bubble burst. Nine were spam accounts offering hot pictures of naked women, five were other musicians trying to raise their profiles, and four were self-published authors plugging their books. The remaining two were middle-aged women who didn't fit the demographic of the young audience he was trying to attract.

As the opening bars of *Kinky Afro* replaced Liam Gallagher's growling vocals, Jackie rolled onto his back. They'd been avoiding the subject of the duet since they retired to his room, but he could no longer take dancing around it.

'I was so sure somebody would bite,' he said. 'Maybe we need to pick another song. There must be something on this album we can do.'

He started to get up, intending to scan the track list. Marie held onto his hand. 'It's not the song. It's us. Would it be so bad to accept we've had our day?'

Jackie pulled her closer, remembering how he'd felt in her bed after the first night together. Maybe it would be okay to curl up in her arms and let the world do without them. Then the floorboards above groaned. He groped for the remote, his heart thudding. His whole life was a series of restrictions: fear of his neighbour, constant fretting over every penny, the doors of record executives that were closed to him, the bars and restaurants that turned him away.

'Don't give up yet,' he said.

He grabbed his cigarettes and walked over to the window. Even that action reminded him of his captivity. He had to blow furtive streams of smoke out of the window, as his mum didn't like the smell leaking into the rest of the flat. He lit up and sent a little cloud puffing out into the cold night air. It drifted across the grassy area between the blocks of flats, a smoke signal from a stranded soul crying out for help.

'I'll find a way,' he said under his breath, 'even if it kills me.'

11

Jackie found his way the next morning after he'd escorted Marie, who had a job singing a jingle for a supermarket advert, to her car at the uncivilized hour of eight am. Normally he didn't rise until eleven, which meant by the time he'd breakfasted and showered he would be ready to watch some TV. After that came lunch, which meant half the day had gone already. He would then spend the afternoon at the keyboard. Now he had an extra morning to fill. He started off by ambling down to the newsagents to pick up a lottery ticket. When he got there, a hefty couple poring over a newspaper blocked his path.

'It's definitely a serial killer,' the man, whose voluminous buttocks consumed the entire aisle, told his partner. 'Taking off the tattoos is like his whatyamacallit.'

'Modus operandi,' the woman said.

'Yeah, that's it. They take souvenirs for their mantelpieces or something.'

Jackie peered over the broad shoulders to the headline on a copy of *The Sun*. Fleur had been murdered.

'Fuck me,' he said.

The woman looked up. Recognition flared in her eyes. 'Here, it's that Jackie Thunder.'

'Who?'

'You know, the bloke that felt Fleur's tit.'

The man leaned around his wife with some difficulty. 'Do you think he killed her?'

'Nah. He looks too soft.'

Jackie ignored them, bought a paper and sat on a bench. Fleur had been missing for days before a dog-walker stumbled over her body on a stretch of waste ground in Enfield. Her manager kept the disappearance quiet. Fleur had shaken off her minder, so he assumed she'd gone off on a bender and would re-emerge, bedraggled but safe.

The Sun wasted no time in proclaiming the second death the work of a serial killer, comparing him to the fictional Buffalo Bill and dubbing him The Tattoo Collector. What caught Jackie's attention was a substory. A journalist had got on the phone to tattooed celebrities to ask them if they were afraid. The image of Fleur taken outside of Embassy—the last picture of her alive, as far as he knew—illustrated the article, although he'd been cropped out of it. Still, it got him thinking. The media would be desperate to fill pages, presenting an opportunity for publicity-hungry celebrities to get themselves in the papers with their fears, real or imagined. There was no reason why Jackie shouldn't be one of those celebrities.

'Sorry about yesterday,' he said when Phyllis answered his call. 'I was out of line.'

'I'm sorry too. I was a bit harsh.'

'You're always harsh. Listen, you've seen Fleur's been killed, right? And they're linking it to the Deckhart murder?'

'Yes.'

'I was thinking we could get some publicity out of it. Call the papers, say I'm worried for my safety. They'll be all over that.'

'Why would you be worried?'

'Well, I was the last person to be photographed with Fleur, and the picture was pretty provocative. I'm concerned it might have set the killer off. I could be his next target.'

'Really, you're concerned are you?'

'Very. In fact, I'm thinking about hiring a bodyguard.'

'You don't need a bodyguard. You've got Agnes. She's the most violent person I know.' Phyllis fell silent for a while. Jackie knew how her mind worked. After the duet failure, she would feel like she owed him one. 'I suppose we can give it a shot. I do foresee one issue, though.'

'What's that?'

'You don't have a tattoo.'

Jackie hadn't thought of that. When he was a kid, tattoos were the preserve of sailors, bikers, convicts and hard rockers: a heart bearing the name of a girlfriend, mum and dad on bicep, a glowering image of a horned Satan on the chest—many of them etched in wonky, faded lines. Down the years, tattoos had morphed from counter-culture to middle class in the same way as smoking dope. It used to be people wore tattoos to stand out. Nowadays, bankers, civil servants and secretaries frequented tattoo parlours to fit in. And the tattoos themselves had changed; now everybody wanted flowers, Celtic bands and cute dragons.

Jackie wasn't immune to the lure of the trend, particularly when it became de rigueur in celebrity circles. He often found himself gazing through windows, trying to decide which design would boost his mystique. Then he would hear the angry buzz of the needle, promising to send searing agony dancing through his nerve endings, and hurry away.

'Nobody has to know I don't have a tattoo,' he said.

'People already know. Those speedos you wore on *Celebrity Public Eye* didn't leave much to the imagination.'

'We can say I've got one on my knob.'

It was Phyllis's turn to laugh. 'You are utterly fucking shameless, you know that?'

'I'll take that as a compliment.'

'I'll give it a shot and let you know.'

Jackie hung up. Now the day stretching out before him didn't seem so bleak. Marie had said the hope got her down. Only hope kept him going. This opportunity wasn't much, but it was something. If he could flag himself up as a possible future victim then people might change their perceptions. After all, if a serial killer ranked him alongside Fleur and Barry Deckhart in the fame stakes, why shouldn't the public?

Three days later, Phyllis called to say not one journalist wanted to talk to him, not when Fleur's death had provoked widespread panic amongst the real elite. Overnight, the crop tops, sleeveless vests and skimpy dresses that had shown off a profusion of body art vanished, replaced by garments that covered every inch of flesh bar the hands and face. Paparazzi snapped the more nervous celebrities emerging from laser clinics, woozy from anaesthetic and the bulge of bandages visible beneath their clothes.

Jackie, who'd half-expected this outcome, hadn't told Phyllis he had a more drastic phase to the plan up his sleeve. Before he could commit himself to the next step, however, he needed some final motivation. He headed over to Primrose Hill and peeked from behind a parked car at his old house on Chalcot Crescent. He'd bought the three-storey corner terrace in 1991 after the album went platinum, throwing almost every penny he'd earned at it yet still having to take on a significant mortgage. He didn't care. The money rolling in was only the beginning, or so he'd thought, and the many best-selling albums to come would pay off the mortgage. In the first year, party followed party and girlfriend followed girlfriend in a debauched haze. Many a star filled the flower boxes below the windows with vomit, the back terrace had been the scene of wild drunken couplings, and enough lines of cocaine had been snorted from the marble kitchen counter to line fifty football pitches.

This went on while Jackie was supposed to be working in the top-floor studio. The hair of the dog he took to tackle the screaming headaches and the temptation of the latest scantily clad floozy meant he spent little time writing. When he did drag himself to the keyboard, he was in no state to compose anything decent. Still, he churned out a second album, concentrating on replicating the winning formula of *Your Eyes Are Mine*. When his record label rejected it, he burst into their London offices with his keyboard and, in shouty song format accompanied by lots of swearing and choppy chords, accused them of being a bunch of stuffed suits who thought Billy Ray Cyrus was a musical genius. They dropped him on the spot.

Phyllis had touted the album around, despite her telling him she considered it a half-arsed, derivative effort and that he should write new songs. Jackie didn't listen. Besides, the rich musical vein he once could tap into at will had vanished down a long, dark tunnel of booze. Nobody bit as first-album sales and concert bookings evaporated. Eighteen months after moving in, he had to sell the house.

He'd vowed that he would buy it again one day, and that this time things would be different. He pictured himself curled up on the sofa with Marie, enjoying the fruits of their labours. He smiled, and knew he had to push on with his scheme. The smile faded when the front door swung open and out flew Tiny Burns, one of the members of boy band Eastside Eazy and the current owner of the house.

'I told you not to hang around outside my window,' the tall, rangy youth shouted. 'What are you, a pervert? Are you banging one off behind that car?'

Jackie backed away. 'I told you, I used to live here.'

'I don't give a shit,' Tiny said. 'Fuck off before I call the police.'

'Tut, tut,' Jackie called when he was far enough away. 'Think what the little kiddies who buy your crap records would say if they heard you swearing.'

Tiny raised a middle finger and slammed the door, leaving Jackie to saunter off to the supermarket to pick up the items he would need.

Jackie sat before a wavering stack of newspapers, a pair of scissors, twenty sheets of A4 paper, some glue, a large book of stamps and a list of celebrity names. As well as keeping Phyllis in the dark, he hadn't told Marie what he planned to do. If it worked out, she would thank him— he intended to bring her back up with him—but she wouldn't approve at the moment. He set to work with the scissors. Half an hour later his first note was ready.

> *Jackie,*
> *I want your tattoo. Soon you will be like the others. There is nothing you can do to stop me.*
> *The Tattoo Collector*

It was short, partly because he had a lot of letters to get through and partly because he couldn't put himself in the head of a serial killer, but it would do the job.

By late afternoon, twenty letters addressed to agents representing the cream of Britain's stars, plus Phyllis, were ready to post. He shoved the evidence into a bin bag, stuffed the letters into a rucksack, and caught the tube to Heathrow. Nobody paid him any attention as he sidled up to the post box and dropped off his load. Now he was committed, which meant he needed to go through with the part of the scheme he dreaded most.

New Wave Tattoo in Muswell Hill sat empty when he arrived an hour or so later, save for a bald man in skull-and-crossbones t-shirt with his feet up on the shop counter.

'Afternoon,' he said. 'Do you have an appointment?'

'No. Do I need one?'

'Sorry, force of habit. Normally you do, but everybody's bloody cancelled since that nutter popped up. Anything in particular you fancy?'

Jackie shrugged, still wondering if he could get away with a temporary tattoo, like the kind you used to get in bubble gum. Alas, for this to work he knew he had to make it real so he picked an Inca sun, the smallest tattoo in the catalogue. The tattoo artist led him through to the back room and sat him down in a high-backed reclining chair. Jackie took off his jacket and rolled up his sleeve.

'First tattoo, mate?'

'Yes,' Jackie squeaked, his gaze never leaving the needle.

The tattoo artist held his forearm aloft. It was covered up to the wrist in a riot of colours. 'I've had hundreds done. Doesn't hurt.'

When the needle buzzed into life, it took every ounce of Jackie's strength not to sprint out of the store. The instant the needle touched his skin, he screamed. It felt like liquid fire was being poured into his flesh.

The artist took the needle away. 'You sure you want to do this?'

'Yes,' he said, squeezing his eyes shut and tensing every muscle in his body.

This time, the needle stayed in when Jackie's scream rent the air.

12

The 1960s

At Murmur's leaving party, his drinking buddies from Souls Receiving filled him so full of harpy piss that when he teleported to an unoccupied toilet cubicle in New York's Biltmore Hotel the next morning, his first act as a field agent was to vomit into the bowl. He stayed there for thirty minutes, groaning and listening to his acidic bile sizzle through the porcelain, before he managed to get his feet under him and stagger out into the lobby. He checked in under the name of Brad Pine—identity and reservations provided by the travel office—and flopped into bed to sleep it off.

When he woke disoriented in the darkness, he found his molecules had snapped back into demon form while he slept. He would have to pay for the sheets his talons had shredded, which wouldn't be a problem, although explaining the damage might. Under the bed sat a suitcase stuffed with $50,000 in used bills, which he had to account for through expense forms. Even field agents couldn't escape paperwork.

He reassumed his human shape to avoid further damage to the upholstery and pulled back the curtains. His pulse raced as he drank in the alien environment. Light-studded buildings, so different to Hell's ragged stalactites and stalagmites, rose straight and true above vehicles that trundled along a grid of roads in orderly fashion. As he followed the lines of one of the tallest buildings to its pointed spire, he became aware of the yawning vastness of the sky above. He dropped his gaze to dampen the dizziness.

Across the busy junction, people streamed in and out of Grand Central Terminal, maintaining an invisible compact to behave in a regularized manner, rather than snapping and tearing at each other as demons were wont to do in similar situations. In Hell, he only saw humans through the viewing screens at torture chambers, a popular pastime amongst the low-borns. His personal favourite was the shit pit. Generally the viewing screen revealed blank brown sludge, but occasionally a human would float against the glass to scrabble goggle-eyed and frantic. To see humans free of torment now felt wrong, but it emphasized the wonderful strangeness of this new world. Here was the clockwork conformity to a system that Satan craved. Yet Murmur felt a giddy sensation of freedom, for he didn't have to conform to this system. Out in that sprawling human world, he could do anything, go anywhere—as long as it involved killing musicians.

Reminded of his mission, he flicked on a light and reached for the radio to sample his first taste of the forbidden fruit. The sense of incredible possibility evaporated as the chunky device unleashed a cacophony that forced him to curl up in a ball, hands clapped over his ears. The din, imbued with unrestrained joy and energy, bludgeoned through his defences. His soul seemed to be trying to claw its way out of his body. It took every ounce of will to uncover his ears so he could reach up with a shaky hand to stab at the "Off" button. Once the music died, the immediate agony vanished. In its place came an indefinable sense of loss and longing. He sat on the carpet, hugging his knees and staring out of the window at the night sky, searching for what, he didn't know.

He spent the next few days in near-constant torment. As he wandered the streets to buy clothes to combat the biting cold, music ambushed him from the doors of bars and restaurants, clobbered him from passing cars and assaulted his senses from the lips of people humming and singing their favourite hits. Only earplugs and a steady intake of sense-dulling whisky allowed him to function as he set about identifying and tracking his first victim. Elvis had been pencilled in as a top target, but Murmur had discovered that he was on military service and all the records being released had already been recorded. There seemed no point killing him, especially since the name on everybody's lips was that of Holly. His choice to kill the bespectacled guitarist proved the right one. The deaths of Holly and his friends caused a huge outburst of grief and despondency and showed the disruptive force his tinkering could bring to bear. When a delighted Satan handed him a six-year mandate in response to the instant success, Murmur set to work laying the groundwork for his long-term campaign.

With the immediate pressure to prove his worth eased, Murmur began carving himself a niche in New York. Despite the music, he found the mad energy of the city exhilarating, particularly after two hundred years in which losing a paper clip counted as drama. His innate demon ability of speaking in tongues allowed him to carry out daily interactions such as finding an apartment, although initially he hid away as much as possible: he still struggled to control the fire that longed to burst from his face. In keeping with his solitude, he assumed the identity of a struggling writer and morphed his human shape to look more appropriate to the role—tousled black hair, pale skin, soulful brown eyes behind thick glasses, and a set of perfect teeth in contrast to his real dental chaos.

Cooped up at home, he engrossed himself in television and radio to familiarize himself with the music scene and thus formulate a longer-term target list. He'd accepted that he would have to listen to music in order to understand it, although he kept the volume low and tried to limit his exposure to an hour a day initially. Like nerve endings deadened by repeated trauma, his soul adjusted and the visceral initial reaction faded. The aching sadness didn't, however. After two months, he managed to get his emotions largely in check and the molecular itch of maintaining the human shape receded to manageable levels, although it never went away. Every time he went to sleep, he woke up in his true shape as his mind and body relaxed. He even began to adjust to the cold, which was a blessing since his heating bill had been eating up a large chunk of petty cash. Finally, he felt ready to pick up where he'd left off with Holly.

As the bewildering number of bands popping up testified, rock music was taking off. Yet only when he began attending concerts, earplugs in place, did he understand the power of music to inspire humanity. Time and again, he felt the collective lifting of woes and worries as the music reached a part of the human spirit inaccessible to the long talons of Hell. Their spirits strained upwards and they began to glimpse the possibilities of change and beauty in their own lives. The afterglow could last for days and be reignited by the simple act of placing a particular song on the turntable and letting the conscious mind, normally so locked-in to the day-to-day grind, unfurl in the soft swirl of melody. Music, he realized, would permit humanity to rise beyond Hell's clutches should they be allowed unfettered access to its buoying swell. He set to his sabotage with grim purpose.

At first, he focused on Rock'n'Roll, careful not to take too many high-profile targets and thus start people asking questions. Jesse Belvin bought the farm in 1960 in an opportunistic moment of tampering with the steering of his car. A blown-out tyre, helped along by Murmur's sharp talons, took out Eddie Cochrane in the same year. Yet the more music he listened to, the more he realized that he couldn't focus on this one strand alone. R'n'B, Blues, Jazz, Soul and many other old and new musical styles were causing similar amounts of enlightenment. He broadened his focus to include them, first sending Patsy Cline down in another plane crash. People killed people all the time, with or without Hell's proddings, so in 1964 he set up a stooge to shoot Sam Cooke. In the same vein of varying his MO, a gaggle of cancer cells implanted into John Coltrane's liver took care of the jazz legend. Then another plane crash, for old times' sake, put paid to Otis Redding. Murmur again toyed with the idea of killing Elvis, but by this point the singer was making formulaic Hollywood films and seemed to be a spent force.

He made no effort to deal with classical music, even though the pain he felt when listening to swelling strings indicated just how powerful it was. Most musicians appeared to be playing music by composers who'd been dead for a long time, and it appealed to such a small group of people that the effort-benefit ratio didn't justify diverting his limited time and resources—although the large size of orchestras would have made it easy to ramp up his body count by collapsing a roof or starting a fire during a concert.

While Baal had warned of Heaven's behind-the-scenes role, Murmur saw nothing to support these fears until 1966, when he killed Paul McCartney in a car crash in an effort to halt the meteoric rise of The Beatles. Murmur had stood over the bloodied corpse, yet two weeks later McCartney was back shaking his mop top as though nothing had happened. Whether Heaven reincarnated Lennon's partner-in-crime or sent down an equally talented doppelganger, Murmur didn't know. But he knew for sure that other forces were at work and so didn't try to kill the new McCartney. While he didn't believe Heaven was on to him, hitting the same target twice would definitely alert them to his machinations. The day would no doubt come when they discovered him, but there was no point in hurrying it along. There were plenty more targets; the new talent that kept popping up far outstripped the pile of bodies he'd created. It was that last fact that made it clear he couldn't manage on his own, so when Satan called him down for a face-to-face performance review at the end of 1965, he resolved to ask for some help.

On the morning of the meeting, Murmur popped into his old office to catch up with his former workmates. Within two minutes of gathering round the water cooler with his two closest friends, Gergaroth and Tarsis, and the rest of his old crew, his jaw ached from the strain of clamping his mouth shut to stop blurting out the details of his mission. With his reticence apparent, the conversation soon turned to the standard old tales of the juicy sins contained in that day's admission forms. Little fires crackled up as laughter rippled around the group, and Murmur felt a burst of homesickness. It lasted until the section boss popped up to herd everyone back to work. His friends slumped in unison and the fires fizzled out. He watched them file back to their desks, all individuality swallowed up the moment they sat down. The injustice he'd nursed down his years as a clerk returned, this time for his friends. He'd escaped, while the others remained trapped in Hell's rigid social structures like flies caught for all eternity in an abandoned spider's web. As he listened to the scribble of pen on paper and the thump of stamps, sounds that sometimes still haunted his dreams, it occurred to him that he could be the claw that cut through that web.

He left the office, mind churning with new possibilities, and flew over to meet Satan on the golf course modelled on Gleneagles, with fire pits instead of bunkers and boiling tar replacing water hazards. Satan was wearing a pair of plus fours in black and yellow tartan and a matching cap. Despite the jaunty headgear, jammed awkwardly between his long horns, Satan looked as morose as ever. In response to Murmur's formal greeting asking after his health, he didn't hesitate to have a good moan.

'I am exhausted,' Satan said, rubbing his eyes to emphasize the point. 'I cannot remember the last time I had a holiday, but nobody from this disorganized rabble can run the operation in my absence.'

'I'm sorry to hear that, my Lord.'

Satan let loose another of his sighs, so old and weary it turned the hair of his human caddy instantly grey.

'We need more demons like you,' he said. 'Demons with a can-do attitude.'

Murmur hid a smile behind his hand. He knew several demons just like him.

After Satan swiped his ball straight into a fire pit, Murmur stepped up to the tee. He'd never played golf, but it seemed simple enough once you figured out the best way to hold the club was to dig your talons into the rubber sleeve rather than try to grasp the slippery metal shaft. His ball sailed onto the green of the par three. They tromped around the course, Murmur filling Satan in on developments upstairs. The boss's mood worsened as Murmur detailed the explosion of new bands and styles, laying it on thick to support his case. By the time they reached the fifth hole, Satan had fallen into a glowering silence. After he'd hacked another ball into the rough, he tossed his club over his shoulder, catching the caddy full in the face. The human began to weep.

'Why does he love them so much?' Satan said softly.

'Sorry?'

Satan snapped his head round, his lips twitching. 'I said, "Why do they love this so much." Humans. This game. There's no combat, no drama. Only lots of walking. I loathe it.'

A faint picture formed in Murmur's mind, like the flickering images amid the static just before his television locked into the channel he was searching for. Satan began to talk again, far louder than usual, and the coming insight slipped back into fuzz. 'Yet play it we must, for so many of the decisions that matter are taken on golf courses. We need to understand it, so we can understand those who govern the world above.'

The by-rote recap of Hell's standard position on Satan's obsession with all things human didn't ring true. Murmur filed the exchange away for later examination and lined up his shot. Satan coughed. Out of the corner of his eye, Murmur saw an avatar drop to the ground, turn green to camouflage itself, and set off in the direction of its master's stranded ball. Murmur pretended not to notice. He'd hoped to wait until Satan played a few good shots before tackling the day's business. That didn't look like happening. So, as they set off in pursuit of the errant ball, he launched into his pitch.

'About the humans, Sir. I could do a lot more if I had some minions.'

Satan looked at him askance. 'You know only Lords of Hell have minions. You are doing a good job, but you are asking me to change millennia of tradition and give a low-born command.'

'I understand that, my Lord, but I can do much more with some help. There are tens of thousands of musicians up there, all of them making people disgustingly happy. I can't tackle them all by myself.'

'What do you propose to do with these resources?'

'We can't kill all of the big stars, but we can take out the next generation before they become big, as well as the best session musicians, managers, agents, everyone who is involved. We don't even have to kill them. We can addict them to drugs, mislead them and otherwise sabotage their careers.'

'I suppose that is a good idea.'

They reached Satan's ball, which unsurprisingly lay on the edge of the fairway. Satan glanced at Murmur, who said nothing. The King of Hell pulled out a five iron, settled into a powerful crouch, and hacked at the ball. It travelled all of thirty yards.

'Execrable human game!' Satan roared. Six-foot-high pillars of flame burst from his horns, setting his hat smouldering. He tossed it to the ground and pounded it with his club. When the hat was suitably chastised, Satan turned to Murmur. 'Fine. I will give you a score of demons to do your bidding. I will take them from Lucifer's house. He has been even more annoying than usual lately, demanding we destroy this and pulverize that. He needs put in his place.'

The mention of Lucifer set Murmur's skin crawling. He hadn't forgotten the boardroom confrontation, if you could dignify his cowering submission to Lucifer's aggression with such a word. Nor had Lucifer. Earlier that year, Murmur had woken to find a pair of red eyes floating in the darkness of his bedroom. Lucifer had said nothing, merely staying there for a few more seconds before vanishing. The message was clear: I'm watching you. Having the minions comes from

Lucifer's legions would give the demon another reason to want to make good on his threat of multiple Filofax insertion, which Murmur supposed at least gave him added motivation to succeed and keep in Satan's good books.

'That would be wonderful, Sir, although I do have one request. There are two demons I used to work with, Gergaroth and Tarsis, who I believe would be valuable additions to the team.'

'More low-borns unattached to a great house? I am not sure.'

'We low-borns are hungry, and that makes us hard-working. I guarantee they will do a great job, as I have done. You did say you needed more demons like me.'

Satan prodded at his charred hat with a yellow toe talon. 'I will release them. Just be aware that this does not make you a Lord of Hell. You are still a low-born, if a capable one. Now, let us proceed directly to the nineteenth hole. We shall call this round a draw, yes?'

Satan stomped off without waiting for an answer and Murmur followed, fire playing around his lips. Yes, he wasn't a Lord, and a score of minions didn't constitute a legion, but it represented another rung up the ladder. And he couldn't wait to see the looks on his friends' faces when he told them they would be joining him upstairs.

As expected, Gergaroth and Tarsis were grateful and far more active than Lucifer's lot, who resented being placed under the command of a low-born. Lucifer's minions—who reminded Murmur of snobby English butlers from movies, servants themselves but somehow believing they were better than everyone else—still did what was asked of them, although far slower and more sloppily than his friends. As well as providing him with drinking buddies, Gergaroth and Tarsis' dedication freed Murmur up to devote more time to research. He began attending as many music festivals as he could. At the 1967 Monterey Festival he finally saw one extraordinary individual whose name he'd been hearing for some time.

He started the evening watching The Who from the back of the crowd, wondering if he could arrange for an electrical fault to fry the lot of them. Inertia brought on by the four joints he'd smoked, a habit he'd initially taken up in the hope it might dull the impact of the music only to find the drug intensified it, stopped him. He couldn't be bothered elbowing his way to the front or sending out an avatar to scuttle through the forest of legs. That all changed when a wild-haired man with God in his hands, sporting a pink feather boa, took to the stage. Murmur found himself edging forward. As the guitar, bass and drums drove out their frenetic and mesmerizing sound, Murmur looked at the rapturous faces of the audience. They'd been transported away from their miserable lives, eyes glowing and tawdry souls reaching out for Heaven. He felt a seductive upward tug on his own soul that made him want to give in to the beauty of the music. Somewhere deep within him, he heard the ancient chime of harps and felt an appalling sadness.

He teleported away from the concert with renewed conviction that Heaven was at work through musicians such as Hendrix. Yes, they had a very public policy of non-intervention, but Murmur had learned in his short time on Earth that governing bodies were adept at saying one thing and doing another. If God created mankind in his own image it stood to reason that Heaven could be just as dishonest.

Murmur bought *Are You Experienced?* and listened to it repeatedly on his Moerch turntable, hurting from the pain the sweet music brought but unable to stop. As soon as *Axis: Bold as Love* and *Electric Ladyland* were released, he snapped up copies. Each record drove home the message that Hendrix needed to go. Yet he couldn't bring himself to do the needful. Instead, he made increasingly half-hearted attempts to snuff out other artists. At the Altamont Festival in 1969, he whispered in the ear of a drunk and paranoid Meredith Hunter before passing him a gun to take out as many of The Rolling Stones as he could. A Hells Angel stabbed the assassin before he got a shot off, and Murmur didn't feel as disappointed at the failure as he probably should have.

He may have been better possessing Hunter, but taking full charge of a human wasn't as simple as stuffing your hand up a puppet's behind, as movies and books seemed to portray. The human mind's intricate networks of neurons, conflicting emotions and hidden desires made it more akin to controlling a feisty, uncooperative puppet with a thousand unlabelled strings that kept getting tangled. It was hard enough sober; drunk possessing was damn near impossible. So, Murmur always preferred to use his powers of suggestion. It wasn't a complete loss, however. It only took a firm boot to the side of a Hells Angel's motorbike to turn the atmosphere sour. There wasn't much peace and love that weekend.

After Altamont, he took the decision to move to London. It made more sense given the number of bands sprouting up in England. He bought a house in St. John's Wood with the stash of money Satan sent up and filled it with all the latest gadgets and trendy furniture, which he used with pleasure now he no longer had to contend with claws and scaly buttocks in his human form. Gergaroth and Tarsis moved in with him, while the other minions were despatched to less salubrious digs in the East End. He kept the cover of a struggling writer, but changed his appearance to bring more of a British feel to go with his accent. He selected dodgy teeth, a shaggy shoulder-length mop, pasty skin and a gangly body, and assumed the name of David Ainsworth. The cold bothered him less than he'd imagined it would, although he still kept the heating in his apartment at full blast for much of the year.

Then in 1970 the moment came when he could no longer put off dealing with Hendrix. Despite his growing record collection, he hadn't killed anybody high-profile for a while, and Lucifer's minions kept asking him why such an obvious target remained unharmed. Concerns would be raised downstairs if he didn't carry out his duty and that could lead to him being recalled in disgrace to Hell, where Lucifer would be waiting. To avoid being ripped apart, he had to ensure he returned a hero. And that meant sticking to his task.

And so, one September night, Murmur stood across from the Samarkand Hotel in Notting Hill as Hendrix and his girlfriend pulled up outside the building's stone façade and intricate black railings. The musician looked haggard and leaned on Monika Dannemann as they stumbled down to the basement flat. Murmur waited another thirty minutes before teleporting into the bedroom, where they were both asleep. An uncapped container of sleeping pills beckoned to him from the table at Dannemann's side of the bed.

When Murmur placed his hand on Hendrix's chiselled cheeks and squeezed to open his mouth, the guitarist woke with a start. Murmur stared into his eyes, rocking his head until Hendrix followed suit and his eyes glazed over. He paused for a moment to inspect the guitarist's long fingers, searching for some residual trace of heavenly tinkering—a white glow or angelic symbol perhaps. He rattled the pills in his cupped hand and then sighed.

'I'm afraid you're just too good,' he said.

Faint traces of fire lit up the frown lines on Murmur's face as the pills went in. He waited, the only sound the soft whoosh of

Dannemann's breathing, until Hendrix arched his head back. Murmur put his hand over the guitarist's mouth, feeling vomit gurgle up against his palm. Hendrix began to choke, his eyes open and panicked now that the hypnotic effect of Murmur's gaze had worn off.

When Hendrix went still, Murmur teleported home. He poured himself a Jack Daniels and pulled out *Axis: Bold as Love.* The warm crackle of vinyl hissed through the speakers before the intro to *Little Wing* soared through the living room. He imagined Hendrix's fingers racing up and down the fretboard like a possessed spider to produce the impossibly complicated and gorgeous riff. Then he thought of Satan, staring upward from Hell's caverns and hating the man who'd banished him and the music he'd created. He knew he should hate it too, if only for the pain it brought him. And yet, although his fingers hovered over the arm of the turntable, he couldn't bring himself to turn the record off.

13

Jackie sat at the kitchen table, doodling lyrics for a song about the horror of being the target of a serial killer. The creative process served as a distraction to the pain in his upper arm, which had backed off from unending torturous agony to unending average agony with occasional bursts of torturous. He'd barely slept, waking up screaming every time he rolled onto the arm. His mother had shown him no sympathy, but Marie mopped his brow as he lay in bed the first day, counting the minutes until he could take the next dose of painkillers. However, her patience ebbed as he continued to whine. Soon he was forced to haul himself out of bed to make his own tea. As for the tattoo itself, Marie seemed indifferent. Jackie told her he felt he needed to get one to update his image, to which she just shrugged.

He had the house to himself. Agnes was off at a friend's and Marie was at her once-monthly gym session. He didn't mind, as it gave him more space to focus on the song, which formed part of his plan to take advantage of being a potential victim. Once his profile rose, he would post the tune to his various social media profiles and, with luck, get picked up again. He'd got as far as 'Death stalks the land, but I'm not afraid, as long as there's music, my soul will be saved' when the MP3 of *Your Eyes Are Mine* he had loaded into the mobile interrupted him. As soon as he saw Phyllis's name on the display, he knew the threatening letter had arrived.

'Phyllis,' he said. 'What's up?'

His manager's breath rasped down the phone for a few seconds before she spoke. 'I just got a letter.'

'That's nice,' Jackie said, keeping his voice neutral. 'I always find it a pleasant surprise to get something through the post these days.'

'You haven't done something really fucking stupid, have you, Jackie? Because if you have, I need to know now so we can limit the damage.'

He tried to keep his voice from wavering as he replied. 'Maybe you could give me a clue which stupid thing you're referring to, since you seem to think I do so many.'

'Somebody sent me a letter made up of words cut out from newspapers. Do you really need me to read it out?'

'It would help, since I have no idea what you're talking about.'

Phyllis read out the letter, her mocking tone making it clear she harboured no illusions about the authenticity of the threat. He paused before replying, hoping she would interpret the delay as shocked silence.

'Oh my God!' he yelped. Then, realizing he may be laying it on a bit thick, he shifted to a hoarse whisper. 'He's after me.'

'You'd like that, wouldn't you?'

'What are you implying?'

'I find it suspicious that only a few days ago you were telling me we should flag you up as a possible victim, and now voila! I also find it odd that you're being threatened at all. I made some calls, Jackie. At least another eight people got similar letters. Every last one of them was a big name. It does seem pretty fucking convenient that you've been included.'

Time to act insulted, Jackie thought.

'Are you accusing me of sending these letters?'

He could almost hear the fatigue in Phyllis's voice. 'Yes, I suppose I am.'

'I'm hanging up now,' he said, and did so.

He felt rotten about lying to Phyllis. Then again, she could at least have had the decency to doubt her conclusion, even though it was correct. Anyway, the die was cast. He launched Twitter and typed, 'Just got letter from #tattoocollector saying he wants to kill me. I'm terrified!!!'

That'll do the trick, he thought, and went off to make a celebratory cup of tea.

Mid-afternoon, imbued with a new urgency, Jackie had finished penning the lyrics and was hunched over the keyboard to see if he could knock out an accompanying tune. It needed to be dramatic: minor chords to indicate the gloominess of the situation topped with the odd diminished chord to add an element of discord and menace.

As a poignant B minor died away, footsteps scuffled on the landing. He hurried into the hallway. The kids downstairs had a habit of lighting dog turds seeped in lighter fluid on the doorstep and ringing the bell in the hope he would try to stamp the fire out. He was looking forward to slapping a few greasy little heads when the door shuddered on its hinges. He jumped. Either the kids had graduated to house-breaking or his upstairs neighbour had come home and was forcing his way in to stomp the crap out of Jackie and his instrument. Before Jackie could hide in the cupboard, the door burst open. Police poured in two-abreast, automatic weapons locked against the shoulders of their bulletproof vests.

'Down on the ground!' the officer in the lead shouted.

Jackie stared slack-jawed down a gun barrel. They must have kicked in the wrong door, but he hit the deck nonetheless. A boot on the back of his head mashed his cheek into the carpet, while both arms were wrenched up his back and handcuffs slapped on. He let out a yelp as the healing skin over the tattoo stretched tight.

'Do you know who I am?' he said, well aware that this phrase carried far less weight than it did twenty years before, but still hopeful.

Two officers hauled him to his feet and jammed him against the wall.

'Archibald Thorpe, you are under arrest on suspicion of the murders of Barry Deckhart and Jane McDonald,' one of the coppers said. 'You do not have to say anything but it may harm your defence if you do not mention when questioned something which you later rely on in court. Anything you do say may be given in evidence.'

'Who's Jane McDonald?' Jackie said, before realizing that this wasn't the smartest thing to say. 'I mean, what are you talking about? I didn't kill anyone.'

'Jane McDonald is better known as Fleur,' the officer said.

That's when it hit him. The letters. They must have figured out he sent them.

'Bollocks,' he said.

Two hours later, Jackie sat in an empty interview room, trying to rub off fingerprint ink on the table. The journey to the police station had been humiliating. They frogmarched him down the stairs in full view of the neighbours, all of whom were typing on their smartphones. News, and no doubt pictures, of his arrest would be all over the internet. He wasn't worried about being found guilty of murder, but the story of him sending the letters would be bound to come out. The phone call to Phyllis was the worst aspect of his arrest, however. He told her he'd been nicked and to get a lawyer down to New Scotland Yard. All she said was, 'Oh, Jackie. I warned you.'

The door clicked open and in walked a man in an ill-fitting polyester suit. A shaggy beard carpeted the bottom half of his face, while thick eyebrows overhung his eye sockets like thick snow clinging to a roof ledge. Given that 90% of his face seemed to be composed of hair, Jackie couldn't read any kind of expression. He was accompanied by a woman in her mid-thirties; her ponytail, wire-frame glasses and tailored blue trouser suit screamed lawyer.

She shook Jackie's hand and settled into the seat next to him. 'I'm Maria Rodriguez, from Williams & Tait.'

The yeti turned on a recording device, checked his watch and read out the time the interview began.

'I'm DCI Jack Rooney, and you, Archibald Thorpe, are in deep shit.' Rooney leaned forward, his equally hairy hands folded over each other on the table. 'I'm curious. What do you do with them?'

'Do with what?'

'The tattoos, once you've cut them from your victims. Put them in a scrapbook? Make them into a pretty little dress and dance around in front of a video camera? Use them as a wank glove?'

'No,' Jackie said, raising his hands.

'What then?'

'I don't do anything with them. I mean, I didn't kill anyone.'

'Then explain this.'

Rooney threw a plastic bag on the table. It contained one of the letters. Jackie's heart sank as he stared at the scrap of paper, wondering if he should claim no knowledge of it.

'Your fingerprints are all over them.' Rooney slid the letter across the table. 'And then there's this.'

The newspaper cuttings had been detached. On the back of the word 'Tattoo', taken from a sub-headline in *The Daily Mail*, was the bottom section of a crossword. Printed underneath was Jackie's name and the first line of his address. He dropped his forehead to the table. Keeping his head down, he turned to look at his lawyer.

She shrugged. 'I would suggest you cooperate, Mr Thorpe.'

Jackie let out an almighty sigh. 'Fine, I sent the letters, but it's not what you think. I wouldn't have sent one to myself if I was the killer, would I?'

Rooney ignored his denial. 'Where were you on the night of January 13?'

'You can't seriously think I killed anyone,' Jackie said, meeting the policeman's impassive gaze.

'Answer the question.'

Jackie searched his memory to place the date, which must have been the night Deckhart was murdered. Then it struck him. 'I was in the *Celebrity Public Eye* house, then out on the town. You've got that photo of me with Fleur as proof, and loads of witnesses.'

Rooney scribbled something in his notebook. 'Fine. Now, February 1.'

'What day was that?'

'A Wednesday.'

After a brief pause, Jackie figured out that was the night he went for dinner with Marie, and told the officer.

'Right,' Rooney said. 'We've also pulled in Marie Stubbs for questioning.'

Jackie felt sick. He could imagine how Marie would react to being sucked into his scheme.

'She had nothing to do with the letters,' he said, banging the table for emphasis, because that's the kind of thing he'd seen innocent people do in police dramas.

'Really? Then explain this.'

Rooney got out of his chair and crossed to the TV and DVD player that were sitting on a table in the corner. He pressed a button, and CCTV footage of the entrance to Tottenham Court Tube station began playing. Amid the crowd, Jackie saw himself and Marie. They embraced then walked off.

'So? That proves I was with her.'

Rooney rewound the DVD and paused it. He pointed to a slim figure lurking against the wall. 'Recognize her?'

'No.'

'It's Fleur.'

The colour drained from Jackie's face. 'I didn't know she was there.'

'You don't think it looks suspicious that you were photographed molesting her and then a few weeks later you're seen near her on the night she disappeared?'

'I didn't molest her. And I swear I didn't see her standing there. Marie and I went for dinner and drinks then home to bed. That's it. The cameras must show we don't talk to her.'

Once again, the officer pressed play. Jackie and Marie walked off camera, ignoring Fleur. Then the image went dead. Jackie looked at Rooney, who said, 'Just wait.'

Three minutes of excruciating silence later, the images flickered back into life. Fleur was gone.

'That doesn't prove anything,' Jackie said.

'It doesn't disprove anything,' Rooney said. 'You could've doubled back after your accomplice disabled the camera and persuaded her to come with you.'

'I don't have an accomplice.'

'Well, somebody turned off that camera, and cameras along New Oxford Street for the next fifteen minutes. That suggests you had an accomplice besides your girlfriend. We want to know who it is.'

'I didn't kill anyone! Come on, the same person that killed Fleur killed Barry Deckhart, and I've got an alibi for both.'

'It doesn't matter if you have an alibi for Deckhart. Your accomplice, the same one who also turned off the cameras when Deckhart was kidnapped, could've snatched him for you to kill at your leisure.'

Jackie turned to Rodriguez, his face incredulous. 'Don't you have anything to say?'

The woman looked down. 'To be honest, I'm a bit out of my depth here. I'm not a criminal lawyer.'

'Oh, for fuck's sake,' Jackie said, aware that Phyllis was probably trying to teach him a lesson. 'I don't have an accomplice. I sent the letters, yes, but it was just an attempt to drum up some publicity. I'm a desperate has-been, not a bloody murderer.'

With this admission, the true extent of how moronic and utterly pathetic he was struck Jackie. He closed his eyes to hold in the tears that were threatening to come.

'I'll be the judge of that,' Rooney said. 'Now, let's go back to the start.'

Rooney fired the same questions at him repeatedly for the next four hours. Though Jackie was exhausted and terrified, the answers he gave were consistent, and he sensed a gradual relaxation in Rooney's approach. Finally, the copper stopped the interview and left the room for half an hour. When he came back, he was carrying three cups of coffee.

'OK, Archibald,' he said. 'Or should I call you Jackie?'

'Jackie.'

'The good news is, after interviewing Marie Stubbs, talking to your manager and checking up on your alibis, we're reasonably satisfied you are in fact just thick as two short planks. The bad news is you're still in the shit, which is now only nipple-high instead of up to your eyeballs.'

'Why? You've cleared me.'

'Do you know how serious it is to send threatening letters?'

'I'm hoping the answer is, "Not very, you're free to go."'

'Wrong. Aside from the threats themselves, you've interfered with a major police investigation. That's perversion of justice. You could get a couple of years.'

'I didn't mean any harm.'

'Doesn't matter. You diverted valuable police resources.'

Jackie's right leg went into spasms. He put both hands on his thigh to get it under control.

'Maybe we can work something out,' Rooney said. 'I have a proposal for you. We need some bait.'

'Bait for what?'

'To catch the killer. We want to make you a star, Jackie. When you're a star, with a very obvious tattoo, this maniac will come for you.

And we'll be waiting.'

'You can't expect me to do that. I could get killed.'

'You'll be shadowed. And need I point out the alternative?'

Jackie looked at his lawyer for support. Once again, she shrugged. 'I would take the deal.'

'You're not much bloody help, are you? Is Phyllis paying you in sweeties?'

'I'm doing this as a favour,' she said.

'I'm going to be honest,' Rooney said. 'We're desperate. We've had leads on this guy. A tattoo parlour owner said some sweaty nut came in months ago asking about magic tattoos. He couldn't remember what he looked like apart from the fact he had a shit mullet, and there are plenty of those around. Then we found a few managers who said they got emails asking where they got their magic tattoos. Those emails disappeared. Nobody has seen him kidnapping or killing these people. The guy's a ghost. We have to be creative.'

'Easy for you to say. It's not your life on the line.'

'Think of it this way: you want to get back in the charts. This is a great chance for you to do that, with minimal risk.'

'You said no risk a minute ago.'

'Would it help if we told you we're going to ask Murray Murdoch to get involved?'

Jackie's leg stopped shaking. Even though he was showing signs of waning influence, the music impresario could still make a career with a snap of his fingers. 'Murdoch?'

'Yes. He'll get you back on the map, and once the killer is caught, you'll be a hero. A megastar.'

'How many officers would be following me?'

'Two, with a backup armed-response unit on call.'

Jackie considered his options. It wouldn't be a whole lot of fun inside, even if he was too old to be prime bitch for the butch queens. Taking the deal gave him the chance of getting back where he belonged, despite the risk of being horribly murdered. 'I'm in.'

'Excellent. Let me get the ball rolling. I'll arrange for you to be released without charge, and we'll keep your role in the letters under wraps.'

'My neighbours took pictures,' Jackie said. 'The media are bound to get wind of it.'

'We can say there was an imminent threat against you and we took you in for protection. That should help get your profile up straight away. We'll be in touch in a few days to set up a meeting with Murdoch.'

As Rooney headed for the door, Rodriguez scampered after him with a hasty wave at Jackie.

'Thanks for all your help,' he called after her.

Freshly disgorged from the shiny metal maw of the New Scotland Yard building, Jackie headed for St. James's Park underground. As much as he dreaded facing the music, he headed for Marie's flat. He figured that once he'd told her he was on the verge of stardom, to which he would drag her along, she would get over the trouble he'd caused her. First, he had to get her to talk to him. It took five minutes of holding his finger down on the bell for her even to come down the hallway.

'I'm not talking to you,' she said from the other side of the door.

'You just did,' he said, hoping to break the ice.

She said nothing, but he could see the outline of her head through the frosted glass. He pushed open the letterbox and put his lips to the gap. 'I'm really sorry. I didn't plan for any of this to happen.'

She responded by slamming the letterbox shut on his fingers. He let out an almighty yell and pulled them from the metal vice. Two of his knuckles were dented, and a third was bleeding.

'Fucking hell, that hurts!' he shouted, shaking his hand.

Marie opened the door, her brows unfurling when she saw blood leaking onto the doormat. 'You deserved that. But I suppose you'd better come in.'

They went to the kitchen, where Marie bandaged his finger in silence. Once she'd finished, she met his gaze for the first time. 'What were you thinking?'

'I wasn't. I'm sorry I dragged you into it.'

He reached for her hand. She let him take it.

'Are you that desperate?' she said. It wasn't a question that needed an answer. 'Are they going to charge you?'

He shook his head, and laid out the content of the deal.

'You can't be serious,' she said. 'You'll get killed.'

'That won't happen. Don't you see? The letters worked. We're talking about Murray Murdoch here. He'll make me huge.'

'He'll make you dead.'

'That won't happen. I'll have a 24/7 police detail.'

'But Murdoch, for God's sake. You told me he was ruining the music industry, or was that only a line to get me into bed?'

Jackie had thought that about Murdoch, but it was different when you were on the outside, your face pressed to the glass looking at the banquet within. Now that he had an invite to gorge himself at the overflowing table, Murdoch didn't seem so bad.

'This is different. I'm not a manufactured star. I'll just be using him as a springboard. And I'll demand they involve you.'

'You want me to get murdered as well? Charming.'

'This guy kills people with tattoos, nobody else. I'll tell the police I'll only do what they want if Murdoch agrees to help your career too.'

'And if they say no?'

'I'll go to jail,' Jackie said with an emphatic nod.

'You'd really do that?'

'Yes,' Jackie said, aware that the residue of coldness in Marie's features had gone. 'We're a team. I wouldn't leave you behind.'

Suddenly, it was as if he were looking in a mirror. Marie's eyes shone with the same sparkle that he knew his own held at the thought of a new start. Even when she'd talked about giving up, he'd known she didn't mean it. She sashayed around the table with an exaggerated swing of the hips to plonk herself in his lap.

'I suppose I can forgive you,' she said, and planted her lips on his.

The kiss developed and before he knew it they were on the kitchen floor. As his reasoning shut down to allow the more primal drives to take over, a little voice, which sounded a lot like his mother's, tugged at his thoughts.

'Don't make a promise you can't keep,' it admonished.

I'll keep it, he thought.

'Even if it means prison?'

This time, Jackie ignored the voice, letting the urgent call of his body's needs wash it away.

The next day, after an evening of excited chatter about the future, Jackie stood outside Phyllis's office. He'd been hovering there for five minutes, unable to bring himself to ring the bell, when the door flew open.

'For God's sake, come in,' Phyllis said.

'How did you know I was here?'

'You're a noisy lurker. Don't ever try to be a Peeping Tom.'

She spun round, leaving the door open. Jackie followed, like a guilty schoolboy shuffling into the headmaster's office. He sat before the desk; she peered at him over the top of her glasses.

'So, they let you out,' she said, her frosty tone of voice conveying the fact she thought the police had made a very big mistake.

'No thanks to that lawyer of yours.'

'She was the best I could get on short notice. I generally don't have to worry about my clients facing murder charges. Anyway, you're lucky I didn't leave you to rot.'

She sipped coffee as Jackie squirmed on his seat.

'I'm sorry,' he said. 'I shouldn't have lied.'

'You shouldn't have sent a bunch of threatening letters to celebrities, you complete and utter tool. Anyway, I suppose you're here to tell me about the deal you cut.'

'Rodriguez told you.'

'Yes, she told me.' Phyllis took off her glasses and rubbed the bridge of her nose. 'Jackie, we've been together for a long time, haven't we?'

He nodded.

'And haven't I always stuck by you, tried to give you good advice?'

Again, he nodded.

'Consider this the most important piece of advice I'll ever give. If you sell your soul to Murdoch, your last chance to turn back the clock will be gone. You had something, once: talent, a musical direction. Then that bloody *Your Eyes Are Mine* came along.'

'What do you mean?'

'I mean it was the worst song on the album, but it went huge and all you could think about was repeating the winning formula. Once you had a taste of fame and money, you lost sight of what made you good. I've told you this a hundred times, in a hundred different ways. You didn't listen. I tried to pull you back, and I still think it isn't too late. But if you go with that evil sod, you'll be gone forever.'

'Don't you think you're being a bit melodramatic?'

Phyllis lasered him with a stare that would have sliced a block of concrete in half at fifty paces. 'I've put up with so much shit from you down the years because I believed in you. I could even forgive you for the letters because I know deep down you're a good man and a real musician. But if you go with Murdoch, we're finished.'

'I don't have a choice. It's either that or jail.'

'God gave humanity free will, which in my view was an incredibly fucking bad idea, so there's always a choice. It may not be one you like, but it's still a choice.'

'You seriously expect me to go to prison?'

'Why not? You broke the law. You made people fear for their lives. You didn't care about that. You couldn't see past your own needs. You need to pay the price.'

'If I do what the police want, I could help catch the killer and save lives. This isn't just about me.'

'Dress it up any way you like, Jackie. This is about you.'

Jackie shook his head vehemently. Yes, sending the letters was a mistake, but he had a chance for redemption. The killer would be caught, and he would be the reason why. And if he became disgustingly famous along the way, so be it. He looked around Phyllis's office, and realized how grubby and low-rent it looked. His gold disc was the only one she had. The rest of her clients were small-timers who'd barely sold a million records between them. She should be grateful to have him instead of constantly ticking him off.

He got to his feet. 'You know what I think? You're jealous because Murdoch can do something you've never been able to do. He can make me famous again.'

'And that's all that matters, right, Jackie? Not the music.'

'Spare me the moralizing,' he shouted. 'I'm fucking sick of it.'

The sharp look in Phyllis's eyes blunted. She got up, crossed to the wall and took down the gold disc. Her finger caressed the frame briefly before she thrust it at Jackie.

His anger fizzed out as suddenly as it had arisen. ' Phyllis. Please.'

She held the disc steady, not a muscle in her body moving. Finally, Jackie lifted his hands and took it from her. It felt impossibly heavy. She sat back down and turned her swivel chair around. He lingered, trying to find the words to express the conflicting emotions welling up within. Eventually, he turned to leave.

'Goodbye, Phyllis,' he said, and closed the door behind him.

He stood outside the office for a minute, unable to believe what had just happened. He needed a drink and some distraction, so he called Marie.

'Fancy some karaoke?' he said.

14

A waxing moon shone pale silver light on Hampstead Heath, where Gareth wound his way through the trees in search of the cruising area. In one hand he clutched a holdall with the tools he would need; in the other he'd palmed a syringe. He'd been tripping over tree roots for fifteen minutes and was beginning to wonder if he'd come to the wrong place when he saw a broad-shouldered figure in a hooded top and tracksuit bottoms in a small clearing up ahead. He dumped the bag behind a tree, double-checked that the syringe couldn't be seen, and headed towards the silhouette.

He'd been sprawled before the television an hour earlier, flicking through the channels in a mindless trance, when the sound faded. His mum's voice, clear and cheerful, came through the speakers. She told him to get his tools together and rush to Hampstead Heath, where he would find Tom Burnett cruising for sex.

They'd agreed that their next target should be a male singer to increase the chances of the tattoo taking, and for the last ten days he'd sat around waiting for the right opportunity to present itself. He should have been looking himself, but the doubts he'd been feeling since Fleur's death sapped his motivation. Her voice had been a shimmering wonder and he'd silenced it. It didn't help that he was now officially a serial killer. The papers said so. Somebody had created a Facebook page dedicated to The Tattoo Collector, with over 50,000 fans, where people posted guesses on which celebrity would be next and suggestions of which one should be next. Bookmakers were even taking bets on the identity of the next victim. He supposed he should be happy to receive so much attention, but he was supposed to be a global singing sensation, not a psychotic weirdo, and the virtual nature of the focus did nothing for him in the real world. He began to spend long hours in front of the bathroom mirror, staring at his reflection and hating what he saw. Even his snipping out of pictures became half-hearted. His new collection of images grew slowly, and his face seemed to leer at him with the snarl of a killer.

Despite all his reservations, he'd stuffed everything he would need into a bag and jumped into the van. The pot of gold beneath the rainbow was too rich to back out now and he would surely, as his mum said, give the world far more in return for the lives he'd taken.

Tom, the openly gay singer-songwriter who'd won *Icon* two years before, looked up at the sound of crunching footsteps on the frosted grass. Gareth couldn't see his face. He didn't have to. Tom's jutting jaw, aquiline nose, light brown skin and soft grey eyes were ingrained in Gareth's memory from the many pictures he'd gazed upon. How his mum had known Tom would be here alone on such a perishing cold night, and why he was shivering in the darkness when he could have his pick of suitable partners, Gareth didn't know. He sensed the hand of Fate.

'Finally,' Tom said. 'I was just about to go home.'

Gareth said nothing as he closed the distance. He had to get near enough to slip the syringe into Tom's neck, and his plan brought him nose-to-nose with the singer. The sudden kiss that followed, so warm and intimate, leached all the strength out of Gareth's arm. His mouth opened like a flower in the first shaft of morning sun. All thoughts of his mission burned away in the heat whirling through his veins as Tom tracked his tongue down his neck and then knelt to fumble with the buttons on his jeans. Still the needle remained unused as Tom freed his now-erect penis and began to suck, first gently then with an intensity that set Gareth's hips to pumping.

Throughout his life, love had been something he got from his mum and sex a vague concept, something that happened to other people. He'd never wasted any time imagining what it would be like, whether with man or woman. Now, as he spurted deep into Tom's throat with a groan so deep he could barely believe it came from within him, he understood what the fuss was about. The sheer physicality of the pleasure pulsing through his groin, of the link between cock and mouth, between human and human, made his fears of invisibility seem a distant and ridiculous dream. When the spasms had passed, he looked down at the grinning Tom and stroked his handsome face with his left hand

'Your turn,' Tom said.

The singer lay on the ground and tugged down his tracksuit bottoms. He wore no underwear. Gareth was unsure how to proceed or if he could bring himself to put another man's penis in his mouth, but he didn't want this feeling of closeness to pass. He went to his knees, placing the needle in the grass, and tentatively grasped the shaft before closing his lips over the end. At first he gagged, then, encouraged by the moans emanating from Tom's parted lips, slurped at it. The penis pulsed in his mouth, an umbilical cord connecting him to the physical world. When Tom grabbed the back of his head and rammed his whole length home, Gareth did not withdraw. Soon warm, sticky fluid filled his mouth and he swallowed reflexively. Gareth dipped his head forward, maintaining the suction, as Tom tried to withdraw. The singer had to place his hand on Gareth's forehead and yank his hips backwards; his penis slipped out with a pop.

'Bit amateurish, but not bad,' Tom said.

Gareth, his cheeks flushed and heart swelling, slid up to cuddle in, thinking he could close his eyes and sleep awhile in this blissful afterglow. Instead, the cold sharpness of the grass pricked his cheeks as Tom rolled away. The singer stood with his back to Gareth and hauled up his trousers.

'When can I see you again?' Gareth said, placing a hand on the singer's calf.

Tom laughed. 'You *are* new at this. We've had our fun. Time to say bye-bye.'

Gareth didn't understand. Yes, their encounter had been brief, but it had also been so special. They'd been inside each other. Surely that couldn't mean so little to this man when it meant so much to him? Yet Tom began to walk away. Gareth threw his arms around the singer's leg and was dragged several feet along the ground before a kicked-back heel struck him on the shoulder. He let go.

'Needy much?' Tom said.

Gareth hugged his knees, staring at Tom's retreating back. His throat felt raw, empty and used. His skin began to tingle, and when he looked down at his wrists they seemed translucent. His thoughts were turning to the scalpel when his mum's voice came whispering out from the trees.

'You won't get love from the likes of him, my boy,' she said. 'He took what he needed from you. Now you have to take what you need from him.'

Gareth's gaze fell on the needle glinting in the moonlight, its point as sharp as the latest rejection. He picked it up and moved through the grass. Tom, intent on hurrying away, didn't hear him coming until the needle was in.

He felt no guilt, no regret as he bent over Tom's still body and sliced off the tattoo. The gauze and antiseptic cream he'd brought to dress the wound remained in the bag, the phone he'd intended to use to call an ambulance in his pocket, as he walked away from the unconscious singer, his heart now as cold as the night.

Once Gareth departed, Murmur emerged from the shadows and walked over to Tom Burnett. The singer's breathing remained strong, the drug concealing the trauma from his body. It didn't seem likely he would die, even given the cold. He would wake up in a while, stagger onto the road and flag down a car. That wouldn't do. Murmur summoned up an avatar. It skipped across the grass, prised open Tom's lips, and disappeared down his throat to block his windpipe.

As he waited for the avatar to do its work, Murmur thought how easy it was to get to the celebrities. They had fame, fortune, respect and admiration, but it wasn't enough. Each sought out dark corners to indulge their hidden desires. Deckhart had longed for an escape from beauty and perfection, seeking it in the arms of the unattractive Prudence; Fleur had sought dissolution to escape the pain of her broken love affairs; and Burnett had trawled the anonymous playground of suck and fuck because the closeness and responsibility a real relationship would bring petrified him. Deckhart had deserved to die for playing for Chelsea, Fleur had wasted her talent and Tom was arrogant and dull. Only Gareth deserved any pity. Murmur had felt the aching sadness when Tom rejected his yearning for a simple cuddle, and found himself wondering why Hell needed to exist. Humans did far worse things to each other than demons could dream up.

Murmur had planned to have Gareth kill at least another two previous *Icon* winners plus Tottenham's star winger, but he didn't want to put his young protégé through any more frustration. It looked likely that his mind wouldn't be able to bear it much longer.

Tom's chest fell still. Just as he'd interfered with the CCTV cameras as Gareth kidnapped his targets and cleaned up the bodies after, Murmur took care of the evidence. He sent the first avatar to the stomach to suck up Gareth's sperm and spat up another to clean off any fingerprints, hairs or fibres that might point the police in Gareth's direction. Although he'd set Gareth up in another house, he didn't want to prompt a manhunt and have Gareth's name and face plastered all over the media before the right moment. The time had come to bring this phase of his plan to a close, and for that he would need just one more celebrity. It was only a question of whom.

When Gareth got back to the house, he laid out the tattoo on his worktable and brushed his fingertips over it. The warmth had fled the skin, but still he laid it flat on his right palm and undid his zip with his left. He spent five minutes trying to recapture the feeling of intimacy that had been given and taken so casually, but he may as well have been flogging his flaccid penis with an old flannel. He threw the limp skin into a corner, feeling as scraped out and hollow as a Halloween pumpkin, and took to his bed.

When he dragged himself up after noon the next day, he forced himself to retrieve the tattooed skin and tape it on. His shudder this time derived from emotional pain rather than disgust. Before leaving, he turned on the news and saw that Tom's body had been discovered by a jogger. He switched off the television, feeling nothing, and headed out onto the streets.

Five hours later, he fought his way up Regent Street, barely aware of the regiments of pedestrians, just as they were barely aware of him other than as an obstacle to step around. Not even the tantalizing red lettering of H&M or the store's glass doors roused him from the black mood that had engulfed him as he realized Tom's tattoo, like those of

Barry and Fleur, had not given up its magic. With each passing person who ignored him, the tingle of pre-invisibility grew stronger. After Oxford Circus, he took a random left turn down a side street, hoping to find a quiet corner in which he could deliver a few quick slashes with the scalpel. He found himself outside The Old Explorer bar. Through the windows, he saw a karaoke machine being set up amid a smattering of office workers catching an early dinner. He pushed open the door, thinking he could give the tattoo one last test and hopefully ward off the symptoms. He ordered a fresh orange and lemonade to justify his presence and then headed straight over to the karaoke machine.

'I need to sing,' he said to the compere, who'd just finished plugging in all of the cables.

'We don't start until seven.'

'Please.'

The compere gave Gareth a long look, then shrugged and handed over the microphone. 'No skin off my nose, I suppose.'

Gareth selected *Total Eclipse of the Heart* and put his all into it. The small crowd took little notice at first, although one or two glanced in his direction—enough for the tingling to subside even though the tattoo still felt lifeless. He was halfway through the song, thinking it would hold him until he got home, when the two men sitting closest to the speakers, their cheeks already flushed as a result of the collection of empties on their table, began to heckle.

'For fuck's sake, mate, we're trying to eat here,' one of them called.

Gareth redoubled his efforts, almost screaming the lyrics.

The other man threw down his fork and got to his feet. 'Has anybody ever told you, you sing like Darth Vader on helium?'

They laughed loud and long, sucking in the people nearest to them. Gareth, his resolve weakened by the draining events of the last twenty-four hours, dropped his arm. The microphone slipped from his fingers as their mocking brays transformed into the poisonous chuckle of the man who'd crushed his dreams, and he was sucked down into the memories of the day he'd tried so hard to forget.

It was supposed to be the best day of his life. For the first time, after years of auditioning, he'd made it to the second round of *Icon*, where the real judges would watch him strut his funky stuff. When he'd passed the first audition six weeks earlier at his eighth attempt, he and his mum had bounced around the hallway, still filled with aspirants awaiting their turn, unable to contain their joy at making the cut. They ramped up their practice schedule to exhausting proportions. Gareth spent six hours each day working at perfecting the tune they selected, a rendition of *Hallelujah* that started slow and melodic but burst into a high, upbeat tempo on the third verse. It was a wonderfully twisted cover, and they had no doubt that Murray Murdoch—a real judge of talent, unlike the bored members of the production team who oversaw the first round—would be blown away.

Four weeks before the audition his mum, who'd had a cough for a few weeks, doubled over and hacked up a clot of blood as Gareth was practicing the knee slide that would serve as the finale to the song. Gareth, still on his knees in the hallway, stared at it glistening on the floor, and looked up at his mum. Her eyes were dull. For the first time he saw the deep, curved lines stacked up beneath her sunken sockets.

'I've got something to tell you,' she said.

The cancer had been diagnosed a month before: a malignant, inoperable mass of tumours in her lungs that she'd hidden to avoid throwing him off his preparations. Within two weeks she lay in a hospital bed, hooked up to tubes and beeping machinery. In another week, she was dead. In her last minutes, as Gareth clutched her wasted hand, she pulled off the oxygen mask and beckoned him closer.

'You still have to go to the audition,' she said in a voice that already sounded like it came from beyond the grave.

Gareth squeezed her hand harder, feeling the bones of her fingers grind beneath his palm. 'I can't. Not without you.'

Her eyes were massive in her skeletal features, hypnotizing him. 'I need to know you're going to make it without me. Tell me you'll go.'

'I'll go,' Gareth said, his voice breaking.

She let out a long sigh and the heart monitor flat-lined. He laid his head on her chest and stayed there until the nurses came in, making no attempt to resuscitate. None of the nurses put a hand on his back, touched his hair, or whispered any condolences. Why would they? They couldn't see him. Nobody would ever see him properly again.

Somehow, he got through the next week. He tried to practice in between making arrangements for the funeral, but when he opened his mouth all that came out were moans. After the funeral, he lay on his bed for two days, unable to summon up the energy or will to go downstairs and eat. Even chocolate tasted sour. On the morning of the audition, only the memory of his promise to his mum got him into the shower and dressed. They'd agreed he would wear a dark blue shirt and red trousers with a white stripe running down each seam. Gareth instead picked out a matching black shirt and trousers with a hint of silver thread running through them.

When he got to the venue, the other hopefuls were pacing the hall, insincerely wishing each other luck. The variety of garish costumes with which they hoped to attract the judges' attention made Gareth's black outfit seem plainer than it actually was. He sat in silence through it all, ignoring the young girls who babbled to each other about how this was their chance to escape the office jobs that crushed their creativity. When his turn came, he dragged himself into the audition room. The three judges—Murdoch, Celine Murphy and Larry Bowen—sat behind a fold-away table, notepads and pens arrayed before them. Gareth stood on the X and stared at the blank, appraising eye of the camera.

Murdoch raised one eyebrow. 'You look like a cheery chap. Are you going to sing us a Radiohead number?'

'My mum just died,' Gareth said.

A long silence followed. Finally, Celine, the judge with the heart of gold whose job it was to offset Murdoch's more outrageous pronouncements, said, 'Are you sure you're up to this?'

'No, not really,' Gareth said.

Murdoch threw down his pen. 'Oh, for goodness sake. Next!'

An assistant hurried over to jockey Gareth from the room, bringing him back to his senses. He'd told his mum he would try. If he let them usher him out now he may never get another chance.

'Wait,' he said, pulling away.

Murdoch gave a brief nod, and the assistant backed off.

Gareth took a deep breath. 'I'd like to dedicate this to my mum. I wouldn't be here if she hadn't supported me all those years.'

Celine gave a loud sniff, dabbing at one eye even though no tears appeared to be sallying forth. Murdoch's face remained expressionless. Gareth closed his eyes and began to sing, imbuing every note, word and syllable with love for his departed mum. At the appointed moment, his eyes flicked open and he upped the tempo and volume. His body took over, snapping into the dance moves ingrained into muscle memory. He skipped back-and-forth, rolling his shoulders and revolving his hips, hoping his mum was somehow watching.

He forgot his pain and the scrutiny of the judges until Murdoch's harsh voice pulled him from his reverie. 'That's quite enough.'

Gareth froze mid-dance, his forehead and cheeks dappled with sweat. Murdoch was staring at him while the other two judges scribbled in their notebooks, heads bent.

'I'm in then?' Gareth said.

Murdoch snorted. 'Absolutely not. I've seen some bad singers in my time, but you take the biscuit. In fact, you take all the biscuits, the cakes and any other teatime snacks in the immediate vicinity.'

Gareth stood there, arms dangling limp by his sides. 'You can't be serious.'

'Oh, I'm deadly serious. You are truly woeful.'

'My mum said I had the voice of an angel.'

'An angel with throat cancer singing through a voice box, perhaps. Seriously, a hyperactive fly stays on a turd longer than you can hold a note. What I just heard was about the most blasphemous thing ever. Whatever possessed you to think you could sing that song, and then make it worse by trying to bloody dance to it?'

Gareth managed to catch Celine's gaze as she glanced up. 'Please, give me another chance. I'm upset. My performance must have been off. I can do better.'

She opened her mouth, but Murdoch cut her off. 'Begging won't make any difference. Get out.'

'I've worked my whole life for this. What am I supposed to do now?'

'Go work for Bernard Matthews. I hear he's fond of turkeys.'

Two assistants were approaching, attempting to shoo Gareth towards the door. He jumped out of range. He knew that if he walked out the door, his mum wouldn't be there to cradle his head and pin him to the real world with her gaze. Only the blade would remain, and both forearms were already crusted with scabs from the last week. Soon even that wouldn't work. He mentally flipped through his back catalogue and selected *Rock DJ*. He began singing again, but his voice warbled as he dodged around the room, trying to flit away from the assistants. They almost trapped him behind the camera, but he nudged the cameraman towards one of his pursuers and slipped through the gap that had opened up, somehow managing to keep the song going.

'Does anybody have a long cane to hook this maniac off?' Murdoch said.

Despite Murdoch's words, Gareth could tell the attempts to usher him out of the room were half-hearted. Celine and Larry were smiling.

He was providing the show they wanted, and this knowledge gave him the heart to inject even more oomph into his voice, which was now so loud it hurt his ears. He was beginning to believe it might work, that he might actually make it to the show, when Murdoch thumped the table so hard that a glass of water toppled, rolled and smashed on the floor.

'It's just as well your mother's dead,' Murdoch said.

Gareth stopped, the smile dripping from his lips. 'What did you say?'

'Oh, that got your attention. If your mother trained you, she did a great service to music by popping her clogs. She clearly had no idea what she was doing.'

Every muscle in Gareth's body clenched; a black hiss of rage coursed through his mind. Abuse about his singing he could take, after all he'd had enough of it from the philistines down the years, but he would not hear somebody talk about his mum like that. His thoughts blinked down to a small spot of light, like an old-fashioned television set, and disappeared.

He ran towards the table and flung himself headlong across it. His hands closed around Murdoch's throat in mid-air and the momentum of his leap sent them both tumbling over the back of the chair. As he bore down on the soft windpipe, Celine began clonking the back of his head with the spiky heel of her right shoe, while Larry tried to prise off his fingers. Screams and shouts penetrated the veil of Gareth's rage, but his fingers continued to tighten around Murdoch's neck. Despite the choking grip, Murdoch lay still, gazing at Gareth with a calm and calculating air. When he winked, Gareth snapped back to himself and loosened his hands. His rage spent, he sat back up, intent only on getting to his feet and running from the room. He didn't get any further, for a burly security guard brought a chair crashing onto the back of his neck. Gareth slumped to one side, his consciousness fading.

'Did you get all of that?' Murdoch asked the cameraman.

Gareth's eyes closed, and for the first time since his mother died he felt nothing.

When Gareth emerged from the memory, tears coursing down his face, silence filled the bar. He dropped the microphone, prompting a spike of feedback, and walked towards the door. Even though there were now several dozen people in the bar, not one of them was looking at him. As he was about to exit, the door swung open and in walked Jackie Thunder, arm-in-arm with his girlfriend.

'Are you alright, mate?' Thunder said, reaching out a tentative hand that didn't quite bridge the gap between them.

'No,' Gareth said, and slipped between the couple and out onto the street.

15

December, 1980

Murmur stirred his coffee in a café on 72nd Street, watching his latest stooge walk robotically towards notoriety. The assassin's bouffant black hair, bushy sideburns, large glasses and wobbling double chin gave him the look of a low-rent Elvis impersonator as he stepped onto the road, touching the jacket pocket where the gun Murmur had slipped him nestled. The brash honk of the yellow cab that whizzed inches past made him start and almost drop the copy of *Catcher in the Rye* he clutched in a meaty fist. The assassination about to take place would be another big one, for even though The Beatles had split ten years ago, John Lennon was still widely loved—thanks largely to *Imagine*. The song had spread like the plague, with the crucial difference that it brought peace and understanding rather than pustules and death.

Murmur took no pleasure in Lennon's impending demise. He wasn't worried about being implicated, as he'd obliterated all traces of his whisperings from Chapman's mind. In their place he left a confused psycho-babble about phonies, Chapman's inner child and a dialogue between God and Satan for his soul. Trying to penetrate that nonsense would keep the psychiatrists busy for years. Rather, his sense of unease related to his greater task on Earth. Over the last twenty years he and his team had killed and hamstrung hundreds of people at all levels of the industry, yet he appeared to be little more than a splattered fly on the windscreen of the musical juggernaut.

New movements, each with its own complicated branch of sub-genres, kept coming. Every one prompted spiritual awakenings across the globe. Take punk, for example. To the uninitiated it would seem like something Hell could throw its weight behind given its nihilism and anti-establishment nature. But Hell's goals were best served by the establishment, which promoted greed, started wars and suppressed creativity. Bands such as The Clash and The Dead Kennedys, full of energy and righteous indignation, made youth more socially and politically conscious and forced them to question the established order. Murmur wondered what such music would do to the ambitions of the low-borns if it were unleashed in Hell.

The music also served as an indicator of the way humanity moved forward at breakneck speed, technologies and societal mores ever-changing as the species jumped from trend to trend like a hyperactive child given unrestricted access to a two-litre bottle of Cola and as many sweets as it could cram into its sticky face. Humanity's lust for change undoubtedly came from Heaven, and while it caused him no end of headaches, Murmur couldn't help but admire it. Humans had an energy the demon community sorely lacked.

He signalled for the bill, planning to head home and figure out a better way forward. As he stepped onto the street, gunshots crackled through the air. Screams followed. He looked across the streaming headlights of the late-evening traffic, demon eyes zeroing in on the arched entrance to the Dakota courtyard. Lennon lay on the ground, Yoko Ono wailing on top of him. Chapman stood nearby, reading from his book as though waiting for a bus. Shoulders hunched, Murmur left the rubberneckers to their panicked squeals and trudged into a nearby alleyway to teleport back to London.

Murmur sat up until the early hours of the morning, staring into space and listening to music. He needed a new direction, and he'd found one of the best ways to spark ideas was to listen to the very bands he'd been sent to destroy. Inspiration failed to come, so he got up to stand in front of his record collection, which covered one whole wall in custom-made shelving. As well as splitting the records by genre, each in alphabetical order, he'd divided them into three overarching sections: artists who really needed to be killed; artists he'd killed; and everyone else. He looked at the hundreds of records in the section of those he should have done something about, gaze settling randomly on the sleeves of the many outstanding musicians it held: David Bowie, Stevie Wonder, Black Sabbath, Funkadelic, Neil Young, Bob Dylan, Sly Stone, Van Morrison, Gil Scott Heron and on and on.

The shelf he'd set aside for those he'd dealt with was much smaller, and as he turned his attention to it he thought for the thousandth time how many of them were still widely listened to. Murdering musicians before their powers waned gave their music greater resonance. In fact, it felt like everything since Holly had been an anti-climax. That assassination was the only one given a name, The Day the Music Died. It also epitomized the pointlessness of killing musicians, as it prompted others to write more songs. Those he had killed, the bare minimum to keep the project going, he'd selected by closing his eyes and running his fingers along the sleeves of the records to stop at random. Jim Morrison, Bon Scott and Ian Curtis all died thanks to his work in the shadows. Bob Marley, while not dead yet, was on his way out thanks to a radioactive wire hidden in his football boots to give him cancer. Murmur had been particularly unhappy about Marley, but he had to kill somebody. Even putting aside his fear of Lucifer, it wasn't just about him any longer. The legions of low-borns were depending on him, even if they didn't know it yet, and to stop now would mean all of his friends would be stuck stamping forms forever.

He turned off the record player, Pink Floyd's *Animals* slowing to halt, and clicked on the radio. The news broadcasts were full of people talking about how much Lennon had inspired them and how his music would live on. Murmur spun the dial until he found a late-night channel playing entries from that year's Eurovision Song Contest and mocking them. The last-placed song, the Finnish entry *Flute Man*, got a particular savaging before the DJ ironically put it on. The song was more bland than woeful. The melody, the beat, the orchestra, even the flute when it came, all managed to invoke not a single feeling in Murmur. It was the worst kind of cookie-cutter song writing, so far removed from the music of the greats that it may as well have come from another planet—one where the inhabitants sleep-walked through existence, barely lifting their spirits above the drudgery of their lives.

An idea hit him so hard that, for the first waking moment in over a decade, his face burst into flames. He damped the fire and sent an avatar to silence the beep from the smoke alarm he'd installed after a vivid dream in which he appeared on the cover of *Fire & Brimstone* set his body, and the bed, on fire.

Music was a language that couldn't be translated. You heard it in the way people fumbled to explain why they loved a song. You saw it in the way people drove with their windows rolled down and radios turned up, the way they pressed their favourite records upon friends, the way courting lovers made cassettes for each other to express the inexpressible. They wanted to share in the only way they could. Yes, a musician could describe what he technically admired about a song in terms of keys, chords and melodies, or look at sheet music to understand the notes that must be played, but it didn't reveal what gave music the potential to be so powerful and infectious. Styles came and went, and different genres and bands did it for different people, but Murmur had come to understand that the common thread could be summed up in one word: heart. All great music derived from this human core; the passion, pain or joy that artist poured into the song and transmitted to the listener. Without heart, a song was nothing more than an empty shell. He could always tell when somebody was going through the motions: he felt nothing. And there lay the crucial leverage point he'd been overlooking.

A quick check of time zones told him he would have to wait eight hours before Hell got up-and-running, so he passed a restless night until he could call down. When he rang Morgane, he booked a meeting with Satan for three weeks' time. It was the earliest possible slot, and although Murmur couldn't wait to put forward his idea, the time would come in handy. He would need to put together a detailed project plan to get Satan to buy in to the scheme, which would require significant resources. He sat at his writing desk with a large sheet of paper and a fountain pen, his inner conflict forgotten amidst the joy of planning.

Satan elected to come up top for the meeting, combining it with a 'reconnaissance mission to check out the latest human trends'. What he

really meant was that he wanted to go on a shopping spree. The first
order of business, however, was a game of squash. Satan strolled onto
the court in a pair of ball-hugging white shorts and a t-shirt that rode a
little too high over his stomach. He'd chosen a squat and unremarkable
body topped by a face nobody would ever look at twice. He could have
passed for a middle-aged banker if not for the reddish tint to his eyes
that hinted at something more sinister.

Murmur began humming *I Wanna Be Like You* under his breath
before he came to his senses and cut if off. He'd been singing the song
at every meeting with Satan since one stoned afternoon in a darkened
cinema watching *The Jungle Book* in the early 1970s. When King Louie
had set forth his desire to be human, Murmur pictured Satan's face
atop the body of the prancing ape. It made no sense for Satan to want
to be like the creatures he set out to corrupt, defile and torment, but
Murmur couldn't shake the feeling that this lay behind his obsession
with human technology. He hid these thoughts as best he could,
fearing what Satan would do were he to peek into his mind and
uncover this theory. Fortunately, Satan never seemed to bother trying
to force his way past Murmur's meagre mental defences.

'How are you today, my Lord?' Murmur said, trying to take his mind
off the dangerous thoughts by getting straight to the point of their
meeting.

'Fed-up,' Satan said. 'Too many problems, not enough solutions, as
usual.'

'Well, Sir, I am coming to you with a solution, one so …'

Satan held up a hand. 'Later. This is called squash, you say?'

'Yes. Everybody's playing it these days. I thought you might like to
give it a go.'

Murmur ran through the rules, and then stroked some gentle warm-
up balls off the wall. Satan only made contact on his third attempt and
even then sent the ball ricocheting off the ceiling. It took two minutes
for the cheating to begin. No matter how fierce the shot Murmur
played, the ball always seemed to land in the centre of Satan's racquet.
When the balls came back to Murmur, they swerved at the last minute.
If Satan behaved this way in Heaven, Murmur wasn't surprised he'd
been kicked out. He resisted the urge to use his own mind to control
the ball, instead reconciling himself to defeat. It would be worth it to
put the boss in a more receptive frame of mind. When the match was
over, the final result 5-0, Satan looked a lot more cheerful than when
he'd arrived. They showered and toured the shops, where Satan

purchased a ZX80. Back at the flat, Murmur poured Satan a large one and settled him on the leather sofa before beginning.

'You've probably noticed that killing musicians doesn't seem to be stemming the tide,' Murmur said.

'I have remarked upon that trend,' Satan said, with half an eye on the ZX80 instructions.

'We'll never be able to rub out good music completely. It has to be damped down to an acceptable level, and that means a change of tactics.' Murmur paused, unsure whether what he was about to say would prompt a fireball in the face. 'I think we should enter the music business ourselves.'

That got Satan's full attention. 'Demons do not make music,' he said in a low growl. 'It is against the laws of Hell.'

'I understand that, Sir, but you yourself said we were too reactive. We're trying to control the symptoms of the disease, rather than tackling it at its root.'

'Go on.'

'I will. First I want to play you some music.'

'No,' Satan said.

Murmur saw something close to panic in the eyes that had once again dulled to deep purple. Satan half-rose, looking ready to bolt from the room. Murmur gave his best reassuring smile, prompting a slight lightening of Satan's eyes, and pressed "Play" on his hi-fi's cassette deck before Satan could scarper. He knew he was taking a chance, that Satan could react very badly, but he figured it was a small one. After listening to the Finnish song, he'd begun searching for music in the same vein. To his delight, he found that while he'd been focusing on finding great songs, major record labels had been spewing out reams of crap.

Satan cringed as the music, for want of a better word, eked out of the speakers. He'd squeezed his eyes shut, but less than five seconds into the tape he tentatively opened one eye, then the other. He relaxed as the predictable, derivative singers Murmur had plucked from the airwaves churned out their insipid tunes.

'Tell me, my Lord, how does this music make you feel?' Murmur said.

Satan gulped his whisky. 'It makes me feel...' He broke off, frowning. 'It does not make me feel anything.'

'Precisely. We've been looking at this the wrong way. Instead of trying to stop good music, we should be making mediocre music. Fill the airwaves with this stuff and the only thing humans are going to aspire to is bedtime.'

'What makes you so sure they will like it?'

'All of those songs were big hits. We just have to expand on it and shove our music down their throats. I've watched trends develop. If people are repeatedly told they should like something, and enough buy into it, then a tipping point is reached and that particular thing—be it music, fashion or film—becomes wildly popular. It's nothing to do with quality; more with the pack mind. In music terms, it's all about airplay.'

Satan still looked unconvinced, so Murmur pulled out his sheets of paper. 'I've made a plan.'

Satan's eyes flared red with pleasure as Murmur laid out the documents, full of charts and arrows and timescales, over the top of the ZX80 manual. Murmur went through his scheme play-by-play, knowing he had Satan when he got out his red pen and started making notes in the margins. It was only when they came to the demonpower requirements that Satan balked.

'You are asking for a lot of resources. We are up to our necks in it down there.'

'If we're going to do this, we have to do it right. Nothing speaks to the human soul more than music. If we take away this inspiration, we remove the bedrock they build their other achievements upon.'

Satan held out his glass for a refill. Murmur obliged.

'What is this style of planning called?'

'It's a Gantt chart.'

Satan picked up the top sheet of paper and cradled it. 'I will make you a deal. If you agree to give a training course on how to use this, then I will give you the demons you need. I suppose you want more low-borns?'

'Yes, Sir.'

The boss drained his glass and stood up. 'Give me your list and I will make the arrangements.' He touched the project plan one last time. 'You know, Murmur, I am very pleased. I am starting to think you may have a future down in Hell once this is over.'

'I hope so, my Lord. You can count on me.'

'It would seem so,' Satan said. 'One last thing, though. Lucifer has been keeping a close eye on what you are up to, so you will have to keep up the assassinations. You know he is never happy unless we are killing or maiming, and I really cannot bear listening to him whine. It gives me a headache.'

When Satan had vanished, leaving behind a faint hint of sulphur in the air, Murmur pulled the cassette out and threw it in the bin so he need never listen to any of those appalling songs again. He flicked through his vinyl in search of something to cleanse his palette and settled on The Talking Heads, cleaning the album with his special cloth before gently lowering the needle into the groove. When *Once in A Lifetime* crackled into life, he danced around the living room and sang along at the top of his voice. Eventually he lowered the volume and sat at his desk. He would push for as many low-borns as he could, but even more delicious was that the new plan would allow him to bring himself more to the fore. He would place himself firmly at the centre of the record label, ensuring that his name became as big as the groups he signed up. He would only be famous on Earth, but that was better than nothing.

To do that, though, he would need a new identity, a fresh young face to front up the label. First he needed to choose a name. Knowing he would never be able to sleep that night anyway, and keen to get the ball rolling, he teleported to the darkened aisles of the nearest library and pilfered a book on Western names, which he leafed through over another glass of whisky. He wanted something that would give a hint to his true identity to those who looked hard enough. It took him five minutes to come up with a name that fit the bill: Murray Murdoch.

16

Murray Murdoch was much smaller than he appeared on television, standing a good four inches shorter than Jackie. Despite the height disadvantage, he radiated strength. The slightly hooked nose, coupled with dark eyes glittering within deep sockets, gave him an intense aura. The real kicker was the way he rarely rearranged his facial features into anything close to an expression. He employed a complex system of eyebrow semaphore to convey emotions as he sat on the *Icon* judging panel. As far as Jackie could tell, outward edges down meant, 'I am bored senseless.' Inward edges down meant, 'This act is dreadful beyond belief.' Eyebrows flat meant, 'I am ambivalent about this act.' Right eyebrow raised meant, 'I am mildly impressed.' Left eyebrow raised meant, 'The other judges are talking nonsense.' Both eyebrows raised meant, 'I am going to make a killing on this.' On the rare occasion he smiled, his thin lips twitched upwards and his hooded eyes remained expressionless.

Murdoch wore such a fake smile as he stood in front of Jackie and Rooney in the *Icon* studios, alongside an assistant named Gerry whose lips were similarly arranged. They shook hands. Murdoch's palms were warm and dry in comparison to Jackie's, which he'd already wiped ten times on his trousers. Jackie's incessant sweating had two causes.

Firstly, the killer had struck again and the papers were full of fevered speculation on who would be next. The process about to begin made it likely that the answer would be 'Jackie Thunder', particularly since he knew Burnett's corpse hadn't yielded a single scrap of evidence. Rooney, who talked far more than he should, had confided he'd never seen a case that so defied the precise forensic science that had made old-fashioned detective work near obsolete. The police had become accustomed to handing over a hair or blood sample to the scientists, and putting their feet up until it was time to arrest whomever they were told to arrest. Now were stumped. They needed Jackie to dig them out of an embarrassing hole. Secondly, he'd decided to get his ultimatum regarding Marie out of the way early.

'So, Jackie, my good man. Are you ready to clamber from your pit of obscurity?' Murdoch said. 'I can't imagine it's been easy being a nobody again for all those years.'

'Yes, but …'

Murdoch cut him off. 'Then let's get started.'

He turned towards the stage, and they all scampered in his wake like obedient puppies. The studio was empty. The real show would begin in six months, after UK-wide auditions had whittled down the thousands of hopefuls—but, just like Embassy, it felt hallowed. Stars were born here, anointed in the font of public opinion and sent forth to be worshipped. Murdoch kept up a cracking pace for a short man, and Jackie was breathing hard by the time they entered a changing room, where a woman with a dyed-red fringe waited.

'Step number one is the makeover,' Murdoch said. 'You need a more mature look. You dress like a fifteen-year-old thinks a grown-up should.' He slapped Jackie's gut. 'And those tight shirts have to go. You look like a python that's swallowed a midget.'

'You should put him in sleeveless tops,' said Rooney.

Murdoch fixed Rooney with a dead-eyed stare. 'Policeman and fashion consultant. What a marvellous combo.'

What little of Rooney's cheeks peeked out above the beard flushed. 'I just meant the killer has to see the tattoo for this to work.'

'Ah, of course. The killer. How thrilling. Let's see what we have to work with. Off with the shirt.'

Jackie slipped off his top, aware of how his gut and chest sagged.

'Hmm,' Murdoch said. 'We'll need to get you pumping iron to put some definition in those dinner-lady arms.' He plucked at Jackie's hair with his thumb and forefinger. 'And this has to come off tout suite.

You look like a trampy Peter Stringfellow.' He turned to the stylist. 'Rajinder, he's all yours. Sculpt me some beauty from this lump of clay. I'll be back in two hours.'

As Murdoch and Gary turned to leave the room, Jackie plunged in. 'I'm not doing this unless you promise to help Marie Stubbs as well.'

Murdoch's eyebrows lowered into a V. 'Who do you think I am, Super Jesus? One Lazarus act is bad enough, never mind two. Count yourself lucky I'm doing this at all.'

Jackie turned to Rooney as the door clicked shut. The policeman was shaking his head.

'I mean it,' Jackie said, his voice shrill. 'You have to tell him.'

'If you want to spend the next five years scrubbing skid-marks off underpants in Wandsworth, feel free to continue making demands. The deal is for you alone.'

The cop had kept his word to suppress the identity of the man who sent the letters, so the road had been clear for Murdoch's PR machine to sweep all before it. Jackie received a full-page spread in *Celeb!* detailing the threat, the move to put him into protective custody and the news he would soon be releasing a single. His Twitter account took an instant boost, hitting over 3,000 followers. Wheels that would bring him to the killer's attention had been set in motion, and the momentum was sweeping him away. Phyllis thought he had a choice. That wasn't true. He had to go along with it. Marie would understand, he told himself. After all, he'd asked. And anyway, once he was famous again he wouldn't need Murdoch's help. They could do the duet then.

He sat down, unable to look at himself in the mirror, and let Rajinder get to work.

By the time Murdoch returned, Jackie had forgotten Marie, instead mesmerized by his new appearance. Rajinder had cut his hair short, yet somehow managed to arrange it in such a way that his scalp couldn't be seen—without even the slightest hint of comb over. She'd also trimmed his eyebrows, plucked his nasal hair, and applied a little foundation. To emphasize his cheekbones, she'd smeared on bronzer, making his face look less chubby. From the wardrobe, she'd selected a loose black vest top with slimming dark blue vertical stripes. The trousers were dark blue suede, and he'd been given a pair of heeled black leather boots to add an extra inch. He looked five years younger.

'That's a start,' Murdoch said. 'Do try to suck your gut in though.'

Jackie obliged.

'Now you look constipated. Forget it. We'll get you chiselled before the video. We're going to record the song and film in two weeks.'

'Fantastic. I've got a few song ideas to discuss. I've written some great tunes.'

Murdoch waved his hand. 'No, no, no. We have a deliciously appropriate cover version lined up.'

Jackie had expected to have some kind of creative input to the process, but the hard set of Murdoch's features told him arguing would be futile. 'What's the song?'

'*Somebody's Watching Me.*'

Rooney snorted with laughter. 'Perfect.'

'Isn't it just,' Murdoch said, his eyebrows dancing upwards.

It could've been worse, I suppose, Jackie thought.

He was wrong.

Marie took the news that she wouldn't be included badly. They still saw each other, but the cocoon-like atmosphere chilled despite the barrage of flowers and chocolates he sent her way. It didn't help his mood that he and Phyllis hadn't exchanged a word. Every time he passed through King's Cross, he thought about getting off and walking to her office. He always stayed on. They'd made their respective choices, and no words were going to heal the rift.

The physical demands were almost as draining. Instead of beer and wine, he drank water and slimming shakes. Burgers, chips and Agnes's greasy fry-ups made way for salads, tofu and grilled fish. Most days, his stomach felt like it was trying to gnaw its way out of his chest to take itself down to the kebab shop. Each morning, a personal trainer rang the doorbell at 6am and dragged him to the gym. He discovered he had at least two dozen muscles he hadn't known existed, all of them clamouring to proclaim themselves the most exhausted and painful.

Afternoons were spent at the *Icon* studios working with voice and dance coaches. Jackie had always believed his voice spanned three octaves, from F3 to F6. The voice coach, a former opera singer, forbade him from entering the third octave. Jackie fought at first, but gave way when she recorded them both singing scales. She hit and held every note perfectly. His voice pulsed and cracked when he hit the high end. The dance lessons were equally demoralizing. On the first day, they asked him to show off his best moves. He let rip, giving it the twirl and point, the shoulder shimmy and the foot slide. The dance teacher banned him from ever doing any of those moves and instead gave him a set of very simple steps that 'a rhythmically challenged clodhopper' like Jackie could do in time to the music.

Bit by bit, Murdoch's team sliced away the Jackie he'd been like a hunk of ham in a delicatessen.

By the day of the recording, he'd shed two stones and found he could climb the stairs to his mum's flat without wheezing. Murdoch had been absent during Jackie's rebirth, but he resurfaced in the recording studio, along with Gerry and another guy called Tarquin. They made an odd trio, with their immobile faces and strange habit of occasionally looking at each other intently. The band had already recorded the backing. It was a typical modern cover, the dynamics and quirkiness of the eighties electro version sacrificed for a bass-heavy rendition. Jackie hated it. While the song was just a throwaway pop tune, at least the way Rockwell half-spoke the verses in a theatrical voice gave it some character. Jackie planned to stay true to this vibe, which would go some way towards adding personality to the track.

He was three lines into the run-through, emoting and declaiming with all his heart, when Murdoch burst into the studio, eyebrows kinked downwards. 'What on earth do you think you're doing?'

'I thought the song was a bit bland. I'm being idiosyncratic.'

'You're being idiotic. If the public wanted idiosyncratic, The Cardiacs would be number one every week. They want bland. They want to anesthetize their minds after a day in the office, not listen to something that's going to make them think or feel. This is background music, Jackie, to be played at parties, in the car, or in the gym as fat people prance about in ridiculously tight shorts.'

'I don't think you're giving people enough credit.'

'I do the thinking around here. How many number one hits have you produced over the last thirty years? Now, be a good boy and sing it properly or I'll call the whole thing off.'

Rooney, who was sitting in the control room, carried out a ridiculous jailhouse pantomime: his pattering fingers indicated a shower; he dropped an imaginary bar of soap; he pumped his hips.

Eyes on the prize, Jackie thought for the hundredth time, and nodded his assent.

If the song was bad, the video proved worse. A location scout had found a derelict building in Old Ford, on the banks of the River Lea. Every window of the graffiti-covered, two-storey brick structure was broken. The neglect was rendered starker by the white modern apartment block next door, whose occupants presumably relished the stench of stale piss that wafted up to their balconies enough to lash out several hundred thousand quid each. Broken glass, crumbling brickwork and the remains of makeshift fires littered the floor. Five stuffed bin bags, overflowing with beer cans and empty wine bottles, attested to the building's normal use.

Jackie's job was to lip-sync while dancing from stinky room to stinky room pursued by a scalpel-wielding actor dressed in a Victorian cape. Feeling increasingly like a performing monkey, he mugged it up as best he could. They filmed him from the right-side as often as possible, and on several occasions the director asked him to flex his new biceps so they could do a close-up on the tattoo. In between takes, he crouched in the corner and smoked, trying to ignore the echo of Phyllis's warning. After their showdown, her words about his first album stuck with him, and he'd gone home to listen to it. He'd run through it three times, a sick feeling in his gut as he realized *Your Eyes Are Mine* was the weakest song on the album. Yet he bit back on the doubt. After all, millions of people had loved it and Phyllis was one woman. Plus, once this unpleasant phase had passed, he would have a new fan base and could regain his integrity by introducing them to the real him. He had dozens of unrecorded songs to regale them with.

Just like that, after two decades struggling to win back the favour of the fickle public, an offhand wave of Murdoch's magic wand put Jackie right back up there. Murdoch's choice of song and video proved inspired. The public loved that one potential victim was rubbing the killer's face in it with no apparent regard for his own safety. Upon the release of the single and video, Jackie's social media pages burst into life with messages. He even became a trending topic on Twitter as, with relentless airtime on Radio 1, the song went straight to number one. He spent the first two days in a fever dream, watching the number of followers shoot up. Each follow was like a drop of soothing rain on an ego parched by almost twenty years in the desert of anonymity. They soon became a deluge, and he was almost overwhelmed and unmanned.

The phone began ringing with invites to parties and requests for interviews. He agreed to them all. During his media appearances, Jackie acted unconcerned. In reality, he spent every waking minute scanning his surroundings and at night woke up at every creak and passing car. No other victims had been claimed since Burnett, due no doubt to the crisped flakes of celebrity skin piling up in drifts in laser clinics and the hard-looking minders with suspicious bulges under their jackets who trailed the big stars everywhere. This made Jackie a likelier target.

He'd been assigned two officers: Hao, a tall, rangy woman with short black hair and a gaze that flitted around, and Alfie, a stumpy man almost as wide as he was tall. Hao was posing as Jackie's stylist, and had been saddled with a wardrobe of clothes in bright primary colours. Her cover allowed her to carry a hefty bag, which instead of hairdryers and make-up contained a hidden camera, two pistols and spare ammunition. Alfie was supposed to be his PA, and spent an inordinate amount of time pretending to talk into his mobile. Hao and Alfie disappeared when Jackie went home, at which point the surveillance team set up in a flat across the road took over. According to Rooney, nobody could get near him.

Even if he managed to avoid the clutches of the killer, he was already paying for his newfound fame in his relationship with Marie. He invited her to every party, introducing her to agents and record producers, and took every opportunity to mention her in interviews. Yet nobody showed any interest in her. She grew ever more silent, resisting all of Jackie's efforts to soothe her, until it all came to a head. And it was all because of that bloody Tandy Carston.

17

In his two hundred years languishing in Souls Receiving, Murmur had filed every human sin imaginable under the main categories of Lust, Gluttony, Greed, Sloth, Wrath, Envy and Pride. People killed, raped, abducted, tortured, abused, lied, conspired, stole, conned, misled, and so on in endlessly inventive combinations and permutations—so much so that filing under the correct category of main sin could sometimes prove tricky.

Murmur had read extensively on the subject, and concluded that all sins flowed from Pride. He'd even popped in a suggestion, roundly ignored, that they wipe out all other sins and replace them with this single category. He'd backed it with a wealth of references on the subject, including the Biblical literature stating Pride as the real source of Adam and Eve's fall from grace, Dante's definition of the sin as 'love of self perverted to hatred and contempt for one's neighbour', and Thomas Aquinas's statement that 'Pride is the first sin, the source of all other sins, and the worst sin.' Wisely, he omitted the most obvious example of Satan's fall from God's grace. He'd seen nothing on Earth to change this belief. There were seven billion people on the planet, each one locked into their own narrative about how special they were, endlessly turning over their petty problems and grievances until they assumed an importance that eclipsed all else.

And here, Murmur thought as he watched Jackie emerge from beneath the deck of the Murdoch yacht in his gold speedos, *comes another one.*

Jackie, who'd whined that Marie wasn't invited to the long weekend on the yacht off the coast of Barbados but came anyway, epitomized why the rise of Murray Murdoch had been farcically easy. Fame, above all else, raised the individual to the level where their pride was validated by millions, proving once and for all they were more important than the rest of the world. Jackie had tasted that once and would debase himself in any way to get it back.

From the moment he'd started his record label, Murmur realized that this desire for fame meant there were few artists whose principles couldn't be bought, while journalists lined up to gush the praises of any given band for the chance to rub shoulders with the elite and have that stink of fame rub off on them. Mammon had also played its part. Virtually every music programmer in radio or television could be induced to put Murmur's dire output on the playlist with a bit of payola. As for those few righteous souls who refused to bend, Murmur had them bumped off and sent a minion in to take their place.

Stardust Records quickly created a production line of stars to sing along to the blandest beats and riffs his team of composers, plucked from the obscurity of writing advertising jingles, could churn out. The over-produced songs were filled with blaring instruments that deadened dynamism and eradicated the quiet space that allowed emotion and passion to come through. He used filters to kill the raw emotion of the human voice. He ensured that the lyrics said nothing of any value, emphasizing predictable threads about love, encouraging songs about mindless fun and having the songwriters chuck in as many repetitive 'lalalas' as possible. He co-opted actors and actresses from TV soaps, using their profiles and fan bases to reach a wider audience with unbridled fluff. No heart ever found its way into any one of Stardust's songs, and when he attended gigs put on by his acts, as many as he could stomach, he noted the complete absence of collective inspiration amongst the crowd. God had assuredly left the building.

By the end of the 1980s, Stardust had scored hundreds of hits, and the profits meant he no longer needed to requisition cash from Hell's financial office. Sure, the label had its detractors, particularly from the snooty music press who referred to Murdoch plus Gergaroth and Tarsis—who were acting as co-producers—as 'the unholy triumvirate'. Only students read those rags anyway, and they in time would succumb once their principles and ideals were eroded by the harsh reality of having to make a living. Nonetheless, Murmur started up his own media empire with the Stardust profits. He filled the pages of *Celeb!*, modelled on *Fire & Brimstone*, with titbits from the lives of the singers in his stable, making more money and boosting record sales in the process. He made sure to feature himself as often as possible, primarily appearing on the red carpet at swanky functions on both sides of the Atlantic.

Despite his ministrations, good music continued to be released in sufficient quantities to keep his record collection growing. From Acid House to Madchester, great bands leaked through the cracks he hadn't plastered. Murmur kept tabs on all of them, adding the likes of The Pixies, Violent Femmes, Underworld, Public Enemy, Spearhead, The Blue Nile and Fugazi to his collection, which now stood at tens of thousands of records. He added the best to the section that had once been set aside for those he should kill, which had now become reserved for the artists he listened to most. That wasn't to say he didn't follow Satan's directive to keep bumping off a few musicians here and there, although he was careful not to kill his favourites. Freddy Mercury and Kurt Cobain numbered among his victims, mainly because Queen's best work was long behind them and Nirvana were, in his view, the least interesting of the grunge bands.

As well as giving him plenty of listening material, his collection served as a useful database for subverting new musical forms. He took the beats and vibe of hip hop and rap, deleted the political messaging, and pumped out his own pale echoes. He took the underground electronic music scene and morphed it from something new and fresh into simplistic jagged bleeps and bloops with pumping beats and repetitive lyrics. He took the raw energy and anger of grunge and the Straight Edge movement, cleaning up their choppy angry riffs and putting pretty boys preaching hedonism at the front of the bands.

Through it all, Murmur still kept an eye out for angels, part of him longing for them to show their faces so he could bring to life his fantasies of heroic battles in which he triumphed. He never had any direct encounters, although he remained convinced they were working on the peripheries—particularly when he first encountered Jeff Buckley. Murmur had heard many amazing singers down the years, but Buckley's ethereal voice came close to how Murmur imagined an angel would sing. The Murmur of twenty years before would have killed this divine creature. This Murmur just kept turning up at his concerts and bathing himself in the sweetness of his voice on the slim pretext that he was looking for proof of Heaven's tinkerings. When Buckley drowned in 1997, an untimely death in which Murmur played no role, he played *Grace* back-to-back for a full day.

Then there was the peculiar case of the American comedian Bill Hicks, who came worryingly close to the truth in a skit that revolved around MC Hammer and Vanilla Ice sucking Satan's cock in exchange for success. Those artists weren't on the Stardust roster, and the only cock sucking going on was metaphorical, but it still hit too close to home. After a bit of humming and hawing—it would've been nice to get the recognition if Hicks really was on to him, but it would have meant the end of the road and a premature trip back down to Hell to face Lucifer—he gave Hicks a dose of cancer. The comedian was thirty-three when he died in 1994, the same age as Jesus upon his demise, which had a rather nice symmetry if Hicks were indeed a prophet.

The creation of *Icon* in 2001 was a logical progression born from the growing conviction that he'd yet to harness fully the power of television. Sure, music shows were plentiful and he'd made certain his flashy, sexed-up videos got the lion's share of exposure, but he still felt there was more to be squeezed from the format. Then one night he flicked from *Pop Group* to *Public Eye*, and his mind made the connection he'd been searching for. The two new shows were part of the growing trend of reality TV: one where judges created a band, the other where members of the public were given a shortcut to fame despite their grubby, unremarkable lives. It was a simple matter to combine the two. The resultant show exceeded his wildest expectations.

Initially, the real singers were what concerned him. He wanted to ensure those with talent were neutralized by making them buy into his bland template rather than take the risk of going out on their own and producing something amazing. It worked in the same way as the National Lottery: why work hard to become rich or famous when there was a chance, no matter how small, that you could attain your goal with zero effort? What surprised him, however, was how many people were prepared to risk public humiliation for a sniff of fame. He'd expected only those with at least some talent to enter, but everybody seemed to think they had what it took. The show was essentially bottom trawling, forcing him to sift through vats of shit to find those few baubles he could polish up and fool the world into thinking were precious gems.

At first this annoyed him, but he soon realized that this was what made the show so popular and deliciously pernicious. Reality TV tapped into the curtain-twitching instincts of humans, who seemed to enjoy nothing more than shaking their heads at the stupidity of others and basking in the warm glow of superiority it afforded them. The human drama, particularly when it revolved around hopefuls having their dreams crushed, mattered far more than the actual music. And so he gave them what they wanted, spending as much screen time as possible on the deluded and pitiful acts, and having Murdoch give them a roasting on behalf of the judgemental watching nation. He ensured that the songs were sandwiched in between long scenes of the performers fretting and sweating over whether they would make it, and kept controversially bad acts in the show for as long as possible to give the public someone to mock.

Even when he did get to the music, the spectacle came first. Every performance was awash with dozens of hot backing dancers, flashing lights and intricate set pieces. He applied all the production tricks he'd used to such good effect down the years, adding in Auto-Tune—a piece of software that corrected for pitch. This not only allowed bad singers to sound just competent enough, but sapped the power out of any performances that came dangerously close to exhibiting real emotion. To add the cherry to his overly sugared, cloying cake he focused heavily on cover versions, which further created a culture of reduced originality and creativity and served the purpose of diminishing the impact of the original by replacing it in the public consciousness.

Each year, queues for the auditions grew longer, and the show dominated the weekend ratings. His human alter ego became one of the most famous people in the Western world, feted and hated in equal measure. The UK's disproportionate musical influence meant the rest of the world was affected, and dozens of franchises and copycat shows sprang up everywhere from Nigeria to Poland. He exported the show to the US, and although it hadn't quite reached the giddy heights of the UK success it was coming along nicely. However, he couldn't shake off a vague dissatisfaction that, for all his work, his real identity remained unrecognized in any of the realms. He regularly Googled for 'Murmur' and found only a few mentions, all of them wrongly listing him as a minor demon responsible for small-scale jiggery-pokery. Essentially, he was big in Japan. That would have to change.

First, though, he had a more immediate problem to resolve: that of the flagging *Icon* ratings. He'd pushed the boundaries of his cruel and sarcastic persona too far when dealing with Gareth. In his defence, the years of approval of such behaviour had made him believe there were no limits to what he could say, and he'd already been forced to listen to three appalling covers of classics on that day. Gareth's mauling of *Hallelujah* had been the final straw. Even had he tried to emulate Leonard Cohen's original, which was spoken in deep, mournful tones, Gareth would have fallen woefully short. But Gareth went for the powerful vocal gymnastics of Buckley and tripped up over every note before launching into his ridiculous up-tempo dance version.

Even paying for Gareth's treatment in The Priory hadn't helped mollify the public, who began to go off the show. Murmur suspected that it wasn't just about Gareth. It was another symptom of humanity's short attention span. They'd had over ten years of *Icon* and other such shows, and were now looking for something new. Even reality cooking and dancing shows were a threat. He probably could have lived with the dip, had it not been for the winner of *Icon* failing to attain Christmas Number One for the first time in seven years. When he first started Stardust records, any time he saw his acts dominate the charts he thought 'I did that' with a glow of pride. Now, when he watched the pitiful bands dancing to the strings he pulled, he thought 'I did that' and felt faintly nauseated—a sign that it was perhaps time to move on. But failing to be the top dog on Christmas Day prompted a flurry of comment questioning whether Murdoch was losing his touch. He couldn't have his reputation besmirched in such a way.

On top of everything else, he found the reaction to Gareth's humiliation a bit rich, since the viewing public was the modern equivalent of the baying citizens of Rome watching the circus. If they didn't want to see public savagings, they shouldn't tune in. Still, it was typical of humanity to deny its own complicity in any tragedy, always finding somebody else to blame, be it a book, a song or the abstract concept of evil. Yet beneath the condemnation of his actions, he detected an undercurrent of self-loathing, as though the public was aware of its own role in Gareth's humiliation. He intended to exploit that to the full, delivering the lovely symmetry of using the man who'd helped kick-start public discontent to bring them back into the fold. And now Jackie was in the mix.

Jackie's meddling had given Murmur's scheme to revitalize *Icon* an unexpected, and welcome, boost. The sad old bugger hadn't figured in his plans, but when he involved himself through his half-baked stunt with the fake letters, it was too good an opportunity to miss. The song they'd recorded further hyped the media attention around Gareth and his little murder spree. Nobody was saying it out loud, but they were waiting for Jackie to be killed and, when the moment of reckoning came, Murmur would hold up the mirror to their bloodlust.

Murmur looked at Jackie, who was now lowering himself into a lounger and reaching for a pink cocktail. Yes, Jackie would serve very well in his master plan.

Jackie could hardly believe the changes the simple act of posting a few letters had wrought in his life. Here he lay on a lounger on Murray Murdoch's luxury yacht—a gleaming white hunk of kit inlaid with sparkling fittings, polished wooden decking that caressed the bare soles, and hushed service from attractive young waiting staff. Tropical fish darted through the azure waters and a few hundred metres away the butter-yellow sands of Barbados soaked up the heat of the sun, which warmed Jackie's skin to a soporific temperature. The odd speedboat and water bike zipped past, sometimes sending playful spray up onto the deck of the yacht. This was the British idyll.

You've got what you wanted, he thought. *You should be happy.*

And yet all he could think of was the lie he'd told Marie. Murdoch had been adamant that she couldn't come on the trip, despite Jackie's repeated pleas. He only shut up when Murdoch reminded him that he could be putting her life in danger since the Tattoo Collector was after him. He'd thought about not going, but Murdoch had been equally insistent that the trip was a compulsory celebration of their success so far. Nor could he bring himself to tell Marie the truth. Instead, he'd spun a yarn about being taken away to a secluded studio in Cornwall, where they would set a trap for the killer. She'd bought it, yet her parting statement that he should make sure he came back in one piece seemed lukewarm. Their relationship appeared very much on the rocks while he sunned himself by the sea.

In an attempt to distract himself, he fiddled with Murdoch's Mac, which was attached to expensive mini speakers on the foldaway table between their loungers. He scrolled through the playlist, finding bands that would look more at home in Phyllis's collection: The National, Massive Attack, Wilco, British Sea Power, The Postal Service, Majical Cloudz, Savages and dozens more.

'I'm surprised at your music choices,' he said to Murdoch, who had his hands folded over his chest as he gazed up at the clear skies.

'How so?' Murdoch said without looking round.

'It seems very … alternative.'

An eyebrow went up. 'Do crack dealers use their own product? I spend most of my working life listening to the dross we produce. I'm certainly not going to bring it home from the office.'

This pulled Jackie up short. He'd always assumed that Murdoch must like the music he produced. 'So why do you do it?'

Murdoch shrugged. 'We all have to work. Besides, having the charts so full of drivel makes the good music more powerful, don't you think? You must have had that feeling when you're listening to something that hardly anybody else knows about. It makes you feel superior, part of the little gang in the know.'

Jackie let the conversation lull, wondering if he could pose the question he'd been itching to ask from the moment he first met Murdoch. The tabloids and celeb mags, apart from Murdoch's own, were filled with low-level speculation about his sexuality. He surrounded himself with beautiful women, but he never seemed to date any of them. While Jackie had been having great difficulty keeping his eyes off the breasts of the models along for the ride—including, to his discomfort, Tandy Carston—Murdoch showed no interest. The girls may as well have stuck postage stamps on their nipples for all the cover their bikini tops were providing, yet when they sashayed past Murdoch, lush buttocks within inches of his nose, he never once let his gaze slither over them. He seemed equally uninterested in the young cabin boy, who was so handsome and chiselled you could have glued a leaf to his crotch, painted him white and put him in a museum. Jackie had just about plucked up the courage, planning a conspiratorial tone asking which one Murdoch was fucking to introduce the topic, when he was thrown off track.

'Isn't it marvellous being famous again?' Murdoch said. He pointed to the shore, where tourists were stretched out on sun loungers, trying not to catch the eyes of the trinket sellers roaming the sands. 'We're more real than they are, Jackie. We'll be remembered. Don't you want it to be this way forever?'

An image of Marie, her eyes cold, popped up in Jackie's mind. He said nothing in response. He was thinking about calling her when the sun glinted off something on the beach. He squinted and just made out a prone figure leaning over a long metallic object pointed towards the boat. There was no doubt in Jackie's mind that it was a sniper rifle. Hao and Alfie were asleep with books over their faces—not that they would have dived in front of him to intercept a bullet anyway—so he leapt to his feet, ready to plunge into the water. The flash came again as he got his leading foot onto the rail running around the yacht, and the assassin rose from his crouched position. The object resolved into the long, fat lens of a camera. Jackie felt like a prize tit. The killer hadn't shot anybody, and of course needed the tattoo. Plus the presence of a large rifle would have caused something of a stir on a busy beach.

Jackie stretched over his extended left leg, trying to look nonchalant even though his rampaging heartbeat was probably visible through his ribcage.

'Pins and needles,' he said in response to Murdoch's raised eyebrow, and sat back down. 'You know there's a photographer over there, right?'

'Why do you think we've laid anchor so close to shore? This isn't just a holiday, Jackie. It's publicity.'

It hit Jackie that a camera could be worse for him than a rifle. If Marie saw a picture of him on the yacht, he'd be in big trouble. He swung his legs down again to scuttle into his cabin, where he would remain until they were somewhere more private.

Tandy, whom he'd been ignoring, rose from her lounger and stood over him. 'Let's give them something to take a picture of, shall we?'

She slid on top of Jackie, her oiled body smooth against his skin. He felt nothing, not even when she planted a kiss on his lips. Oh, she was beautiful, his roving eyes told him that, but she was poisonous. And she wasn't Marie. Jackie tried to squirm out from underneath. She wrapped her hands around his waist and arched her back upwards. His knees came up as he tried to lever her off, and their groins met. His traitorous cock stirred in response as she slid her crotch up its length and, for a moment, his resolve weakened. Somehow the signals from upstairs overrode the hot-blooded roaring from downstairs. He stood up, Tandy still clinging to him like a randy limpet.

She winked at him. 'That ought to do it, don't you think?' She released her hold, stepped back and looked down at his bulging speedos. 'And you might want to get some cold water on that before the periscope pokes out of the water.'

'Stop teasing the poor man,' Murdoch said.

Jackie wiped his mouth and stared off at the beach. While he'd been struggling with Tandy, he could almost hear the shutter clicking, capturing frame after frame of what would look like a steamy clinch. He thumped down to his cabin and locked the door. He dialled Marie as his erection wilted. The phone rang only twice before cutting off. He couldn't blame her for not answering. At least his penis had only betrayed him in the heat of the moment. His betrayal of Marie by not keeping his word had been cold and pre meditated. He shrank away from the shaft of sunlight pouring in through the porthole and curled up on his bed.

18

Three days following Jackie's return from Barbados, after he'd left dozens of messages on Marie's answer phone, she showed up at his door to deliver the killer blow he so thoroughly deserved. As soon as he opened the door, she thrust a rolled-up copy of *Celeb!* into his chest.

'How could you do this to me?' she said.

He'd avoided buying any of the magazines, knowing all too well what he would see within. Still, he tried to act innocent. He didn't know what else to do. 'Do what?'

'Page 15.'

She waited until he'd thumbed through the magazine to the page in question. He saw Tandy Carston on top of him, the picture snapped at the moment their groins kissed, the hands thrown around her back apparently trying to wrestle off her bikini.

'She jumped on top of me. I was trying to get her off.'

'How stupid do you think I am?'

'You know I hate that woman after what she did to me. Why would I get involved with her now?'

'Because all you care about is fame. It's funny how we were all loved-up when you thought there might be a duet in it, some little straw to grasp at. Now you've got what you wanted, you've dropped me.'

'That's not fair.'

'Really? Then explain what you were doing in Barbados of all places when you were supposed to be in Cornwall staked to a post for the killer.'

'Murdoch told me I had to go and he wouldn't let me invite you. I asked. Repeatedly. I have to do this until the killer is caught, or else I go to jail. My life's in danger, or have you forgotten?'

'Spare me the poor victim schtick. Your life was never in danger, or have *you* forgotten you sent out those letters yourself?'

'No, but do you think he hasn't noticed me by now?'

'Oh, please. Some desperate old has-been appears out of nowhere with a big tattoo he jams into the camera at every opportunity, virtually demanding to be killed, saying he received death threats. The guy knows he didn't send those letters himself. Do you really think he's stupid enough to fall for that?'

Until that point, Jackie had been prepared to take his medicine and try to repair the damage. Now, stung by the verbal barb that had pricked at the heart of his worst fear, he felt his face pucker up. 'Desperate old has-been? Is that what you think of me?'

Marie's glower wavered for a split second, and came back on just as strong. 'If the shoe fits…'

'That makes two of us then,' Jackie said, his voice raised for the first time. 'You wanted to be famous as badly as I did, and you're jealous because you aren't getting it.'

Marie took a step back and butted up against the balcony wall. It took him a few seconds to understand the tears welling up in her eyes were not from rage.

'You're wrong,' she said, all the heat gone from her voice. 'I wanted you more.'

She half-ran to the lift. Jackie took one tentative step forward, but the echo of her words stopped him going after her. He shut the door and listened to the faint hum as the lift descended. When he turned around, his mother stood at the end of the hallway.

'Do you want a cup of tea?' she said.

'Mum, tea isn't some cure-all fucking medicine!'

She advanced, hand raised. As she went to slap him, he caught her wrist. 'Don't do that to me. I'm not a child.'

'You're acting like one. I thought we'd raised you better. Now I wonder if you're just a spoiled brat. Your father would be ashamed of you.'

She pulled her wrist free, and left him alone in the hallway. A familiar surge of self-pity bubbled up like lava. They'd all turned their backs on him: first Phyllis, then Marie, now his mum. Even the favour of his dead father had been withdrawn.

Is it really worth it? he thought.

He got no further with this train of thought, as his mobile rang. The caller was Murdoch, who launched into a spiel with no greeting. 'Good news, Jackie. I've put you on the bill of the finale to the *Icon* tour in the O2 arena next week. You'll be singing one song as a special guest. You up for it? We've sold 20,000 tickets.'

Ten minutes ago, perhaps he would have dithered in his choice between the love of one woman or the love of 20,000, no matter how fleeting. Now that Marie had made her feelings clear, he didn't hesitate.

'I'll do it,' he said.

19

Gareth would have needed to be in a coma to miss Jackie's precipitous rise to fame. From anonymity a few months ago, his grinning mug was now plastered over every celebrity magazine and tabloid in Britain and his song seemed to be on the radio every ten minutes. The buffoon the public had kicked off *Celebrity Public Eye* for being horrendously irritating was now a whisker short of becoming a national icon.

The apparent spark for the re-found fame, a threatening letter sent by The Tattoo Collector, heightened the sense of unreality. Gareth at first wondered if he'd sent the letters and simply forgotten. The black mood that had settled over him since Tom meant that several times he'd found himself sprawled on the sofa in darkness, amid the rubble of decimated chocolate bars, with no memory of the preceding hours. He could find no evidence around the house to support this theory, however. He felt conflicted about what happened in the park. The encounter had removed the doubts about the correctness of his course of action, for it showed he meant nothing to those celebrities, who would use and betray him. And so they meant nothing to him other than in their role as a means to an end. At the same time, he couldn't shake the feeling that there must be somebody out there who could deliver the sweet closeness Tom had shown him.

Jackie's rise at least gave him hope. There could be only one reason for this loser reaching number one: the fresh tattoo on his upper arm. As soon as he'd seen the camera zoom in on the flickering sun in the video, all of Gareth's seemingly coincidental encounters with Jackie had come flooding back. Yes, fate had already misled him several times, but perhaps he and his mum had been misinterpreting the messages. Jackie had shown up three times, on each occasion as Gareth was about to take a tattoo or had just taken one. Four, in fact, if you counted that he was on *Celebrity Public Eye* as Barry Deckhart sat unconscious in the chair. That had to be more than chance. Yet the previous failures had left him sceptical and the depression paralyzed him, so he sat at home growing fatter on chocolate and revisiting his old tactic of using teddy bears and toys to create a captive audience. He sang for them every day and talked to them when the crushing loneliness got too much, though the scalpel still saw regular use.

He was only roused to action when one night he spoke to his teddy and it answered back in his mother's voice. She hadn't been in touch for weeks, apart from a brief appearance after Tom died to exhort him not to give up and trust in her to find the right tattoo. Her warm tones dispelled the solitude.

'Hello, my boy. How are you keeping?'

'Not too good, Mum. I'm lonely.'

'Don't worry, love. The end is in sight.'

'What do you mean?'

'You know what I mean. We've found our tattoo.'

'You mean Jackie Thunder's?'

'You're a smart lad. Yes, Jackie Thunder's. We've been looking in the wrong places. All of the tattoos you took came from people who already had talent. Thunder has none, yet he's famous. This man doesn't deserve his tattoo. It should be yours, Gareth. It is yours. You just have to take it.'

'Are you sure this is it? You told me all of the others were the one.'

'I'm sure. There won't be any more after him, I promise.'

'Cross your heart and hope to die?'

The teddy chuckled. 'I'm already dead, my boy. But I cross my heart.'

Gareth considered his options. He'd thought about joining a book club or yoga class, as he understood that was what people did when they wanted to find love and companionship. Maybe if he'd got a job after leaving school, perhaps in a call centre where he would have been forced to interact all day, things would be different. He hadn't, and he knew that even if he did join a club he would once more stand in silence on the periphery, befuddled by the mysterious rules of human engagement. A celebrity never had that problem. No matter how banal, their words always carried weight. And to refuse his mum now would mean that he would have nothing left but the scalpel and growing silence. He had to go on.

'How am I going to get to him?'

'Don't worry about that. I know exactly where he's going to be and when. And when we get him …'

'…I'll be famous,' Gareth concluded, with far more certainty than he felt.

20

The roar of the crowd rumbled through the O2 arena to where Jackie sat, head bowed, in front of his dressing room mirror. He should have been giving the hair and make-up one last check, but he felt so sick he could barely sit up straight. On the way over, riding in an ostentatious white limousine with Jackie Thunder stencilled on the side, his chief concern had been whether The Tattoo Collector would attempt to grab him. They'd pulled up in as quiet an area as possible and let Jackie wander on ahead, feeling completely exposed. Nothing had happened. Once he was in the arena amidst the bustle of pre-concert preparations, his mind had turned to the show, which made him feel even more terrified.

In his pomp, he'd never played to a crowd this big, or live to a nationwide television audience. Then he'd spent years playing venues little larger than this dressing room. In those circumstances, the odd bum note or wobbly dance step didn't matter. Now his every move would be transmitted to millions of people for instant mockery should he falter. Even with the recent polishing, he wasn't sure he had what it took to get through the show. Had his old band been around, it would have helped, as they would have been laughing, joking and drinking heavily. Instead, he sipped on a mineral water—Murdoch had forced him to drink litres of the stuff and stay off the booze, insisting that proper hydration would help his performance—picturing all the ways in which he could show himself up.

A stagehand popped her head through the door to give him his ten-minute warning.

'I need to hit the loo,' he told his escorts.

'I'll come with you,' Alfie said.

Jackie shook his head. He needed a few minutes alone to conjure up his calming image before going on. 'I'll be fine. The toilet's just outside and there are people everywhere.'

Alfie, who'd been enjoying a sneaky vodka and Coke, sat back down with no argument. When Jackie ducked out into the corridor, Murdoch was sauntering past in the direction of the stage. He took one look at Jackie's pale features and raised an eyebrow.

'Don't worry. It'll be over in a jiffy,' he said, and continued on his way without a backward glance.

The toilet lay ahead on the left, but an out-of-order sign swung from the handle of the locked door. The need to pee was now real, so Jackie scanned the corridor for another lavatory. A sign pointed into the bowels of the building. Jackie clattered down the metal stairs and found himself in what appeared to be a maintenance corridor. He followed the next sign, trailing his hand across the pipes and wires. He came to a junction and guessed left. At the end of the corridor, the passageway kinked right. He followed it for fifty metres and came to another junction, where he decided to get the job done. With a quick glance up and down the corridor, he pissed against the wall.

He was shaking off when footsteps echoed down the passageway. He zipped up and stepped around the corner, waiting a few seconds until he heard the approaching person hit the corridor. When Jackie came back round, a chubby youth dressed in black, with an access-all-areas pass dangling from his neck, was frowning at the puddle. Jackie brushed off the twinge of recognition he felt, figuring he'd seen him around at the sound check.

'Disgusting, isn't it?' Jackie said. 'Some people have no class.'

The man, either a stagehand or maintenance staff, looked up. 'You're absolutely right, Jackie,' he said in a high-pitched voice that set off a fresh burst of familiarity. He dropped his black holdall, went down on one knee and unzipped it. He pulled out a copy of Jackie's album. 'I was hoping to bump into you. Would you mind signing this for me? I'm a big fan.'

'Sure,' Jackie said. 'Let's do it quickly, though. I'm due on stage.'

The worker held out the CD and pen. Jackie snapped open the plastic case. 'What's your name?'

'Gareth.'

Jackie finally made the connection and looked up. He remembered Gareth's performance at the *Icon* auditions, his attempt to kill Murdoch and the mental illness it sparked. Unbidden, the other occasions he'd literally bumped into the man without placing him snapped into focus.

'I know you. You're the guy …'

He tailed off when he saw Gareth slide a syringe out of his jacket pocket. This was the moment they'd been working towards, but he couldn't believe it was happening, particularly since the killer had found him without his guards. Jackie resisted the screaming instinct to turn and run. He'd witnessed a stabbing from his balcony once and it was only when the victim gave the attacker his back that the knife found its mark. He took a step back as the syringe swung round and pointed at his neck.

'There's no need to be afraid,' Gareth said. 'I only want your tattoo. This …' he inched the syringe closer '… is just so it won't hurt.'

'You killed all those people.'

Gareth's cheek twitched. 'I didn't mean to. Let me take your tattoo, and you'll be in hospital getting fixed up in a few hours.'

'Do you promise?'

'I promise,' Gareth said. 'It's not fair what the papers are saying about me. I'm not a bad man. I'm just hungry. You should understand that.'

'I do,' Jackie said. He lowered his arms and, against every instinct, stepped towards the madman.

As expected, Gareth smiled and relaxed. Jackie seized his moment and swung his foot with all the strength he could muster. He aimed for scrotum, but misjudged the distance and instead found kneecap. It was enough. Gareth yelped and reached for his knee. Jackie ran, fumbling for his phone until he remembered he'd left it on the dressing room table. He turned right, hoping to find another right turn that would connect him back to the corridor leading to the stairwell and safety. The recent fitness regime gave him a speed and stamina he didn't think himself capable of. He took the next right, the rough concrete floor giving him enough purchase to turn without slipping, and pelted ahead. He chanced a look back, and saw that Gareth was a good thirty metres behind him, hobbling and panting. The passageway turned right again, and Jackie took it at full speed, confident he was on the road to escape.

Instead, he almost ran straight into a door. He rattled the handle, his breathing ragged. It wouldn't budge.

'Help!' he yelled. 'Somebody help!'

Either there was nobody there, or the music, louder now, drowned out his voice. He spun around, his only option to fight. Gareth hadn't looked in good shape and the knee would incapacitate him further, but Jackie's condition meant he'd always wormed his way out of physical confrontation. He didn't know how he would stand up in a battle that could be to the death—or his at least.

'You can do this,' he told himself as the irregular footfalls drew closer.

Jackie closed his eyes and conjured up his calming image. The microphone, the blackness and the shaft of light all came instantly. At that moment, the song above ended and the whistles, clapping, screaming, yelling and stamping of the crowd intruded upon his attempt to find peace. A flash flood of clarity engulfed him. He'd adopted this technique in his mid-teens from his father, who'd shared it on the eve of Jackie's first gig. Only now did he understand that for all his waking fantasies of fame, this image contained no people at all: no loving audience, no screaming fans, and no legions of adoring eyes. It was all about the beauty and purity of the music.

Now he remembered how it had felt in the early days to hammer out songs to a handful of spectators in a sticky-floored dive. When he'd closed his eyes and sang, his fingers finding the right keys effortlessly, he knew he'd found his place in the world. Then came growing recognition and success and with it the expectation of thousands of fans and the need to please them all, and countless others beyond. He tried to recall any moment since then when he'd recaptured that feeling of being lost in the music. All he could remember was performance after performance where he had one eye on the audience, his voice and keyboard mere accessories to his quest for approval.

Most likely he was about to die, but the dread of the impending darkness was not what consumed him. Instead he felt shame at the way he'd treated his loved ones. He knew his own stupidity had brought him to this point. Part of him had always known it. When Phyllis told him how bad his music had become, how he'd pursued a course set by what he thought would make people love him rather than what felt right, it had resonated within. Yet he'd pushed it aside and carried on regardless.

Jackie had gone to the dog races a few times over the last few years, dragged along by one of his pals down the local. As he watched the greyhounds lolloping after the hare, he'd wondered how many times they would go around the track if the stuffed imposter kept on going, and what they would do if they actually caught it. Now he knew. He'd been running round the track for twenty years, not noticing he was going in a circle or that the stadium had emptied. Finally he'd caught that hare, and the taste of dry sawdust filled his mouth.

So much of his adult life seemed futile, filled with pathetic attempts to get attention when he had as much love as he needed right in front of him—even more true over the last few months with Marie in his life. They'd all tried to warn him. He'd been too pig-headed and foolish to listen. It was so ridiculous and predictable that it took this, the near-certain end of his existence, to shine the light into the dark recesses of his psyche where the truth had been cowering all of these years. If the lunatic wasn't trying to kill him, he would probably thank him.

If I get out of this alive, I'll make it up to everybody, he thought.

Gareth was close now and Jackie bent his legs, ready to sprint and hopefully take his would-be assailant by surprise. Yet Gareth never made it to the corner. Jackie heard a cry of pain and the clang of something hitting metal. There came the sound of stomping on concrete, another yell, and the slap of running feet receding down the corridor. Jackie moved forward and chanced a peek. Gareth was running away, slapping at his hair. A dazzling white shape, which appeared to be a tiny humanoid, squirmed in his mullet. It pulled out a handful of purple hair and screamed with delight in a high-pitched voice. Another two of the little white men, one of them jabbing at Gareth's heels with the syringe, scampered after him as he disappeared around the corner. Jackie leaned against the wall, blood pounding in his ears and his mind frazzled, as the door swung open. He turned, expecting a stagehand. Instead, he saw Phyllis. She looked him up and down, and then smiled.

'Lucky for you I was passing,' she said.

Jackie ran to her, momentarily forgetting the bizarre scene he'd just witnessed, and enfolded her in a huge hug. 'I'm so sorry, Phyllis. I was a complete arsehole.'

She laughed into his shoulder. 'I know.'

He leaned back and looked into her eyes. 'What are you doing here?'

Phyllis focused on Jackie's nose. 'Oh, I pulled a few strings to get a pass. I wanted to see your show.'

'Really?'

'Fine. I was worried. I had a bad feeling about tonight and wanted to keep an eye on you.'

'I thought you hated me.'

'I could never hate you, Jackie. Even if you are a prize bell end sometimes.'

He couldn't resist doling out another hug. 'God, I missed you. But look, we need to head back and get the police to lock down the venue. He's here.'

Phyllis tried to squeeze past. 'I heard. In fact, I think half of London heard. I didn't realize you had such a good falsetto voice.'

'I was shitting myself.'

'Understandably so. Now, why don't you go alert the police and I'll chase this loony.'

Jackie gripped her arm. 'No. He'll kill you.'

'You do know I'm really fucking hard, don't you?' Phyllis said, trying to pull away, her eyes distant.

Jackie tightened his grip. Phyllis was surprisingly strong, and he found himself being dragged a few feet along the corridor. He dug in his heels. 'Seriously, don't do it. Let the police get him.'

She snapped her head up, eyes now clear. 'You're right. Let's get back to the dressing room.'

Without waiting for Jackie to follow, she set off at a fair old lick back through the door.

When Gareth felt the soft impacts on his head, he at first dismissed it as water dripping from the ceiling. Then two little white men leapt onto his shoulders and ran down his arm. Their appearance froze him, the white light they radiated so bright it left spots on his eyes. Even so, he could make out little eyes, ears and teeth. His fear that he'd lost his mind after all returned, but when one of them sank its teeth into the sensitive skin between his thumb and forefinger, the pain—so like that of the cuts that anchored him to reality—told him this bizarre occurrence was as real as his mum's return from the grave. These had to be the agents she'd warned would oppose him, sent by the guardian of the magical tattoos. And that could mean only one thing: Jackie's tattoo was the real deal. Despite being under attack, he let out a scream of delight as he realized that his goal was within sight.

He shook his hand to dislodge the biting creature, dropping the syringe in the process. The two attackers leapt down to land lightly on the concrete. Gareth stamped on one of them, flattening it to the ground like a sticky mass of chewing gum. The other picked up the needle and shouldered it like a soldier preparing to fire an RPG. Gareth raised his foot, ready to crush it and run after Jackie in one motion. As he did so, the little man he thought he'd killed reformed and bit his ankle. The other charged at him with the needle. He managed to catch it with his toe, and it skittered to the side. It jumped up, aimed the needle again, and crept towards him.

Fire burned in his scalp as another mini assailant landed and began to yank at his roots. Gareth, all thoughts of reaching Jackie abandoned for the moment, ran back the way he'd come. As his legs pumped, he snatched at the creature hauling out clumps of his beautiful hair. Any time he grabbed hold, it melted through his fingers like hot wax and reformed to recommence its attempts to pluck him like a chicken. He stopped trying to catch it and instead waited until it had jerked out more hair. As it hooted, he dealt it a strong flick. Out of the corner of his eye, he saw it sail through the air and rebound from the wall. When he chanced a glance back, he saw it had formed up behind its two accomplices.

Gareth was panting, his diet of chocolate snacks and lack of exercise slowing his gait. The syringe crept ever closer, until he felt the sharp tip prick his sock. Panic gave him an extra burst of speed and he took the metal stairs ahead two at a time, shoving a man loitering at the top of the staircase out of the way. The five teenage boys who'd just left the stage bustled down the corridor, sweaty and excited. He could hear the voice of Murdoch onstage, exhorting the crowd to give it up one more time. As the group surrounded him, he looked down the stairs. The three white men shrank back, although they held their middle digits aloft in unison.

Gareth pushed his way into the heart of the scrum and let it carry him down the corridor in the direction of the backstage bar area, cutting glances back for signs of pursuit. The man he'd shouldered past stared after him, but didn't follow. He ducked out halfway, heading for the backstage exit. He smoothed his hair as he approached, feeling the little bald patches that dotted his head. He'd been so close to getting his hands on the tattoo and now not only had he been foiled but his beautiful mullet, which he'd maintained even during his month of letting his body and mind go to seed, had been ruined. He pushed open the door, nodding at the bouncers manning the entrance to prevent over-exuberant fans from trying to sneak in, and hurried towards the tube station.

It took Jackie and Phyllis two minutes to get to the dressing room, coming up a different set of stairs from the other side. When they burst in, Alfie and Hao leapt to their feet, reaching for their guns.

'The killer just tried to get me,' Jackie said. 'You need to shut the place down.'

Hao pulled her radio from the bag and talked into it urgently. While the cops tried to sort out a blockade, Jackie picked up his smartphone and Googled, 'Gareth Icon Murdoch strangle.'

'This is your man,' Jackie said, handing the phone to Alfie. 'His name is Gareth Jones.'

'You sure?'

'Positive. I recognized him before he pulled out the syringe. He was all over the news last year. Do you remember? Murdoch gave him a roasting after an awful *Icon* audition. He snapped and tried to kill him.'

'Excellent work, Jackie,' Alfie said. 'You've probably saved a lot of lives.'

Rooney burst into the dressing room in response to the call over the radio. He had what looked like vol-au-vent crumbs in his beard.

'You saw him?' he said.

Alfie handed over the phone with the picture of Gareth still displayed.

'Right,' Rooney said. 'I'll take over coordination of the lockdown. I want you two to go out and look for him.' He addressed Jackie. 'He attacked you near here?'

'Yes, down in the maintenance corridor. Then he ran back this way.'

'Ok. Alfie, you take the backstage exit and check the car park. Hao, you head for the tube station, see if he's there.'

Jackie's bodyguards zipped off, brushing against one of Murdoch's assistants, who said, 'You're back. Thank God. You're due on stage.'

Jackie looked at Rooney. 'Do I have to keep doing this now you know who he is?'

'Not unless you want to.'

Jackie thought of the huge audience waiting for him, ready to lap up every word and move. He imagined himself in the crowd, watching the clown on stage mugging his way through a soulless rendition of a song he hadn't written himself.

'I think I'll pass.' He looked at Phyllis. 'I need to catch up with my best friend.'

The assistant looked at the cheesy grins on both their faces. 'Silly twat. Murdoch will destroy your career for this.'

'He's welcome to do whatever he wants,' Jackie said.

'Thanks a lot. Now I'm going to get it in the neck. Wanker.'

The assistant disappeared.

'I'm glad you didn't give on up me, and not just because you probably saved my life,' Jackie said. 'You were right; about Murdoch, about my music, about everything.'

'I'm always right.'

Rooney looked from one to the other, and handed back Jackie's phone. 'I'll leave you two to your love-in.'

He headed off, whether back to the vol-au-vents and free bar or to do his job, Jackie had no idea.

'So, what now?' Jackie asked. 'Looks like I'm back to square one.'

'Not quite,' Phyllis said. 'You can still make good music.'

'Speaking of music, I want to watch the videos of this nutter again.'

As Jackie loaded the YouTube videos of the audition, the memories of the bizarre little creatures that had been forgotten in the mad dash back to the dressing room came back. It must have been the stress of the moment playing tricks on his eyes. What he'd seen was physically impossible.

They were rats, he told himself. *Just albino rats with unusually dexterous hands and a remarkable resemblance to tiny people.*

Gareth crossed Peninsula Square, all too aware his waddling speed walk was almost as suspicious as a run. In twenty minutes the place would be heaving with concert-goers leaving the venue. For the moment, the large concrete plain outside the brightly lit dome was near-deserted, save for a few people drinking and smoking outside Costa Coffee and

Café Rouge. He felt horribly exposed. He knew Jackie would have alerted the police and he wanted to be in North Greenwich tube station before they got going. To have come so close to the real tattoo without getting it stung, but he clung to the knowledge that he was on track. Once he'd made good his escape, he and his mum could strategize on how to get hold of Jackie now they knew what they were up against.

He'd made it halfway across the square when a tall young woman sprinted out from the arena. When she saw him, she redoubled her speed, shouting into a walkie-talkie. He'd been too slow. Gareth, whose legs were still sore and heavy from the intense run, took off in the direction of the station. The slap of her flat shoes grew louder.

'Stop!' she yelled.

He chanced a look back and saw she had a gun in her right hand. His legs turned to jelly, but somehow he kept his feet. As he began zigzagging to dodge the expected bullet, his mother's voice hissed in his head. 'Make for the river, Gareth.'

'They'll catch me there,' he said between heaving breaths.

'Trust me, son. Just do it.'

He cut left and took the gap between two buildings. His legs refused to carry him forward at the speed he needed, and the woman's footfalls were close behind him now. He wasn't going to make it. He could almost feel her breath upon his neck when he heard her grunt. Glancing over his shoulder, he saw her entangled with a homeless man who'd appeared from nowhere. She was still trying to extricate herself when Gareth took the corner, heading back up towards the covered walkway leading to the pier.

The overhead lights shifted from puce to purple to yellow as he weaved through a few pedestrians, who made no attempt to stop him. By the time he got to the top of the pier, the woman's long legs were eating up the ground along the walkway. He blundered through the metal gates and ran down the gangplank. When he got to the floating platform he realized there was no clipper docked. Even if there had been they would just have followed him on and arrested him.

'What now?' he shouted.

'Jump into the river,' his mum said.

'I can't swim.'

'Do it. I won't let anything happen to you.'

The policewoman was closing in, gun pointing in his direction. He had no choice. He took a deep breath, ran to the waist-high fence and vaulted over. His trailing foot caught the rail, and he pitched head-first into the water. The shock of the cold sucked all the air from his lungs. He sank to the bottom in a matter of seconds, feeling the insistent tug of the current pull him away from the pier. He opened his eyes, blinking against the murky waters. He saw nothing.

Had he not seen the proof of Jackie's magical guardians, he would perhaps have succumbed and gone to the other side in search of his mum's embrace. Now he had something to fight for. He kicked his feet hard, but in the darkness he didn't know if he was heading up or down. Only when his flailing hands sank into the sucking mud did he realize he was going the wrong way.

I'm going to die a killer, not a star, he thought.

He opened his mouth to rail against the injustice of it all, and the river took the chance to jam its cold fingers deep into this throat. His mind, already oxygen-deprived from the sprint, began to lose its grip on consciousness. Just before he blacked out, he felt a warm hand close around his wrist. Then there was nothing.

21

Jackie was driven off in a police car, staring out the side window at the yellow tape cordoning off the walkway leading to the pier. Hao had watched the Thames swallow Gareth and hadn't budged from her vigil until reinforcements arrived. She saw nobody surface. According to Rooney, he'd either drowned or choked to death on a rogue turd. Divers were now scouring the muddy bottom of the river for the body, which was either trapped beneath the pier or had been washed downstream and would surface in a few days.

Jackie had spent the time waiting for his escort home reading articles about Gareth, from the details of the attack to the backstory on his life. Gareth had been an isolated man, his mother seemingly his only friend. When she died, all that remained for him was the forlorn hope of making it as a star. At Jackie's lowest moments, there had always been people around him, even if he didn't fully appreciate them or listen to them. He couldn't imagine what it must have felt like to face such failure alone. Small wonder Gareth had cracked.

While it was too late for anybody to put an arm around Gareth and lead him in the right direction, Jackie had that option and he intended to let the guiding arm take him where it would. He'd left Phyllis back at her car with a promise to call the next day to discuss career options.

Jackie was going back to his roots, away from the awful *Your Eyes Are Mine*. He shook his head, marvelling at the human capacity for self-delusion. He'd convinced himself all his efforts to recreate the song that propelled him to stardom were in the same class as Radiohead and such bands, when they were nothing but tosh. He borrowed paper and a pen from one of the policemen. As the car jiggled homeward, he wrote down a shaky list detailing the way music had made him feel, vowing only to create songs that engendered such emotions in others. By the time the car pulled onto his street, his list read:

It gave you a sense of endless possibility
It cradled you when you felt low
It inspired you to play yourself
It could bring you out of a funk
It helped you relate to other people
The lyrics gave you a new worldview
It filled you with a sense of poignancy
It expressed feelings you couldn't express yourself
It transported you to a higher plane
It gave you a soundtrack to your life
It made you feel you weren't alone

The list wasn't complete, but it would serve as a starting point. He still kept in touch with the boys from the old band and he planned to get them together to share his vision. He would play the bars again, essentially restarting his apprenticeship. Two weeks ago, the prospect would have depressed him. Now he couldn't wait to get started. It would be immense fun, and this time he planned to have the woman he loved share it with him. Presuming it wasn't too late.

He called Marie's mobile for the fifth time that evening, leaving another message professing his love. If she didn't call back, he would go round to her house tomorrow. If she didn't open the door, he would email, text and generally stalk the crap out of her until she understood that he'd changed. In the meantime, he contented himself with the knowledge that his mum would be there to listen to his apology. Mums didn't have a choice in that kind of thing. When he got upstairs, the police car remaining outside to watch him until Gareth was confirmed dead, Agnes opened the door before he had a chance to put his key in the lock. He moved in to hug her the way he'd hugged Phyllis. Before he could get his arms around her, a stinging slap connected with the side of his head.

'You could've got yourself killed, you numpty,' she said.

Jackie rubbed his burning ear. 'I take it you saw the news, then?'

Now his mum planted a big kiss on his cheek. 'Aye, son. I saw it. So, now you're a big hero are you too important for a cup of tea?'

'Hero?'

'They're saying they wouldn't have caught him without you.'

Jackie felt as heroic as a deer staked out to catch a rogue lion. Still, if having his mum view him in such a way meant a few less slaps around the lughole, he was willing to let her believe it.

'I'll have a cuppa,' he said.

They went to the kitchen hand-in-hand. As his mum busied herself with the kettle and teabags, Jackie leaned on the counter. 'I've got a lot of apologizing to do. I've already started with Phyllis, so now it's your turn. I'm sorry I didn't listen to you.'

'Does any laddie ever listen to his mum?'

'No, but …'

She cut him off. 'Let's not make a big fuss. You were daft, that's true. But I've always known you were a good boy. Just tell me one thing. Are you done with all this being famous nonsense?'

The media would no doubt be all over him the next day and, while the old Jackie would gladly have embraced the frenzy and talked up his role, he had no intention of saying a word to anybody. He'd deceived enough people. 'Yes, I'm done.'

'Good. Now, go sort things out with that lassie of yours.'

'I tried to call her. She's not answering.'

'Did you not watch *Notting Hill* and all those other romantic films? You're supposed to dash over there and convince her.' She paused. 'She's not about to catch a flight abroad is she?'

'Not that I know of.'

'Shame. Still, get your behind over there.'

'Can I have my tea first?'

'Of course. You can't do anything important without tea.'

One hour later, Jackie stood outside Marie's house. The lights were off, so he hesitated before applying knuckle to wood. This would be hard enough, never mind with the added difficulty of waking Marie. She slept deeply, and nothing made her angrier than being roused—well, apart from being neglected, betrayed and humiliated, and he'd already ticked all of those boxes. He'd spent the taxi ride over trying to recall various last-ditch romantic speeches made by Hugh Grant, Tom Cruise and other male leads of that ilk. None of them really applied to his grubby situation. He only had the simple truth to offer: I've been a despicable, selfish human being and I'm sorry. He wiped his palms on his trousers, inhaled, and rapped on the door. When Marie didn't answer, he shouted through the letterbox and then graduated to banging on the windows. Finally, as Jackie's voice grew louder and shriller, Marie's neighbour yanked open his door. His hair was tousled and his eyes rimmed red.

'Pack that in,' he snapped. 'I'm trying to sleep here.'

'Sorry,' Jackie said, for the umpteenth time that evening. 'I need to talk to Marie. Do you know if she's home?'

'If she is, she's either stone deaf or doesn't want to talk to you.' The neighbour looked at Jackie's face, and what he saw there softened his attitude. 'Her ex came to pick the boy up, and then she went out with her glad rags on.'

Jackie checked his watch. It was after midnight. She might not be home for hours. So much for the big romantic moment. 'If you see her tomorrow, tell her I need to speak to her. And tell her I'm sorry.'

'For what?'

'She'll know.'

'Sure.'

Jackie turned to go. The neighbour stopped him with a question. 'What happened tonight anyway?'

Jackie thought of what he'd seen as Gareth sprinted up the corridor. Try as he might to rationalize it as his mind playing tricks on him, he couldn't shake the image of the tiny little men scuttling after his would-be killer.

'I have no idea,' he said.

Murmur stood over the prone Gareth, watching filthy Thames water drip from the hand that lay limp over the edge of the bed. He hadn't regained consciousness since Murmur teleported him from the bottom of the river. Murmur was shivering, and so dialled up his body heat just short of the level where he would burst into flames. It wasn't difficult to do, since he was fizzing mad. While Gareth hadn't come to, he'd been feverishly muttering something about little white men. That meant only one thing: Heaven was on to him.

In a way it was a relief they'd shown their hand. Now he had his confirmation. All the same, they'd chosen an inopportune moment. He'd arranged a backstage pass for Gareth and stayed close to the dressing room, waiting for the moment Jackie would have to come out before sticking up the fake sign leading him down into the maintenance corridors. At that point, he'd thought it was all in the bag and gone off to attend to his MCing duties at the concert. After all, he'd left Gergaroth at the top of the stairs to stop anybody else following Gareth and Jackie down. It had seemed a simple matter for Gareth to drug Jackie and drag him the short distance to the nearby unguarded delivery entrance, where the van waited. In retrospect, he should also have put an avatar on Gareth, but that would have meant diverting a tiny bit of consciousness and he needed his full charisma to wow the crowds. Of course, he couldn't have known that Heaven would choose that moment to get involved, and he wasn't entirely sure how they'd figured out his move. All the same, he'd been sloppy. He'd counted on Jackie being taken at the gig, creating the drama of a star being snatched under the noses of so many thousands of people as he was about to return to the big stage. It would have been perfect.

There was a human saying about there being more than one way to skin a cat. Murmur knew what they meant. There were 14 ways to skin a human, which was much the same thing. He didn't need that many options, but he still had a decision to make. Sure, he could teleport across town and bring Jackie to Gareth himself, but he didn't want to run the risk of bumping into the angels that were sniffing around. Besides, there was still more drama to be squeezed from this saga, and he knew just how to do it. He put a hand on Gareth's back, funnelling heat into his chilled body, and whispered in his ear.

22

When Jackie's phone rang early in the morning, he snatched it up without looking at the display, sure it must be Marie. The voice that came over the line was not hers, but it was all too familiar.

'Hello, Jackie,' Gareth said. 'You were a naughty boy last night.'

Jackie should have been surprised to hear the voice of a man who was supposed to have drowned, but somehow he wasn't. He'd seen enough last night to know something very strange was going on. 'Aren't you meant to be dead?'

'I'm not dead, Jackie. Just a bit soggy.'

'Why are you calling? Do you want to give yourself up?'

'Don't be a silly billy. I've come too far to just stop now.'

'But the police know who you are.'

'It doesn't matter. Soon everyone will know who I am. They won't be able to touch me. But never mind that. We have things to discuss.'

'No, we don't. Maybe it slipped your mind when your bonce hit the water, but you tried to murder me last night.'

'Don't be like that. We need to talk about your tattoo. You see, I've been taking the wrong tattoos. Those others had talent. You, Jackie, are complete pants.'

'You can talk,' Jackie snapped, too vexed by the insult to figure out what Gareth was trying to tell him. 'I saw your audition. If I'm pants, then you're scabby old y-fronts with a big skid mark on the back.'

'You're not going to throw me off the scent by getting me angry. You were nobody until you got that tattoo. Its magic must be powerful, and I want it. I deserve fame more than you.'

Jackie's eyes widened as he understood the full scale of Gareth's insanity. The police believed The Tattoo Collector was a garden-variety serial killer, taking the tattoos as mementoes. But the deaths were just a side-effect of getting the tattoos, which Gareth seemed to believe would make him famous. Jackie briefly with pretending that his tattoo was indeed some mystical key to glory and trying to set up a meeting where the police could grab the nut job. Then he thought of how close he'd come to ending up a corpse, a scrape he would much rather not repeat. He'd done his bit. The police would catch Gareth soon enough.

'If you think I've got a magical tattoo then you're off your rocker,' he said. 'Where am I supposed to have got one of those?'

'I don't know. Maybe a wizard gave you it.'

'Yeah, spot on. I looked up "Wizards" in the phone book. It's right between "Witches" and "Wookies for Hire". There are loads of the buggers, all with degrees from Hogwarts.'

'Trying to pretend this is all just a big joke won't work.'

'You want the truth? I'm not famous because of the tattoo. I'm famous because they made me that way. The police set me up with Murdoch so I could become bait. I was the wiggly worm, you were the hungry trout. That's it. The tattoo had nothing to do with it. It's just some ink jammed under my skin in an excruciatingly painful manner.'

Gareth snorted. 'I've heard a lot of lies from you people, but that's one of the best.'

'For fuck's sake. I'm going to say this very slowly. There is no magical symbol that can make you famous. Either you have talent and you make it, or you get that ballbag Murray Murdoch to turn you into a performing monkey. End of.'

'I don't believe you.'

'It doesn't matter what you believe. As soon as we're off the phone, I'm going to call the police and tell them you're still alive. They have your picture. You won't last a day.'

'You won't call the police. I have something you want.'

'What can you possibly have that I want?'

Muffled movement followed, and Marie's jittery voice flooded down the line. 'Jackie, is that you? Oh God, he's got me, Jackie. He's got me.'

Jackie almost dropped the phone as the full consequences of his selfishness hit home. Like a termite gnawing at the foundations of a building that would one day crash to the ground, he'd never looked beyond his needs, not understanding the way every action ripples out into the world—or worse, not caring. Now he knew. Marie, the one good thing that had come into his life as a result of his dumb quest for recognition, was now in mortal danger. He wrapped his numb fingers tighter round the handset.

'I'm going to get you out of there,' he said. 'No matter what.'

Marie's sob receded into the background as Gareth reclaimed the handset.

'Are you going to help me?' Gareth said.

The insanity of Gareth's narrative was plain, but there would be no convincing him of his error. Jackie briefly revisited his idea of setting up a meet where the police could snatch Gareth. He rejected it. Gareth had Marie and for all Jackie knew he had an accomplice, as the police suspected, who would kill her as soon as Gareth didn't come back. That meant he couldn't pretend to take Gareth to a place where he would get a tattoo, for when he found out it was a set up Marie would be dead. There was only one thing he could do to save her.

'You got me,' he said. 'I was lying. My tattoo is magical.'

Gareth squealed. 'I knew it! Come to Teddington Lock Footbridge tonight at 1am, alone. You come with me, she goes free.'

'I'll be there.'

'And Jackie. If you tell the police, I'll know. Then you'll never see her again.'

The phone went dead. Jackie let it slip out of his hand to plop onto the pillow. Fear wafted an icy breeze through his body, coalescing into a cold, tight knot in the pit of his stomach. Yet his mind was clear. His actions, and nobody else's, had brought them to this point. Only he could fix it. At least now he had a clear path to Marie's forgiveness. It was a shame it would probably cost him his life.

Jackie said his goodbyes to his mum as best he could without raising her suspicions. He told her that he loved her three times, that he was grateful for all she'd done for him twice, and kept sidling up to grab sneaky hugs when she wasn't looking.

Finally, she laid down the wooden spoon she was using to mix scone batter and looked him in the eye. 'For God's sake, son, will you give us peace? I know you're feeling guilty, but we got by perfectly well for forty years without all this emotional rubbish. Why don't we assume you love me until you tell me otherwise?'

'I just …'

She picked up the spoon and advanced on him, dripping gooey spots of batter in her wake. 'I'm warning you. I'll belt you over the head if you don't shut it.'

Despite her aggressive movements, a warm smile played at the edge of her lips.

'Point taken,' he said, and turned away so she wouldn't see his eyes glisten. 'By the way,' he said, trying to sound casual. 'I'm heading out tonight to meet Marie.'

'Great. So you're going to sort it all out then?'

'It's going to be fine. I'll make sure of it.'

'That's my boy.'

The spoon tapped against the glass bowl as she returned to her mix. At least he would have a tasty last meal. He'd always been partial to a jammy scone.

Stars pricked the clear sky and reflected off the slow waters of the river as Jackie waited on the bridge. He'd arrived ten minutes early, going out the back door and sneaking through the basketball court to avoid the mob of journalists who'd set up a twenty-four-hour vigil outside his house. Hidden up his sleeve was a solid wood rolling pin, still sprinkled with flour, which he planned to bring thumping down on Gareth's skull when he was sure Marie was free and unharmed.

As requested, Jackie had told no one, not even Phyllis when he rang to call off their meeting, saying he needed to patch up things with Marie first. He didn't repeat his coded farewells. Phyllis would have picked up that something was amiss. Instead, he'd promised to meet her in a few days' time. He could have used some of his manager's feisty attitude as he stared up the riverbank for some sign of life. Not even the heft of the makeshift weapon could dispel the belief that this would be the last night of his life.

Headlights spilled along the dark road running past the river, catching a fox's glowing red eyes in its beam. Jackie watched it disappear into the gloom with envy. When danger came, the animal could run with no fear of consequences. Self-pity gained a foothold as he wished his life were that simple. He pushed it away. He'd spent his life feeling sorry for himself, wishing that fate had dealt him a different hand and blaming everyone else for his problems. It had gotten him nowhere and only brought pain and upset to his loved ones. The bitter fruits he was about to taste fell from a tree he himself had planted and nurtured. He could not, would not, shy away from them.

The van rolled to a halt close to the bridge, the engine still running. The window slid down and a shadowy head stuck out.

'Over here,' Gareth called.

Jackie walked towards the van, keeping the arm with the concealed rolling pin pressed against his side. With luck, Marie would be in the back of the van. As soon as she was free, he would make his move, and just hope that Gareth didn't turn out to be a black belt in karate.

'Get in,' Gareth said.

'Let her go first.'

'Do you really think I would be stupid enough to bring her? You don't seem very trustworthy. Who knows what you're planning?'

Gareth looked at Jackie's right arm.

'How do I know you'll let her go?' Jackie said, turning his body to shield the arm from view.

'Why would I keep her when I have you? I promise I'll let her go if you drop whatever you're hiding up your sleeve and get in.'

Jackie, all too aware he had no choice, let the rolling pin drop to the ground and climbed into the cargo space. The van smelled of aftershave, chocolate and too much hairspray. Gareth clambered over the seat, holding up a syringe. It took every ounce of Jackie's will not to fend it off. He felt like an old dog in the vets, watching helplessly as the death-bringing needle inched ever closer.

'Please, tell Marie I love her before you let her go,' he said.

'Stop being such a drama queen. I don't want to kill you. This will just knock you out until we get to where we're going. Then we'll get down to business.'

The needle stung Jackie's neck. In the few seconds it took for him to lose consciousness, he prayed that Gareth was telling the truth.

23

Gareth could barely contain his excitement as he dragged Jackie, still insensible, from the garage to the studio. Jackie had given up the secret, admitting that his tattoo contained some mysterious, arcane power that made the public love him. Not that he could deny it, since a cohort of magical, miniature bodyguards were at his beck and call. And in a few minutes this power would be Gareth's. His mum, as always, had come through for him.

It had been a stroke of genius to kidnap Marie. When he came to on the bed late in the evening, still damp with foul-smelling river water, he'd suffered a brief period of grogginess when he wondered why he was safely at home instead of drifting along the bottom of the Thames. The instant his head cleared, however, the plan popped up fully formed. The question over his mysterious relocation from riverbed to bed disappeared even as he picked a stray weed from his trouser leg and deposited it in the bin. Yes, he should have thought of Jackie's weak spot sooner, especially since the relationship had been so public, but sometimes the most obvious ideas were the last to occur.

In his elation, he hadn't questioned why he now knew where Marie lived, pausing long enough to change his clothes, slip on a hat to cover his ravaged scalp and grab a syringe before jumping into the van. Seizing Marie was simple. She had no detachment guarding her and was so pissed she could barely make it up the stairwell to her flat. The needle was in her neck and the plunger down before she could do more than issue a vague grunt of surprise. Once he'd got her home, he kept her bound and gagged, only allowing her to speak when Jackie came to the phone the next day. He hadn't enjoyed threatening to kill Marie or causing Jackie so much upset. He still remembered the day in the karaoke bar, when Jackie had at least asked him if he was okay. And he had no intention of killing the innocent woman.

Now she would be on her way to hospital in the back of an ambulance. Gareth had been watching the bridge through a set of night-vision goggles donated by his mum, and he'd dumped the drugged Marie on the pathway when he saw Jackie arrive. When Jackie was in his custody, Gareth had dialled 999 and told them he'd seen a woman lying unconscious by the lock. Now he could concentrate on fulfilling his destiny.

Jackie was beginning to stir as Gareth hauled him into the chair, stripped off his jacket and tied him hand and foot. He busied himself with arranging the instruments. In a strange way, Gareth didn't want to hurry. He'd waited so long that he wanted to savour every second of this, the moment of his ascension. So, when Jackie moaned and called out Marie's name, Gareth put down the scalpel he'd been testing for sharpness on his forearm, knowing he would never need to cut again, and strolled over to the chair.

Jackie's eyes still looked fuzzy, but the clouds were receding.

'Marie,' he said again, focusing on Gareth. 'You let her go?'

'She's free.'

'Thank God,' Jackie said, his voice stronger. His gaze flicked over to the table where the instruments lay before he looked Gareth straight in the eye. 'I can tell you the truth now. The tattoo isn't powerful. I just needed you to think it was so you would exchange me for her.'

Gareth rolled his eyes. 'Do we have to go through this again?'

'I'm serious. If you take this tattoo, all you'll have is a scrap of wrinkly old man skin. It won't do you any good.'

'Jackie, you don't understand. It was always you. Fate kept trying to tell me, but it took me a while to listen.'

'What are you talking about?'

'You were always there. The morning after Barry, when I was trying out his tattoos, I saw you. Minutes before I took Fleur, you were there. After Tom, you ran right into me in that bar.'

'That's just coincidence.'

'Right. In a city as big as London, we just happened to bump into each other at critical moments. And then suddenly there you are, famous and with a shiny new tattoo, threatened by The Tattoo Collector, even though I didn't send any letters. Doesn't that seem odd?'

'There's nothing mysterious about it,' Jackie said, although to Gareth's ear his voice lacked conviction. 'I wrote the letters myself to get a bit of reflected glory. When the police figured it out, they told me I could either go to jail to enjoy a spot of vicious anal rape or be bait to catch you. I got this completely normal tattoo in a completely normal shop so I could have some excuse to pretend you would be after me. It's not magical.'

'How do you explain the little white men then?'

Jackie's brow crinkled. 'I was hoping they were a hallucination brought on by stress. But since you saw them too, I guess that's out. I've no idea what they were, and I don't want to know. All I can tell you is that they had nothing to do with me.'

'Liar, liar, pants on fire. So why are you famous now?'

'Good God, I'm getting dizzy from all this wandering around in circles. I told you why. But that doesn't matter. What matters is that I was a vainglorious buffoon who wasted years of his life. Now I know.' Jackie looked up, his eyes bright. 'Do you understand? Now I know.'

'Know what?'

'That chasing fame is pointless.'

Gareth frowned. This didn't sound at all like the Jackie he'd expected. In a way, he'd seen in Jackie a kindred spirit, a man who spent years fighting tooth and nail to regain fame. Sure, Gareth was far more talented, if more unlucky, but he'd thought they shared a common goal. Now Jackie was spouting heresy.

Jackie squinted at Gareth, who'd remained silent as he tried to make sense of what his captive was saying. 'Why do you need to be famous?'

'You of all people should know why. People only see you if you're famous. They only love you if you're famous.'

Jackie shook his head. 'I lost myself thinking exactly that, Gareth. And you've lost yourself too.'

'You're wrong.'

'Am I? I thought they loved me, but they didn't. None of them really knew me. They loved the idea of me, this cardboard cut-out they saw prancing around on television. It didn't last. As soon as I began to fade, they jumped on to the next big thing. Maybe every now and then one of them would hear my songs and wonder where I was, but do you think a single one of them pined for me or had their heart broken when I was gone? Of course not. And do you want me to tell how much happiness fame brought me? None. It's a drug. The more you get, the more you want, and you're never satisfied. The only love that matters, the only love that lasts, is the love that comes from the people around you. Your family. Your friends. Your partner. That's what you should be looking for. I just wished I'd realized that sooner.'

Gareth thought of the way he'd felt with Tom Burnett's penis in his mouth, and for a moment he was almost convinced. Then he remembered how it was taken away from him, and how barren he'd felt. Now that his mum was a ghost, the only path to love lay a few feet away, trying to fib his way out of the chair. Gareth's hand moved away from the syringe. This man needed to be awake to see his transformation, to know that he was wrong.

'It's time,' Gareth said.

Jackie strained against his bonds, his voice rising in pitch. 'Don't you get it? You don't need my tattoo. The others worked. You're already famous. Everybody knows who you are. There's even a Facebook page dedicated to you.'

'The Tattoo Collector isn't me. I want to be famous for being a singer. And that's about to happen.'

Jackie's gaze flitted between the scalpel and Gareth's eyes, unable to settle on one or the other. 'For fuck's sake! Even if this tattoo was powerful, it wouldn't work. They know who you are. They'll never let you put out a record.'

'Yes they will. Famous people can do anything. They're above the law.'

'Bullshit. Loads of them have been arrested. George Michael, Robert Downey Jr. and Hugh Grant for starters.'

Gareth picked up the scalpel and advanced on Jackie. 'And they're all more famous than ever.'

Every nerve in Jackie's body screamed, like an air raid siren warning of an impending bombing, yet he forced himself to keep his eyes open as the scalpel approached. If this was the end result of his actions, he wanted to face it head-on rather than scuttling away as he'd done for his whole life. Gareth's forearm muscles bunched as he pressed the point against Jackie's skin, ready to make the first cut. Jackie willed himself not to scream, although he knew from the pain he already felt that he'd never be able to hold it in once the slicing began. The cut never came, for the door to the studio flew open and cracked against the wall. There in the doorway stood the last person Jackie had expected to see.

'Hello boys,' Murdoch said. 'Surprised?'

The scalpel fell from Gareth's hands and embedded itself point first in Jackie's thigh. It felt as though it had gone right through his leg and out the other side, but even his bellow was eclipsed by the deranged screech Gareth let out. Gareth charged, his clawed hands searching for something to gouge, but Murdoch moved so fast he seemed to blur. Gareth grasped at thin air and ran out of the open door before he could stop. He returned immediately and made another lunge at Murdoch, who slipped away. The game of matador and bull went on as Jackie jiggled his leg, trying to dislodge the blade before he disgraced himself with a flood of tears. He'd just managed to shake it out, bringing a slight dialling down in the torture, when Gareth sat down on the floor to pant.

'Now, now, Gareth,' Murdoch said. 'There's no need for all this unpleasantness. I'm here to help.'

'I'm going to kill you,' Gareth said. 'When I get my breath back.'

'Why would you do that when I can give you the special tattoo you've been searching for?'

Gareth grew very still. The uncertainty on his face reflected the expression Jackie knew was painted on his own. How could Murdoch possibly know that Gareth believed the secret to fame lay in magical body art? Nobody knew except Gareth and Jackie. And how did he find them?

'You know about the tattoos?' Gareth said.

'You're not the only person your mum has been talking to. She's quite chatty for a dead woman.'

'She didn't tell me about you. And why would she talk to you after what you did?'

'Because she realized I'm the man she should have been talking to all along.'

Jackie stared at the two men, trying to make sense of this turn of events. If it hadn't been for the slit in his leg, seeping blood and twanging his nerve endings, he would have been convinced he was having a cheese dream.

'Why can't I take his?' Gareth said. 'I know it's one of the special ones.'

'Right, because you've had a lot of success with that strategy.'

'But Mum said ...'

'She was right about the tattoos, but wrong in her approach. You can't gain power by taking somebody else's tattoo and sticking it on with a bit of tape. That's like equating plastic surgery with wearing a Halloween mask. The tattoo has to be personalized, lovingly inked in to your own skin by the shaman. Guess who pays that shaman, Gareth? Me. And he's waiting next door right now.'

Gareth looked towards the door, wetting his bottom lip with his tongue as he did so. 'Why would you help me?'

'Believe it or not, I'm not a monster. I feel positively dreadful about the things I said during your rehearsal. I was a bit cranky that day. I want to make it up to you.'

'How do I know I can trust you?'

Murdoch was swaying from side to side like a snake charmer, and Jackie noticed that Gareth was following his motions exactly. Even though he wasn't looking directly into Murdoch's eyes, Jackie could feel his own trunk start to sway.

'Because making you famous will be good for me too,' Murdoch said, his voice now sonorous and warm. 'You'll be huge, and I'll be the man who made you huge. Don't you think you've waited long enough? Don't you deserve it?'

'Yes,' Gareth said, his eyes glassy.

'Don't just take my word for it. Ask your mum. I know she's listening.'

Gareth didn't bother getting up. He simply hunched over and began whispering, pausing as though listening to responses. Jackie looked at Murdoch, who put his finger to his lips and leaned in to say softly, 'Don't say anything. It'll just antagonize him. Trust me. I'll get you out of this.'

When Gareth finished his communion with thin air, he jumped to his feet and clapped his hands. 'Mum says it's okay. What do I have to do?'

'Give yourself up.'

Gareth began to get agitated again. 'Then I'll go to jail.'

'No,' Murdoch said, swaying again. 'You'll go to hospital for a little while. Once you're famous, we'll get you out. Celebrities are above the law.'

Jackie's feeling that he'd somehow wandered into the middle of something very peculiar deepened as Murdoch aped the words Gareth had spoken a few minutes before. A suspicious man would think Murdoch had been outside, listening and waiting for the most dramatic moment to enter. As much as Jackie wanted to ask what the hell was going on, he kept his mouth shut. He was extremely glad to be alive and didn't want to say or do anything that might change that.

'Now give me a hug,' Murdoch said, walking up to Gareth with his arms held out. 'You look like you need one.'

Gareth snuggled in to Murdoch's chest, sighing as a hand stroked his hair.

'Let's go next door for a nice Mars Bar and get that tattoo on you,' Murdoch said, and shepherded the youth from the room with a fatherly arm.

When Murdoch returned ten minutes later, the open door let in the sound of a buzzing needle and muffled whelps of pain.

'You really have a tattoo artist next door?' Jackie said.

'Of course I do.'

'Isn't that taking the charade a bit too bloody far?'

'Oh this isn't a charade. At least, not in the way you think.'

'Well why don't you untie me and tell me exactly what it is? And while you're at it get me some painkillers. My leg knacks.'

Murdoch raised an eyebrow. 'What, you don't like bondage? First I want to have a little chat. I'm sure you must have lots of questions.'

Jackie suspected he didn't want to know the answers to the many questions he'd formulated, but at the moment Murdoch was the only man who could actually get him out of this bloody chair, so he played along. 'Are you really going to help that lunatic become famous, or was it just a ploy to get him to hand himself in?'

'I am going to help him. I have been helping him. You see, Gareth's a few sandwiches short of a picnic, so to speak. He needed a little nudge here and there to set him on his path.'

'You mean you helped him kill those people?'

'Yes.'

While Murdoch's sudden appearance was suspicious, Jackie hadn't been expecting such an admission. Sure, he'd seen the way Murdoch treated people as commodities, reducing hundreds of wannabes to blubbering wrecks for the sake of good television. Yet becoming an accessory to murder seemed to be taking it too far, even for a man who clearly had a cold, jagged rock in place of a warm beating heart.

'Fuck me. Why?'

'Ratings. The whole thing with Gareth was a mistake. It created a backlash. You must have seen the figures. They're down ten percent.'

'How is having that maniac kill people going to fix that?'

'Now, now, Jackie. I can't possibly give away the ending. Let's just say we're close to the big finish.'

'Why bother telling me anything at all? You know I'll go to the police. Unless you're going to let him kill me after all.'

'What's the point of having an evil plan if you can't boast about it a teensy bit? Don't worry, you're not going to die. Saving your life at the eleventh hour will make me a bigger hero. Plus you won't talk to the police.'

'Why not?'

'Because I'm a big, scary demon.'

Jackie snorted. 'Yeah, everybody knows you're evil. I still don't see how that's going to stop me.'

'You misunderstand me, Jackie. I really am a demon. Watch.'

Once upon a time, Jackie had taken a lot of acid. His tabs of choice were Pink Floyds—innocuous thumbnail-sized cardboard squares that smelled of cheap perfume yet turned reality into little more than a flat background upon which a mad impressionist frantically smeared shimmering and shifting colours, sometimes smudging away the world entirely and daubing tableaux that were both insane and compelling. When he was on the drug, music became rich and complex, his ears seemingly operating in six dimensions, and his sense of touch grew so sensitive that even the slightest whisper of wind on his arm hairs sent thrills of pleasure scampering up his nerve endings.

Jackie stopped taking acid when one night he found himself out on the street, entranced by shimmering globes of light that had been flitting back-and-forth outside his window. The dancing illuminations turned out not to be spacecraft piloted by beautiful female aliens desirous of mating with mankind, as he'd imagined, but the headlights of oncoming cars. Fortunately for Jackie, the drivers were not on hallucinogenic drugs and swerved to avoid him as he swayed down the middle of the road, offering himself up as a willing participant in the visitors' interspecies experiments in multidimensional copulation. Only when he awoke the next morning did he understand how close he'd come to death and vowed to stick to speed, dope and booze.

Yet sometimes that sense of infinite possibility, of the world consisting of layers that could be peeled off at any minute to reveal something startling and beautiful, came flooding back. When that happened, he had to clamp down hard on his mind to stop it skipping off into the painted canvas for a frolic. What he saw next felt like a flashback, although it had a nightmarish tinge he'd never experienced.

Murdoch disrobed and laid his clothes neatly on the table. Wisps of smoke drifted up from his hair and his skin began to blacken, first on the tip of his nose, then all across his face and hands. Jackie, nostrils twitching with the sweet tang of cooking flesh, found his brain stuttering between the gears of the everyday and the downright strange. In the seconds that followed, his mental gearbox began screeching and squealing in anguish. Blisters popped up on Murdoch's skin, like the expanding throat of a frog, before bursting open. Instead of puss, out came spouts of flame that joined forces and consumed Murdoch's entire body. Charred skin floated up as his flesh bubbled away to pool on the ground. Great leathery wings unfolded from his back and the flames died down to reveal a body coated in mottled brown scales. The face was two pulsating slits above a lipless mouth brimming with unruly teeth, and eyes that were red, reptilian and full of intelligence.

Jackie became aware that he was screaming. The sound of his own voice, producing a perfect high F in the extremities of his terror, brought his straining mind into focus. It also helped that Murdoch, now transformed, clapped his hands and flung himself into the campest of showbiz poses—right leg forward, arms thrown out like the hands on a clock, head turned to profile and chin raised.

'Ta da!' Murdoch said.

For all the mind-frying unreality of the situation, Jackie realized this was no flashback. Murdoch lacked the shimmering, other-worldly feel that acid brought. His demon form appeared concrete, locked-in to the reality they both inhabited. Jackie had already tried, and failed, to rationalize away the little white men. Their appearance had nudged open a doorway in his mind, and the knowledge of Murdoch's true identity kicked it wide open and sauntered through. Sometimes you had to accept the reality of what your eyes presented you. And Murdoch hailing from the depths of Hell explained a lot.

'You're a demon,' Jackie said.

Murdoch dropped his arms, an incongruous pout swelling his flat lips. 'I thought you might be a little more freaked out.'

Jackie, who was still freaked out despite his acceptance of what two days ago he would have dismissed as impossible, did his best to act nonchalant. 'I've seen better special effects in a B-movie.'

Murdoch laughed, causing flames to re-emerge around his mouth. 'Jackie, you're a real card. I knew I liked you. Well, now I've convinced you, I'd better get back into costume in case Gareth comes wandering in to see what Mummy and Daddy are up to. We don't want to tip him over the edge.'

There were no fireworks or histrionics in the change back. Murdoch blurred, like a hologram in a power surge, and then he was back in his normal form. The smell, the ash, and the pool of melted flesh all vanished.

'Why didn't you just do that before?'

Murdoch shrugged. 'Presentation counts.'

Jackie looked Murdoch up and down as he dressed, the image of the demon still burned into his retinas making it impossible to deny what he'd seen. 'Who are you?' he said.

'Please allow me to introduce myself. I'm a man of ... hang on. That's already been done, I believe, and anyway I'm not Satan. Have you ever seen a boss do his own legwork? Consider me more of a project manager. My name is Murmur. That's spelled M-U-R...'

'I know how to spell it,' Jackie said. 'I'm more interested in what you're doing up here.'

'I'm the second mightiest demon in Hell, behind Satan himself. The hordes refer to me as Lord Murmur. I've been dabbling in humanity's history for millennia.'

'Doing what exactly?'

'This and that. You've probably heard of some of my work: the Crucifixion, the Bubonic Plague, World War One, George W. Bush.'

Something about Murdoch's off-hand tone gave Jackie pause. 'And now you're running a talent show. Forgive me if I seem a little sceptical.'

'*Icon* isn't simply a talent show. It's the musical equivalent of Armageddon. I started out killing off just about every famous musician you can think of. Then I realized it would be much better to drown them out. I'm helping bring about the end of all good music—my modest contribution to keeping humanity's collective soul mired in its everyday existence.'

'I still don't see why this is going to destroy humanity's soul. Sure, the music in *Icon* is pitiful, but it makes people happy.'

'Murder and rape make some people happy too. Simple happiness makes people content. It makes them stagnate. Give them the promise of a weekend of fun and frolics watching *Icon*, and they'll put up with their soul-crushing jobs without any thought of escape. Humanity isn't going to attain enlightenment if you're all plonked in front of the television on a Saturday night, drinking beer and watching talentless drones churn out cover versions. What inspiration are they going to draw from repeating self-referential lyrics about being famous? I've killed your creativity, Jackie.'

'So all those artists you produced have been working for Hell?'

'Yes. Although in all fairness they didn't know it.'

'What about me?' Jackie said. 'Am I one of your little minions?'

'You're just an idiot who involved himself. But it has worked out rather well for me, and it could still work out for you. You've given distinguished service to the banal, and for that I'm going to offer you a chance to stay involved. All you have to do is keep being yourself. Work with me and I'll make you a massive star. I'm thinking you could do a duet with Gareth. Killer and near victim. Imagine the sales!'

'You want me to sell my soul?'

'Oh, please. Nobody sells their soul, and if they did they would be idiots. Not much of a deal is it? A few decades of success in exchange for an eternity of being stuck on a big fork and roasted over a fiery pit like a human marshmallow. This is a simple transaction: you help me, I help you. I must admit the big guy upstairs won't be in a hurry to give you a welcoming hug if you sign on with us. You'd be like Carlos Tevez going from Man U to Man City. You'll never get back into Old Trafford again, if you catch my drift. But that's okay. If you join us, I'll make sure that when you come down you'll be made an honorary demon and avoid all that torture unpleasantness. You might even get wings.'

'Like I could trust you even if I was stupid enough to say "yes". I'd rather take my chances.'

'Are you sure? I've heard Heaven is really boring, plus all that piety would really get on your tits. Do you really want to spend all eternity hanging out with the kind of people who're always banging on about all the charity work they do? Plus nobody has to go to Mass in Hell. We play topless volleyball with super models instead.'

'Now you're just talking shit.'

'You got me. We actually play strip canasta with porn stars, winner gets to go on top.'

Jackie just shook his head. If Murdoch seemed put out, he didn't show it.

'Ah well. Your loss,' Murdoch said.

'So, what now?'

'I call the police.'

'And you're just going to let me go?'

'Well, I could wipe your memory, but it's so much more fun having you know but not being able to say anything. Although, I must admit, I would very much enjoy seeing you on the news coming across all bug-eyed and barmy as you try to tell people I'm a demon. But I think you're too smart for that. Anyway, I'd better get on the phone. Time's moving on.' Murdoch quickly undid Jackie's bonds. 'Don't think about trying to leave before the police and media get here. I need you to be my wingman on this.'

'And why exactly would I do that?'

'If you don't, I'll take your girlfriend's soul.'

When the police came, beating the television vans and hordes of newspaper reporters by a matter of minutes despite the flashing lights and cacophony of sirens—making it clear whom Murdoch had called first—Jackie had no choice but to play along. He listened to the chaos next door, the reading of rights and Murdoch's voice above the babble stridently calling for Gareth to be treated gently, before two officers came into the room for him. The police bundled everyone outside, to be taken straight to the station to give their statements. Gareth, his head covered, was deposited into a waiting van. There was no sign of the person who'd been operating the tattoo needle. Murdoch stopped in front of the Sky Television camera. Jackie could tell the police wanted to jockey him along, but Murdoch wouldn't be moved until he'd spoken.

'Can you confirm that the suspect is Gareth Jones, the man who tried to attack you?' the Sky reporter asked.

'Yes,' Murdoch said. 'I've been in touch with Gareth on-and-off since the unfortunate incident at the *Icon* auditions, which I must share the blame for. But it was only tonight that Gareth called me to confess to his crimes and issue a cry for help. He wanted to stop, you see. And when he called I had to come. I'm so glad I did.' Murdoch reached out an arm and pulled Jackie alongside him. 'If I hadn't, then my dear friend Jackie may well have been the next victim. Now he's safe.'

A single tear dribbled onto Murdoch's cheek, squeezed out from the poisonous pool of demon bile that formed the dirty little shit's soul.

Fucking shameless, Jackie thought.

The reporter turned his attention to Jackie. 'Do you have anything to add, Jackie?'

The urge to blurt out the whole insane story was near overwhelming. He looked at Murdoch, who raised an eyebrow.

Just remember that I am a monstrous beast from the darkest depths of Hell, it seemed to say, *and I can take you or Marie any time I want if you do not acquiesce to my will.*

It was a very expressive eyebrow.

Jackie put his own arm around Murdoch's neck, keeping his squeeze a notch under throttle.

'This man,' he forced himself to say, 'is a hero.'

'No, you're the hero,' Murdoch said. 'You gave yourself up in exchange for the woman you love, even though you knew it meant certain death. All I did was listen to the desperate plea of a sick man.'

Jackie's face puckered up in disgust, which he hoped would be interpreted as any one of the other emotions that could be attributed to a man who'd narrowly escaped death at the hands of a lunatic. Fortunately, the attention had turned back to Murdoch. Jackie slipped away, beckoning his police escort.

'Can we get to the station to give my statement, please? I'd like to see my girlfriend.'

If she still is my girlfriend, he thought.

Murmur, still laying it on thick for the viewing millions, watched Jackie go out of the corner of his eye and suppressed a smile. After the episode in the O2, it had been obvious that Heaven was onto him, even if they didn't quite have the full picture yet, so he'd decided the moment had come to get his side of the story out. He'd very much enjoyed spinning his yarn to Jackie, unable to resist one or two embellishments. He'd been itching to tell somebody for a long time, but all he had was a bunch of minions already in the know and Satan, who continued to insist they keep it under wraps. Well, now Jackie knew, for all the peace it would bring him.

Jackie had played along with the insincere request for secrecy for the moment, but with the knowledge now nestling in his tiny little brain he wouldn't be able to keep quiet for long. Jackie wouldn't be stupid enough to go to the mainstream media with his story, but he would tell somebody: perhaps Marie, perhaps his friends. Maybe he would even post anonymously on one of those conspiracy theory websites. No rational person would believe the story, but the countless religious nuts would lap it up. Rumours about a powerful demon named Murmur pulling the strings of humanity from behind the scenes would spread. It would only be a matter of time before he became a regular on the religious websites. Then Satan would have to acknowledge their little secret and his name would be writ large among the great demons. He'd been putting together his memoirs down the years, and felt confident that *Fire & Brimstone* would snap up the serialization rights. It would be the first time a low-born had appeared on the cover of the magazine. He and his peers had shown what low-borns could do, given a chance. Once that was public knowledge Hell would have to change.

Sure, it was another calculated risk, as Satan would be displeased that there'd been a leak. When Satan grew displeased, some unfortunate demon usually ended up being peeled like a juicy blood orange and his body parts tossed out of The Stalactite to be fought over by the harpies. Yet Murmur wasn't worried. He would blame the leak on one of Lucifer's minions. Satan knew that Lucifer both opposed Murmur's ascension and would love to spark another war, so it would be believable.

It would also mean that this particular adventure would end sooner rather than later, a realization that brought him relief. He'd always publicly framed his record collection, which was now so large it needed its own room, in the context of research. Privately, he'd long admitted to himself that he loved good music. Yet the wave of bland bullshit he'd created had brought complicated, meaningful and beautiful songs to the point of extinction. Even though the odd great band broke through to the mainstream, he had to plough through social media, independent music magazines and forums to find the real gems. Lately, he'd found himself longing for the glory days of the sixties and seventies, when great new acts sprouted like bluebells in the spring. He'd begun to wonder whether he was on the right side of this particular struggle.

Regardless of his feelings, he had overriding concerns. To bring about the emancipation of the low-borns and gain the recognition he deserved, he had to ensure that his plan for Gareth reached fruition. Then he could go to Satan and suggest that they find a role suited to his talents in Hell—something nice and senior, where he could use his planning skills and be beyond Lucifer's reach, as well as ensure that he retained all the comforts he'd grown so used to up on Earth. He'd earned it, after all. There was just one problem, however: there was no music in Hell. He'd have to find a way to smuggle in his tens of thousands of records, CDs and MP3s.

Marie was sitting up in her hospital bed, where they were keeping her in overnight as a precautionary measure, when Jackie crashed through the door. He didn't have to persuade the nurses to let him in after visiting hours. They'd watched the news broadcasts and were delighted to see him. One of them even gave him a peck on the cheek, and he could hear them whispering outside the door as he and Marie looked at each other. All the things he'd wanted to say slipped from his mind as he saw her, looking small, frightened and old under the hospital sheets. Fortunately, he didn't have to say anything. It turned out that giving up his life in exchange for hers had bought a lot of brownie points. She simply opened her arms, and he fell into them. She squeezed him so hard he struggled to breathe.

'I love you,' he said once he managed to get some air into his lungs.

'I love you too, Jackie,' she said.

He smiled. 'Call me Archie.'

And that was all it took.

24

In the days that followed Murdoch's Scooby Doo-style unmasking, the feeling that nothing was what it seemed remained with Jackie. From the gnarled and liver-spotted old woman who shuffled below his window with a Zimmer frame each morning to the pack of journalists laying siege to the flat, everybody seemed poised to slough off the cocoon of human flesh and unwrap wings, talons and teeth. No matter how hard he tried to get back on an even keel, the electrical signals so used to following a humdrum path along the synapses of his brain would hurtle down these strange new pathways like pissed-up joy riders.

The story took up at least a third of every newspaper and news show. Commentators, analysts and celebrities were interviewed and re-interviewed as the media hounds chased their own tails in search of new angles to keep the readers coming back. It was worse than the phone hacking scandal, which at least had new revelations to keep it fresh. And this, for Jackie, was the fundamental problem. He had a new revelation that would fry everybody's brain. But nobody would believe him.

Gareth had confessed in gory and insane detail: the dead mother exhorting him to search for a magical tattoo, fate pointing him in Jackie's direction, the little white men attacking, the mysterious transportation from the river bed and Murdoch giving him the tattoo he so desired. That final detail could have implicated Murdoch, but he'd played it beautifully. He told the police and media that Gareth had laid out the whole sorry tale when he called—something Gareth backed even though Jackie knew it was a lie—and that he realized he could only save Jackie by pretending to give the killer the tattoo he so craved.

When the police interviewed Jackie, he edited out all of the supernatural details and stuck to Murdoch's version of events. Privately, Rooney told Jackie there were things the investigation team couldn't explain: how Gareth had got his hands on so much sodium pentothal, how he'd disabled the security cameras without an accomplice, how he'd managed to find such perfect moments to strike, and where the money had come from to buy and outfit the house on Sandy Lane. Gareth told them that his mum sorted it all out, and he clearly believed this to be true. Jackie could tell these loose ends made Rooney uneasy; the policeman had asked several times if Jackie was sure he hadn't seen anything out of the ordinary. Jackie knew the inconsistencies would be set aside quietly, however. Rooney was far too pragmatic to go all X-Files and be mocked as the loony cop who suspected supernatural shenanigans.

Jackie and Marie were prisoners in the flat due to the baying media mob, whose cameras and voice recorders bristled upwards at every twitch of his curtain, and Phyllis's phone rang all day as the tabloids promised increasingly vulgar wads of cash for the exclusive story of their ordeal. On the Wednesday after Gareth's capture, Jackie came out of the shower to find Marie putting down his phone, her cheeks drained of all colour. 'That was Phyllis. *The Sun* has offered a million.'

The towel Jackie was clutching around his waist slipped to the ground. If they took the offer, his financial problems would be solved in one fell swoop and he would be close to being able to buy back his old house in Primrose Hill. But the money would be tainted. He bent over to kiss Marie. 'We've got everything we need right here.'

She squeezed his hand. 'They aren't going to leave us alone until we say something.'

'So let's make a quick statement and get it over with.'

Jackie threw on some clothes and they went down the stairs hand-in-hand to face the media scrum.

'As you know, we've been through a traumatic time, and we would like to be left alone to come to terms with everything that has happened,' Jackie said, wiping away the tears brought on by a big furry mike that had been poked into his eye amidst the initial surge. 'So, this is the only statement we're going to make. We're happy to be back together, and we'd like to thank Murray Murdoch for his intervention in making it possible. If it weren't for him, I would probably be dead.'

'Did The Tattoo Collector tell you why he did it?' one reporter shouted

'All I know is that Gareth Jones is seriously mentally ill. That's it.'

As they turned their backs on the flashbulbs and dashed to the lift to avoid being trampled by the chasing mob of hacks screaming follow-up questions, Jackie knew this would be the last time he would ever receive such attention. Murdoch was talking enough for everyone and the media would soon get sick of standing around in the rain and the wind. After that, given the musical direction he and Marie were going to take, there would be no more paparazzi for them. He gripped Marie's hand tighter and stepped into the lift, letting the door slide closed on the press pack for the last time.

Any time somebody made the mistake of entrusting Jackie with knowledge that shouldn't be passed on, begging the question why they'd shared it in the first place, it was only a matter of time before he cracked. Secrets grew inside him like pearls, expanding day-by-day, layer-by-layer until they became a hard, uncomfortable presence that had to be expelled. With this particular secret, which began so large it could barely be contained, it was always a question of it coming out sooner rather than later.

He couldn't tell Marie, as he'd put her through enough already. Nor could he tell his mother, who would slap his head and tell him to stop making up daft stories. That left Phyllis. She wouldn't believe him either, but it would create the least damage and give him the chance to lance the mental boil once and for all.

They met in her office one week after that surreal evening. Jackie and Marie had already begun writing, and he'd found a few useable gems in his father's back catalogue of original compositions. With Marie by his side and the knowledge that he could help get his father's music out there, listening to the cassettes brought him a warm fuzz of nostalgic happiness. The plan for the meeting was to discuss small gigs they could play to introduce their music. It didn't take Phyllis long to realize that Jackie had other things on his mind.

'Out with it,' she said.

'Out with what?'

'Whatever it is that's giving you that creepy thousand-yard stare.'

Jackie took a deep breath and, unable to meet Phyllis's penetrating gaze, looked out the window. He could see no easy way to segue into the conversation, so he came straight out with it. 'Murray Murdoch is a demon.'

Even though he knew he was about to be ridiculed, just saying it aloud made him feel better.

'I would have used the term "cunt", but that's just me,' Phyllis said.

'It's not a metaphor, Phyllis. He's a demon. As in scaly, scary and from Hell. He showed me what he really looks like.'

Silence followed. Jackie risked a glance at Phyllis, expecting to see her face snap back into an attempt at a neutral expression from the twisted incredulity that must be gnarling her features. She was looking at him steadily, a strange smile on her lips.

'Tell me,' she said.

Jackie told her, leaving out no detail of the strangeness that had begun with the mini squadron that saved him from Gareth. At no point did Phyllis look at him as though he were a raving lunatic, snort in derision or try to interrupt.

When he'd spilled his guts, she threw down the pen she'd been toying with and put her hands behind her head. 'Murdoch. I should have known. All that lack of emotion is a dead giveaway.'

'Why is it a giveaway?' Jackie said, forgetting to ask Phyllis why she was so quick to believe him in his relief at not being dismissed as a gibbering loon.

'When demons smile or frown, their faces catch fire. It's an automatic response. The only way to stop it is to show no emotion.'

Now it occurred to Jackie that Phyllis not only buying his tale, but proving herself an expert in demonology, pointed to another surprise. He said nothing, afraid to invite a further round of craziness. Phyllis didn't wait for an invitation.

'I have something to tell you too,' she said.

'Christ, here we go. Don't tell me, you're a paranormal investigator. No, you're a former nun, turned demon slayer. You probably know ten different martial arts and have a silver crucifix knife jammed down your knickers for emergencies.'

'Actually, I'm an angel.'

'Fuck off,' Jackie said.

Phyllis grinned. 'Let me show you.'

She crossed to the window, pulled the blinds shut and turned to face Jackie. He had a horrible sense of déjà vu as she stripped off to reveal a rather shapely figure. One second he was looking at his naked manager, which in itself was bizarre enough; the next, the invisible hand of the acid painter was unleashed. Through lidded eyes, he looked at the apparition before him. Her body was slim yet powerful, shades of white roiling across the smooth surface like milk about to boil. Tucked-in wings protruded over the top of her shoulder blades and curled out either side of her hips. The incandescence she gave off, like a light bulb about to blow, made it difficult to discern her facial features. Just about all he could make out was a full mouth kinked into what looked like a smile and oval eyes that somehow managed to glow brighter than the rest of her. His eyes drifted down to her bare breasts, which were like two little lumps of unbaked dough with no visible nipples, and stayed there.

This can't be Phyllis, he thought as he leaned back as far as he could in the chair, shying away from the light. Again, though, the vision had too much clarity to be the product of a flashback. What the angel said next clinched it. 'Are you looking at my tits, you grubby little pervert?'

It was definitely Phyllis.

'Not you too,' Jackie said, and tipped over the back of his chair.

When he managed to get to his feet, Phyllis had returned to human form and was calmly putting her clothes back on.

'I wasn't looking at your tits,' he said, trying to rub away the bright spots floating in his retinas.

'Can't blame me for thinking it. You do have history. Anyway, believe me now?'

This was the third outrageous, improbable and credulity-stretching event Jackie had been exposed to in the space of a week. Somehow he found it the hardest to believe, for one simple reason: Phyllis was the proud owner of the foulest mouth imaginable. Admittedly, it had been a long time since he read the Bible, but he was pretty sure he would have remembered if the angels in the Good Book had used words like ballbag, big hairy dog's cock and wankfest.

'But you swear like a trooper,' he said.

Phyllis scowled. 'If you were me, you'd swear too. Angels are God's warriors. We're supposed to swoop through the sky, wielding flaming swords and swiping off demons' filthy bonces. Instead I'm stuck down here doing lots of Cold War behind the scenes bullshit. I've not had a good fight for millennia. Let's just say I'm a little fucking frustrated.'

Jackie tried to imagine Phyllis on the battlefield, cutting a bloody swath through hordes of capering, gibbering demons with a giant sword. He found it remarkably easy to do so. Also, now that he knew she was an angel it occurred to him that her appearance at the arena and the intervention of the little white men had to be linked.

'Was it you who saved me in the O2?'

'Yes. Through my friendly little avatars.' She cleared her throat and spat into her palm. One of the little white figures swelled up from the gooey mess. 'Say hello,' she instructed it.

'You're one ugly bastard,' the avatar said in a voice that was a soft, higher-pitched replica of Phyllis's.

She slapped the avatar back into her mouth and swallowed. 'Sorry about that. Sometimes they have minds of their own.'

'Seemed pretty similar to yours,' Jackie said. 'So, are you my Guardian Angel?'

'On a part-time, self-appointed basis, yes. I followed you to make sure the maniac didn't get you. It's just as well I did.'

'And what is it you do when you're not saving my life?'

'Just what you think I do. We have a little posse of managers, agents and producers across the globe, all sent here from upstairs.'

'God sent you to Earth to manage bands?'

'Manage, encourage, pass on the odd little gift of divine inspiration where required. We've got shares in NME and Pitchfork. We helped start Myspace, GarageBand and ReverbNation to help independent bands bypass the big labels and get their music out there. We even had a scientist create LSD to help with inspiration—a little addition to the dope plants God seeded back in the day.'

The thing about ridiculous, unbelievable situations was that they very quickly became commonplace, and Jackie had been through so much that he found himself swept along by the conversation. 'So who did you give your gifts to?'

'Just a few pioneers in soul, funk, rock and whatnot. I don't think you really need me to name names.'

'I thought rock was supposed to be the devil's music.'

'Are you kidding? Harps got binned in 1965. The cherubs play electric guitars now.'

'Why are you doing all this?'

'It's all part of your evolution. Can you imagine what would happen to the human imagination if all you had to listen to was manufactured pap? Your souls would be barren wastelands. A bit like Didcot.'

'Was I part of this scheme?'

'I had hopes for you. We know how that turned out. Maybe God was up to something, but he tells me fuck all.'

'Can't you ask him?'

'No point. He'll just smile mysteriously and say, "Well, I am omnipotent." He always does that. If something goes well, he can claim the credit even if he knew nothing about it. If things go tits-up, he can pin the blame on free will. Pretty sweet deal, eh?'

'He must have known about Murdoch, though. He sent you down here after the little twat started his antics, right?'

Phyllis sucked in her cheeks. 'Actually, no. We had no idea what he was up to.'

'But you told me not to sell my soul to Murdoch.'

'That was a figure of speech. Rock stars dropping dead seemed pretty natural given their lifestyles and we never imagined for a second that Hell would make its own music. They're not supposed to be able to bear listening to it, although the stuff *Icon* churns out doesn't really qualify. Which, I suppose, is the whole point.'

'Well, they're making music. What are you going to do about it?'

'That's a very good question. My preference would be to kick the shit out of them, but I think we need to refer it upstairs. What are you doing this weekend?'

'Nothing much. Marie's taking her son to Alton Towers. I'm not going. Can't stand rollercoasters.'

'Great. Meet me outside Barfly on Saturday night, 8pm.'

'Why?'

Phyllis grinned. 'I want you to meet God.

25

Phyllis was leaning against the wall of Barfly on the Chalk Farm Road side, blowing cigarette smoke up into the soft purple glow that spilled from a light above a fire exit, when Jackie arrived just after eight o'clock. Youngsters were filing in through the entrance beneath the simple white neon sign on the three-storey brick building. There appeared to be some law that decreed nobody was allowed to wear trousers that fit properly. They were all either incredibly loose, exposing the tops of underwear, or so tight that their feet must be turning blue from the lack of blood. Jackie, in his simple white shirt, black silk jacket and appropriately sized denims, felt two decades too old and horrendously overdressed.

Glances kept shooting his way, followed by whispered conversations. It was strange: now that he no longer lusted after fame, everybody recognized him. Despite his silence, he was still being bombarded by requests from the media, who'd resorted to interviewing old friends and casual acquaintances. Jackie could see that the motley crew of commentators, some of whom he barely knew, were trying the same trick he had of gaining publicity from a major media event.

'So, is God meeting us here or is he keeping us a table?' Jackie said.

'He's already inside. They needed to sound check.'

'He's in the band?'

'Of course he is. He's the singer and one of the lead guitarists.'

'Two lead guitarists?'

Phyllis rolled her eyes. 'There are a few egos at play. The other one is Hendrix.'

'Hold on, Jimi Hendrix?' Jackie said, aware that he'd spent a lot of time asking incredulous questions recently.

'The very same.'

Jackie pinched the cigarette from Phyllis's lips. 'Who else is in this band?'

'Keith Moon on drums. John Entwistle on Bass. Miles Davis sometimes plays the trumpet on some of the jazz fusion numbers, although he's not in the line-up tonight. Janis Joplin sings a few songs when God wants to nip out for a fag. Joe Strummer pitches in too. Beethoven used to be on the keys, but he was kicked out for musical differences. Now all the Grateful Dead keyboard players who popped their clogs take turns.'

Jackie took a long, shaky draw on the cigarette, holding it away from Phyllis as she tried to snatch it back. 'I'm wondering if I should stub this out on my palm just to make sure this is real.'

'I'll help you with that,' Phyllis said, and delivered an eye-watering smack to Jackie's cheek. She pinched back the cigarette while he was cursing her. 'Feel better, now?'

'That was decidedly un-angelic,' Jackie said, rubbing his face and glowering at his manager. 'Can we go inside?'

The semi-circular leather sofas in the downstairs bar each housed around ten people, faces orange from the lights above; dozens of youths were clustered around the stools and higher tables; and the serving area was three deep. Jackie and Phyllis pushed in at the back of the thirsty masses, too far back for even a wafted fifty-pound note to get them noticed.

'I don't suppose you can magic up a space to the bar?' Jackie said.

'I'm sure you've heard the quote about power and responsibility.'

'Yeah, Uncle Ben said it in Spider-Man.'

Phyllis rolled her eyes. 'I despair. Voltaire wrote it. Stan Lee nicked it.'

'So, you're saying you can't do anything because of something a scroty old French bloke wrote hundreds of years ago? Personally, I believe that with great power comes the great responsibility to get your friend a drink, pronto.'

A tousled-haired boy slid his insect-like frame into the sliver of space between Phyllis and the third row of the queue. She glared at his back. 'Well, when you put it like that ...'

She waded in and the crowd parted like the Red Sea. Jackie played the role of the Israelites, trailing in her wake and marvelling at the way nobody grumbled even though queue jumping normally prompted passive-aggressive elbow jabbing, or a fist in the eye if the night was further down the line. Phyllis ordered a G&T and a Zubrowka from an unusually attentive barman. Once they had their drinks, she walked to a small round table, which cleared of punters as they approached.

'What will God make of you messing with mortal minds in order to feed your alcohol habit?' Jackie said.

Phyllis shrugged and took a large swig. 'He'll be too busy warming up his vocal cords to notice. Besides, I think all this omni-this, omni-that stuff is over-egged. You've seen the mess the world is in, but he seems to do nothing except listen to Led Zeppelin and watch *Hedwig and the Angry Inch*.'

'What's that?'

'It's a rock musical about an East German transsexual that names her backing band after the remnants of her botched sex change operation. Great film and great songs, although you'd think it would wear a bit thin after the 500th watch.'

'I thought God didn't approve of transsexuals.'

'The Church may not, but we're all God's children. Even those who aren't sure what they want between their legs, or where they want to put it for that matter. All orifices are equal in the eyes of the Lord.'

'Those nutters from the Westboro Baptist Church will be livid when they get upstairs and find out Heaven doesn't have a no-fags policy after all.'

'Oh, those hateful sods will never make it to Heaven. They're all on an express elevator to the gay spit-roast dungeon in Hell. Within five minutes of kicking the bucket, they'll have demon balls swollen with fiery spunk slapping off their shapeless chins.'

Jackie cut in before Phyllis painted an even more graphic picture. 'So why doesn't God just tell the Church what he does and doesn't approve of?'

'Direct communication would ruin the whole man of mystery thing he's got going on. He probably should tell them, so they won't waste their time with all that praying. They'd be better off cranking up the amps and playing a guitar solo. That would get his attention.'

Jackie resisted the urge to neck his whisky, instead taking decorous sips. 'I can't believe I'm about to see God play with a bunch of dead rock stars. I don't even believe in God.'

'You'd better start believing, because he's onstage in twenty minutes. Come on, we'd better head up.'

Up they went, drinks in hand, and secured a position in front of the monitors in the tiny gig space. The Marshall stacks were only a few feet away, and Jackie could see something odd about the dials. 'Do those amps go up to eleven?'

Phyllis shrugged. 'Jimi wasn't happy—he's a bit of traditionalist about these things—but God insisted on it.'

Even angels needed to pee, so Phyllis nipped off to the loo and left Jackie to soak up the atmosphere. He'd never been to Barfly, but it gave off the same intimate vibe as the now-closed Camden Falcon, where he'd played several gigs as he cut his teeth. It struck Jackie that this was the first time in almost twenty years that he'd been in the crowd for a performance. Back in the day he'd gone to at least three gigs a week, not out of a desire to learn or copy but for the love of good music. He first stopped going when he made it because he was too busy. When he fell from grace, he couldn't bear the thought of being one of the throng instead of commanding the stage himself.

Something else my lust for fame took from me, he thought.

He tried to push away all the lost years by immersing himself in the moment, reaching back through the decades to the time when he loved nothing more than to be buffeted and barged to the soundtrack of the eighties pumping out hard, loud and fast. He just felt old and out of place, at least until the band took the stage. Phyllis had just returned with fresh drinks when the lights went down and out they filed. Hendrix's hair was less sixties, cropped down to his skull, and the trademark headband was missing, but to Jackie's eye he was unmistakable. Jackie couldn't believe that none of the crowd recognized him, although the average spectator age of about nineteen and the fact that Hendrix was dead probably explained why nobody made the connection.

Once the backing band had taken their places, out walked the man Jackie presumed to be God. Decades of religious imagery had sowed an image of a bearded, stocky figure in a robe and sandals—rather like a hippy Santa—in Jackie's mind. The creator turned out to be clean-shaven with eyes that sparkled blue even in the dim lighting, a square jaw and tousled curly hair that fell onto his shoulders. He was wearing a paisley pattern shirt unbuttoned to reveal a hairy chest and a rippling six-pack that sat above the large silver belt buckle holding up a pair of dark blue denims.

Jackie nudged Phyllis. 'He looks exactly like …'

'… a young Robert Plant,' she finished for him. 'Like I said, he's a big Led Zep fan.'

'Did he always look like that?'

'No. He can take any shape he wants. Sometimes he likes to appear as an impossibly white, diffuse cloud. Just when he wants to make a big entrance.'

Jackie cut his gaze from the stage to the crowd and back again as God took a swig of water from the bottle he was clutching and leaned over to talk to Keith Moon. The band, mostly decked out in the style that had been fashionable when they were huge, didn't look like the kind of outfit painfully cool kids would normally listen to.

'I thought this place was supposed to be for up-and-coming bands, not old rock farts,' he said.

'What's the point of being God if you can't pull a few strings?'

God turned to face the crowd, giving Phyllis a quick nod and Jackie an appraising stare, before snatching the microphone from its stand.

'Are you ready to Rock'n'Roll?' he yelled.

The crowd stayed silent, so God tried again, this time making a small gesture with his right hand. Every throat in the room, including Jackie's, bellowed back with an involuntary 'Yes!'

'That's cheating,' Jackie said when he'd regained control of his vocal cords.

Phyllis just grinned.

When the band burst into the opening bars of *All Along the Watchtower*, there was no need for divine intervention. The crowd surged forward, and Jackie forgot all of his problems. The band ripped through a pantheon of rock, punk, new wave, grunge and indie classics: *Back in Black*; *Immigrant Song*; *War Pigs*; *Shot by Both Sides*; *Holiday in Cambodia*; *Another Girl, Another Planet*; and on and on and on. At times Hendrix and God soloed simultaneously. It should have been a cacophony, but their licks twisted around each other like long, passionate tongues in perfect synchronicity. The Who's legendary rhythm section kept it all together—Entwistle's thumping bass filling the gap left by the rhythm guitar and Moon, somehow loose and tight at the same time, driving the songs on. Jackie's spirits swelled like a water balloon under a tap and he embraced the delicious shivers and chills. Occasionally, he would get turned around by the throng and see a rapturous grin on every face. The gig passed by in a delirious daze. By the time the third encore was over, every person and every surface was coated in a slick of sweat. Jackie couldn't remember the last time he'd felt so young and alive. It would have taken an industrial sander to wipe the smile off his face.

Phyllis slung an arm around his shoulder and planted a big kiss on his sodden cheek. 'Now that was fun. Anyway, come on. We're expected backstage.'

Phyllis led them past the bouncer and knocked on the changing room door. Unreality washed over Jackie again as he stepped inside. Hendrix had a towel draped around his neck, and was still noodling on his guitar. Janis Joplin was massaging Keith Moon's shoulders. Entwistle was pulling out earplugs, while Joe Strummer was cracking his jaw. Jackie had met the Queen at a Royal Variety performance once and this experience was exactly like that, only magnified a hundredfold. The Queen probably could have had him arrested and thrown into the Tower of London had he done anything to offend her. God, on the other hand, could disintegrate him or turn him into a slug.

God blew at a bead of sweat dangling from his right eyebrow, loosening it so it dripped down onto his chest and soaked into the hairy thatch.

'Jackie Thunder,' he said. 'Do not be nervous, my son. Phyllis has told me that you are one of the righteous, even if you did make some woebegone music for a while. Now, sit.'

Jackie perched on a stool. 'That was the best gig I've seen.'

'Man, you should have seen us in the Bull & Gate two weeks ago,' Hendrix said. 'We were on fire.'

'That was indeed a righteous gig,' God said. 'But come, Jackie, we did not summon you here for praise. You have a story to impart, I understand. Phyllis has given me the basics, but I want to hear it in your words. Pray tell.'

Once Jackie had laid out his whole story again, God turned to Phyllis. 'Why did we not become aware of this sooner?'

'If he'd been one of the usual suspects, we would have spotted the signature, but the sneaky fucking cock monkeys used an unknown demon and hid him in plain sight,' said Phyllis, grimacing.

Jackie glanced at God, to see if he would react to the colourful language. His face remained impassive.

'And all the planning that went into this is so unlike Hell. Normally they're all about the big impact,' Phyllis continued. 'And who could have imagined the dirty fuckers would start making music?'

'This is most vexing,' said God, who looked distinctly unvexed.

'It's a fucking travesty, is what it is. I've been telling you for a long time that we have to do something about *Icon* and all these other talent shows it spawned. Now we know Hell's to blame, it's time to take some action. And by action, I mean we need to crack some skulls.'

'You know the policy, Phyllis. No direct intervention.'

'Right, because you've never broken that rule when it suited you. You resurrected Paul McCartney, for fuck's sake.'

'That was a special case. I loved The Beatles.'

'You could at least have killed him again after the Frog Chorus. Anyway, my point is that we're already intervening. What do you think I do all day long?'

'That is just helping a natural process, like taking vitamin supplements. You are suggesting surgery.'

'You do understand what's happening, don't you? This music is like an uncapped oil well on the sea bed. It's going to keep spewing out noxious black clouds until every single thing of beauty is dead. Do you know how hard it is to find good new bands these days? Everybody is too busy queuing for *Icon* auditions, and those that aren't are struggling to make an impact because the airwaves are filled with this muck. If we don't do something, your record collection isn't going to get any bigger, because there won't be anything worth putting in it.'

For the first time, God's eyes wrinkled up in consternation. 'That would be most unfortunate. Tell me, Jackie, what do you think this demon plans to do with the young man?'

Jackie had replayed his conversation with Murdoch many times, and had a pretty clear idea where it was all going. 'He's going to make him a star and flog his shit records. He hasn't done anything yet, but I think he's biding his time until the *Icon* season finale. He even told me that I should watch the show until the end.'

'That's ridiculous,' Phyllis said. 'Nobody's going to buy a record by a serial killer. In fact, I doubt it's even legal for him to release one.'

'This is Murdoch. If anybody can pull it off, he can.'

'It's a moot point anyway,' Phyllis said. 'Whether he succeeds with Gareth or not, we have to stop him.'

'Whatever you're gonna do, I want in,' said Hendrix, who'd stopped noodling to clutch the neck of his guitar with his shovel-like hands. 'I told you I was murdered, man. It must have been this dude. I wanna shove my guitar up his ass, body first.'

'There will be no violence, Jimi,' God said. 'Whatever we do must be indirect, otherwise we risk starting another full-scale war.'

The mere mention of war perked Phyllis up, and her fists clenched as though around the handle of an invisible weapon. 'What's wrong with another war? We'd pulverize them.'

'You have anointed your sword with enough demon blood down the years. We must find another way.'

The room fell silent. Jackie looked around Heaven's assembled forces, each one of them lost in thought, features momentarily devoid of expression. Just like Murdoch's. An idea tickled the base of Jackie's neck. 'Phyllis, you said that Murdoch never shows emotion because his face would go on fire, right?'

'Yes.'

'Then we just need to get him all fired up in public. If his face goes all crispy, that's going to be hard to explain away.'

'We'd need to get it on camera,' Phyllis said.

'The *Icon* finale is televised live isn't? That's where we get him.'

'How exactly?'

'Maybe tell him a joke?' Jackie said, aware of how lame his suggestion must seem.

Phyllis pinched a cigarette from Joplin's packet and took several deep puffs. Then she smiled. 'He told you all of this stuff and revealed himself unprompted, right?'

'Yes.'

'And all that stuff about the Crucifixion and the plague is utter bullshit.'

'So?'

'So he was trying to make himself look good. Obviously part of him wants the universe to know who he really is. Look at his names: Murmur and Murray Murdoch. He was trying to leak it out all along. He wants the recognition. And we're going to give it to him in spades.'

'How exactly?' God said.

Phyllis jabbed the air with her cigarette. 'Pride.'

26

Murmur's finger hovered over the laptop's touchpad, which with one click could mark the last task complete on his Microsoft Project file. Only this evening's denouement, the inexorable product of the bars and arrows that flowed down the project file, remained. The temptation to bear down, and achieve that moment of anal satisfaction a ticked box always brought was near overwhelming, but he held back. Even though only an hour or so remained until the culmination of the work of the last year, in many ways of the last five decades, a premature click would be tempting fate.

He'd seen neither hide nor hair of any angels in the months since his public persona captured Gareth. He'd been sure the avatar-led intervention that stopped the attempt to seize Jackie heralded the beginning of a campaign, and sent out his minions to comb the city for the angelic forces that must be massing. They'd sensed no secret cabal plotting to attack, which relieved and disappointed him in equal measure. He didn't want his plan derailed, but a confrontation, which he would have won of course, would have added spice to the narrative of Murmur the Conquering Hero when he returned to Hell. Whatever had prompted the action to save Jackie, Heaven appeared to have reverted to its pathetic passivity, no doubt trusting the fundamental goodness of humanity would shine through. How wrong they were.

However, there remained the faint possibility that they would try to intervene, and a good project manager prepared for every eventuality. For this evening's festivities he'd called in every minion at his disposal. These demons comprised a quarter of the audience, ready to tickle the spectators in the direction they must go and act swiftly if anything went awry. It was doubly important to get it right, as Satan had said he might come up for the big finale. Murmur suspected he would arrive once the singing was over. As far as he knew, Satan hadn't heard a single note since the mix tape in 1980. He checked his watch, and saw he still had a few minutes until the show began. He fired up the internet and Googled his real name for the tenth time that day, just in case anything had changed. The search engine turned up the same old inaccurate mentions. He thumped the touchpad to close the window and sniffed. It appeared Jackie was capable of holding his tongue after all.

One of his human flunkies bustled into the room. 'Time, Mr Murdoch.'

'Is the video link working?'

'Yes.'

'Check it again.'

He followed the assistant out into the corridor, forcing himself to walk slowly and breathe deeply as he approached the entrance to the stage. As the *Icon* theme tune struck up, he steadied himself on a gantry holding up the backdrop, slapped his face, and then strode out onto the stage.

In the last row of the banked seats lining the auditorium, Jackie was squeezing his thighs together to stop his legs from trembling. To his left, Phyllis stared at the stage, clenching and unclenching her sword hand. To his right, Hendrix and the rest of God's backing band were sprawled in their chairs. The only one missing from the night at Barfly was God himself, who'd decided his awesome presence would set the demon's antennae twitching and alert him that something was afoot. He would be monitoring events from afar, he said. Whether that meant he was watching it on TV or would just use his Heavenly powers,

Jackie didn't know.

Phyllis had tried to dissuade Jackie from coming, but he brushed aside her concerns about possible danger. Ever since Murdoch revealed his true identity, Jackie had ached to witness the moment the demon would be brought low. He couldn't forget how Murdoch gambled with Marie's life by delivering her into the hands of a disturbed killer. Every time they kissed, he remembered how close he'd come to losing her. Sometimes the ferocity of his embrace threatened to choke the air from her. Since Jackie had jettisoned his pursuit of public affection, their relationship had flourished. He'd moved in, tip-toeing around her son at first until he realized that the mature youngster was just happy his mum had found someone. The gorgeous music they were writing together, soon to be unveiled at the Dublin Castle, drew them ever closer as their love found expression in the way their voices meshed.

His suspicion that Murdoch would attempt a public rehabilitation of Gareth in the December season finale only strengthened in the long months they had to wait before striking. At first, the media coverage had been of the predictable serial killer kind. The papers wheeled out everybody who'd known Gareth, from his school teachers to his neighbours, to claim retrospectively they'd always thought he had 'evil eyes'. Then Murdoch launched his media blitz, portraying Gareth as just as much a victim as the people he'd killed. His life story was serialized in *Celeb!*, playing up on the loneliness, the unfulfilled dreams, the death of his mother and the trauma of his audition. Murdoch whipped out Cynthia Deckhart, who was signed up to Stardust and had probably been told to play nice or be dropped, to write of the forgiveness she was prepared to offer. Even Jackie felt nothing but pity for Gareth. He knew better than anybody the sad loner had been manipulated into carrying out the atrocities.

Murdoch's secondary tactic seemed to be to hog all the blame. He displayed unprecedented humility, apologizing left, right and centre and presenting himself as a reformed man who'd made a mistake with tragic consequences. All the way through the early rounds of *Icon*, Murdoch had displayed a softer side to his personality—praising rather than criticizing, letting bad acts down gently and engineering close-ups that caught him staring off into the distance, his eyes filled with pain and remorse. The public bought into the reinvention of a penitent man scarred by the consequences of a few unthinking words. When Jackie eavesdropped on the tube, he increasingly heard people talking about how refreshing it was to see Murdoch display this human fallibility.

Through it all ran a sense of collective guilt, driven by a slew of commentators who pointed out that the public hunger for rubbernecking had fuelled the machine that chewed Gareth up and spat him out. No doubt Murdoch planted this seed as well. Britain was desperate to forgive Gareth, and in doing so forgive itself. And once that cathartic process was over, everybody could go back to behaving exactly the same way.

With the stage set, hints had been dropped in the media about a 'very special guest' on the finale. They cited 'sources close to Murdoch' and never named the guest, although there was little doubt in anybody's mind as to who it would be. How Murdoch would swing getting a guy who was locked away in Broadmoor Hospital, deemed unfit to plead, to appear on the show was another matter. Then again, Murdoch was a demon. Virtually the entire nation would be tuned in to the show, boosting the ratings to levels never seen before.

Jackie's inside knowledge made the whole ploy seem so transparent, yet he could do nothing but wait. How Phyllis had controlled herself, he didn't know. Every time he met her, all she could talk about was how much she would love to rip Murdoch's head off and mount it on her office wall beside Jackie's gold disc, which had regained pride of place. Her swearing grew even more colourful and frequent, and he often found her sitting in the office throwing darts at a blown-up image of Murdoch, embellished with horns and a tail in red pen. Yet she'd stuck to the plan, somehow holding her rage in check to deliver the killer blow.

As the *Icon* theme tune struck up, Jackie shrunk down in his seat. He'd been sporting a goatee beard for a week, grown under the pretext of Movember, and wore thick-framed glasses with clear lenses. He didn't want to give Murdoch even the slightest opportunity to recognize him—at least until the moment of his defeat, when Jackie planned to make sure he knew exactly who'd dumped him in the shit.

The crowd followed the cues upon Murmur's appearance, their claps, cheers and whistles fed through the speakers to ensure a resounding welcoming din. He put his hands behind his back and stood motionless as lights flashed and bouquets of red pyrotechnics sprang up around the stage. The huge iron letters of the *Icon* brand spat out red sparks that fizzled out before they set fire to anything. He could sense the electric expectation, further enhanced by the fact that he was onstage himself instead of letting the presenter get the show on the road. After the theme tune died, the hubbub continued until he held up one hand. At the same time, two assistants flashed cue cards. The crowd fell silent.

'Ladies and Gentlemen, welcome to the finale of this season's *Icon*,' he said. 'We have an unbelievable show lined up for you on this, the night you get to choose who will emerge triumphant from the wonderful acts who have made it thus far.'

He brought his arms out. From the wings on either side ran the finalists, fresh-faced, clean-cut and oh-so-dreary. One of the teenage members of the boy band T-Dreamz got a little carried away and overran his allotted spot on the stage, almost putting himself between Murmur and the camera. Murmur stepped forward and pinged an eyebrow upwards. The boy, chastened, shuffled off to the side.

'As you may have gathered, we have an extraordinary guest performance in store this evening,' Murmur said. 'Let me assure you, this will be a night none of us will ever forget. But first, on with the show.'

Murmur took his seat at the judges' table. As the show commenced, all he could think about was the impending big moment. The acts were strangely muted and the audience response half-hearted. Everybody knew that this was just an aperitif. After what felt like decades, the last of the finalists took a bow and departed. Murmur suppressed the jittery heat rippling below his skin and took to the stage as the lights dimmed to the appointed sombre level.

'Ladies and Gentlemen, you all know the tragic story of the marvellous talents who lost their lives this year, and the equally tragic story of the man who ended them. I know it is easy to hate Gareth for what he did, but I stand here before you asking you to think again. If anybody bears responsibility for what happened then it is me. At a time when he needed kindness, I showed him only cruelty and unhinged his mind with my barbarity. Gareth was little more than a gun. I inadvertently pulled the trigger.'

He paused, reaching for the glass of water on the table set out for him. He dipped his fingers into the glass as he lifted it for a sip, and then ran his hand over his eyes as though overcome by emotion. When he took it away, water glistened on his cheeks. He waited long enough for the cameras to zoom in.

'I can't take back what I did,' he said, allowing his voice to break a little. 'All I can do is stand before you today, humbled, and ask for your forgiveness.'

He'd considered having cue cards saying 'Forgive' held up at this point, but decided that would have been a bit much. Instead, he'd contented himself with setting up his minions to get the ball rolling. Sure enough, after the first forgiving shouts from his plants, the crowd joined in. All the months of recasting himself and Gareth in a sympathetic light, while hinting at the responsibility each individual bore, had set the stage beautifully. Their voices soughed down to the stage like the whisper of prayers.

Murmur bowed his head, his shoulders heaving from the strain of holding back a smile rather than the wracking sobs of grief and relief they would be taken for. When he had himself under control, he raised his head. 'Thank you. I can't begin to tell you how much that has eased my pain. But there is one other person whose forgiveness I must beg.'

The huge screen showing Murmur's face flipped to a video feed, direct from Gareth's room at Broadmoor. Even though everyone had known it was coming, a collective intake of breath hissed through the crowd. Gareth's mullet had grown back, and the make-up artists had done their job, bringing some kind of life and definition to his flaccid face. For the first time since Murmur had known him, Gareth looked at ease. Murmur knew this was down to both the tens of millions of eyes staring at him in wonder and the tattoo on the small of his back, which was a hodgepodge of Sumerian Cuneiform symbols inexpertly etched by Gergaroth, done up like a B-movie wizard in robes and pendants hired from a fancy dress shop, before the police arrived. Murmur had told Gareth that he would publicly deny that the tattoo was magical, but that he should hold nothing back from the police. In order for the public to forgive him, they must believe he was insane, he'd explained. He only made one minor change to Gareth's memory, adding in a fake recollection of calling Murdoch to plead for his help to stop the killing.

Murmur waited, allowing the full impact to sink in for the audience, both in the studio and at home. He'd had to pull a lot of strings to arrange for the video appearance. Fortunately he had many strings at his disposal, each one attached to a minion he'd recently placed high within the government and criminal system. Gareth still believed that celebrities didn't have to answer to the laws of mere mortals and that he would be freed. He didn't understand that there were limits to what even Murmur could do. Gareth would enjoy this one brief taste of fame. They would never let him out.

When he was sure that people had digested what they were seeing, Murmur raised his head and got straight to the point. 'Gareth, I am sorry. Can you forgive me?'

For one horrible second, Murmur thought Gareth was about to smile—something he'd been forbidden from doing—but he contained it and nodded solemnly.

'I forgive you. And I apologize to everyone, from the families of those who died to the entire nation, for the acts I carried out. I was mentally ill. I never meant to kill anybody, but what I did was still wrong in every way imaginable.'

Murmur turned back to face the spellbound audience. 'This man has been brave enough to face up to what he did. What do you think, Britain, can we forgive him?'

This time his minions didn't have to lead the way in the misty-eyed 'Yes' that followed, a word Murmur could almost hear echoed across the country.

'Thank you,' Gareth said, lowering his head.

Murmur interlocked his fingers, aping an aspect of prayer. 'We can't bring back those who lost their lives. But we can honour their memory in the way they would have wanted and carry on the charitable work they all engaged in. Gareth has agreed to sing *Hallelujah*, the song that started it all, to pay tribute. The single will be released on December 18, with all proceeds going to charities chosen by the victims' families. I can only hope that some good may yet come from this awful tragedy.' He swept his arm towards the screen. 'And now, I give you Gareth Jones.'

The room dimmed further until the only light came from Gareth's shining face, so childlike and peaceful that nobody could see any malice continued therein. The band struck up the sweeping, ringing chords and Gareth began to sing. Murmur had ensured that Gareth received just enough coaching to stay vaguely in tune, but not even Auto-Tune could have done anything to conceal the cracked, grating voice. Yet the all-too-obvious imperfections lent the song the character of being sung by somebody who could barely contain his sorrow. Murmur looked at the rapt expressions of the front row and knew he was seeing a snapshot of Britain's public. Here they were, approving of a man who'd killed three times, a man who was the worst singer ever to appear on *Icon*. It was the ultimate corruption of music. Forget Buddy

Holly. This was the real day the music died. Even the little voice that had been chiding him for allowing such a beautiful song to be defiled fell silent as he floated in the warm waters of success.

When the song finished, the applause was deafening. Murmur, remaining in his posture of humility, battled hard to suppress the grin that attempted to bubble up around his lips. As the applause grew louder, a woman stood up at the back of the crowd, and began to chant his name. He hadn't arranged this, nor had he expected it. When his minions joined in, the rest of the crowd followed. Soon it became a thunderous chorus. As he spread his arms to soak up every inch of the adulation, the chant grew faster and the emphasis appeared to change subtly. Before he knew it all he could hear was his real name: 'MURrayMURdoch, MURrayMURdoch, MURMUR, MURMUR...'

He closed his eyes, imagining himself promenading through Hell at Satan's side. A mass of low-borns thronged the side of the road as it wended past the fire pits. The ticker tape they threw flamed up in the heat so that sinuous fiery snakes appeared to be writhing in the air around him. The hordes of low-borns roared his name, surging against the barriers to get closer to the demon who'd emancipated them, the demon who was now even more famous than Lucifer. Murmur's face erupted into a roiling conflagration of joy.

He snapped out of the fantasy as the chanting gave way to panicked screams. Opening his eyes to the studio, he saw people half-out of their seats, hands clasped over their mouths in horror. A human assistant was running at him from the side of the stage, fire extinguisher in hand. That was the moment he realized his face really was on fire.

'It's just a special effect,' he said.

He strode towards the audience, intending to mollify them somehow. The front row reeled back in panic and his fellow judges scrabbled away from him. He looked down as the molten globs of flesh sliding from his face splattered his shoes like candle wax.

'This is really bad,' Murmur said, just as a stream of foam smacked him full in the face.

He lost control completely then; his cells scattered apart and rushed together again in his demon form, wings, teeth and all. He stumbled backwards, the claws that had burst from his expensive shoes scrabbling for purchase, and landed on his behind. His Armani suit was completely ruined. Those who hadn't started screaming yet found their voices as he got to his feet and spread his wings. The foam beard he wore probably detracted somewhat from his evil aura, but it was still enough to spark a stampede for the exit. The assistant who'd tried to put the fire out wasted no time in joining it.

'Block the exits!' Murmur yelled, spitting foam into the air.

Gergaroth and Tarsis, who'd come sprinting onto the stage, were the first of his demon crew to react. They blinked out of existence, swiftly followed by the others. As the crowd thinned, Murmur saw that a small group remained, amongst them the woman who'd begun the chant. It took him a few seconds to realize the goateed man standing next to her was Jackie Thunder.

'Bit late for that,' the woman said.

Murmur said nothing for a moment, reaching out with his mind to the minions now marshalling the crowds. The exits were secure, and the audience stood calmly under the collective thrall of his demons. The ban he'd placed on all mobile phones to prevent anybody taking unauthorized pictures or video ensured nobody would be texting or calling out.

He walked to the edge of the stage and addressed Jackie. 'So you did talk. Bad move, my friend.'

'He's under my protection,' the woman said.

'And who might you be?'

'I go by the name of Phyllis down here.'

Murmur realized then who she was: Jackie's manager, a horribly aggressive woman he knew only by repute. She kicked off her shoes and yanked her dress over her head. She had no underwear on. Murmur was momentarily confused, wondering how getting her kit off was supposed to scare him. Then she shimmered and, in an instant, her true form was revealed.

'But you can call me Ananchel,' she said.

It was the first time Murmur had seen an angel in the flesh. He wasn't too impressed. In the religious texts, and his imaginings, angels were powerful, haughty and graceful creatures—often depicted astride horses, flaming swords held aloft and eyes glowing with righteous fury. Sure, this angel was all very white and shiny, but that was a cheap trick anybody could pull off with some fluorescent paint and strategically placed fairy lights. Underneath the glamour, her body looked slim, weak even. Even her folded wings looked more sparrow than eagle. The fire he'd been trying to suppress intensified around his lips. He could totally take her.

'At last,' he said. 'Finally grown enough spine to reveal yourself, have you? I knew you lot were floating about out of sight, like turds just around the u-bend.'

'You can talk, you scaly bell end. You've spent decades skulking up here in that skin. But now everybody knows what you really are. I mean, apart from an egregious cunt, which we all knew. Pride always was my favourite of the deadly sins.'

Murmur frowned, his delight at finally having the confrontation he'd longed for dipping briefly. She was right, damn her. His desire to gain credit for his actions, manifested in revealing himself to Jackie, had brought him to the brink of disaster. It was even more stupid when he thought of all the times he'd shaken his head in wonder at the way pride had brought humans low. Even worse, Heaven probably hadn't been onto him at all. The avatars turned up when Jackie was threatened, and now it turned out his manager was an angel. She was only protecting Jackie, yet her intervention had prompted him to reveal himself. Still, he would have time to beat himself up later for almost destroying fifty years of work. For now he needed to deal with this situation, which was nowhere near as bad as the angel thought.

'I wouldn't be too sure about that,' he said.

'The entire nation just saw you turn into a demon on live television. Are you going to claim it was just showbiz? A theatrical dance number to liven up your boring show?'

Murmur laughed. 'Oh, dear. You really don't understand television, do you? Nobody does live anymore, not since all those dismal youth presenters kept effing and jeffing in the nineties. We run a transmission delay. As soon as my face flamed up, the cameras were cut. The worst thing the public is going to see is short break. We'll put it down to a technical gremlin. And all those people out there will have their memories wiped.'

'You're lying,' the angel said.

'Then why am I not panicking? Gareth's performance has been transmitted across the nation, nothing else. When the single comes out, they'll buy it in their millions. *Icon* is going to be back where it belongs … at Christmas Number One.'

'Hold on, you made that poor lunatic kill three people just to engineer Christmas Number One?' Jackie said.

'This isn't just any Christmas hit, Jackie. It's the antithesis of everything music stands for. It proves once and for all that humanity cannot be saved. I can almost feel the souls withering.' He addressed Ananchel, whose aura had dialled up to white-hot intensity. 'Face it, love. You've lost.'

The angel leapt into the aisle and stalked to the front of the stage, wings unfolding further to brush against the seat backs with a whispery tone. Suddenly they didn't look so small. A smile blazed on her lips as she approached. 'You've got a big fucking mouth, demon. But you're neglecting one thing. I can still kick your teeth down your throat.'

The angel turned into an arrow of white light streaking through the air. Murmur didn't even have time to teleport out of the way, catching the full force of the assault in the chest and sliding across the stage. Her body, incredibly heavy despite its slimness, pinned him down and her blurring fists hammered into his face. He bucked and thrashed, trying to free his arms to fight back. His entire skull was burning, now with fear rather than elation. Here was the glorious battle with the forces of Heaven he'd long dreamed of. Now he was actually in it, he found he was singularly unprepared. His only chance lay in calling back his minions, so he sent out a mental distress signal, and waited for his boys to save him.

Jackie watched Phyllis pummel Murmur, her body a white blob of light above a pair of thrashing legs. The warrior angel was finally unleashed and the demon had no chance in the face of thousands of years of pent-up frustration. Jackie didn't know if Murmur could be killed, but he certainly hoped so. Coming to the finale and showing his hand had been a mistake. The only way to be sure Marie wouldn't suffer from it was for Phyllis to put the demon out of action permanently.

Hendrix and the others were edging towards the stage, the guitarist in particular wearing a look of grim satisfaction at the brutal beating the man who'd killed him was suffering. Jackie followed, all too aware of his isolated position near the exit. He was standing just beneath the judges' table, the grunts and thuds sickeningly audible, when everything changed.

Three demons popped into existence above Phyllis and dragged her off. Another two appeared behind Hendrix, who leapt onto the stage and snatched up a guitar. He clubbed Murmur, who was groggily trying to rise to his feet, across the head with the instrument before the two demons caught up with him and began tearing at him with their claws. Hendrix ignored the slashes, which seemed to pass right through his body, and set about his attackers with the guitar, neck grasped in both hands. They fell back under his torrent of blows.

The trio of demons was meanwhile struggling to contain Phyllis. She beat her wings and rose in the air, taking all three with her, and began to spin. Faster and faster she rotated, until one of the demons sloughed off and walloped the huge *Icon* sign, birthing a shower of sparks. The whirlwind of angel and demons spun away as the sign first creaked, and then toppled. It narrowly missed Murmur, who again was wobbling to his feet.

Murmur's face was battered, yet as Jackie watched his wounds began to heal. He coughed up a huge glob of red phlegm, which split into five avatars that scampered up Hendrix's legs to claw at his face and pull his hair. The second attack was enough to distract the guitarist and the demons he'd been warding off leapt on him. Entwistle, Joplin, Moon and Strummer were all engaged with other demons who'd entered the fray. Phyllis, momentarily free, spat out her own avatars. The other demons followed suit, and soon the stage was swarming with what looked bizarrely like little Jelly Babies wrestling, biting and kicking each other.

For all the noise and fury, nobody seemed to be taking any real damage. It felt like a bar brawl in an old movie, where the antagonists could club each other over the head with bottles for half an hour without causing even the slightest contusion. Jackie, who suspected he wouldn't be quite so immune, sidled towards the fire exit. He'd almost made it when Murmur caught sight of him.

'Not so fast, Jackie!' the demon shouted.

Murmur held up his right arm, palm outwards. The hand began to glow red, then burst into flames that condensed into a ball. Jackie sensed the projectile coming rather than saw it, and dived for the floor. He was still in the air when the fireball whistled just over his head and connected with the front row. Floor, wall and ceiling swapped places as the concussive impact threw him up and into a somersault. He crashed down on his back, all the air knocked out of him. He felt no pain as of yet, the shock cutting off the connection between his nerve endings and brain, but he knew it would arrive soon enough. Somehow he drew enough breath to rise to his hands and knees and crawl for the fire exit. He got less than two feet before a pair of shiny leather shoes studded with demon claws thumped to the floor in front of his nose. He looked up groggily to see Murmur above him, jagged yellow teeth protruding from the middle of a ring of fire.

'You should've kept your mouth shut,' Murmur said.

Another crackling, spitting fireball began to grow in the demon's hand. From this range, there would be no missing. Jackie had already experienced near-death, so this time there was no epiphany—only the weak-legged surety that he was about to die. He closed his eyes and hoped it would be quick. Instead of a fireball came a whoosh of air and a grunt. He opened one eye to see Murmur splayed on the ground and Phyllis looming over him. She held her arm aloft, muttering something under her breath. In her hand appeared a long sword, glittering and shimmering with white fire. Now Murmur backed away, his gaze never leaving the weapon. Phyllis brought both hands onto the hilt of the sword and pulled it back over her right shoulder, her intention to swipe Murmur's head from his shoulders clear.

'Ananchel!' a voice boomed.

Phyllis looked over her shoulder. Even in her ethereal angel face, Jackie could detect bloodlust. He followed her gaze to the source of the voice. A bank of mist, a white light pulsating in its centre, had formed near the ceiling. The cloud drifted towards them, descending until it touched the ground and coalesced into God in his Robert Plant form.

'Put the sword down,' God said, this time in a normal voice. 'If you kill him, the truce is violated.'

'I would say it has already been violated,' another voice said.

The demon who'd spoken was stooped and moving slowly, yet his eyes burned with an internal fire that seemed to suck all of the oxygen from the room. Jackie was pretty sure he hadn't been there a second ago.

'Satan,' God said. 'It has been a long time.'

Sure, Jackie thought. *Satan. Why the fuck not? Who's next? Santa? The Tooth Fairy?*

Satan stopped a short step away from God. He shuffled his feet and his arms came up from his sides as his eyes dulled down to purple. For a moment it looked as though he was going to reach out and hug the supreme creator. Instead he folded his arms and his eyes returned to fiery globes.

'What is going on here?' he said.

'I could ask you the same question,' God said. 'You have been up to no good, it seems.'

'You created me. If you are pointing any fingers, you would do well to point them at yourself.'

'Let us not have that argument again. The simple fact is you have been meddling in human history when you are not supposed to.'

'And you have not?'

God shot a glance at Phyllis, who still held the sword aloft. 'What are we going to do about this situation?'

'She started it!' Murmur said.

'And I'll bloody well finish it too,' Phyllis said, waving the sword.

God pointed a finger. The sword shimmered and vanished. Phyllis, deprived of her weapon, delivered Murmur a sneaky kick when God turned back to Satan.

'She broke the truce when she attacked Murmur,' Satan said. 'You know what that means.'

'Are you ready for another war? You must remember the trouncing you took the last time.'

Satan blinked three times in rapid succession, but otherwise held his face impassive. 'If it is to be war, we shall not shy away. You know that.'

'So, it is war then?'

'If you wish it so.'

'I asked you first.'

'Oh,' Satan said.

The leaders of the opposing forces stared at each other. Jackie watched them closely. For all their big talk, he got the impression that war was the last thing either one wanted. He was with them on that score. This small fight had created chaos in the studio. If they brought a large-scale battle to Earth, the result could only be devastation. Surprisingly, and much to Jackie's relief, God blinked first.

'There is another way,' God said. 'A battle of the champions between the two who started this.'

'Yes!' Phyllis said. 'I'll slice him up like the old ham he is.'

Satan shot a sideways glance at Murmur, who still cowered at Phyllis's feet. Even though Jackie's expertise in demon expressions was somewhat lacking, the dilated pupils and quivering lip told him exactly what Murmur thought of that suggestion. Fortunately for the demon, Satan thought much the same thing.

'I do not think so,' he said.

God spread his hands in acquiescence. 'So let us settle it with music. I suggest a battle of the bands.'

With his gaze transferred to the collection of dead musicians, Satan growled and shook his head. The stand-off looked like it was about to edge back to war. Perhaps it was the proximity of the miraculous, or perhaps his creativity had finally been unleashed once more after decades of hibernation, but Jackie had an idea. It was a bad idea, one that would most likely fail, but it seemed better than the alternative.

'I have a suggestion,' he said. The leaders of Heaven and Hell looked at him, their combined gazes making his voice wobble as he continued. 'Murmur here thinks he can get Gareth to number one with that cover version. I'm willing to bet he's wrong.'

'Go on,' God said.

'I suggest a different battle of champions. Gareth's cover version versus a song we nominate. If Gareth wins, then Heaven backs off and lets *Icon* continue. If we win, Murmur has to close down *Icon* and stop interfering.'

Murmur climbed to his feet and edged around Phyllis to stand by Satan. 'Take the challenge, my Lord.'

Phyllis, who saw God was about to open his mouth, hurried over and led him and Jackie away by the arm. 'Are you mental?' she said. 'His grip on the charts is so tight you can see its camel toe.'

'Hush, Ananchel,' God said. 'What are you thinking, Jackie?'

'They're putting out their version of *Hallelujah*. I think we should campaign for people to buy the best cover there is: Jeff Buckley's.'

'It is a very good song,' God said.

'Yes, but how would we get people to buy it?' Phyllis said.

'You're the one who said you guys ran half of the social media and independent music press. So use it. Twitter. Facebook. You Tube. Myspace. Google Plus. Tumblr. Blogs. Pitchfork. The full bhoona. People were sick of *Icon* before all this happened. Maybe all we have to do is remind them, sell Buckley as an antidote to this manufactured tosh.'

'Come on, you saw the reaction tonight,' Phyllis said. 'We don't stand a chance.'

Jackie knew she was right, but he pressed on, still mindful that this challenge may be the last chance to ward off conflict. 'Do you believe humanity is fundamentally good?'

Phyllis answered with a curled lip, but God didn't hesitate. 'Yes.'

'Then let's prove it. Consider it the ultimate test of free will. If we get Buckley to number one, it could be the spark that gets everyone back into good music.'

'And if it doesn't?'

'Then you keep doing what you're doing and hope it takes root. The worst-case scenario is that you come out if it even, whereas for them it's win or bust. Just look at them. They're so convinced they're going to win. Don't you think proving Murmur wrong will be a lot more satisfying than chopping his head off?'

'No,' Phyllis said, arms crossed.

God, who'd been twiddling his chest hair, nodded. 'You are wise, Jackie Thunder. Humanity must be allowed to choose which path to follow. We shall take the challenge.'

Phyllis let loose a long stream of swear words without even bothering to try and create a meaningful sentence, but followed when God walked back to where Murmur and Satan stood side-by-side, identical fiery smirks creasing their lips.

'We accept the challenge,' God said.

'As do we,' Satan said.

'Excellent,' God said. 'Let us reconvene here when it is decided.' He looked around the stage. The curtains were burning above the wrecked *Icon* sign and the floor was littered with the debris of the makeshift weapons the warring factions had put to use. 'And good luck tidying up.'

Murmur surveyed the wreckage of the studio after God and his crew had teleported away. The minions had been sent off to wipe the memories of the audience and non-demon members of the production team, and plant recollections of an electrical fire, but there was no way they could salvage the rest of the evening's show. Not that it mattered. They could reschedule for the next Saturday, and the main task of rehabilitating Gareth and announcing the release of his single had been completed.

Now that he was calmer, Murmur realized that his fury at Jackie had been misplaced. He'd been angry at himself and smarting at the beating he'd just taken. In actual fact, he should probably thank the singer for blabbing to Heaven and bringing God to the party. They'd been foolish enough to suggest a duel they could never win. Jackie had handed him Heaven's head on a silver platter.

'How did they uncover you?' Satan said.

Murmur walked off and made a show of inspecting the ruined *Icon* sign. 'I've no idea,' he said. 'Perhaps there's a spy in our ranks. You know Lucifer never liked me, and he has been looking to start a war. This almost did it. He probably had one of his minions tell Heaven.'

Two little sparks of fire appeared on the end of Satan's horns. 'I shall deal with him this evening. You have done well, Murmur. If we win, this will put Heaven firmly in its place. Your story will be an example to every demon under my command.'

'Oh, we'll win, Sir,' he said, and turned his back so his grin could not be seen. It seemed Lucifer wouldn't be a problem for much longer.

27

Mince pies, bottles of sparkling wine and scraps of Santa wrapping paper littered Phyllis's desk, which obscured much of a ratty plastic Christmas tree dug out from the bowels of a cardboard box. Above a string of lights, on which half the bulbs sullenly refused to twinkle, perched an angel that Jackie had modified by sticking a photo of Phyllis across its face and gluing on a small plastic sword. It sagged to one side, clinging onto the thin wire that crowned the tree. It was hardly the cheeriest of festive scenes, but then again there was little to be cheerful about. Jackie and Phyllis were huddled up on the love seat, half watching *Kung Fu Panda* as they waited for the *Top of the Pops* Christmas Special they hoped would unveil a seasonal miracle. The one being who could have wrought that miracle still hadn't shown up. He was springing a surprise birthday lunch on Jesus, which made Jackie wonder how engaged he was in their doomed campaign.

The day after the *Icon* fiasco, Phyllis had called in all of her angelic cohorts for a crisis meeting and instructed them on what needed done. They launched a Facebook page, ran dozens of articles and blogs, tweeted incessantly and arranged for interviews in every publication they controlled or could persuade to listen to them. Jackie bombarded the 100,000 Twitter followers his escapades had brought him with links to Jeff Buckley's version, exhorting them to buy it instead of Gareth's. That was as far as he was prepared to go. Both he and Marie had been assigned angelic bodyguards dispatched from Heaven's warrior caste, and he'd seen just how ineffectual Murmur was in a fight, but all the same he worried that prodding the demon too hard might goad him into living up to his threat to take Marie's soul.

At first, it looked promising. The campaign received support from the noisy minority who'd never liked *Icon*, as well as many respected musicians. In the social media, left-wing press and independent music blog bubble, it was easy to imagine they could pull it off. Yet Jackie knew that even Twitter, trumpeted as the tool that gave voice to the masses, was only representative of a small section of the population and that the impassioned voices of the journalists and bloggers didn't reach those who would buy Gareth's records. The tone of the campaign was wrong too, Jackie felt, full of the kind of high-minded preachy pronouncements that the average Brit couldn't give a toss about. To compound it all, they started advocating too early to concentrate sales in the final week, when they would really need them. Then again, they'd had no choice. Had they waited until the same day as Gareth's single went on sale, they would never have been able to build up enough momentum. So, when the first figures came out with ten days left until Christmas, Buckley sat at number three, still a few hundred thousand sales off the top spot.

Anyway, it was a moot point. Even before Gareth's record was released, Jackie could see it would be like *50 Shades of Grey*: panned by the critics, loved and purchased in its millions by the public. The months Murdoch had spent recasting himself and Gareth created just the right mood, particularly with a bout of Christmas-induced soppiness in the post. Phyllis's intervention had made it even worse. The drama of having the show cut out just after Gareth sang only swelled media attention and gave Murdoch the chance to re-run the whole show to its conclusion the next week, replaying Gareth's song at the break. Murdoch was also savvy enough to delay the release of the *Icon* winner's single until January to avoid splitting sales. The end result was that when Gareth's record came out, it began shifting in massive numbers.

They were going to lose.

Jackie at least had something to look forward to. Marie was in Barbados visiting her family and he'd arranged to join her on Boxing Day, saying he should spend Christmas Day with his mum. He still hadn't told her anything of the insane world he'd been plunged into or the danger she could still face. He wanted to, but couldn't think of how he would bring the subject up without making himself seem like a nutter and scuppering his plans for their future together. Hidden at the bottom of his already packed suitcase was a modest engagement ring, which he intended to present at a suitably romantic moment on the island. Had he kept the proceeds from his cover of *Somebody's Watching Me*, he could have splashed out on something more extravagant, but every time a royalty cheque came in, he donated it to Save the Children.

As they awaited the final confirmation of the defeat, Jackie tried to cling to the slender comfort that he'd averted a full-scale war and probably saved millions of lives in the process. All he could think about was that he'd handed that despicable prick Murdoch victory and made Phyllis utterly miserable. The Marks and Spencer's premium mince pies he'd brought were part of his attempt to cheer her up and thus assuage his guilt. A deep sigh prompted him to reach for the box again, all too aware he was copying Agnes's tactic of using sweet delights to treat ailments of the soul.

'Another mince pie?'

Phyllis looked at him out of the corner of her eye. 'Is it poisoned?'

'I'm afraid not.'

'Then I'll have more booze.'

Jackie poured two cups and re-joined Phyllis in the silent vigil.

Murmur traced a circular trail in the soft shag of his wool carpet, the chatter of the television silent for once, as he awaited the imminent arrival of Satan. At the end of each circuit, he eyed the bottle of Dalmore Astrum 40-Year-Old Highland Whisky he planned to crack as soon as the announcement was made on *Top of the Pops*, wondering if he could get away with a cheeky early snifter. After all, his supposed greatest moment was swift approaching. They didn't even have to cheat to make it happen, although Murmur had indulged in a little jiggery-pokery to satisfy Satan's desire for some underhand dealings, dishing out a wad of cash to his minions to buy up copies of Gareth's single.

While he wanted to see Ananchel's face pucker in on itself as she was forced to acknowledge her defeat, the toll of the victory bell would have a hollow ring. Just as his efficiency as a clerk had kept him chained to his desk, it seemed his triumph as Murdoch would keep *Icon* alive. After the night in the studio, he'd begun dropping hints about wanting to retire, but Satan had ignored them. He wanted Murmur to finish the job and kill good music forever. Britain was effectively conquered, meaning much of the rest of the world was also affected given the small island's disproportionate influence, but *Icon* had yet to reach the same giddy heights in the US. That would at least be a challenge, but it was one he didn't think he could face.

He stopped circling and put Gareth's song on in an attempt to remind himself of just how astonishing his achievement had been. He lasted thirty seconds before he had to silence the appalling din. To cleanse his palate, he scrolled through his song list to *Grace* and put Buckley's version on instead. The guitar rang out like a harp beneath Buckley's pure and emotional voice and that familiar mix of pleasure and pain ignited in Murmur. The lyrics suggested forces outside human understanding, rich emotions reserved for the privileged few and the deep sorrow of loss, which only reinforced the power of love. It was a testament to the awfulness of Gareth's voice that this poignancy had been killed in his version.

He was so engrossed in the song that it took him a good minute to notice the air had become charged with an unfathomable sorrow. He swivelled and beheld Satan, his mouth parted to reveal his chipped fangs. Deep purple light swirled in his eyes. Murmur reached for the remote to turn the song off, but something in the way Satan seemed transfixed stopped him. Little puffs of steam began to rise from Satan's cheeks. Murmur had never seen a demon cry, didn't even know it was possible, but he knew they were tears, evaporating on the heat of Satan's face the moment they left his eyes. Murmur sat still, barely able to believe what he was seeing.

When the song ended, he waited for the most powerful demon in history to stop weeping like a child who'd lost his mum in a shopping mall. But as the accordion intro to *Lover You Should've Come Over* swelled, Satan cried on. Murmur could barely breathe in the air that had become as oppressive as that of a summer's day before a thunderstorm. Satan's eyes deepened in colour, the purple becoming the dark blue of the depths of the ocean as the mournful lyrics to a lost lover drifted through the room. Satan lifted his head to the sky and roared, setting the glasses on the coffee table jingling. The light in his eyes deepened and the bellow grew in volume and intensity, matching Buckley's rising pitch as the song built to a crescendo. Car alarms on the street bleated in response. Murmur looked away, but he could not escape the sounds, images and feelings that began beaming into his head.

He saw Satan in the moment before The Fall—a lithe, sinuous angel standing erect, too proud to prostrate himself at the feet of an impassive God and ask for forgiveness. An impossibly beautiful melody plucked on a harp floated through the gentle mist that swirled around them. Then the ground opened up beneath Satan's feet and he accelerated downwards, his eyes straining for one last glimpse of the blessed land he'd been banished from. As he fell, his body withered and changed: his feathered wings ripped free to float above him; new leathery wings, still too feeble to bear his weight, began to form in their place; scales rippled across his once perfect body; horns, teeth and claws burst bloody from his flesh. Satan, too late, reached up with one pleading hand as the agonizing transformation seized him. The last thing he heard before the searing light pouring from the hole from which he'd fallen faded was the mournful ring of the harp. Then there was only darkness, the scouring whistle of the wind and a pain so heavy it carried him downward ever faster into the pit.

The vision died, leaving Murmur on his knees and clutching at his body where he could still feel his flesh rending from the transformation. Now he understood. He'd been blinded by Satan's reputation as the epitome of all evil and darkness, unable to read the signs that had been there all along. He'd been wrong about Satan hating God. Satan had loved him then, and loved him still. Music reminded Satan of what he'd lost and could never regain, and so he'd wrapped himself in the cold comfort of silence. Satan transmitted this anguish to those who served beneath him, which was why music pricked so sharply at the demon soul. Now Satan's conflicting desires to destroy humanity and be more like them made perfect sense. He was no more than a spurned lover, seeking both to harm and become the species who now commanded the love he craved. Murmur's whole mission on Earth, every single thing that Hell did to corrupt humanity, stemmed from Satan's jealous hurt.

Murmur, reeling from this revelation, crawled over to the hi-fi and switched it off. Only then did he manage to get his feet beneath him and rise.

'It's so beautiful,' Satan said, his voice wavering.

'I know.'

The puffs kept coming, drifting up to dissipate and add to the heaviness of the air. It was all Murmur could do to keep from breaking down and weeping himself as Satan's torment radiated outward.

'Humans don't deserve this music,' Satan said.

Murmur thought of his possible futures. He could remain on Earth, doomed to destroy the one thing he loved above all else and become just as damaged as Satan. He could return to Hell as a hero, but have to face living in a soulless void where no guitar would ever ring out. Or he could tell Satan how he really felt and hope for the best.

'No. But we do.'

'What do you mean?'

'It doesn't have to be this way. Don't you think you've suffered enough?'

They stared at each other, and Murmur played his last gambit. He opened his mind, holding up the mirror of his knowledge to the Lord of Hell. Satan looked deep within, and his fists curled up. Murmur screwed his eyes shut, half-expecting to be torn apart. The silence lasted as long as one of the *Icon* pauses before a winner was announced. Murmur forced himself to have a peek. Satan shuddered once, and the weight that had accrued infinite bitter mass with the passing of the years lifted. Murmur felt as though he could float in the air without the aid of his wings.

Satan's eyes were a soft rose colour when he stepped close to Murmur and reached out a hand to rest on his shoulder.

'Play them again,' Satan said.

God and Phyllis, each holding one of Jackie's hands, teleported onto the stage at exactly 4pm. The lights were off, and they stood in the gloom, peering out among the rows of empty seats for any sign of life.

'Where are they?' Jackie said.

'They probably want to drag it out,' Phyllis said, her voice flat. 'That's what I'd have done.'

As expected, they'd lost. Badly. While their song reached number two with over a 100,000 downloads, Gareth's version had sold almost a million copies in a week. God, who seemed unconcerned, not to mention half-cut, had tried to console them when he finally turned up just after the announcement. It was a good effort, he'd said, and showed that all hope for humanity was not lost. Phyllis had said nothing, her fingers again curling around the shaft of an imaginary sword.

The air shifted, and suddenly Murmur—in his human form—and Satan were standing five feet away. Phyllis stiffened, but God laid a soothing hand on her forearm.

'You look different,' God said to Satan.

The lights flickered into life, and Jackie saw that God was right. Whereas before Satan had looked like an elderly relative on the verge of being chucked into a retirement home, now he had the air of a perky uncle who tap-danced unasked at family gatherings after having plucked half a dozen glasses of fizzy wine from passing trays.

'We need to talk,' Satan said. 'In private.'

'I thought you'd never ask,' God said.

They strolled away and began to conduct a whispered conversation. Phyllis glared at Murmur. 'Aren't you going to gloat?'

'Should I?'

'Yes, if you want another smack in the kisser.'

To Jackie's surprise, Murmur laughed, fire playing across his cheeks. 'There's no need. It looks like everybody's going to win.'

'What do you mean?'

He raised an enigmatic eyebrow and said nothing.

Jackie looked over to where the devil now had his head on God's shoulder. God was patting his back just below the point where his powerful wings sprouted. If he didn't know better, he would have said the shaking of Satan's shoulders meant he was crying. Jackie, Murmur and Phyllis stood in silence until the clinch broke apart. Jackie was treated to the incongruous sight of a scaly, mighty demon holding the hand of a Robert Plant-lookalike as they walked back.

'That's all sorted then,' God said.

'What's all sorted?' Jackie said in lieu of Phyllis, whose gaping jaw precluded her from speaking.

'You'll figure it out,' Murmur said, clearly enjoying Phyllis's confusion.

'We'll talk soon,' Satan told God. He put his arm around Murmur. 'Are you ready to go home, my friend?'

'Can I bring my music collection?'

'Only if I can borrow from it.'

And with that, they vanished.

God dusted down his palms. 'Well, if he had done that in the first place, we could have saved ourselves a lot of trouble.'

Phyllis, now an alarming shade of puce, shouted, 'What the fuck is going on?'

God shrugged. 'He apologized. I forgave him.'

'Apologized for what?'

'Pretty much everything. Oh, and *Icon* is cancelled.'

'Just like that?'

'Just like that,' God said. 'It seems he accidentally listened to Jeff Buckley and had an epiphany. Never underestimate the power of music.'

Phyllis looked at Jackie, a smile spreading across her face. 'Fuck me. We won after all.'

'Not exactly,' God said. 'Hell's interference was only part of the equation. Much work remains to be done. Still, thanks to Jackie here we have some breathing space.'

'But I didn't do anything,' Jackie said.

'Do you think any of this would have happened if it were not for you?'

'He's right,' Phyllis said. 'We'd never have known what was going on if you hadn't involved yourself.'

Jackie looked at God, who was exuding smugness. He thought back down the months: how his path had crossed with Gareth so many times, how the police had delivered him into Murdoch's arms when they could have used any number of high-profile celebrities without angels as agents to trap Gareth, how the idea for the race to Christmas Number One that seemed to have triggered a sea change in Satan had popped up out of nowhere. He'd been a tool, in every sense of the word. Now he was beginning to wonder if perhaps they all hadn't been tools in a larger game.

'Did you plan all of this?' he said.

'Well, I am omnipotent,' God said with a mysterious smile.

EPILOGUE

Hell's first-ever Minister for Music put his feet up on the desk in his new office, just one level up from Satan's spread in The Central Stalactite, and beamed at the shiny picture frame on the wall, from which his own face looked out at him on the cover of January's edition of *Fire & Brimstone*. The magazine told of his exploits on Earth in exhaustive detail, save for the humiliating pounding Ananchel had handed out, which he'd glossed over in the interview. A dozen copies lay on the coffee table in the adjoining room where his secretary sat. As in a dentist's waiting room, they would remain there for decades for visitors to thumb through. The same magazine was being read voraciously throughout Hell, and Murmur could barely leave his new private stalagmite without being mobbed by low-borns eager to slap his back.

The hi-fi was playing the album Marie and Jackie had just released on a small independent label. It was surprisingly good. It seemed Jackie had a musician buried inside him after all. Murmur was rather glad he hadn't killed him. Since Satan's epiphany, the residual anguish he felt when listening to good music had faded, although enough remained to add a certain spice. He would miss this sting when it disappeared completely, presumably once God and Satan had completed their kiss and make up. Still, it was a small price to pay for the new order that was beginning to emerge.

His ministry, populated exclusively with low-borns, was responsible not just for the dissemination of music, but for educating all demons in the back catalogue of humanity's efforts down the centuries. The programme was still in the planning stages, with roll-out expected within the month. He'd resisted the temptation to go in chronological order, and planned to start Hell off on a diet of Hendrix, Black Sabbath and Led Zeppelin through digital jukeboxes in the bars, radios in every office and free distribution of MP3 players. From there he planned to move forward to indie bands, then jump back-and-forth between blues, funk, punk, classical, country, electronic, rap, hip-hop, folk and pop as he saw fit.

The demon community was still coming to terms with the abrupt change in the stance on music, although the real surprise was yet to be publicly revealed. Heaven and Hell's long cold war was at an end. Background negotiations were going on between God and Satan as to the exact form the new relationship would take, although it had been agreed Hell would continue to fulfil its primary role of punishing sinners under God's preferred carrot-and-stick model. Murmur suspected Hell would become more like a low-security wing, with televisions, meditation and counsellors instead of eyeball gouging and pushing rocks up hills. It would be hard to throw your heart and soul into flaying a screaming being when you were whistling a happy tune.

The effects would take longer to be felt on Earth. After all, the legacy of Hell's meddling would linger on and humanity was more than capable of corrupting itself. *Icon*'s many imitators—from talent shows, to cooking contests to celebrity dance-offs—would continue, even though the original show would not. Murdoch had staged a tearful retirement, saying his troubled conscience would no longer let him continue now that the show was tainted by death, even with the final redemption. He still popped up now and then to show face at a party or Manchester United match, knowing that to disappear completely would prompt investigation. In a few years, he could probably back off on that too. Murdoch was already fading into history.

Murmur didn't know how it would all turn out. Thrown back together after millennia of inflicting petty hurts upon each other, God and Satan still had a lot of issues to work out; they'd been disguising themselves as human and attending weekly couples' counselling at a practice in Harley Street. And on a personal level, Murmur had Lucifer to contend with. Satan hadn't been able to prove that the leak came from Lucifer's camp, which was perfectly understandable since it hadn't. The demon had fallen out of favour nonetheless and knew where to lay the blame, although he couldn't touch Murmur at the moment. The gradual flattening of Hell's society, with low-borns now being given opportunities they could once only dream of, further enraged Lucifer. And, finally, he was hurting over the knowledge there would be no war, as were many of the more aggressive demons. Murmur suspected there were those on Heaven's side who would also be a tad miffed at not being able to exercise their martial training. As the new order unfolded, there would no doubt be upheavals and alliances ranged against Satan's softening of his position, which could spell trouble further down the line. Still, for the moment at least, Murmur intended to enjoy himself.

Jackie and Marie's album finished and he put his iTunes onto shuffle. Next up came Spiritualized's *Broken Heart*, and he remembered that he had one last loose end to tie up on Earth. He pressed the intercom to tell his secretary he would be going out for a few hours and teleported upstairs.

Life in Broadmoor wasn't so bad for Gareth. When they realized he displayed no violent traits, the staff treated him gently, and the daily routine of meals, therapy and mingling with the other inmates kept him occupied. And of course, he had the tattoo. Its location meant he never got to look at it, but he could feel its powerful heat every waking minute. It served as a constant reminder that he was a star, even though he was never allowed access to the newspapers or the internet. A sympathetic orderly told him the single had gone to number one and his face and name were household currency not just in Britain, but across the world. It was frustrating not to be able to bask directly in the glory, and he still craved physical contact, but just knowing that every minute of the day somebody was listening to his song, watching his video or reading about him kept him visible.

Among the other patients, he enjoyed something of a celebrity status. They repeatedly asked him to tell his story and lay out juicy details of the celebrities he'd encountered. He sang regularly to a rapt audience in the common room, and there was even a groundswell of support for a proper concert—although his doctors were still blocking that particular event. The one thing he really missed was talking to his mum, who hadn't returned since the night of his *Icon* appearance. The psychiatrists kept telling him that her reincarnation had been part of his psychosis. He tried to go along with them, but could tell they knew he still believed her visitations had been real. To accept the version of events that could lead to his eventual release, he would have to admit she was gone forever. That he could not do.

So, when he lifted his head from the pillow to see her standing in his cell, he clapped his hands and leapt from the bed to run to her. It was the first time she'd appeared to him physically since she'd died. She stroked his head as he whooped in huge lungfuls of her scent, his muscles melting to butter as she squeezed him tight.

'Didn't I always say you would make it?' she said.

'You were right, Mum. You were always right.'

She pushed him back to arms' length. He drank in her face. There was nothing of the grave about her. She looked exactly as she did in the picture from the back garden: her hair long and curly, her wide green eyes full of love, her mouth softened with a smile. He wanted to hold onto her forever and tried to squirm his way back into her embrace. She held him off.

'I've come to say goodbye,' she said.

Gareth fought even harder to close the distance and cling to her. Just as he'd never disappeared when she held him in her arms, she couldn't vanish if he didn't let go. She was stronger than he remembered, though, and pushed him across the room until the back of his knees hit the bed. He sat down.

'Don't leave me here,' he said.

She stroked the bridge of his nose. He closed his eyes, the urge to press every inch of his body against hers receding.

'My work here is done. I need to move on to the other side.'

'To Heaven?'

'Yes.'

He'd never thought deeply about his mum's reappearance in religious terms, for they hadn't been brought up believing in an afterlife. Now here she stood telling him that Heaven, and by extension Hell, were real. As a killer, there would only be one final destination for Gareth. Yet it wasn't the thought of endless torment that made him swat aside the soothing finger and bury his face in his mum's stomach.

'Then I won't see you.'

His head so close to the portal through which he'd entered the world, he entertained feverish notions about climbing back up inside and nestling in the womb where nobody could touch him. He'd even begun scrabbling at the buttons on her skirt when she put a warm hand on his head. A strange heat flooded his scalp and his frantic thoughts stilled.

'God knows it wasn't your fault,' she said.

'He does?'

'Yes.'

'Then take me to Heaven now.'

'No. You'll get out of here one day, and then you can enjoy your fame properly.'

'They aren't going to let me out.'

'They will. But only if you can convince them you believe I wasn't real.'

'I can't do that.'

'You can. We'll know it was true, and that's all that matters. It'll be our little secret. Can you do that for me?'

The heat from her palm intensified, and his thoughts grew fuzzy. He tried to remember what he'd been so upset about, but kept coming back to an image of his mum standing before the gates of Heaven, as wide open as the arms that welcomed him home.

'Yes,' he whispered.

'Good boy,' she said, and planted a kiss on his forehead.

When he opened his eyes, she was gone, but he knew he would see her again one day. He took a deep breath and began to sing.

Acknowledgements

As with Apocalypse Cow, this book wouldn't have existed without the support and encouragement of my wife, Nats, who has spent years listening to my doubts about my writing abilities. At first she was sympathetic and patient; now she just belts me round the earhole (rather like Jackie's mum) when I start to moan. Strangely, this works very well, although I may now be a little deaf on one side.

I would also like to thank the family of Bill Hicks for granting permission to start my book with a quote from one of the greats of comedy. I'm not big on using quotes to start books or chapters, but this statement sums up one of the key themes of *Wannabes* and exactly defines how I feel about music.

Immense gratitude is also due to my team of readers, who found many typos, inconsistencies and generously offered up ideas on how to improve the work: Nats, Leah Kohlenberg, Rebecca Dempster, Kat Urbaniak, Scott McDonald, Dani Solomon and Mick Sailor.

Pam Howes also deserves big thanks for advice given as I started out on the journey to becoming a hybrid author. Thank you also to John Hudspith, who copy edited this book in pursuit of those ever-elusive typos. I am equally grateful to Michael Homler, my editor at St. Martin's Press, who kindly gave me permission to release this labour of love ahead of the publication of *World War Moo*.

And finally, thanks again to Nats for designing the cover and interior bells and whistles, which I think are decidedly groovy.

If I've missed anybody, it's not because I'm not grateful. It's because I'm forgetful. So, consider this a big thank you to all you who have encouraged me throughout my career.

About the Author

Michael Logan is an award-winning Scottish writer, whose career has taken him across the globe.

His debut novel, Apocalypse Cow, won the Terry Pratchett First Novel Prize. Since then, the sequel, World War Moo, and an unrelated standalone novel, Wannabes, have hit the shelves. His fourth novel, Hell's Detective: Lost Angeles, will be along presently.

Michael's short fiction has appeared in publications such as The Telegraph, Chapman and Underground Voices. He won Fish Publishing's 2008 international One-Page Fiction Prize with We Will Go on Ahead and Wait for You—at 295 words, the most difficult thing he's ever written.

During his time as a foreign correspondent, Michael lived in Scotland, France, Bosnia, Hungary, Switzerland and Kenya, which points to itches that can only be scratched by moving around. He has also reported from many other countries, including South Sudan, Somalia, South Africa, and other places that don't begin with an 'S'.

He currently lives in Nairobi, Kenya, and is married with three young children.

Michael likes books, fencing, guitars and cheese. This is not an exhaustive list, but it tells you pretty much everything you need to know.

www.michaelloganbooks.com

Printed in Great Britain
by Amazon